LESSONS IN LOVE

PENNY ASHER-DARKE

Published by Miller Publishing.

eBook ISBN 978-1-7396481-6-9

ISBN 978-1-7396481-7-6

Cover Design Scott Gaunt.

A CIP catalogue records this book is available from the British Library. 100525

"Love is composed of a single soul inhabiting two bodies."

—*ARISTOTLE*, GREEK PHILOSOPHER

CONTENTS

FOREWORD

A contemporary, paranormal romance with fantasy elements for adult readers.

Themes include: emotional abuse, miscarriage (off page, side character), physical abuse, bad language, a love-triangle of sorts, a past life, fantasy elements, and a taboo, age-gap relationship between a consenting doctorate student and her hot professor.

Because you absolutely would too, given the chance ;)

1

KIT

For Reasons Unknown - The Killers

Pushing open the door to Josh's office, instead of the quiet, celebratory drink I thought we were having, I'm met with exploding confetti cannons, the pop of champagne corks, and those ear-screeching party blowers.

"Surprise!"

"Congratulations!"

To the small assembled crowd's amusement, I jump with surprise, and then I shake my head at them for being secretive assholes. Grinning, raising my hands in a *you got me* pose, I look across at Josh Cusack, my friend and colleague.

I bet this was his idea.

"Thanks everyone."

"We definitely got you," Daisy rejoices, grabbing my shoulders to give me a little shake.

Looks like the languages department has been hiding out in here. There must be twelve staff squeezed in the small office, made up of PAs, adjunct professors like me, our respective bosses, and some of the language assistants. Daisy, the French Department's PA, swiftly finds me a glass of champagne.

"I thought the hallways were quiet," I offer, shaking an array of colored confetti out of my hair as I take the glass. "Thanks, Daisy."

She beams at me before flicking her head; it makes her long blonde hair fly around her shoulders in homage to ubiquitous shampoo commercials.

"I can't believe you're going. I'll miss your handsome face around here."

Personally, I'm ready to leave Brownlow behind. As luck would have it, Josh will be following me to Jacquard University in a few months' time. He might have got the job offer before me, technically by seven weeks, but I'm starting my tenure this side of the summer break. Our lives have intersected and followed each other's for so long that the thought of working in different colleges filled me with an inordinate amount of sadness. For a time, it had looked like his professorship path had accelerated faster than mine, leaving me languishing behind. My boss, who was meant to retire this summer and allow me to advance up the academic ladder, decided to postpone her gardening and writing plans for three years.

Three years.

I'm not waiting that long. I haven't worked my ass off for the last ten years, publishing as many papers as I have for low pay and zero reward. It's why I accepted a tenured position at Jacquard, because, well, it's *Jacquard*.

Pete Gallagher had called me out of the blue. He'd spoken my name as if it meant something, sounding out each word with entitlement and reverence. "Professor. Kit. Chevalier."

"Pete. To what do I owe the pleasure?"

There was no need to call him by his title when we were on

first name basis—another reason why his formal greeting surprised me.

"As you know, I've been following your career closely; I have an opportunity for you."

Certain it was needless flattery, my heart swelled nonetheless at his words. It wasn't often distinguished professors from institutions like Jacquard University called me up during office hours.

"I'm flattered, Pete. I've long been an admirer of your work myself." His early work. The past seven years he'd been coasting but I planned on keeping that to myself.

"A position at Jacquard is opening up and you're my first pick."

My interest was piqued. "What position is this? I wasn't aware of any openings."

I had been keeping a close watch on vacancies in my field over the past six months, but it's so niche, rarely anything comes up. And top-level positions, ones I'm gunning for, have several contenders.

"Your ideal job, Kit. Professor of European Medieval Literature. Interested?"

My heart stalled. "Well, of course, Pete. Does this mean you're retiring?"

"First, tell me—do you still fence?"

I doubt he needed to ask. Four months ago I saw him at a state tournament I'd entered. After accepting the victor's shield, Pete Gallagher shook my hand and congratulated me.

Referencing my love of fencing was strange, shoe-horned into the conversation but I didn't care to dig any deeper. "I'll only give up fencing when my knees or hips do," I answered with a chuckle.

His answering laughter was low and delighted. "Good. It's your passion."

"It is," I replied, ready to move on to the many questions I had about the post.

But he was too quick, asking, "Remind me of your personal email, Kit."

I rattled it off and he grunted with approval.

"Expect a message from me in the next few minutes. I anticipate your acceptance within twenty-four hours or the offer expires."

Those questions multiplied. Alarm bells sounded in all fucking directions because just what the hell was going on? "Wait, Pete. What's this about?"

"Your inauguration as Knight into The Duel will be July first. Get ready, and for the love of God, learn to use a rapier."

The line disconnected, his gravelly voice disappearing into the ether. In shock, I looked at the work on my desk, spread out before me like a buffet to whatever god had just granted me everything I could ever want.

Want professionally, anyway.

And the reference to rapiers was concerning. Few people train with the dangerous metal blade alongside the more common fencing foils. Scars on my hands and body prove the years of drills I'd endured at my father's instruction, often with a host of blades most people happily avoid.

Pushing my father from my thoughts, I refreshed my email a hundred times in the following minutes. Finally, there it was, documents to prove I hadn't been hallucinating. And there was one hell of a welcome bonus, one that would help Gramps and still give me change to upgrade my apartment.

But then came the doubts. The guilt. Five years ago, I turned down a job at Jacquard for all the same reasons that are bothersome second time around. Did I want to accept this position, one I've been aiming towards for years, when I abhor everything about the philanthropists behind this particular university?

Devereaux money founded that college. Built it. And I—or rather, the Chevaliers—were owed some of their wealth, for past dues. But apart from that, the university was as renowned as Harvard and Yale. It was the pinnacle of a career most professors could only hope for and yet, here I was, reading through a generously packaged contract which stated I had carte blanche for the department I'd inherit.

In the end, it was the reputation, the opportunities that persuaded me that I had to overlook everything else. The family dispute was generations ago and I needed to let it lie. Derailing my ambitions was nonsensical. Irrational. Stupid. It would be astonishingly inept of me to decline twice.

Accepting the job, I hoped I wouldn't regret it.

Standing at the far side of his desk, Josh raises his glass in my direction, his other hand raking though his dark blond hair, dislodging confetti. That stuff is fucking everywhere; it covers his desk, the papers he's working on, and an untidy stack of German literature books in one corner.

Edging closer to where he stands, I nod towards his workspace. "Someone's got shitty aim."

Regarding his desk, he nods like it's a lost cause. "Yeah," he agrees before bringing his hand from behind his back, the item he's holding making me close my eyes in defeat. "Not this time, though," he declares with what sounds like a shit-eating grin, firing the confetti canon over me until I'm covered head to toe.

And I'm back to shaking my head like a wet dog, a perverse sense of satisfaction rushing through me as I cover Josh's carpet with even more mess. "I'm so glad we're in your office," I tell him.

My colleagues laugh, Daisy zealously brushing tiny shreds of paper off my shoulders. "This just doesn't want to let go," she murmurs, her hands smoothing through my hair and sweeping down my back.

I knock back the champagne, acknowledging her help with a brisk, "Thanks," before glad-handing various colleagues. They're all busy, and I'm happy to speed things along so that they can get to the next seminar, lecture, or book.

A few minutes later, Stephanie Santos, my boss who doesn't know when to retire, gives an impromptu speech. It's pretty dull as speeches go, but it's brief, something I can admire. She ends with, "Congratulations, Kit. We're so happy for you and wish you every success. But not too much," she adds on, referencing the colossal rivalry between colleges.

Knowing laughter surrounds me, and I join in because, thanks to academia's paranoia, I'm starting gardening leave tomorrow. University league tables are no joking matter.

"Before you all head off," Josh begins, glancing my way with an unmistakable sparkle in his light-coloured eyes. "As Kit's closest colleague and friend, I can't say goodbye without sharing one of my favorite memories with you all."

"Uh oh. I think you need a top-up," Daisy suggests, filling my glass as I find some patience from somewhere.

Commanding the room, Josh continues, "Picture this: Christopher Tristan St Pierre Chevalier, AKA Kit, the man with the world's most incomprehensibly long name—"

My colleagues—ex colleagues in precisely two hours and forty-three minutes, according to my watch—titter at his joke. It's not the first time I've been ridiculed for my name, and part of me agrees—it's as pretentious as fuck, but family names passed down through the generations often are.

"A man who embraces the incomparable court of chivalry."

The anecdote is one he loves to spout at any opportunity, and it is kind of funny—well, maybe the first time you hear it. Thankfully, his joke lands well, everyone deciding to head off on a positive note. After reassuring Daisy that I won't go without saying a *proper goodbye,* I sigh with relief. Making a bee-line for the nearest chair, I sink into it, saying a heartfelt, "Thanks for the send-off."

At six three, a half inch taller than me, there are not many chairs that Josh doesn't look stupidly big in, but somehow he fits the one behind his desk.

"You're welcome. You still on for beers tomorrow with the guys?" He rubs his hands together. "It'll be a real party."

"You bet."

"You can say goodbye to Erica," he says with a sly lilt to his voice.

I don't rise to the bait. Erica was a regrettable fling for a couple of weeks but she's not who I'm looking for. "Let's avoid Bar Midnight. There are plenty of other places to go."

"We'll start somewhere else, but we'll probably end up there. It's the best spot for a beer and you know it."

"Fine," I say on a long-suffering sigh. "We can end up there." With any luck, Erica won't be working.

Josh scans the trashed floor and blows out a breath. "Fuck. Is OCD catching? I'm starting to feel agitated."

"I don't have OCD," I scold fondly, even though he's well aware of that. And that it's not catching. Winding me up is his favorite hobby.

"Maybe neat freak genes are catching."

"Nothing freaky about liking a tidy space."

He scoffs. "Show me one tidy office—apart from yours," he quickly amends. "Research like ours means books and papers and manuscripts. That stuff mounts up."

Josh kicks his enormous, brogue-covered feet up on his desk and leans back in his ergonomic office chair. He slides open a drawer, a pitying smile forming as he withdraws a silver-wrapped parcel and hands it to me.

"What's this?" I ask, leaning forward to take it from him. There's even a bright pink foil bow on top.

"Santos asked me to make sure you got this."

The floppy, A4-sized parcel is not really a gift at all. "She left me work, didn't she? Figures."

"Why break the habit of a lifetime? She won't know what hit her when you leave and she actually has shit to do until your replacement arrives."

"She'll just leave it for my successor."

"You got any more intel on who that'll be?"

I pull off the bow, launching it at Josh's face but he easily dodges the lightweight projectile. "Not my problem," I murmur, my concentration entirely on the papers—correction, the application forms.

"Anything interesting?" he asks, finishing his drink.

There's a sticky note stuck to the top of the pile. It reads: *I really want Devereaux. I hope you agree. She is my top choice followed by Ferrera, Watson, and Secker. Send out the acceptance emails. Stephanie.*

My heart stumbles as I read the message. When I flip the print-outs in my hand, little bits of confetti scattered across Josh's desk rustle in the blow-back.

"Could be," I offer. Thanks to his recent job offer at Jacquard, Josh is fully aware of the animosity I have for a certain Devereaux family. Out of loyalty to me he was going to reject the job. Thinking it nonsensical, I urged him to take it. And thank God I did considering I got Pete Gallagher's call a few weeks later. In all honesty, it made accepting the job a hell of a lot easier.

Devereaux. It can't be *her,* surely? Why Madrigal Devereaux has applied here, to work with *me,* is beyond curious.

Leafing though the stapled papers, I find the one my heart seeks, if only to put it out of its misery. I go entirely still as I read, then re-read, the full name at the top of the document. There's no mistaking who this person is. There's no tricking my body, my pulse, my arteries as blood pumps round my body in an agitated torrent.

Madrigal Iseult Georgette Devereaux.

Madrigal *fucking* Devereaux.

"Shit."

"What's up? Someone you know—or worse—screwed?"

I laugh humorlessly. Josh has worked his way through scores of women, and the fates seem to have a wicked sense of humor because he keeps bumping into them at really inconvenient moments. "That's more your area of expertise, Professor," I remind him, scanning over her application with a keen eye.

Like any niche or field of interest, the world of academia can be a small one at times. Conferences are ripe for blurred lines. Bumping into any number of colleagues and associates from our years in education happens all the time, and to Josh's horror—his exes too.

"You're no different. In fact, you're worse. Going home with the bar staff means you're running out of places to drink," he accuses. "Just as well you're heading off to a new city."

I shoot him a smile as we argue over familiar territory. My friend's always been less guarded, less careful about the consequences of who he sees. I prefer to keep my work space conflict-free. "There's always another bar or restaurant to walk into," I rebuff, my eyes bouncing between him and the desk fan on a nearby credenza. "The same can't be said for interviews or meetings when the previous weekend's lay is on the other side of the table."

"That happened twice!" he objects.

"Twice *last month,*" I respond before adding, "That you know of."

He sits upright and holds out his hand. "Show me what's got you so riled."

Teasing aside, I clue him in. "An enmity that goes back decades."

I toss Madrigal's stapled papers across the desk. Snatching them up, Josh gives me a long look as he straightens the ruffled, overturned pages and looks down at the front page, seeing her name.

"Jesus. For real?"

For. Real.

"I thought I had the mother of all pretentious names but hers takes the crown."

I simultaneously love and hate her name. Love it for its ridiculous originality, and yet I hate it for how it calls to me on an intellectual level. This name has meaning as deep as hell's pit. It's a distraction, a lure to trap me.

And I will not be turned.

Josh whistles on an exhale, his words cutting too close to the bone. "The Iseult to your Tristan. How positively chivalric," he says wryly. "And she wants to study here." His eyes make quick work of my expression which is hopefully projecting inner calm. "Does she know you work—worked—here, or do you think she's applying because you're leaving?"

Without question, her parents must know every detail about where I reside, work, eat, and shit. A grudge as deep as ours goes back at least a century, and time won't let it go.

"Doesn't matter what her motives are. Either way, she's not studying here."

Josh leafs through the pages of her application, his eyes avidly scanning the details of her studies. By the gigantic hike of his eyebrows, I know when he's read the astonishing and wholly surprising detail I'm trying hard to ignore.

"She's on *financial aid*?" he asks incredulously. "What's wrong with the family money?"

"I don't know and I don't care."

Josh frowns before his eyebrows smooth out again. "It doesn't make sense. A student of her calibre should be on a full scholarship."

He continues to read her application and it's a fascinating play by play. There's an occasional nod, an impressed press of his lips, a raised, intrigued eyebrow.

"Valedictorian. And—interesting, she's also a tennis pro."

Yeah, I caught that too with my lightning quick read of the first page. "She sounds like a cliché." Middle class, a personal tennis coach, educated at the finest private schools—and it's all been on the Devereaux dime.

"Don't be bitter. Just because you're shit at tennis."

"I'm not shit—I'm just not a pro."

"Technically, I misspoke. She's not a pro either, just a college athlete at the top of her game. Literally," he adds, seeing her ranking as he flips the page. "And besides, you had lessons," he leads, "which makes *you* a cliché."

"Whose side are you on?" I challenge, reaching forward to snatch the papers out of his hand.

He chuckles at my discomfort, because although I'm irked by her family history, by her application to Brownlow, I'm not upset at *her.*

I don't think.

"Not everything can be bought you know." He turns to his laptop, his fingers flying over the keyboard. "It's her only college application so she's not studying *anywhere* right now. If you're moving to Jacquard, what would it hurt to let her come here?"

An age-old grudge simmers under my skin. At no point will our families resolve their differences. At no point will I forget how much the Chevaliers lost because of her corrupt, thieving ancestors. Her career, academic or otherwise, will receive *zero* assistance from me.

"Because her family made mine powerless, Josh. They stole

from us. For once, I have a small amount of influence and I plan on wielding it."

With her family name, influence and wealth, she can go to any college in the world. Why does she have to pick this one? The fact that she hasn't applied to Jacq U, her father's alma mater and the college that the family built over two hundred years ago, doesn't even register as a thought. Seeing as I'm heading there next, I'm just happy to see Jacquard is not in her sights.

We lock eyes, Josh nodding when he sees the determination on my face, though I'm not sure why I'm being this petty. Maybe I'm more like my father than I thought.

The thought makes me frown. Makes me reconsider my position.

Nodding towards the pile of applications still in my fist, he asks, "If she's out, who's in?"

I check my watch. 3 PM. Before I leave tonight, I've a shit-ton of work to do. But at least all of my books and belongings are packed and ready to be shipped. "That's for Stephanie to worry about," I tell him with a crooked smile.

"That's the spirit," he cajoles, rising to his feet. "I'd better ring Estates and ask them to bring a vacuum."

Josh rounds the table nearest the credenza. I stand, pulling him in for a shoulder bump.

"See you tomorrow night," he confirms, turning for his chair. "No tears please. Save them for when I have witnesses."

"I'll bring the extra large, man size tissues, shall I?"

Throwing himself into his seat, he chuckles, watching me retreat backwards with only one goal in mind.

Guessing my next move, Josh pleads, "Don't do it," as I reach for the fan switch. "I threw you a party!"

I flick it to max speed. A million pieces of paper swoosh up into the air, creating a confetti blizzard that swirls around Josh until he's all but lost to the naked eye.

"That's for recounting your favorite anecdote."

"Dude, it's a compliment. They don't make men like you anymore," he stresses.

Ignoring the mess I've created, I don't need to wonder why I'm in such a destructive mood.

Madrigal Devereaux—what am I going to do with you?

2

MADDIE

Sweet Nothing - Florence and the Machine

My cell chimes with an incoming email and my current state of play each time I hear it ding like that, is to lunge for it and hold my breath at the same time. Blood pounds through my ears as I read the name of the sender. It's just the person I've been desperate to hear from.

Professor Stephanie Santos.

I unlock my screen and open the email, my pulse frenzied. This is it! This is the defining moment of the next few years of my life. Quickly, my eyes scroll over the first few lines of the email and my world screeches to a halt.

What the hell?

I've been *rejected?*

Mouth open, I read the email again just to be sure the past few hours I've spent in a tensely fought three set match hasn't depleted me of all intellect, but the heaviness to my heart tells me I'm out.

"Shit."

Tossing my mobile to the desk, I follow it, slumping to the graffitied surface as I wonder how this happened. Wondering what to do next. I mean, I could reply and ask Santos to reconsider. *Beg* her to rethink her decision. She's not even given me any reason why—just some story about the exceptionally high standard of candidates. When I emailed her a few weeks ago, she was delighted how knowledgable I was of her colleague's work and thought I was a really positive fit for Brownlow's program.

Dread pools low in my gut as I reach for my phone and call Perrie. This ruins all our plans and somehow, I must find the courage to tell her.

"Hey! I was just about to call! I'm in!" she shouts in her bright, chirpy voice. "This is gonna be so great!"

Her easy laughter has my gut twisting. She doesn't know my news yet. "That's great, Perrie, but Brownlow *rejected* me."

I wonder if my mind is playing tricks on me or if I've entered an alternative universe to the one I was born in. None of this makes sense. My research has been meticulous. My tutors at Princeton have written glowing reports about my work. I'm predicted a distinction, and yet Brownlow don't want me?

"What? Noooooo! Wait, I'm on my way. Are you still in the library?"

"Yeah. Usual spot."

"I'll be two minutes. Who's the email from?"

"Professor Santos' office."

I hear doors closing, a multitude of voices as Perrie rushes from her class towards the library. "Well, shit. Are you okay?"

I mull that question over for all of one second. "No. This ruins *everything*."

"No, it doesn't," she reassures me, steel creeping into her voice. "It just *changes* them."

I blow out a breath, knowing she's probably right, but right now it feels like the floor has fallen from underneath my feet. "Fine. Consider them changed."

"What reason did she give?"

"The usual crap. You know, the quality of candidates has been exceptional this year and blah blah blah, we regret to inform you blah blah blah, we wish you all the best with your other applications." I suck in a breath. "I literally said I had only applied to Brownlow. That there were no other colleges I was interested in."

"Those bastards. There's no way I got a spot and you didn't."

"The rejection email says otherwise."

"Well, I'm not going if you're not."

A subdued burst of laughter rips free. Perrie's so stubborn sometimes. "You should. It's a good school."

We were so excited about committing to a doctorate together, albeit different areas of French literature. Over the previous months, we've endlessly debated our academic plans, even deciding which student accommodation we wanted to live in. And we'd earmarked bars to work in to supplement our loans and financial aid.

With my eyes glued to the staircase, I easily spot Perrie when she reaches the top and turns towards my row of tables.

"I can see you," I tell her.

"Get ready for the best hug of your life."

Somehow, I raise a smile. Standing, I struggle to hold back tears as she jogs towards me, tosses her bag to the floor, and envelopes me in a bone-crushing hug.

"I'm so sorry," she murmurs, her peroxide hair tickling my cheeks. "But we'll fix this."

"How?"

Perrie scans my red-rimmed eyes, her lips smooshing together in sympathy. "Plan B."

"There wasn't one."

"Make one."

She directs me back to my seat, her heart-shaped face full of concern. There's a tiny pause before she asks, "Like, will you reconsider Jacq U?"

Jacquard University is a niche, ancient institution specializing in European literature, history, and the arts, bringing its own unique traditions. My father, John Devereaux went to Jacq U, as did his father and *his* father before him. When he knows I've not got into Brownlow he'll pull every string, gift obscene sums of money, and harass the Dean on a daily basis to ensure that his only child follows in his footsteps. To say that we had the mother of all arguments about where I planned to study for my PhD is an understatement. Christ, my ears are still ringing.

Shit—why didn't I have a back-up plan like Perrie? Not the Jacquard back-up plan, but I should've had the foresight to apply to another school. Let that be a lesson for me and my over-confidence.

I rub my hands over my face and stare at the desk when I'm still none the wiser of how to deal with this setback. "Still not going to Jacquard, Perrie."

"Come on, Maddie," she urges, taking a seat beside me. "Think about it. They might accept late applications."

"I bet they're full."

Full of people who are exceptional, unlike me.

"It's worth a try."

Doubts creep in, my thoughts turning dark. Perrie found out three days ago that she was accepted to Jacquard, and if I get rejected from there too, I'm not sure my confidence will survive it. We're competitive in a healthy way, spurring each other on. And mostly, we get similar grades, so it's hard to be the one who's not winning right now. I feel wrong-footed and it's disconcerting. Friends since day one at Princeton, our whole friendship has been based on one of study and a love of academic research.

"Maybe I don't need a PhD. Maybe I should get a job. I could support you, you know. Feed you and make sure you're not drowning under all those books and essays."

Perrie's tinkling laughter raises my spirits a little. "You could, or you could get on the phone to Jacquard and see about late applications. They'd be mad to turn you away."

"Madder than Brownlow?"

"Certified *crazy*."

I scoff, unconvinced, full of wretchedness. Standing, I walk to the balcony that overlooks the foyer and peer down, trying to get a fresh perspective.

"Wait, doesn't Harrison coach at Jacquard?"

Thinking of Mark Harrison Tait, who goes by his middle name, makes me curl inward with uncertainty. A few weeks ago he came to see me for New Year. It was a total surprise, and mostly a good one, but we have a fraught relationship.

Toxic, Perrie calls it.

A simmering tension has existed between us for so long I'm not sure if it'll ever go away. Sometimes I wonder if I'm the only one who can feel the tightness of that space between us. A tiny gap brimming with hurt, dashed hopes, and an indecisive kind of love.

"Yeah he is. He's been coaching there for ten months now."

He took the job hoping I'd choose Jacquard over Brownlow. Hoping I'd choose him, choose tennis, choose us.

Perrie joins me at the balcony and, for a few quiet moments, we people-watch. "I thought so. Well, this is perfect—you'll have two friends at Jacquard, and only one of them will yell at you to move your ass faster across court."

I chuckle. She's not wrong; Harrison constantly berated me from the sidelines. And although Perrie knows much of the detail about my former relationship with Harrison, she doesn't know the worst of it. She doesn't know that I was only sixteen and he was twenty-eight, and if I lost a game after being in the lead, he'd take his anger out on my body in the locker room, his thrusts rough and punishing as he yanked on my hair and whispered furiously what a bad girl I'd been.

There was never a time when he made love to me in celebration. There was never a victory fuck, gentle or sweet. So I thought it was love. A perverse kind and complicated, but love was passionate, wasn't it? But I got older, wiser. I realized his love was one dimensional, negative emotions fueling his behavior.

I wanted the red hot kind borne of feral *love.*

"Harrison's yelling aside, I reeaaaaally don't want to go to Jacquard. The work ethic they expect from their students is legendary and I'm not sure I can afford it alongside my tennis. Plus, I'm still cross at Dad, and ending up at Jacq U feels like submitting."

According to my staunchly feminist friend, submission is a dirty word. Everything to do with men is on her terms, and while I like that, in principle, I also like a man to dominate. But there's a scale, one that needs to be balanced.

And my parents' marriage difficulties are hitting Mom hard. The fact that Dad's been seeing another woman while *still married,* leaves me inconsolable. It's no different for Mom I'm sure, but she's bottling it all up, refusing to speak about it.

They're my problems, Maddie. I love you but I can't involve you in my marriage. You wouldn't want your father and I entangling ourselves in your relationships either. Some things are meant to be between your husband and you.

And while I understood Mom's perspective, it still bothered me. These were my parents. People I loved. And seeing them hurt and angry and not talking, hurt me.

Softly, Perrie sighs. "I know. But I need to make a choice

soon. Your enquiries could take some time so you need to make some tough decisions."

She needs to accept either Brownlow or Jacquard by the deadline, and I need to work out what I want to do. And she only applied to Brownlow because I wouldn't apply to Jacquard which was always her top choice. And now they've rejected me, my pride won't let me beg them to reconsider. They had their chance.

"Sorry for letting you down."

"Don't be ridiculous," she says kindly. "But you know," she says, a sly curl to her voice, "there is a very big way you can make it up to me."

Blackmail? "You're the worst."

"The best. The absolute best," she dismisses with a charming smile. "Do it. Come on, you know it's meant to be. You, me and Jacq U. It'll be epic!"

Those doubts keep plaguing me, telling me I'm not good enough. "I haven't got in!"

"I'm confident enough for both of us. At least *try*."

Squeezing my eyes closed, I rub a hand over my face. "I'll try."

Her squeal of delight has heads from nearby desks turning our way.

"You'll get us kicked out," I admonish, elbowing her gently.

"Let me know when you've called and what they say."

I nod, even though I'm still conflicted. Standing by my principles is important to me. And I'll need to secure loans and financial aid and probably a job.

"Now," Perrie begins. "Are we going to Paris for spring break, or what?"

Her excitement is uncontainable. We traveled extensively in our semester abroad, funds allowing, but her father promised to foot the bill as a special treat if she secured her place at Jacquard, even if she didn't accept.

I love Paris, so of course, I agree, to an ear-splitting, excited scream.

It's noisy in Arrivals, the happy sounds of people reuniting flooding the hall as I continue to scan the crowd for Mom and Dad. They've always been there for me, even when I fall out with Dad about college choices or my studies. It takes me a few seconds to locate them but the smiles on my parents' faces are broad and contagious.

I hug Mom first because she deserves it. She carried me, nursed me, and raised me. She gets priority every time. That's not to say I don't love my dad, because I do. But absent, empire-building husbands can't expect the same relationship as nurturing mothers. There's a point when a daughter realizes she's never quite enough, and nothing she does will change her father's priority.

I want to be a priority. When I find my forever guy, I want to know that I'm *it* for him.

Mom feels frail under my embrace, and I know she's always been slim, especially now she's competing for attention from her husband, but this is a concerning difference to when I saw her a few months ago.

"Darling, it's so good to have you home."

"Hi Mom. Thanks for coming."

Her hands slide to my shoulders as she pulls back to study my face. She's always looked at me like I'm precious. And while I know I am loved by her for all the many reasons a parent loves a child, the seven miscarriages which came after me must factor into it.

"Of course, I was coming to meet you." She kisses me on the cheek, her lipstick leaving a sticky mark on my skin before her eyes lift to Dad.

We close the gap between us at the same time, his patience finally paying off. I throw my arms around his shoulders and breathe in his cologne of sandalwood and musk.

"Maddie, we've missed you."

"Hi Dad," I mumble into his shoulder. "Missed you both, too."

I pull away, scanning the dark eyes set amongst handsome features. The crow's feet when he smiles are endearing, the salt and pepper shades in his hair complimentary. "You look good."

"You too, honey."

Mom threads her arm through mine and we set off towards the exit. Behind me, my father gathers up my cart and follows.

"Remind me," he begins as I slow my steps so that he's not left behind. "Why flying on the company jet is so much worse than this circus." He waves an indignant hand at the crowd around us.

"One: carbon emissions. Two: it's cheaper to share transport. Three: I can get the Air Miles."

"And all the germs, apparently," he responds fondly, knowing this is an argument I'll never let him win. Still, he tries his best to persuade me each time. "So, how long have we got you for?"

"A week. Maybe two, if that's okay?"

"Of course, it's okay." Dad looks sad and subdued when our eyes meet, those words spoken tenderly between us. Even with the hubbub of the airport and a million people rushing around us, they transmit to me as if the entire world stopped and held its breath. "It's your home."

It's hard to maintain eye contact but I do, because he needs to know I still stand by my decision to leave home when I was seventeen and hadn't even graduated high school.

"What are your plans afterwards?"

"I got a job, so I'll be busy."

"Are you seeing Harrison?"

The answer to that is no. Firstly, there's the job I secured. Secondly, I don't know how I feel about him, even with all the time and space I've created to cure the heart and steel the mind.

I'm not sure I've been all that successful.

"Doubtful. I'm hoping to house and dog-sit." And coaching tennis to middle-schoolers in the spare hours I have in between.

"A friend of ours?" Mom asks as we exit the airport.

"No, a widowed businessman who's away for two months. He's got a black Labrador called Monty."

Mom thumbs my cheek, whispering. "Clever girl."

I squeeze her hand, letting her know I understand. She's not congratulating me on staying away—that hurts us both. *All.* No, it's because she's proud I'm not giving in to Harrison's requests for another chance.

After a short drive we pull up the wood-lined driveway of our house on Summit Circle. The views over the city from up here on Westmount are incredible.

"Needless to say, the boxes you shipped are in your room," Mom reminds me as we exit the car. "Did you buy more books?"

"I needed them," I say. Like always. "I couldn't resist the *bouquinistes*," I admit, referencing the two hundred or so Paris quayside booksellers from spring break. "I'm sure I got some really rare finds."

"And I'm sure you paid handsomely for them," Dad remarks with a knowing smile.

While I'll haggle the price over most things, when it comes to a limited edition book I will gladly pay over the odds. "You know me."

"I can understand the appeal."

I grin. "Right."

Dad's a collector of many things, but antique, rare books are his absolute weakness. And the beautiful thing about studying in London for my junior year was access to all of the University of London's libraries. And while I saw plenty of rare manuscripts at Brownlow, the privilege of looking at, of touching, medieval books and manuscripts is one that will give me goosebumps as long as I live.

Dad pops the trunk and lifts out my two bulging suitcases. "Not sure if all the boxes of books will fit in your bookcase. Maybe I can extend that for you?" he offers.

Swallowing my pride, I murmur, "Thanks, Dad."

A few hours later, I've unpacked and sorted out a pile of clothes that I need to throw in the washer. Mom keeps me company the whole time, but her exhausted demeanor has me concerned.

"Let's get these clothes to Céline. She'll be happy to have something to do."

"Mom, I'm pretty sure Céline's busy enough." Without doubt, our lovely Québécois housekeeper is cleaning any number of the thirty rooms this gigantic house boasts. "And I can do my own laundry."

"I know that, Madrigal, but she's dying to see you too. I fill her in on all your news."

I smile at Mom. Her dark hair is loose but not as glossy as normal as I curl my arms around her shoulders and give her another hug. Guilt steals through me for not being around more, and while I know she would never want to hold me back or keep me from my passions, I'm pleased to be back.

Pulling away, I look her in the eye. "Mom, I'm sorry I've been away so much. At least I'll be closer now and can see more of you."

Softly, she shakes her head. "Maddie, I don't want you to worry about that. It was good for you to get some distance. To experience all that you did." Affectionately, she slides a hand over my hair.

"It's greasy. I need to shower away the flight."

"Dinner first." Mom checks the time on her Patek Philipe, an anniversary gift from Dad when things were better. "It will be ready shortly."

"Okay, after. Besides, I need to speak to Dad real quick before dinner."

"Jacquard?" Mom suspects.

I nod. "Did he interfere?"

"He told me he didn't."

"Do you believe him?"

She sighs, her hand lifting in a gesture that I interpret as *I have no influence here, what can I do.*

I kiss her soft cheek. "Let me go speak to him."

Leaving my bedroom, I head down the sweeping stairs and turn left towards Dad's office and the library. I'm comforted to be in the family home and in familiar surroundings again. Growing up, I only ever knew this house. It has been a constant beacon, a bastion of emotional and physical security. And yet, at the same time, the grip this house had on me slipped, my life taking a new, unexpected course.

Shivers of anticipation grip me as I near the library, a room that has felt like hallowed ground. Inside, the air is a cool 62 degrees as I cross the beautiful parquet floor. Dim light filters in through a screened window, while endless bookcases made from a sumptuous American walnut are stocked with novels, tomes, and texts. Mainly, the collection consists of British, American and French authors, but the best books, the rarest, are in the museum, alongside other items from the Devereaux Collection.

The faint, intimate smell of leather and ink and age permeates through the room, my mind unspooling as I reminisce about the rare moments I'd spend in here when I wasn't training on the tennis court. Sliding out a random book from a shelf, I carefully flip through the fragile pages as I cradle the spine. Words and phrases catch my eye before I replace the book and turn for the door; I can't put off speaking to Dad any longer.

I knock on his study door. My father's deep voice rumbles from within. "Entrez."

"C'est moi," I announce as I enter the wood-panelled room, closing the door behind me. When we're alone, my father and I speak French. "I wanted a quick word before dinner."

Dad rises from his leather chair and rounds the desk. Out of habit, I walk to the matching leather couch and sit.

My eyes catch on the huge family tree that hangs on the wall. Going back as far as the eleven hundreds, it's a rich tapestry of prestigious lives lived amongst the French aristocracy, then the upper echelons of the Republic of France before my recent ancestors settled in Canada.

At the very top of the document are four names.

Marc Devereaux, who married Iseult Auclair, and Tristan Chevalier who married Gisèle DuPont.

Not much conforms to the usual rules of genealogy, the descendants of the Chevalier and Devereaux families listed instead of those of just my ancestors. Of what I can determine, Tristan Chevalier loved Iseult Auclair, as marked by the letter A for *amour* next to their names, but she married Marc Devereaux as stated by the M for *mariage*. Why the Chevalier names are detailed, their lives lived in parallel down the length of the document, is anyone's guess.

Both of noble birth, Marc and Iseult had a son and daughter, the children and grandchildren that followed listed. But so is the family that Tristan and Gisèle had. It's curious. Dates of births and deaths are not always legible or available, but it's fascinated me since I first discovered it.

Presumably, the indecipherable words written in cursive in a bottom corner might be a clue. All I can determine is *Âme du.* I've always assumed the missing word was *coeur,* the phrase *soul of the heart* seeming to fit. And there's another phrase which I found intriguing—*Honneur aulx Digne.*

It's Norman French, meaning honor the worthy.

"Shoot," Dad encourages as he sits next to me. I drag my eyes away from the wall as my pulse skyrockets.

"As you know, I got into Jacquard."

"And I couldn't be happier."

I nod, knowing this. Obviously, my doctorate plans were confirmed many weeks ago but there's some detail I'm unclear on. So I play the only hand I've got and pretend I'm not sold on Jacquard. "I'm still deciding."

Dad stills. His eyes don't move from mine. "But your inheritance comes with a degree or doctorate from Jacquard."

My inhale is long and deep. When I decided not to go to Jacquard like my father did at eighteen, it coincided with his decision to change his will. I didn't really care, so I didn't take much notice of the details, but there was a hefty trust fund that I would've gained access to. There were antiques of international importance that were going to be signed over. He promised to review his decision if I went to Jacquard for a masters or doctorate, so naturally, I didn't apply. His wealth wasn't a motivator; books and knowledge were my currency.

If his wealth was meant to be a carrot, it turned into a stick, one that I beat *him* with.

"I don't care about that, Dad. I never have."

He blows out a beleaguered breath. "So, what is this about? Is it Harrison?"

I shake my head, though it's a lie. And because I detest lies, I admit, "Maybe. He's a complication."

Dad nods slowly, understanding the difficult relationship I've had with my ex. With the Taits long-time friends of the Devereaux family, Dad has always championed Harrison, even my young, illicit relationship. "Would it hurt to reconnect?"

"Yes, Dad, it would!" I protest, cross at him for even suggesting such a thing. "He was a serial cheater."

"Learning from his mistakes has taken him some time, but I'm convinced he's changed."

Getting advice on my love life from my father is very low on my priority list.

"Interesting that a man who cheated on his wife thinks I should forgive the man who cheated on me." Dad's eyes flair in outrage. "Is that what you think I'm worth?"

"Of course not. You're worth far more than he gave you. And for the record, I haven't been unfaithful, it's—" Dad flounders for a moment, clearly embarrassed. "It's not like that," he stresses. "I promise you."

After Mom told me not to interfere in their arguments, I could only assume the worst. But I'd like to believe him, I really would.

"If Harrison is committed to you, if he's seen the error of his ways, can't you give him the opportunity to prove himself? It would be gracious of you. It would be fitting of a woman of your pedigree."

His audacity has me raising a brow. If he puts so much stock into the character and lineage of our family then he should've behaved better himself.

"Jesus, I thought having a daughter would be easier than this," he mutters, his tone exasperated but lighter.

I smile warmly, knowing how difficult I can be. "You and Mom didn't raise a wallflower."

Dust settles over our disagreement. Honestly, I feel resigned about Harrison and me. We keep falling back together and I'm tired of fighting against it. But I'm not going to *knowingly* give Harrison another chance; he's going to have work hard to convince me of the merits of another, final try.

"So, back to the fact that I'm still deciding about Jacquard, which Harrison may or not be partly responsible for." I take a breath. "Did you promise the college money? Or a gift from the Collection?"

Conviction alters the line of his brow. "No, Maddie, you got the spot and your tennis scholarship because you're worth every penny. Don't undersell yourself; any academic worth their salt would see your credentials the moment your paths crossed." Unconvinced, I take a steadying breath, but he comments, "Did I do such a terrible job as a parent that you can't bear to follow in my footsteps?"

I shake my head. "Don't guilt me. You know how important proving myself is."

"Of course, I do. It's a family tradition."

Dad relaxes into the couch. Briefly, I consider if I'm being unfair. After all, he had to live with the Devereaux name hanging over him too. Making his mark on the world in a separate, defining way was an ambition he had for a long time. It's why he donated a large number of antiques and artefacts our family held to the college. To MOMA and to the Smithsonian. Some even went abroad.

"Professor Santos wrote to me a few months ago," I begin. She said there had been a terrible mistake and that if I wanted a place on her program at Brownlow, she'd make it happen."

Dad's eyes narrow. "Are you accusing me of being involved in this mistake?"

"Were you?" I demand. It would make sense. If I'm rejected from my one and only choice of university then I'd have to give up on my dream—which was never going to happen, or look at other colleges. I might've toyed with the idea for all of five glum minutes in a somber library, but my stubborn heart and resolute head would never lose sight of my ambitions.

"No. Next question."

My heart gives a loud, brisk pound before I soldier on. "The professor I spoke to at Jacquard—Pete Gallagher—who I found out is a friend of yours," I accuse, "has since retired. His replacement is someone who I wanted to work with at Brownlow, alongside Stephanie Santos," I say slowly and carefully. "Kit Chevalier's entire professorship has been based on medieval love poetry, chivalric epic poems and other European texts. It just seems very coincidental."

"Is there a question, darling, because I don't hear one."

"Are you sure you didn't influence this? Your friend retires," I begin. "A spot opens up at Jacquard for a professor I've admired from afar. Brownlow reject me, Jacquard accept me—well past the deadline. I'm at your alma mater, something you've been angling for since I was fourteen. It's so slick," I point out carefully.

Dad looks fatigued by our conversation. "That would be one hell of a feat, even for a resourceful man like myself." He clasps his hands together and leans in a fraction, giving me all of his attention and ensuring he has all of mine. "I can't help that Santos fucked up. That's on her, and I had absolutely nothing to do with it. As for Pete Gallagher, I do know *of* him, that's true. Apparently, he's had a serious heart complaint for over a year now, so I guess he decided it was worth retiring early for. The way I see it, you're winning here because you get to work with someone who's passionate about the same literature as you. He looks good on paper."

"How do you know?"

"I looked into him."

Of course he did.

I open my mouth, ready to berate him for stalking, when he says, "And before you scold me for stalking, I will remind you that *researching* who my daughter will be studying alongside, who she will be working with for the foreseeable future, is every parent's right."

I bite my tongue because he has a valid point.

"You are my only child, Maddie. And while I know I let you down by not being around much when you were younger—which you have, rightly, never forgiven me for—this is how I make it up to you." Reaching for my hand, Dad gathers it in his. With sincerity that has my resolve dwindling, he tells me, "I love you, Maddie. My empire is yours—everything I've inherited and built for this family. There's nothing I wouldn't do for you."

"Nothing?" I question, wondering if he's been bullshitting me since I entered his study.

"Nothing," he confirms.

I play the hand the dealer just gave me. "Stop seeing other women, including *that woman*, and make Mom happy again. She's thin, Dad. Broken. I don't need to know the detail, just love Mom like she deserves because I'm pretty sure she deserves it."

For the first time in a while, true emotion, emotion of the heart where Mom's concerned, shifts across his face. "I do love your mother."

"Then prove it."

He nods, his hand tightening around mine with affection. Or resolve. "And you'll go to Jacquard?"

Of course, he saw right through my demand. My blackmail. Sometimes, it scares me how much like him I am. "I'll stay for the duration as long as you're faithful *every day*."

A smile, slow and creeping transforms his face into one that's charming and irresistible. "Clever."

I swallow, his praise making me feel ten feet tall. And while he's always championed me, either at state tennis competitions or through my studious accomplishments, this feels different. For the first time, it's like we're equals.

No, I decide while I reflect on what I've negotiated here. For the first time in forever, it feels like I've won.

3

MADDIE

Uninvited - Alanis Morissette.

It's Friday night, and, just like old times, Perrie and I are getting ready to go out. We moved into our dorm a couple of days ago, and so far, despite fighting it, despite grave doubts, I'm beginning to enjoy Jacquard. The fact Perrie is right here with me is a huge bonus, but there's something else that has anticipation simmering through every breath I take. Maybe it's down to the fact that my decision has been made, that I'm committed to being here, but there was a growing sense of excitement when I arrived on campus. Some kind of innate feeling that attending Jacquard University was *right.*

Monumental things are going to unfold here, I can sense it. There's the doctorate, for sure, my classes and people to meet. And of course, there's Harrison. Is this building awareness I have about being here, this prickling expectancy, down to him?

Unable to answer that question, I look around the eerily familiar room Perrie and I share to the one we had in Princeton.

The same linens are on the beds, the same poster art adorns our walls. I still have the cerise neon heart affixed to the wall by my head, alongside a red sign reading *Love* in curly letters. My vintage art and numerous curiosities are sprinkled about the room. Packed away for the summer, the sight of all our decorations and familiar things have waves of nostalgia running through me.

Shimmying into a short, black cotton dress, Perrie says, "We're back in business, baby. You, me and a whole lot of studying in front of us."

I smile happily. "And bars."

She flashes me a grin. "A hundred percent."

"I'm so happy we're here together."

"You are?"

I nod, working my way through a myriad of tough emotions. It's strange to think that two days ago I was in Montréal. "Leaving Mom was hard, but she looked brighter the past few weeks. And I've decided to embrace Jacquard. I'll have my tennis to keep me sane, new friends to make, new studies to dive into. And you, of course. "

"Well, thank you," she says in a faux-coy voice. "But don't forget the hot professor to work alongside."

I roll my eyes. Perrie never changes and I love that about her. "You have to stop looking everyone up online before you meet them. It steals the mystery."

"I'm telling you, you need to check him out. Mahogany hair, eyes like whiskey, cut jawline. Let's hope he's tall to go along with the dark and handsome."

Perrie does this every time. Got a doctor's appointment? Dentist? Well, Perrie looks them up on the company website before she arrives. Sometimes before she even books the appointment.

"It helps," she insists. "Trust me. If my dentist is a guy and, somehow hot, I need to know in advance. I don't want there to be any misunderstanding when I'm laid out on my back and he tells me to *open wide*."

"Of course," I deadpan, fighting an image of Perrie in the dentist's chair, spreading her legs. "An easy mistake to make, I get it, but choosing your college based on the staff photos is a step too far."

Perrie pretends to be outraged. "Fine, but I chose Dr Hurren not only because she's a woman, one who looks approachable and like I could have a beer with her on a Friday night, but because she's the best in her field."

"I know," I say, peering at my reflection in the mirror and smoothing down my hair. Jacquard is known for hiring the best. "Your strong feminist ideals wouldn't let you apply to male professors."

Perrie's speciality is female novelists of the eighteenth, nineteenth and twentieth centuries. While I can appreciate the topic, and even enjoy reading novels of that era, by women, it's never held my interest to the same degree as medieval literature, which, much to Perrie's disgust, is written by men.

"I'd much rather *bang* a hot professor." She sighs, zipping up her dress. "Okay. It's on. How does it look?"

"You look great. You've got to stop worrying."

"Some of us need help."

"Shut up. Three guys already have your number!"

"Zac was cute."

Zac has already invited Perrie—and by default, me—to a bar tonight. It should be fun.

"What happened to being *boy-sober* for a few months?"

"A girl can change her mind," she replies with a wink.

I laugh. "Cool. I want to meet him. It sounds like you're into him."

Perrie aims some perfume at her upper chest and spritzes, liberally. "First impressions were good."

I slide my phone into the back pocket of my jean shorts and flick through one of Perrie's textbooks on her desk. Mentally, I map out the next few years and what they'll look like for me. Studying for a doctorate seems like a lifetime of work, but I know the years will fly by. And then what? What comes after? I think I'll have reached my limit by then, and instead of learning all I can, maybe I'll just teach all I can.

I decant the last of the wine we've been working through into our glasses. Tennis training begins in earnest after this weekend and I've not played competitively all summer long. I miss it, despite knowing it'll take up all my spare time, but most days I wouldn't want it any other way. Hoping the enthusiasm for my sport continues at Jacquard has me thinking cautiously.

"Don't let me drink too much," I entreat my friend. "I need to keep hydrated."

"Give yourself a night off. You've got all weekend to recover."

My cell alerts me to an incoming email, one addressed from a Professor Chevalier. I give my phone all of my attention as I click the email open.

Dear Madrigal

I'd like to review your interest in a doctorate at Jacquard and to discuss your schedule. I am free on Monday at 8.30AM.

I shall see you then.

There's no sign-off except the automated email signature in the footer, listing his name, titles, and contact details.

"What's up?" Perrie asks, studying my face. "Bad news?"

"An email from my professor."

"Speak of the devil."

"Going by the tone of his email, he might be."

"What?" She thrusts out her hand. "Let's see."

I pass her my phone and she scans the message.

"A man of few words," she surmises, handing my cell back. "It's early. Can you make it?"

She's referring to my tennis schedule. After checking my calendar, I tell her, "Just," and then type out a reply.

Dear Professor Chevalier

Thank you for your email. I have tennis practice until 8.15 and will be with you as soon as I can after that.

I look forward to meeting with you.

Regards

Maddie

Fifteen minutes won't be enough time to cool down, change out of my kit and get to the faculty, but I'll have to make it work. Maybe Coach Tait will let me leave ten minutes earlier?

He'd better.

"I bet he dishes out detentions."

"What detentions?"

Perrie makes a face. "Haven't you read the student handbook? The department gives out detentions if you already have extensions for two essays and you ask for a third or more."

"You're shitting me."

"Nope. It's in black and white."

Well fuck. "I didn't get detention at high school so I'll be fine."

Convinced, Perrie nods. "Are you sure you don't want to have a peek at his photo before you meet him?"

"No!"

"Don't say I didn't warn you." She throws out a finger for each of her next points. "Deodorant, a change of clothes, and dry shampoo will sort you out."

"Whatever. It's not like he'll throw me out of college because I've come straight from practice. Besides, all the paperwork's confirmed."

"Yeah, but still," she argues kindly. "You need to impress him, otherwise he might wonder why the college made special dispensation for you. He might be one of those people who like to shit all over their predecessor's work and decisions. What if he's difficult?"

Hmm.

It's a thought, a concern I've been toying with for some time. Letting my memory spool back a few months, I run through the conversation I had with my father. If he's to be believed, my rejection from Brownlow and acceptance at Jacquard had nothing to do with him. So maybe, I think to myself, maybe Professor Chevalier was! But as soon as the thought pops into my head, I dismiss it. That hypothesis can't be right because he had no way of knowing I would apply here. It was never on my radar and certainly not on my application. Besides, my doctorate was approved by Pete Gallagher.

I sigh, abandoning that hypothetical conversation and toss my phone to Perrie's bed. "I'm used to difficult men," I remind her. "Ones in position of power. I'm a resourceful, determined woman who can forge her own path, right?"

My best friend beams at me. "Does that mean you're ending things with Harrison?"

"I didn't say that," I hedge. "I'm going to see how it goes."

Her smile fades. "Just watch out for those red flags. Don't be a bull," she reminds me, which has always been her favorite metaphor when we discuss toxic masculinity. "Run *away* from the red flags. Run the other way."

Dusk is upon us when we head for the pre-arranged bar, the sky a murky purple. The illuminated sign for Midnight Blue guides us down the busy street. Inside, it's close to standing room only, most tables taken. Music plays in the background as we scope out the neon-lit interior, looking for Zac and his friends.

Perrie spots him, tugging on my hand as we head towards a booth table where three people are already sitting.

As she introduces me to Zac, he checks her out in the summer dress. He thinks she's cute too.

"Nice to meet you," I say.

"Likewise. This is—" he turns to a bi-racial woman with auburn hair and a band of freckles across her nose. "—Mimi, a European politics and diplomacy major. And this—" he says, pointing to a slight-built guy with a patchy beard and light hair, "—is Dylan. He's a journalism major."

We exchange hellos and grab a spot on the bench seats. Just then, the waitress approaches our table and introduces herself as Erica.

"What can I get you?"

The others are drinking beers, so we order the same.

"Hey, are you hiring?" Perrie asks Erica.

"Not sure. The manager's fixing the CCTV but I can ask."

"Thanks so much," Perrie enthuses before telling Zac, "Working here would be pretty cool. It's got a good vibe."

"It's Friday night," I object. "And everywhere looks good after a bottle of wine."

Mimi laughs, her tightly coiled hair bouncing as she looks between Perrie and I. "A friend of mine works here. The manager's known to be nice. You could do a lot worse."

Maybe I'll ask too, but late nights don't really work with my early starts in the gym or on the court. And I bet Harrison would have a fit if I seemed off my game due to lack of sleep.

A few minutes later, Erica returns with our beers. She drops off a card with the manager's details on. "Email for Hank is on there," she tells Perrie. "Let him know your free hours."

"Great, thanks!"

"Let's hope your work shirt is bigger than Erica's," Mimi

offers dryly as our waitress sashays back to the bar, her luscious curves spilling out of her uniform.

"I have no objection to the size of the uniform," Zac murmurs, a grin on his mouth just for Perrie.

We settle into the night, the bar busy due to its recent opening. Must be why there are electrical problems. Evan, a friend of Mimi's ex's former ex, or something like that, joins our table. He has dark hair and a square jaw and looks like my next boyfriend, if I wanted one. Which I kind of do. It's been a while since I got laid or kissed a guy, and he looks down for the role. And he's got that arrogant, overly-confident vibe about him that I should avoid at all costs, but still have a weakness for.

I always suspected Harrison ruined me for other men and tonight I'm wondering if he actually has. Seeing him again on Monday morning leaves me conflicted, but I've only got myself to blame—I avoided him for the entire summer. Since New Year's. A few texts and voicemails don't count as *contact.*

I make a mental note to call him over the weekend. He's tried to reach me, to set something up, but so far, I've kept my distance, wanting to keep things professional.

When another round of beers arrive I learn Evan's on the fencing team. My interest is immediately piqued. "For real?"

"Yeah. Been training and competing since I was seven."

"You ever learn to swing a broadsword, or maybe a rapier is more your style?"

He chuckles, revealing dimples that should only make him more appealing. "You thrust with a rapier. Definitely swing a sword, but no, partly because a rapier is too deadly and a sword too cumbersome. I'm no twelfth century knight."

And fuck, he winks at me too. This man is über confident and sexy. Why the hell am I not getting sucked into his orbit?

I'm on the cusp of living and breathing medieval literature, so a man who's learnt the art of swordplay, even if it's a lighter foil designed for sport not slaughter, is a real turn on. I don't need a man to go about his day slaying dragons for me, but knowing he *could,* breathtakingly effortlessly, is an entirely different matter.

I should be jumping his bones. Dragging him in for a kiss.

What's wrong with me tonight?

Just then, Evan gets pulled into another conversation. It means he moves away slightly, the space next to me opening up. Now, I can see several people that were blocked from view.

And that's when I see *him,* an inexplicable tug from my center making me turn my head in his direction.

Our eyes seem to find each other at the same time. I catch just a hint of movement from his body as his whiskey gaze falls on me. Mahogany hair glints under the lights, framing a face made for heartbreak because he is hands down the most handsome man I've ever seen. He's dark perfection, his expression unreadable as he shamelessly studies me. His jaw is defined, his mouth an appealing full shape. In many ways, he's too much to look at so I glance away, embarrassed at how our eyes met so strongly, tied for so long.

But then I look back, to find him doing the same, his head lifting in my direction. He's got to be early thirties, late twenties at best, and he's utter temptation. His lips part fractionally as if he's lost his breath, his mien turning sharp and astute which does powerful things to the rhythm of my pulse, my body liquifying. And his aura is a consuming blend of dark and dangerous, my blood igniting at what that promises.

Then all of a sudden, his eyes sharpen, his jaw flexes. He looks to his blond-haired friend who's peering at me over his shoulder, words exchanged between them. I feel his friend's eyes rake over me, appraising, cataloging, but the dark-haired stranger doesn't look my way again. He does, however, turn his attention to Evan, where it lingers for a hot second, and then he's back to looking at his bottle of beer.

Left confused, I look down at my empty beer bottle on the table. I've never felt so discarded before. Seen and then unwanted. And damn, if I don't immediately think of Harrison.

Loud conversation around me drowns out coherent thoughts, so, head reeling, I rattle off a text to my coach. *Should we talk before Monday's meet?*

Finally. Where are you? I'll pick you up.

I release a sigh, wishing I'd thought this through. *Midnight Blue,* I text back, adding the street name.

Ten minutes, he replies, giving me time to use the bathroom. When I glance at Mr Handsomely Confusing, hoping that I imagined his disinterest, it's to see Erica standing by his seated body, smiling happily. By the cross look on his face, he's an unfeeling asshole to all women he comes across. But he gets to his feet to speak to her so I know I can add *tall* to his description.

At that point I'm turning, heading for the signs that take me down a short corridor to the restrooms. At the end, there are three unisex cubicles. Two of them are locked so I take the only one available.

That's when I realize the light doesn't properly work.

Great.

I lock the door, opening up my front-facing camera to take a look at my reflection, the bathroom flashing light and dark thanks to the busted light. Being dismissed by that guy has stung my confidence. Propping my cell on the wainscoting behind the sink, I give myself a stern talking to: do not sleep with Harrison; do not give in to Harrison; do not think about unattainable, undoubtedly toxic men like Mr Handsomely Confusing. Or Harrison. Think of Evan, I remind myself, who's a hot postgrad, closer in age, and makes me feel wanted.

Despite my own personal talking to, my heart is skittering and I can't work out which man from tonight is making me feel so disorientated. Deciding to splash my face with water, I lean on the wainscoting with my elbow when it comes away from the wall, my phone crashing down behind it.

Crap!

The wainscoting ricochets back into position, so I put my hand on it and force it forwards. But there's no way I can reach behind the paneling to collect my phone—I'd have to pull the woodwork off the wall to do that.

And then I remember: I need to find Hank. Hank who's fixing the CCTV.

I unlock the door, murder on my expression as I stalk towards the bar. I'm just about to push through the door at the end of the hallway when two people beat me to it.

It's Erica-needs-a-bigger-shirt and *him* from the bar.

Refusing to look at him for longer than a cursory glance, I walk past. I don't want to know what they're getting up to. At the bar, I ask a member of staff for the manager, and thankfully, Hank is right there. He has a kind, stubble-rough face and I keep my fingers crossed he doesn't tell me to come back tomorrow; I need my phone.

"Hey, I'm not sure how it happened exactly, but my phone has fallen between the wall and the wainscoting in one of the restrooms. Can you help me get it back?"

He frowns, circumspect. "How'd you manage that?"

"I was leaning on it and it pinged forward."

His frown hasn't lifted, but at least he says, "Let me grab my tool kit. The contractors rushed things," he mumbles by way of explanation.

"*Thank you*," I say, full of gratitude.

He nods. "Meet you down there. Maybe stop people from using it."

"Good idea," I say, immediately turning for the doorway. Harrison will be here soon and I'd rather not keep him waiting.

Back at the cubicles, my heart drops to my toes when I see the door is closed but I try the handle anyway.

Locked.

Suddenly, I hear a woman's raised voice. It was hard to hear what she said but then the door is unlocking, a woman exiting. It takes me a couple of seconds to recognize Erica. Her cheeks look flushed, her brow scrunched up. She spies me at the door, peering at her when a choked sob sounds. Deciphering what caused it has my mind flipping, and then I notice that there's someone else inside the cubicle.

My pulse kicks out in shock when I realize who it is.

In the strobing light he looks angry. Furious. And I don't know if it's because he spots me at the door, taking it all in before I have the good sense to avert my eyes, to step back a little, or if it's because I've interrupted something.

"Sorry," I mumble.

A metallic sound has me looking, investigating what that noise is, but I wish I hadn't because he's buckling his belt.

Buckling. His. Belt.

"Excuse me," he says quietly, moving past, purposefully eyeing the vacant stalls next to us.

I debate with myself, wondering if I should just let the moment pass as unmarked as possible, even though this moment feels lashed to my bones. And then, stupidly, I worry he thinks I've got a bad stomach. "I needed this one. My cell—"

"No problem."

Like a roiling thunderstorm he strides away, disappearing down the corridor and passing Hank and his toolkit.

I loose a breath. Hank is beside me a heartbeat later.

"Thanks," I say, trying to ignore the goosebumps prickling my skin and focus on the task in hand.

He eyes the light with irritation. "Another job to add to the mile long list."

I follow Hank inside the small space and show him how the woodwork pulls away from the wall. A few minutes later, he's managed to prise it away from the corner and guide my phone into that same corner by using a wooden baton to extend his reach.

"Hank, you're a lifesaver, thank you so much," I declare as I pick it up.

Shaking off flecks of dirt and balls of fluff, I check my screen for damage only to see that, somehow, I've managed to video the last seven minutes. Sighing, I toggle straight to my messages to see the latest string of texts from Harrison.

The most recent message reads: *I'm outside.*

I don't want to examine why nerves ride me hard on reading that. Why suddenly seeing him has me hot and cold.

I type out: *Slight hitch. Be there in two.*

4

MADDIE

Miss Me Too - Griff

After updating Perrie on my plans, I head outside and scan the sidewalk. A powder blue Porsche is parked a few cars down the street, so I head towards my ex, my coach, my possible future. When I reach for the door handle, I do a double take.

Waiting outside the shop front to my right is the guy from the bar. He's watching me. Our gaze tangles, his face a picture of implacable ambivalence. At his side, the friend looks on with bemused indifference.

I hop inside the car, letting the weight and momentum of the door pull it closed. Immediately, I feel some relief at getting away from the intense presence of that man, but it's not enough to chase away the flustered emotions striking my body from the person next to me.

"Maddie, it's been a minute."

Harrison's voice wraps around me, choking the air from my

lungs. To hear his voice is so good, and so unbearably bad at the same time. "Hey, Harrison."

"It's good to see you," he says with what sounds like genuine emotion.

Leaning in, his fingers grip my chin as his lips meet mine, his tongue sliding into my mouth. A hot palm rests on my bare thigh, stroking up and down before his fingers curl around my quad. His lips continue to curve over mine because I'm returning his affection which has always been in short supply, and even now I still want it. Want it because I'm weak and stupid where he's concerned. Because I loved him hard. And being with Harrison reminds me that insanely handsome men are not only found in bars called Midnight Blue.

Harrison pulls away. "Damn, babe." Raking his lust-filled eyes over me, he adds, "You look good."

"So do you," I reply automatically because he's never looked anything but impossibly beautiful. Blond, with ocean blue-eyes, tanned and athletically built, his intoxicating smile has been the fantasy of many adoring tennis fans for years. He had a hold of my heart for eons too, even when we broke up. Even when I was cross and hurt and wondering how I could ever be enough for him. Ever keep him.

"What do you think of the car?"

His hands grip the steering wheel, running gently down the sides as if caressing the rounded hips of a woman.

"It's beautiful."

"*She*," he corrects, even though I know his preference to refer to his cars this way. "Cars this gorgeous are always female."

When I was younger I asked him why he referred to his Ferrari as *she* and *her* and *beautiful.* The car I drove at the time didn't have a name. It didn't have a discernible personality or character. Harrison told me, *Sports cars are always female because, one: they're beautiful to look at, begging for my hands to run over their sleek lines, and two: men like to ride their cars* hard. *We race them, push them to their limits and get a serious hard-on whilst we're at it. This car does exactly what I want and is at my complete control, tamed by the power of my touch.*

At the time, I was too enamoured to see how dangerous his metaphors were. Too willing to be tamed between the sheets.

I fix my seatbelt because Harrison is pulling away from the kerb and heading down the street.

"Where are we going?" I ask.

"You can stay over."

I dither for all of a second, cursing the kiss and that I let it happen. "Harrison, I can't."

"New Year's was a long time ago, Maddie. I need you."

New Year's Eve in Princeton didn't end in just a kiss at midnight, but with lots of regret, soul searching, and sore body parts. "I'm not sleeping with you, Harrison," I say, careful of his fragile ego. "Let's see how things go."

"Don't," he cautions, his eyes finding mine under the strobing street lights as we zip down the road, the engine roaring like my heart. "That kiss wasn't a no."

"It was a hello."

As excuses go it was weak, and he uses it against me. "Don't lie to yourself. You know we'll cycle back to each other for another five years. And again after that. It's you and me."

If only that were true.

"I can't go back to yours, Harrison."

There's a ghost of a smile. "Because you know you'll give in. You know this is right and pretending otherwise is pointless. Come on, you're *finally here*. We're a team, the best doubles out there."

"The only team we're in right now is that of coach and athlete. Anything sexual would be inappropriate."

"Like I fucking care."

And there is the crux of the problem; even underage and in his professional care, Harrison abused his position. He always will.

"It never bothered you before," he points out when I remain silent. "And that kiss wasn't a no."

I have no answer to his first statement. I encouraged his pursuit. I was infatuated with him, loving him beyond all reason. At some point, I realized I was a challenge, then someone to pass time with. He didn't love me the way I wanted him to.

We stop for the lights. The powerful engine idles, vibrating through my body as I work out how to move forward from here.

"We'll be discrete," he suggests. "We're good at that."

Having the same relationship all over again is not appealing. And anyway, I've not agreed to reconcile. When, and if, I do decide we have a future, it will be different. Honest. Anything else is just going backwards.

"Can you take me back to my dorm please?" I point which way he needs to turn. "It's been a weird night."

"No. We need to talk and we're not doing it in the car."

"Then come to Jolie Hall and we'll talk there."

A jaw muscle grinds as he calculates. He's never liked it when I stood up for myself. When I refused to play into his hands. Fear whispers through my mind and I try not to encourage it, to allow it to develop into something more tangible. Harrison was always quick to anger; placating him became my mission. And while I know I won't be inviting him inside, he doesn't. But I offer it up, if only to get to where I need to be which is the safety of campus.

Those ocean eyes trail over my face, a sigh leaving him. "I knew you were avoiding me. I hoped you coming here was a sign for us to patch things up and move forward." He frowns, confused. "I thought—finally—that you and I were on the same page, but looks like I was wrong."

There's nothing to say—I *have* been avoiding him. And while my heart is skipping in my chest to be near him, next to him, it's also thudding like a warning drum roll.

"Your father wants this. He'll be happy for our reunion."

The light turns green, Harrison turning in the direction of the dorms and I release an anxious breath.

Dwelling in happier times seems like a good strategy, so I say wryly, "Do you honestly think Dad's approval of my relationships keeps me in line?"

He chuckles, glancing across at me with a smile that usually preceded him doing wicked things to me. And boy, is it hard to keep my resolve. But recently, I've been wondering if toxic relationships are the same as abusive ones, or if there's a difference. Are they mutually exclusive? Maybe for some, the words are interchangeable. It's hard to understand. I just know that Harrison is black-hearted compared to a morally gray man, and it's a shade too dark for me.

Harrison's eyes sweep down my body. "It's why you let me take that tight virgin pussy of yours," he says into the dim-lit car, his words echoing, surrounding me like a physical, unyielding embrace. "Your sweet ass, too."

Memories flicker past my eyes as if I can physically see them: the locker rooms; the bathrooms; the reclined seats of his various sports cars and the endless dark corners of glitzy parties and events. Our relationship always felt like a dirty secret. I thought it was what I wanted, but that infatuated young girl I was grew up. She learned of other types of love, ones to aspire to. Ones to find for myself.

"Pretty sure I didn't have much say about my virginity."

He chuckles out an *Ooohhhh*, like pointing out the truth to him is somehow below the belt. "You were asking for it. You asked for it plenty."

It's the truth, but I hoped it would be closer to what I asked for—softer, with more romance involved. It was the *man* I wanted. The connection. The relationship. The emotion.

"You definitely wanted it," he adds when I don't respond.

Arguing with Harrison is pointless. And this little trip down memory lane isn't making me feel like reconnecting is in my best interests. Our conversations always managed to shred my heart, my resolve, and my opinions.

A few moments later, Harrison pulls up alongside Jolie Hall. I don't need to see the outline of his pants to know he's hard.

Gently, I tell him, "Let's keep this professional."

He puts the car in park and twists in his seat. An arm lifts, his hand coming to rest on my bare shoulder. Wearing shorts and a vest top as it's hot as hell in Boston, his fingers idly draw on my exposed skin. I don't know this version of Harrison. This person who gives me gentle touches.

"You don't want to keep things professional," he murmurs, his heated gaze sliding over my breasts. "You loved getting fucked by your coach. It got you hot. And guess what, I'm your coach again."

I shake my head and avert my gaze, looking for anything to distract me. To avoid any truth to his words. The sidewalk is empty of people. Lights are on in the dorms . . .

Quiet laughter sounds, his fingers digging into my skin. *There he is.* "In fact, you loved me riding you so much you asked me to marry you."

The car empties of air. Of sound. I look him dead in the eye, channeling everything I know about keeping my game face. "That's true," I admit, because I did, stupidly, ask him to marry me when I was young and foolish and thought we were in love. How he laughed in my face. "It was a ridiculous suggestion."

For a moment, he looks at me with a kind of fondness. Of nostalgia, maybe, for how things used to be. "Pretend all you like that you don't still love me. That you didn't love my rough kind of love. But if that's how you want to play it, I'll indulge you—for now—because you're my fucking weakness." Reaching for my thigh, his fingers dance over my skin until I feel a pinch. "And when you ask me to marry you again, I'll never make you regret it. The ball's in your court."

I gather his hand in mine, not because I'm caving to his advances, but because I hate him leaving reminders of himself on my skin. "Don't pinch me."

A scoff sounds as he looks out of the window dismissively, pulling his hand free. "It's like you expect to see a different man every time we meet up." He looks back at me. "I never lived up to your demands, your high standards. Take me as I am, Mads. You used to love that man."

Desperate to understand how I'm feeling, I stare out of the window. Why can't I just quit him? And why is he making sense? It's not often Harrison speaks with such profound insight but it's the God's honest truth—I do expect more from him, something different. But he's not going to change and I'm not going to accept less than what I deserve.

"So, Coach Tait. What's the plan for next week?"

Sighing wearily, he clips out, "Gym work Tuesday and Thursday. We'll get on the courts if we can. Match practice Monday and Friday. The match schedule has already been emailed."

"I got it, thanks. When will seed positions be decided?"

"A week or two. We'll play some sets and see who's strong."

"Who looks good?"

"Robyn is a strong contender for first seed but you need to make it yours." I nod, wanting that first spot. "First seed gets extra time with me."

Yeah, I'm not loving that idea. "I have some early sessions with my professor. I might have to cut practice short here and there."

His lips quirk. "That didn't sound like you were asking your coach nicely, Maddie."

"Oh come on. You know what I'm asking for."

"A good fuck?" His voice drops low. He takes hold of my nearest hand and rubs it over his engorged cock. "Cos' you know I can deliver, baby."

Normally, those words made me melt for him. Being his *baby* was all I ever wanted, but I came to realize the sentiment lasted as long as his orgasm.

I pull my hand away. "Can I please leave early so that I'm not late for my professor?"

"What's it worth?"

"Not that," I mutter.

"Dinner. Have dinner with me and I'll be flexible."

Light from a nearby lamppost distorts his face and I can't decide how to proceed. Whether to be nostalgic too, or to remember the devil he is under the beautiful exterior.

"I don't think dinner is a good idea."

"Then no getting out early. I expect the same commitment from you as everyone else."

Of course that's his response, and part of me knows it's fair. I'm on an athletic scholarship. I need it badly—which Harrison also knows—so I have to pay my due. But come Monday morning, my professor will be hugely disappointed. Now that Harrison knows I need to leave early, he'll make me stay late just to piss me off. To spite me for turning him down.

"Don't take too long to take me back. I won't wait around forever."

The tightly spoken words dangle like tiny weights on the strings of my heart.

Reaching for the door handle, I say, "It was good to talk. See you Monday."

Frustrated silence is all that answers.

5

KIT

Found What I've been Looking For - Tom Grennan

The lock to my office door twists and I push the handle down, entering into a space that feels, until only recently, like mine. Tidy, exact, clean, with no confetti bombs in sight. It's a corner office with three windows that overlook the college and the paths that criss-cross the lawns. There's a big, century-old desk, two entire walls dedicated to books and texts, and by the second window, a couple of old leather sofas offer a chance for more informal discussions. Nearby, a seminar table to seat six takes up the last bit of floor space.

Curiously anxious, I check the time on my watch, then I drop into my desk chair and log on to the network. From my bag, I pull out Madrigal's file to review—again.

It was her, the other night in the bar. It took me a few seconds to recognize her, but once I had, I knew I was going to cut my night short. And it was a night that went from good to bad to worse.

Erica Reid, who has never meant anything more to me than a consensual, sometime release, has relocated to Boston. She tried to convince me it was what I wanted. Clearly delusional, I was having none of it. My evening had already turned sour after locking eyes with Miss Devereaux, but the evening ended by falling off a cliff. Letting Erica down, ensuring she knew there was no future between us could've gone better, but after seeing Madrigal, I wasn't in the right frame of mind for pleasantries or patience. And fuck my cursed luck if Madrigal wasn't on the other side of the door when Erica stormed off.

I blow out a sharp breath as I consider all the ways that encounter could've been misconstrued. The look of wry disapproval on my student's face tells me she's made up her mind about events.

With Josh's move to Jacquard, it was a long overdue opportunity to catch up. So we went out to celebrate his new job and that the two of us were working alongside each other like the good old days. Neither of us realized Bar Midnight had a sister bar, Midnight Blue. Neither of us knew Erica had asked for a transfer, ostensibly to be closer to me. To pursue something with me.

There was so much to learn about the department when I finished gardening leave that I only looked at my new student files a week ago. I was shocked to my core to see Pete had accepted Madrigal to my course.

Concentrating on the the file in my hands, I re-read the French paper Madrigal submitted alongside her application. It's annoyingly impressive. Considering she only took three relevant classes at Princeton it was faultless, actually. Her knowledge of the subject is vast, her analytical mind showing a maturity older postgrads struggle with. Still, her capabilities are entirely bothersome. As was the picture I stumbled across online when she'd turned eighteen. It was unintentional, but there it was, on the news site that I had been scrolling through.

Devereaux Heiress Celebrates Eighteenth Birthday.

Instinct made me look away, but then curiosity, the morbid, sickening kind, dragged me back to the photograph of the new adult with her parents either side of her. Dressed in a pale gold sequin dress that hugged her body, she looked every inch the starlet I expected her to be, the progeny of a family superpower. She was undoubtedly pretty—and young—and so beyond my sphere of existence that I slammed my laptop closed and went to a bar for a much-needed drink. But that image of her haunted me, her eyes beckoning me to take another look, a *longer* look, like they were fucking talking to me.

But no. I couldn't. Couldn't, because I feared that in looking, it would make me want.

For four years since that night I have avoided seeing her face.

I glance at my watch again to see I've wasted too much time thinking about someone I've denied existed. And yet, here I am, waiting for that denial to sit opposite me in a matter of moments.

8.43 AM

She's very late.

I dash out a text to my grandfather, who, at the age of eighty-one, manages to communicate by text message, even sometimes sending me gifs, video, and memes.

The man has skills.

Hey Gramps. Don't forget to take your meds today. I want video evidence.

My message returns a *Read* receipt. Then I see that he's replying.

I'll get to it. You just concentrate on you and your work.

It's followed with: *And concentrate on making me a great-grandfather. Neither you or Hélène seem to be in any hurry.*

Hélène is my older sister by two years. She doesn't want children which is a point of view I fully understand. Loving people hurts, especially when you lose them young in tragic accidents that seem to happen too often in my cursed family.

There's an abrupt knock at my door, the door handle already lowering as I call out: "Come in."

The door sweeps open, Madrigal's bright hazel eyes flying to mine as she steps inside. The amount of time it takes her to do this is barely two seconds, but her arrival distills into microseconds, her quick movements, her arresting beauty that confronts me like a car crash, condensed into a slo-mo film.

Last night, her thick hair was loose and wavy; now it's tied back in a high ponytail. Her face holds an old world appeal, an icon of the golden age of film, even without last night's red lipstick accentuating her mouth. Still, I'm met with a graceful, ageless beauty, thanks to the smooth curve of her cheekbones and the shape of her sensuous eyes. And there's an openness to her face, a beguiling mix of curiosity tinged with nerves, in stark contrast to last night where she sat sparkling and amused with her friends, or dismayed at my bathroom exploits.

I'd spotted her before we'd locked eyes. At that stage, all I had was a profile. And when that asshole, Evan, had moved out of the way, I willed her to turn. To look my way. To *find* me.

I'd almost given up hope. I'd stopped staring at her, looking at my beer in consolation. But then, suddenly, she turned, just as I looked up again. A few seconds later, realization struck.

Rising from my chair, I shake her hand and introduce myself formally. It's almost comical the way the curiosity in her features morphs into one of shock, concern, and then passive professionalism. Still, she shakes my hand firmly, her eyes invasive and searching, a mirror to how she looked at me when our eyes met across the bar.

"Madrigal, I'm Professor Chevalier, though I go by Professor Kit if you'd prefer."

"Hello. I'm Maddie."

Ignoring her correction, I gesture to the red-cushioned chair opposite my desk. "Please, sit."

Only now do I notice the waist-length zipped tennis jacket covering her top half, but aside from a scrap of material, there's nothing on her legs. Long, tanned legs, which are highly distracting, not least for the definition in her quads and hamstrings, the sleek power strikingly obvious, but because her skirt is Very. Dangerously. Short.

I hide my discomfort with a reprimand, uncaring of her email warning me of her tight schedule. "You seem to have mistaken my office for the tennis court."

Surprise passes across her face before she apologizes, her following answer brief. "Practice overran."

From out of her padded, oversized racquet bag she pulls out a pen and notebook. She leans the bag against my desk before sitting on the chair. Crossing her legs discretely, I can't see anything from behind the table and I congratulate myself that I chose to sit here and not on the deep-cushioned couch.

She seems a little out of puff. Her chest rises and lowers, her cheeks carry a light blush, and I wonder if she ran here.

"What's the name of your coach?"

No longer staring at her shoes, her eyes fly to mine. Is she protective of him? She wouldn't be the first student I've taught who prioritizes sport or parties over college, the coaches idolized.

"Harrison Tait."

Of course, I know this. I saw her get into his car Friday night. Saw him kiss her, though I can't be certain. I was already walking away but it looked like he was leaning in towards her.

What I didn't already know from his short, professional

career, I looked up online. A former US tennis pro, he was injured at twenty-four, having won five grand slams which earned him the moniker *King of the Court*. In that time, he was fined several times for his oncourt outbursts. He coached for a time, privately, before turning his hand to commentating. Still a bachelor at thirty-four years of age, I'm not convinced about him. And I'm not sure how his job as coach compliments that at a national broadcaster.

"Okay, so I wanted to resolve your teaching schedule which will be three classes a week."

"I thought it was two," Madrigal challenges.

She's correct, but it's not up for discussion. Choosing someone else is an option, but her mother-tongue language skills means she's the superior choice. Passing her a copy of the department's timetable, I say, "Mrs Pantazis has highlighted your classes. I trust there won't be a clash with your studies but let her know if there is."

"I'll let her know there's one too many."

I school my face, disliking the entitlement. "Failure to meet teaching or academic commitments will mean that your athletic scholarship is in jeopardy."

Her face falls, her eyes flashing fire.

Deciding honesty might be best, even though part of me doesn't want to go easy on her—the Chevaliers didn't have it easy, I offer, "We do need someone with your skills to pick up this session. I was hoping you wouldn't mind."

"Fine, I'll do an extra session."

Fleetingly, I consider asking why she's on financial aid when her father is richer than Croesus, but then I remember that the less I know about her the better.

It doesn't make sense, Josh told me. Well, it'll have to remain a mystery.

One mystery I've managed to solve was The Duel, my induction as Knight at Club VX taking place several weeks ago. The fencing bouts were just as tough as the tournaments I enter, but I won convincingly enough. A brief interview followed, after which I was enthusiastically welcomed.

Rumors of secret societies have always been rife amongst ancient institutions. Old clubs like VX have been the preserve of old money and prestigious families for generations. And while my name is as old as they come, it's a name that no longer carries the pedigree or prestige that it used to.

At some point I'm going to have to tell Josh about the club, though I'm sworn to secrecy. The confidentiality agreement was weighty and complex, but I'm not sure I can't *not* talk about this to someone I trust implicitly.

Snapping out of my thoughts, I see Maddie tugging at her tennis skirt, agitated.

"I know I didn't apply here within the usual timeframe, but you should know that I am extremely passionate about European medieval literature. My transcript details my grades and statements from my tutors which should allay any fears that I've come to this half-hearted. Tennis won't get in the way of my work. I'm dedicated to both and divide my time carefully."

"That's very reassuring, Madrigal," I say dispassionately.

"I go by Maddie," is her steel-coated answer. After all, it says so at the top of her application, but being named after a medieval short lyrical poem, a vocal piece, is far too complex and intriguing a name to be shoved to one side.

As she brings out a drinks bottle from her racquet bag and downs a third of it in greedy gulps, I consider if there's anything poetic about Madrigal.

Even though she's provided a well-rounded essay on why a doctorate in my chosen field appeals, I ask, "Why medieval literature?"

"Tristan and Iseult is the most famous, oldest legend, crafted into an iconic piece of literature. It predates the Arthurian legend of Lancelot and Guinevere which was influenced by this tragic romance. Which gets all the glory," she tags on as if annoyed.

I've heard uninspiring answers before but that was pretty lame. "Some would argue to the contrary, seeing as Wagner composed an operatic masterpiece on Tristan and Isolde."

"Some would argue that," she confirms, and I wonder if she's referencing me in that statement. And if she is, I don't care for her opinionated ass.

As a professor and a department head, only I have that privilege. I don't rise to it. "And what interests you specifically about the works of De Troyes?" It's a standard interview question, one of many I never got the chance to ask.

"Chrétien de Troyes' poems of courtly love have dominated the West's view of romance ever since they were written, influencing countless Minnesänger in the German court and wider still. This era is page zero of the history of literature."

Page zero is debatable but I don't argue the point. "Do you consider the works from this era tragic or romantic?"

"Undoubtedly tragic. Tristan and Iseult have to overcome so many obstacles, not least adultery and poison, war and exile, betrayal and death. She loves King Mark, but she loves Tristan too. *More*. It's not a pretty love story."

"Are love stories ever pretty?"

An eyebrow arcs which stirs my blood in confusing ways. "Of course. Western civilization thrives on happy ever afters."

"But you're not sold on them?" The inflection in her voice tells me she's uninterested.

Bitterness creeps into her tone. "Love is meant to be all conquering, so it's gratifying to see it reflected as such. But courtly love is underpinned by adultery. And I know the noble ladies were often unhappily married due to necessary alliances, but adultery is villainous, the antithesis of the expected morality these knights were held accountable to."

"Marriage was often out of necessity, it's true. But not all relationships were sexual. Often, they were expressions of admiration and esteem. Deeds enacted to show a knight's valour, honor, and worth." She should know this. Perhaps she chooses to ignore the tenets by which knights lived.

Madrigal looks unconvinced. "Then it shouldn't be termed courtly *love*. I always come back to this: *When it hurts and destroys its follower, Love is worse than Hatred.*"

It's an apt choice of quotation and only confirms that she's either jaded as all fuck about love, or is on a real downer today. Feeling charitable, I offer her something to reflect on. Something I should heed more today and stop baiting Madrigal. "*When a man fails to honor ladies, his own honor must be dead.*"

"Well, that's true." She bites her lower lip but it's too late: the words are out there. She swallows, asking, "Do you mind if I open a window? It's hot," she continues, unzipping her jacket and rising to her feet to shrug out of it.

And damn me to hell and back but my eyes linger and trace over her blood-stirring physique before I walk to the nearest window and open it as far as it will go. Then I move to the second window and do the same, needing a hit of cooler air myself. When I return to my desk, a light summer breeze stirs the papers on my desk.

"Better?" I ask, trying not to notice her cute tennis dress as I retake my seat. Is that a bruise on her thigh? Her shoulder?

"Thank you," she says, catching me noticing her clothing, her body, and, presumably thinking back to the other night where she saw me emerge from the bathroom re-doing my belt, is unimpressed.

"You've chosen two of my courses this semester."

She sits back down and nods, a total lack of enthusiasm on her face. "They fit with my doctorate aspirations."

Fair enough. I glance at the other courses on her schedule: historical linguistics, Italian literature. "And the postmodern feminism lectures with Professor Hurren do too?"

A genuine laugh, soft and seductive reaches toward me across the desk. "My good friend, Perrie Secker, is doing a doctorate in this field. It's not something I'm nearly as enthusiastic about, but I need to keep up with her arguments."

I know of Perrie Secker. And annoyingly, I like Madrigal's answer. "You're competitive." And I understand competition. I live it. It drives me too.

"We disagree frequently so it's more . . . combative," she offers with an arched brow. And fuck me, if my pulse doesn't kick out again at that tiny gesture. At the thought of getting lost in academic arguments, debating intricacies and contradictions. Could Madrigal be an equal, young as she is? Her confidence is astounding.

I dismiss that errant thought. She's not my equal, for three reasons. One, she's an heiress to a dynasty. Two, she's descended from actual fucking nobility. And three, I'm a tenured professor who's published multiple papers and she's a freshman postgrad of twenty-two. Not to mention I find her annoying and vexatious. Clearly she knows the literature, the code, but seems intent on challenging every single thing about it.

"Everybody should be a feminist," she continues, glancing at me strangely as if she heard my inner thoughts. "But I don't always agree with every argument a feminist has, which in many ways," she counters, "is anti-feminist."

"I promise not to tell your friend."

"Thanks." A tentative smile emerges. I want to wipe it off her face. *With my cock.*

"Most of my students, Madrigal, come here with a sense that chivalry and heroism are a lost art. Many postgrads have written a thesis on these themes. Yours included," I add, knowing her intentions for her doctorate as specified in her application.

"Actually, I've changed my mind on my thesis." I look up, waiting. "I, er—" She looks around the room as if it, this place, is to blame for her change of mind. "Over the weekend I, well, that is to say, I had a change of heart. I want to focus on research behind missing manuscripts and passages from the medieval era."

"This isn't a history PhD."

I stare at her, waiting for an answer to my dick statement.

Hearing it, her eyes narrow. "Sorry, was there a question?"

Internally, I growl. I'm undecided if it's a purring growl of want or one of warning.

Before I answer, she continues, "And actually, I think you're wrong. The very nature of medieval literature is historic. The languages these poems were written in old versions of modern French, German and English."

"A valid point," I concede, because she's infuriatingly right, and I can be reasonable. "Why the change of heart?"

A shrug. "I don't know. It just felt right, coming here."

She fidgets in her seat, so I ask, "What's your view on chivalry?"

"It's hard to read literature written nine hundred years ago and not view it through twenty-first century eyes. As a modern woman, the idea of chivalric, gallant men is highly appealing. But, De Troyes and his contemporaries wrote in a time where society viewed woman as needing protection, descriptions of their virtues or beauty all encompassing. Doesn't that imply we're fragile? Do we really drive men to acts of bravery?" A knowing look. "Or stupidity? As a feminist, I would say I don't need to be rescued. As a modern woman, I would argue that chivalry goes both ways, that it's still appealing, but that women want more than gallantry alone."

Her candidness is too appealing. "More than gallantry?"

It's a deeply personal question, and she lets me know it.

"You can't expect to know the inner workings of a woman's heart, as represented in medieval texts, or now, Professor Chevalier."

The use of my more formal title brings the telling signs of a smirk to my face. And she was right—she is combative which I've always found incredibly attractive. My mind deviates to a place where I command her to get on her knees and suck me off for that sass. Instead, I use my position of power in a more appropriate way. "Sounds like your first essay. You have a week to hand it in."

The smile on her face is deceptive, as if I've met preconceived ideas.

"As you know, academia doesn't view the works of De Troyes et al with modern eyes. They can only be considered illustrative of their time."

"I know. Chivalric love has a lot going for it, that's true. And a lot to answer for. Just imagine all those broken hearts because we were sold a lie a millennium ago. A lie so embedded in our mainstream media, literature, and music that we're forever disappointed. What man can live up to that? What woman?"

"Not many," I wager.

"I need convincing. Anyway, it's why I like puzzles," she admits. "Finding missing manuscripts which would answer vital questions from a period of history where so few records remain, is a long-held ambition. Who knows—maybe in those last stanzas, De Troyes wrote that it was all horse shit and men should trample over the hearts of women. Should disrespect them because, haven't you noticed, women like unattainable, damaged men?"

Our eyes lock. The silence is so damning, I can hear every soft inhale as the seconds tick by. And I swear I can hear her eyelashes flutter as she sits there, unable to look away.

"Only in their fantasies," I begin, "which is an entirely different seminar given by a colleague. You can sign up next semester if it's of interest."

She laughs and shrugs a shoulder as if the idea is anathema. "I'll pass." And under her breath I'm sure she whispers, "I could teach the class."

Hmm. Mademoiselle Devereaux is perplexing, infuriating, and inconveniently taking up a much larger space in my head than I wanted her to occupy. And while I wanted her at least two thousand miles away from me, in another college, for the first time in months I might be the slightest bit grateful that my ploy backfired.

Attractive eyes dance about my face, but when I catch them up in my own, they jump to my obsessively tidy desk, then the qualifications hung on the wall, then the scars on the backs of my hands thanks to a life spent learning the art of the sword. She smooths down her tennis skirt as I cast my mind back to what she said about puzzles and missing manuscripts. Her interest is also one of mine. Ironically, historians have long argued that alongside the known missing pages, entire stories might yet be unearthed, ones stolen from knights of the French court.

Ones named Chevalier.

"Is there anything else you'd like to discuss?" I ask before I think it through. Discussing literature from this time period is no hardship—I could do it for hours. And learning the perspective of my students is always refreshing. Debate is healthy. Academia is a process of continual learning, and I'm not complacent enough to think I can't learn something from those just starting out in their academic careers.

And frustratingly, I don't want her to go. I haven't met a woman with such depth of character, or candidness. She possesses an intoxicating vulnerable complexity that I want to explore. Normally, women bore me, or are too busy agreeing with everything I say.

Madrigal swallows. "You were at Brownlow before you came here?"

I nod, anticipating her line of enquiry and regretting offering up the window of opportunity.

"You were a big reason why I applied. Do you know why I was rejected? It stings a little," she says with such brutal honesty, and with such a dejected smile, it makes me sick to my stomach for my actions. It makes me take a long hard look at my preconceived opinion of her.

"Did you not ask them directly?" I divert.

"No," she responds, though I'm not entirely sure I believe her. And why doesn't that surprise me, a Devereaux lying to a Chevalier?

Thinking it fair game, I lie right back. "I started gardening leave when the acceptance and rejection emails went out, so I'm not sure, Madrigal."

Abruptly, she stands. "It's Maddie. Call me Maddie, please."

Jesus, *okay*. I quite liked Madrigal as a name but, whatever. The lyrical tones of her voice are exactly what a complex, unaccompanied vocal piece brings to mind. "Is it a family name?"

"No."

"It's an apt name. Can I ask why you don't like it?"

"Can I lie?"

"No. Lying is against the chivalric code," I respond with heavy irony.

She scoffs, bending to collect her things as I rise to my feet. By the looks of things, our meeting has ended but I don't recall drawing it to a close. She leaves, those long, toned legs carrying her swiftly to my door as a heaviness, the source of which I can't place, settles in my chest.

Depressing the lever, the door yawns wide. Over her shoulder, her eyes latch to mine. "Then I guess neither one of us is a hero."

6

MADDIE

Something to Someone - Dermot Kennedy

"How'd it go?" Perrie asks as soon as she spots me. We made plans to grab some lunch before we hit the library and she's a sight for sore eyes.

Slumping into the seat opposite her, I sigh. "As expected."

By the looks of her crumb-laden plate she's already eaten, which confirms being late is the story of my life right now.

Ravenous, I unwrap my turkey salad sub and take a huge bite. "He gave me some shit for being late, so I gave purposefully unimaginative answers to simple questions."

"Dick. Him, not you," she clarifies with a self-congratulatory grin.

"It's okay. I can be a dick too."

"Only when pushed."

"And he was pushing," I assert. "Being provocative and obtuse. But, to his credit," I point out, suddenly remembering a significant moment, "and this is the *only* positive, he stood up when I walked in and shook my hand while introducing himself."

"Very gentlemanly. I like it."

"Yeah, I did too. But the best bit is that I realized a nano second after walking into his office that I saw him in Midnight Blue."

Looking back on that night, I wonder if it took him a few seconds to recognize me as his student. It's the only thing that makes sense. Why else undress me with his eyes and then look at me like I'd just run over his dog? And his cold expression didn't change when I bumped into him in the corridor, the bathroom stall, or outside the bar.

The next few years are going to be difficult. It is an inconvenient truth but Professor Kit is ridiculously nice to look at. And the occasional agreeable moment today aside, he's mostly antagonistic and difficult, which is not much of a deterrent for someone predisposed to assholes like me. The bombshell waitress is clearly involved with him, though I'm really curious why she was upset. If I hadn't got a look at his personality today, that small insight into his life told me he's got toxic written all over him.

And that's not good for me.

Still, there's one other thing that I keep to myself for a moment. Another highlight from meeting him today. His voice is a double bass, resonant and warm. It comes right from his chest, full of sensuality and power and is far too appealing. There are echos of familiarity to it, prickling my senses.

With a jolt, I remember the recording my phone made while stuck, hidden in the wall. That's getting deleted ASAP because there's no way I want to listen to them having sex.

Right?

"No way! I missed him? The man in the flesh?" Perrie pouts. "Guess I only had eyes for Zac that night," she jokes.

"He lives and breathes and isn't just a pretty picture."

My friend chuckles gleefully. "Told you. I'm looking forward to our epic poem class on Wednesday. I want to meet him. I bet his body count is sky high," she suggests, waggling her eyebrows at me.

"Eww. Please don't say things like that."

"Just stating facts," she challenges before changing tack. "So you were late? Is that because you got a chance to change and look presentable?"

After my meeting with Professor Chevalier I returned to my dorm and got ready for the day, agreeing to meet Perry here after her classes. "Funny," I respond. "No. Harrison was also being a dick and wouldn't let me leave on time. It's been a double dick day, and not for any fun reasons."

Perrie snorts into her cup. "The worst kind of day. You called it though. With Harrison."

I demolish my sub, famished from an early start and busy morning. After my brief car ride with my ex, I filled Perrie in on the conversation we shared. I sigh, tired of feeling so topsy-turvy when I'm around him. And his BS attitude this morning, purposefully making me late, is going to get old very quickly.

"Yeah. I did. And you called it with the prof. How do you know so much about guys?"

It's a rhetorical question, but Perrie says, "Handsome guys have no trouble getting women, so they're shit at keeping the one they've got."

"True."

Denying I still love Harrison, however shallow or deep that runs, is pointless. The reality is that I can't shake him. And the effort it takes to regather all those bits and pieces of myself when we see each other, to try and remain strong, is exhausting. Why do I put myself through this?

While I sip at my hot chocolate—a treat to myself for the

epic day I'm having—Perrie updates me on her morning. Unhelpfully, I find myself thinking about my dream last night, the one that starred a faceless man. Remembering the details alludes me, but as soon as I woke up, I knew someone important to me had featured, his form and voice and presence drifting away like smoke until there was nothing left of him at all.

Who is that man, and what is he to me? And why does the distant memory of his voice make my heart ache?

Perrie takes a deep breath. "So, enough about random people I meet. What does your schedule look like?"

I roll my eyes. "He gave me *three* classes."

"For real?"

"Yup! When I said I'd let his PA know there was an error, he threatened me."

"What'd he say?!"

I don't bother sharing the comment about my skills being required. That was desperate flattery to make me reconsider. I don't have time for extra sessions, even if it earns me kudos with my professor. "He flat-out told me that scholarships were in jeopardy if teaching or student commitments weren't met."

"Dick."

"You were right. You said he'd shit all over his predecessor's work and make it hard for me."

Perrie frowns. "We're in red flag territory."

Zac and Evan enter the coffee shop, looking around as if they're expecting to meet someone.

"I told them we might be here," Perrie confesses when I whisper across the table that they just walked in. "Is that okay? Evan looked crestfallen when you ran out on him at Midnight Blue."

I check the time. "Ha, sure he was! Anyway, I promised to call Mom."

Evan and Zac make their way over to our table where I say a

quick hello before making my excuses, Evan's dimpled smile not delaying me one bit. Then I head outside to make my call. Mom'll want all the details of the past few days but I'll stick to the facts and keep things simple and upbeat.

A low wall nearby provides me with a seat as I wait for Mom to pick up.

"Maddie, darling. How are you?"

"Good, Mom. Things are good."

Quickly, I mention practice and that Harrison is still a pain in my ass, and that my professor seems likeable and interesting, for reasons I don't elaborate on.

"That's good. I'm pleased. It's a new chapter, exciting and daunting at the same time."

"Sure is," I agree down the line. "Did you and Dad have a good weekend?"

"Yes, we had lunch with the Duvals at that French restaurant we like so much on Lavalle Street."

"Yeah, what'd you order?"

Please be eating. Please be eating.

"The lobster. I'm predictable, I know."

"Good choice. I remember their puddings were divine."

"They still are. I had the pana cotta this time and I wasn't disappointed."

I'm so happy, I beam into my phone. House-sitting for the widower was a gamble, but Dad and Mom accepted my decision. Working full-time is still a long way off but I need to earn money in the holidays when I can. And although I'd only managed a couple of nights at home after my dog-sitting gig ended, Dad has been good to his word, and importantly, it's had an immediate affect on Mom's well-being.

"Any plans for the week?"

"Well, I have my day at CanTRA which I'm looking forward to." Mom's voice becomes enquiring. "Will you come to the charity event next month? Some very interesting people attend and I'd love for you to meet them."

Supporting Mom is high on my agenda, so I say, "If it fits with my schedule, Mom, I'll be there."

"Oh thank you, darling. I saw the perfect dress for you."

"I'm sure I have something—"

"My treat. Let me, please."

I take a breath. "Okay, Mom."

The happiness in her voice when she continues telling me about her week patches up the little holes in my heart like mortar in a brick wall. "And then your father surprised me by suggesting we go away for Thanksgiving, or Christmas, but I didn't know your plans. I would want to see you."

It's too early to make plans for the holidays and I tell Mom just as much. "A weekend away sounds great though, Mom! Book something while there's still a chance."

"Yes," she agrees. "That's what your father said."

I laugh softly. "Well, I'd better go. Let me know what your plans are once you've booked."

"I'll message you the date for the ball."

"Can Perrie come too?"

"Of course. Bring your darling friend."

We say our goodbyes and I toggle to my text messages. Pulling up the latest thread to Dad, I write: *Mom seems happy. Thank you. Can I suggest Tennessee for Thanksgiving?*

Mom's sisters are in Tennessee and she doesn't see enough of them, mostly because Dad doesn't like going. I rise from the wall, my ass numb. As I reach the door to the coffee shop I get a text back.

Spend Christmas at home, Maddie, and I'll take her.

I reply, *Deal.*

Five nights minimum, he adds which makes me smile. He's always locking down those loopholes.

I send an emoji of a contract and pen. *I agree to your terms.*

My first week at Jacq U speeds by. Wednesday's class with the man of the hour was less problematic than I thought it would be. Kit Chevalier played it down the line.

He was tolerable. Pleasant.

I answered his questions to the best of my ability, occasionally debating my point of view with him alone before he opened it up to the class. At no point did it feel unnecessarily combative, even if I felt his eyes landing on me too often, an eagerness to demand more opinions from me hovering on his lips.

It's progress.

Perrie, who seems to be less of a fuck-up when it comes to matters of the heart, found him genuine, intellectually extra, and too next level for the good of womankind.

He's *extra* alright. An extra pain in my ass.

Thursday is spent in the library. Afterwards, Perrie decides to go to the gym, so I head back to the dorms, lost to my rambling thoughts. My mind churns over a thousand things: how I feel about Harrison; tennis commitments; the years of work ahead of me; Mom and Dad's happiness. But those questions are overshadowed by my frequent dreams and the man at the center of them. Who is he? And where are all these dreams coming from? Are they linked to my arrival at Jacquard and my new life here? At that brewing sense of anticipation?

I cast my mind back to the dream, of the fuzzy outline of a man who captivates me. And while I can't picture him, my pulse quickens when I think of how strong and virile he is. Love for him lights me up in a way I can't fully comprehend as I re-live a series of brief moments where we read, debate, make love, or dream of an untroubled future.

I don't see the auburn-haired woman waiting by the doors

until I almost walk straight into her. Dressed in a sky blue pant suit with a pretty floral blouse, she looks nothing like the casual student population around here.

"Madrigal Devereaux?"

The woman pronounces my name in perfect French. "Yes?"

It's then I see the white envelope in her hand, which she extends towards me.

"My name is Sophie Bouchard. We have selected you for a unique opportunity, Miss Devereaux. The log-in details to view this opportunity remain accessible until 11PM only. My contact details are enclosed should there be further questions. I trust you will accept."

Baffled, I ask, "What's this about?"

Looking at the envelope, I notice my full name hand-written on the front. My pulse careens. Is this a legal document?

"Have a good day, Miss Devereaux."

Walking to a silver BMW, she hops inside and drives away.

What the hell?

I flip the envelope over to see an image of a shield, a sword speared through the middle. A black horse rears on either side of the shield, their dark manes flowing out behind them. Intrigued, I check the time on my phone.

8.17PM.

Doubtful it's anything interesting, I tear open the envelope. Inside is a slip of paper with Sophie Bouchard's cell number and email address. The company name is VX.com.

There's a website I need to log onto, a code typed out on the piece of paper which grants me access. Curious, I climb the stairs, enter my dorm room and sit at my desk. When I log onto the website, a simple white page loads, black text inviting me to enter the login details.

I type them in. As long as I'm not asked to provide any personal or bank details, what's the harm? And Sophie knew me on sight and by name. That's not insignificant. How does she know me? My middle names are not public knowledge, though they're listed on my application to the school.

Is this anything to do with Jacquard?

The first page to load is entirely black. Words like a watermark appear across the screen.

Société d'honneur.

A message box pops up, silver text greeting me with *Welcome Madrigal.* Then a *play* button appears. Just that. No text, no obvious video, just a small silver triangle in the middle of the screen below the society's name.

Taking a moment to think about this, of Trojan horses and malware, I steel my spine, click on *play,* and watch as a video comes to life onscreen.

Atmospheric music accompanies a series of slow-mo videos, each morphing into the next via stylish editing. Nothing is easily discernible. All I can make out at first is the flow of dark-colored fabric, or a blurred light, the slow opening of an iron-studded door. The notes of the music strike me, something dark and tempting as a dimly-lit room is revealed. Thick pillar candles housed in black lanterns circle the interior as haunting piano notes give way to drums, the tempo evocative and sensual.

My breathing turns shallow, the panning camera offering a glimpse of a man's form. Slowly, it becomes clear that he's wearing black chainmail, the metal glinting from what little light there is. A sword is gripped in his hand, the sharp, silver edge shining. There's a fleeting image of an opponent robed in silver. Helmets cover their faces, their features indistinct.

The video segues into one that shows those swords meeting, battling, clashing with a ferocity I've only ever seen in films. The prowess of those men, of their raw power, stirs my soul in a way that has my pulse accelerating. Flashes, short scenes of chandeliers, gold-filigreed cornicing, and wood-paneled walls give me some idea of what type of room, of building this *duel* is taking place in. When I see the coats of armor mounted on the walls, I know I'm on the right path.

A sword clatters to the floor.

Hands raise in surrender.

The thump of the bass drums crescendo as a circle of men—also wearing silver armor—congratulate the black-clad victor, clapping or thumping a fist into their armor.

In direct contrast to my heart, the beat of the drums slows as a woman walks towards a wooden throne.

Fucking hell, there's a *throne.*

Her dress is long, an elegant cream. She sits, the angle of the camera obscuring her face. Golden hair cascades down her back, a simple tiara crowning her head. A series of short clips consist entirely of the silky material of her dress, the sensual movement of it playing in perfect synchronicity with the swelling, seductive strains of the violins. The scene merges sinuously with the next, the black-dressed knight approaching the throne. There's a far-off shot of the room emptying, of the knight stepping up onto the dais where the woman waits in a position of power.

I don't need to see what comes next. The scene has already played out in my head, the music, the brief, short glimpses of muscled physiques, of weapons, of secrecy all leading to one conclusion. So when the knight kneels, when the woman on the throne undresses, I feel relieved.

This was expected. Wished for, even.

He went to war.

She is his prize.

A sharp throb in my core has me sucking in a mesmerized breath. The music fades out, the film slowing down until the colors turn entirely black, the writhing bodies of the knight and his lady melting into the outro.

Heart racing, wanting more, I wait for what feels like forever.

Words appear onscreen. *Do you wish to join? Type YES.*

A blank box appears, the space where I type my answer has three corresponding dashes.

A sense of desperation hits me. Searching the screen for a *watch again* button, I wonder if I'll lose this page if I reload the video or hit the back button. It's a potential error I want to avoid because my mind is already made up.

I knew as soon as the woman appeared.

No man I know ascribes to this code; I want a glimpse of it, to understand why the theme of chivalric love has such a hold on the world.

On me.

Sophie Bouchard told me I had been selected, and it would be easy to think I was chosen based on my specialty. To the contrary, the study of knights and courtly love has a much stronger connection to me than my doctorate. Because that dream I can't seem to visualize manifests more brightly in my mind's eye. Not the indistinguishable person with a profound link to me, but I become aware of the era my dream is set in.

Of the century.

It's like I lived a life at court, breathed it.

I want to be the woman on the throne.

Without pause, my fingers find Y - E - S.

7

MADDIE

Mixed Emotions - Chase and Status

Already, my first week has passed, albeit in a blur of long days where early gym sessions, practice, classes, and study had me whizzing about campus like a pinball. I gave up trying to negotiate an early release from my tennis commitments because Harrison is still demanding dinner.

The only highlight is that Sophie Bouchard called. It transpires she's French Canadian, our conversation in our mother tongue reminding me of home and weirdly homesick. But underneath that, it means she's also acquired my cell number. We arranged to meet at the club in ten days, where she promised to detail what exactly I'd agreed to. After being assured I could back out at any point, and that there was a hefty compensation for my time—twenty thousand dollars—it's an opportunity I can't easily turn down.

Ten days is a long time to wait but there's no way to speed things along.

Perrie would be appalled at my decision so I've decided not to tell her. Sophie explained I'd have to sign a NDA, so discussing it with a friend looks unlikely anyway. And while I have doubts, fears, and a motherload of caution, I remind myself that I'm young and single with zero commitments. Harrison doesn't deserve my abstinence—we're not together—so there's nothing to consider. Besides, the secret society has me beyond intrigued, and the money will fund any financial losses should my professor follow through on his threats.

I need this money, but more importantly, I need this dark, mysterious experience. Sophie explained there's an opening available soon, or it's a four month wait. Waiting is not my forté.

The languages department is a beautiful Victorian square building with drafty windows and creaky staircases. My linguistics seminar is due to be held in room 2.4, but there's a note on Dr Philpott's door saying she's had a family emergency, and that the class will now be held in Professor Chevalier's office.

Sigh.

At times, it feels like I see him more than I do Perrie, and we share a room.

I remind myself that there's been a noticeable détente between the professor and I. Or rather, he appears less stick-up-the-ass and more of what a teacher should be: approachable, engaging, smart beyond measure, with an appealing quiet authority about him. And although things have mellowed between us, I can't forget the extra session added to my timetable, nor the essay he assigned me, plucked from thin air. Professor Chevalier definitely decided to bust my balls when I first met him and I wonder if it's because I caught him with his pants down—literally. Okay, *almost*. But if that's not the reason, then what is?

Whatever it is, his knowledge is a turn on. He knows the literature inside out, quotes tripping off his tongue and the history behind the stories, the comparisons between authors of long ago so clearly marked in his brain it's a thing of beauty.

Smart men are a compulsion. The fact that Professor Kit looks like an AI bot created him in real life, helps an awful lot too.

Thankfully the class is late-morning, and I've had a chance to shower and change into normal clothes: loose jeans and a tight t-shirt with the word *Paris* across the front.

Walking to the far corner of the building, I enter his office to find him by his desk, presumably waiting to greet us individually. When he spots me, he shoves his hands into the pockets of his navy pants.

"You got the short straw?" I ask with a wry smile.

The corner of his mouth quirks. "Appears so. Grab a seat."

I recognize a sophomore called Oliver so I sit next to him, though to my horror, Gemma follows me in and sits opposite. She's a freshman with bright blue eyes and black curly hair who seems to be in all my other classes, even the early ones. The other day, I overheard her refer to Oliver as an extra from *The Lion King*, which I had to presume was down to the scars on his face.

Witch.

"So you *do* have other clothes," she jabs. "Let's hope your tennis dress is in the wash."

All she gets in return is a closed-mouth smile because I don't want to waste my breath on anyone doling out abhorrent remarks about my new friends.

Yves joins Oli and myself. Another freshman doctorate student, he has sandy hair and muddy brown, soulful eyes. We catch up over nonsense as I place my notebook and drink on the table, getting comfortable before the seminar begins. Professor

Kit is still leaning against his desk, waiting for the last straggler to take her seat.

"Professor, is it true about the detentions?" Gemma asks.

"Yes. While we recognize your workload is heavy, you get two passes. A third request means an immediate detention. It will allow you to make progress on your missing or delayed work."

"How long is the detention?" Yves asks.

"Three hours."

"Will it be with you?" Gemma's voice is thick with hope. "If our third pass relates to your assignment, that is," she amends.

"It will be with whoever is on duty."

Pushing off from the desk, Professor Chevalier introduces himself properly, explaining Dr Philpott's absence as a temporary, one-off occurrence. For today only, he's taking the class.

I can't think that tenured professors normally fill in for ill colleagues and I'm trying to work out what that tells me about Professor Kit's character. Does he enjoy teaching that much?

"Welcome to Historical Linguistics 101. Let's start with the basics. French is known as a Romance language, but why?"

"It's the language of looove," Gemma coos.

I roll my eyes and somehow find Professor Kit silently watching me.

Oli answers: "It's one of several that stem from Roman—basically Latin. They're known as Romance languages," he says, giving Gemma some serious side-eye which makes my heart smile.

"Correct. Thank you, Oliver."

The minutes trickle by, the professor's voice a compelling blend of steely precision and warm encouragement. The roots of the words we use is really interesting but it's an area I'm less confident in. So I'm not thrilled that the questions are often directed at me—or that's what it feels like.

When class finishes, most people rush off stat, clearly

unhappy with the huge piece of work we've just been given five days to complete. The academic demands shouldn't surprise me, but already I'm feeling the strain of all the assignments. It makes me wonder if Professor Kit took the class purely to see the look on my face when he gave me my fourth assignment in five days.

I pack up my few personal items only to hear Gemma's grating voice ask, "You got a match this weekend?"

Debating whether to answer or not, I reveal, "Only against the squad. First competitive game is next weekend."

She zips up her laptop case. "I wish I had your confidence."

"About what?"

"Not everyone can arrive red-faced and sweaty-haired to class and carry it off like you." She starts to walk away, calling, "Bye, Professor Kit."

He acknowledges her with a murmured *Bye.*

Gemma is as transparent as glass. All she does is stare at Professor Chevalier the entire duration of the class and it's plain embarrassing. Before she's made it to the door I ask, "You never get a glow going, Gemma?"

"Sweat isn't attractive," she returns, slinging her rucksack over her shoulder, three steps from the door.

"Ahh," I draw out. "You're one of *those* girls. Girls that make the guys do all the hard work."

She turns to me, her face bright red, which is poetic. Then her eyes fly to Professor Kit, the suggestion of a smile on his face as he pretends to read book spines. "Don't be crass," she bites out.

"Gemma, I like to get physical and work up a sweat. And playing sports is nothing to be ashamed of either," I add on, just to fuck with her. Just to stress that point one is totally separate to point two.

"Whatever."

She rushes out of the room, her bag banging into the door frame as she whistles through.

Slowly, I follow in her footsteps, though I stop by Professor Kit's desk where he watches me, that hint of a smile still there. He's not pulled me up on the fact that I basically called him the anti-hero and a liar after our initial meeting. If he was bothered by it, I'm sure he would've spoken to me already. After all, he's had plenty of chances this week. Maybe that's what he's planning on doing now.

"Don't judge me," I tell him. Isn't attack the first form of defense? "She was cruel to Oliver and she deserved it."

My professor folds his arms across his chest and all it does is accentuate nice biceps, a broad, hard chest, and a stance that exudes power and authority. "About?"

Hesitating, I say, "His scars."

He nods. "And she was cruel to you," he points out.

True. "I can handle her sly barbs. That was for Oli."

"I see. Well, it makes sense you're good at backhanders."

Wait—is he insulting me? I'm just about to challenge him when I realize he's referencing my sport.

My laugh comes out a little nervous and I don't think it's entirely down to his joke. That was a joke, wasn't it? And if I remember correctly, not the first one he's made.

Whether back-handed compliments from classmates, or the professor's intellectual hits, if someone's not playing fair, I'll fight. For my friends too. "Down the line or cross court is where I prefer to play them, but sometimes you've got to stick up for other people."

"And yourself," he amends, his shrewd focus never wavering.

For reasons unknown to me, his attitude, which bordered on dickish five days ago, feels more penetrating. More intense. Before, I felt dismissed by him, someone he had to tolerate. But now, he studies me like he's discovered something new about me. It makes me feel young, which is perplexing. Flashbacks of younger me, when I was impressionable and naïve and flattered by a powerful man's sexual interest hit me like strobe lights. I thought I had become immune to older, attractive men, capable of dismissing the way they make me feel.

Until now, I never perceived Professor Kit as a threat to my stupid heart. I take a steady breath, thoughts worrying me. Why does he make me feel like this—young and uninhibited?

My mind casts around, inconveniently landing on the fact that I probably have video of him having sex with the waitress. With Erica. But it's not why the barriers feel non-existent between us right now, conversing like acquaintances, maybe even friends. Is it because I've seen the human side of him? The man outside of his work. He's not so terrifying without the protection of his title.

Professor.

It holds gravitas, but he's just a man. I need to remember that. His student I may be, but we will be working closely together. Maintaining equality and my position in whatever dynamic is currently in play, is important.

He perches on the edge of his desk, leanly muscled legs stretched out in front of him, his arms still crossed. Body behavior experts say it's a defense mechanism and my brain takes a diversion, wondering why he'd be protecting himself. And the open stance of his lower body is in complete opposition to his upper body.

I rest my ass against the back of his couch as silence holds us in a state of perplexing anticipation. I don't know what we're doing or why I don't just leave his office. Perhaps it's because it's the end of the week, and even hard to read professors think *Thank fuck, it's Friday.* Maybe I just broke the cardinal rule of inviting him into a conversation that he probably wasn't even interested in and he's being polite.

"Have you ever wondered," he begins, and I almost sigh with relief as his measured voice fills the space between us, "if your interest in courtly love and literature has translated into the modern day equivalent?"

"I don't follow."

"Your court is not Tintagel or those of Norman kings, but it comes with white lines, a net, and a game that involves love all the same."

He's referring to the tennis scores. *15-love.*

Surprise hits me right in the belly, followed by a bright smile. "I like that," I admit. "The symmetry." He watches me absorb his observations. "I've never noticed," I murmur, noticing too much about him right now, like the glimmer in his light brown eyes that makes them very alluring, the light stubble on his face which has me considering how soft or scratchy it would be if I kissed him. No wonder Gemma stares at him all day long. "Must be why I make so many faults."

Surprised at my confession, his brow rises. But he doesn't ask anything further. He just studies me like I'm unfathomable.

A memory tugs at me, but it doesn't bloom into anything tangible so I move the conversation on. "Do you know why the score of zero is called love?"

"A theory, surely."

"Well, sure. And there are a few of them, that nerdy etymologists still argue over today."

He looks exasperated. "Nerds? Really?"

"Undoubtedly professors," I suggest, "as evidenced by the class I just sat through."

He smiles, but it's coupled with disbelief, like he can't decide whether to chastise the student or laugh with a friend. And I'm unclear on which one of those two camps I want to fall into. Professor Chevalier's motives towards me are unclear.

"I know the one," he asserts. "In the 1800s, the French

imported the game from England and they pronounced love as l'oeuff—the closest pronunciation on account of the difference in vowels. The egg looks like a zero."

I put my hands on my hips. "I know, but the one I prefer, especially when I'm on a losing streak and it's 40-love in my opponent's favor, is the fact that I'm still playing, still here, all for the love of the game."

He lifts a shoulder. "Commendable, Maddie. But I don't buy it."

"Why not?"

"Firstly, because it lacks finesse. More importantly, the likelihood of the first theory is superior. Approximations of words are how languages develop. Us nerdy professors like to teach this to our students."

I smirk. "Pretty sure tennis has got nothing to do with eggs."

"Agree to disagree."

Thanks to several surreptitious glances this week, I'm well aware that Professor Kit has an athletic shape with lots of muscle definition where it counts. It's obvious he works out or does sport to offset all those hours at his desk, reading, writing, translating.

"If you played, you'd understand why my theory is best."

"I played tennis plenty."

"At college?"

"No."

"What's your sport?"

Fucking women in public bathrooms?

"How do you know I have one?"

If that wasn't an invitation to eye-fuck the hell out of him, I don't know what is. However, I don't need to because like I said —well aware already.

Our eyes connect, something crackling in the air. "You work out."

He stands, shoving his hands in his pockets, a habit of his. Or a tell. "My sport requires stamina and precision."

That could be *anything*. "Playing coy, huh? Okay, I'll bite. But, I should point out that tiddlywinks is *not* a sport," I respond dryly. "Though the number of times I've launched one of those plastic discs at someone's eye lends weight to your argument about precision."

He tries to hold in a smile. Fails. And boy, does it knock the air from my lungs and the floor from under my feet when he unleashes it directly at me like that. That smile is *dangerous*.

"You've got an answer for everything."

"I like to talk."

"I noticed."

"And you like talking to me."

I'm pretty sure I didn't mean for that to slip out, but I've not seen him talking to any other students.

He tips his head, like he has to think. "Debatable."

I chuckle, channeling a fuck-ton of bravado. "Lying goes against the code of chivalry, Professor."

He laughs at that, briefly, but it came right from his belly. It was mellow and deep and had goosebumps dancing down my back. I stand there looking at him as time expands until there's almost an audible *snap!*

In the space of a blink, the good humor in his features disappears. The lines of his face sharpen, a muscle in his jaw grinds. Flat-voiced, he turns for his desk and tells me, "Make sure I have your essay by Monday, please."

Aaaaand we're back to him being a hard-ass.

"Will do," I answer breezily, uncaring for his mercurial personality. Walking towards the door I call, "Have a good weekend."

"Good luck in your inter-squad competition," he murmurs looking through a pile of papers.

I stop dead. So he *was* listening. *I knew it.*

With his hand in a pocket, Professor Kit looks entirely at ease. Yet, somehow, I've rattled him. Still, the confidence with which he wears his indolence suits him. And while I know no one becomes a professor because they're work-shy or lazy, as he stands there so comfortable in his skin, I can't help but wonder if it all comes easy to him.

I asked him not to judge me, and I'm trying to live by my sword, but he holds all the cards; my future is in his hands, and he shouldn't look at me with a bristling intensity only to replace it with cool dispassion the next.

On the cusp of exiting his room, I turn towards him. "Everything's a competition, Professor. Study your ass off to get into Jacquard, earn the scholarship, win every game and walk away victorious. But competing in a game you don't know exists, where the rules change from one day to the next, is exhausting. Even if it's for the love of it."

And then I leave that handsome, confusing man behind.

8

KIT

Use Somebody - Kings of Leon

As soon as Madrigal leaves my office, I close the door and sit at my desk in a state of mild distress.

What the fuck am I doing? Why is she pressing my buttons so hard? And why the fuck am I flirting with my student? But then, I reason, I'm pretty sure she was flirting with me. I mean, it's hard to say for certain, but overhearing her chat to Oliver and Yves was different. The back and forth we have is suggestive, probing, challenging.

Her intellectual curiosity is a fucking turn on.

My thoughts are stuck on her *one of those girls* comment, my brain refusing to release a very indecent image of Maddie straddling my thighs, riding my cock until we hit oblivion, her skin dewy with sweat. And I didn't miss her point about enjoying tennis *and* getting sweaty. A chuckle escapes as I dwell on that. As I consider if her feistiness translates to her sexual appetite. To her tastes in bed.

Blowing out a breath, I focus on recalibrating my train of thought. But it's a futile exercise; Maddie has swept into my life like an exploding star, expanding, filling the entire horizon until there's only her.

I wasn't expecting her. I wasn't expecting this reaction to her. My aim was to tolerate her, but for a variety of reasons, I can't unsee her. Can't dislodge her from my damned brain. Pursuing her goes against every regulation and code I live by. Having only recently got this position, ignoring my attraction to Maddie is the safest thing to do. My career is in jeopardy, my reputation, my livelihood. And then there's my duty to my other doctorate students. If I went down this path, and it's a big *if*, where would my forced expulsion leave them?

Talking to Josh, urgently, is my first thought, but I buzz Mrs Pantazis, or Mrs P as I've been allowed to call my outstanding PA.

"Yes, Kit?"

"Can you get ahold of someone in student finance please? I need to speak to them urgently."

"Will do. Anything else? A coffee perhaps?"

"That would be a god-send, thank you."

I've lost track of the number of times I've told myself I don't care about Madrigal's backstory. She's wheedled her way into my head, hijacking my thoughts and winning my gaze every time she's near. Smart and beautiful, I'm losing myself to her just as I feared.

How long can a family hold a grudge? It might be centuries in the Chevalier case but I've tried to not let it consume me. I wonder what my ancestors would think if they knew I was devoting so much time thinking about Madrigal Devereaux, wondering what she was thinking. Wondering if she was thinking about me.

Mere minutes ago, she called me out. I'm making her play a game she appears to have no knowledge of, my moods zigzagging like a car traveling switchbacks up a mountain. For the sake of my sanity, I need to drop this infatuation with the Devereaux family, with the bewitching heiress of their empire, and concentrate on my work.

Nothing can happen between us anyway. Or rather, nothing *should.*

In a floral, knee-length dress and her short, curly hair looking immaculate, Mrs P comes in with a coffee and a couple of cookies. "I'm on hold but I thought I'd just whizz these through while I wait. I'll bring you some lunch at one, shall I?"

I barely manage to respond in the affirmative before she's gone, closing the door softly behind her.

Distracting myself with work is pointless. It feels like I can't breathe until I know more about Madrigal's financial situation. Thankfully, in a matter of minutes my phone rings, Mrs P patching someone through.

"Hello?"

"Hello, is that Professor Chevalier?"

The woman butchers my name but I don't care. "Yes. I need some information on a student please. Madrigal Iseult Georgette Devereaux." I spell out her utterly ridiculous name to save repeating myself.

From the other end of the line, nails clack on a keyboard.

"Mmm. Let's see." There's a pause that seems interminable. "Yes, here we go. The student has been awarded a partial athletic scholarship and she's on financial aid."

Most parents try and support their kids to some degree so I'm unclear why John and Pippa Devereaux are letting their daughter rack up hundreds of thousands of dollars in debt. Affording the fees is easily within their means.

As if a mind reader, the woman on the end of the line tells me, "There's a copy of her Declaration of Emancipation on file."

Well, there we go. "How old was she?"

"Seventeen and . . . seven months."

I'm not sure knowing when she applied for the declaration helps me understand what happened when she was a minor, but I ask, "Any reasons given for her emancipation?"

"It's been redacted."

"Is that normal?"

"No, but I've seen it before."

"Who redacts the document? The court?"

"Highly likely. A lawyer on someone's behalf."

The family's lawyer, wanting to keep things private, I imagine. Or maybe Madrigal is protecting herself. But from what? I hoped this enquiry would answer questions, but all it's done is bring up more. I check the time, my thoughts rushing to Josh and whether he's free right now. He might have an opinion on this.

"It says here she turned down a full scholarship."

Wait a second. Josh raised this at Brownlow. "Turned down?"

"Yes.'

"Do we know why?"

"No. Guess she's too rich to need it."

With Devereaux as a surname, there's no hiding here. Still, confusion and questions swarm me and I end the conversation. "Thank you for your help . . .?"

"Ailsa."

"Ailsa. I appreciate it. Bye."

I hang up and blow out a long breath as I digest what I've heard. *Jesus.* No wonder the athletic scholarship is important to Maddie. Briefly, I wonder if she has a job alongside her tennis and studies. Would she even have time?

Brushing my concerns aside, I dwell on my deeds over the

past week. Of the assumptions I've made about her and the way I've piled on to the burdens she already carries. As her reporting professor, I owe this woman a duty of care. I have begrudging respect for her participation in my classes, her answers thoughtful and structured, even if sometimes they're off the mark. And while I don't want to acknowledge it, she breathes life into my routine day.

After a quick call to Josh, who's no help whatsoever, I throw myself into my work and vow to do better by her. Swiftly, the afternoon arrives, Mrs P bringing me a turkey sub and numerous cups of tea in much-needed sustenance. I only leave my desk to take a leak and to retrieve books from the heavily stocked bookshelves in my room, but the one I want isn't where it should be.

Its misplacement bugs me. Losing things irritates the hell out of me. And I know Josh likes to rib me about a tidy space, to roast me about my OCD tendencies, but the reasons why go pathologically deep. So deep, I'm clueless as to why I have such fear of misplacing important items.

For a prolonged moment, I stare at the shelf where the book should sit. Having organized these books upon my arrival, this is frustrating beyond measure. For the next twenty minutes, after Mrs P tells me she has no idea where the book is, I turn the place upside down, and then I knock on some of my colleagues' doors. Eventually, I track it down in the language assistant's classroom. I remember telling her I had a copy she could borrow if she needed one, but she didn't confirm either way. I bet she *appropriated* it when I had momentarily left my office.

"I'm so sorry," Margot says, dragging it from the bottom of a pile of books. The sight of it being manhandled like that gives me hives. "I forgot to return it."

"Thanks," I tell the raven-haired woman instead of a reprimand, and head back to my work.

At my desk, I email Estates and Mrs P, asking for a new latch to be fitted on my office door, one that secures the door without a key. Staff stealing my treasured things when I'm taking a slash is a worry I don't need.

When the clock tells me it's just gone 4PM, I decide to call it a day. More importantly I decide to tell Mrs P to head home. She's looking after her one-year-old grandson, Cody, this weekend and she's overjoyed, if a little daunted by how tired she'll be at the end of it.

Standing, I stretch my arms above my head, loosening the muscles in my back. I roll my shoulders for good measure and then head in the direction of Mrs P's office. The hallway is quiet. Doors to offices are closed, probably locked. I'm about to turn left into the admin office when I hear Maddie talking.

Hidden by the doorframe, I stop just outside the room.

"You're welcome, Mrs P. I hope Cody likes it."

Mrs P? I thought only I had special dispensation to abbreviate the über efficient Mrs Pantazis' name? What the hell? Do all the students call her that too?

"I'm sure he will. It's so kind of you, dear."

"No problem," Maddie says confidently, like they chat like this all the time. "Does he still hate peas?"

"With a passion!"

Their easy laughter makes me smile. I know Mrs P can laugh —we share a funny anecdote in quieter, less rushed moments. And I recognize Maddie's laugh. It's contagious and lyrical, like her voice. When she was talking to Oliver, she laughed a lot which, curiously, I didn't like.

"Add some parsnip to them," Maddie suggests, "and purée them together."

"Good idea."

"On Monday, I want a full report of your weekend. It's going to be so fun!"

"Exhausting, dear. Fun but exhausting."

I can sense Maddie's smile, a soft puff of laughter carrying towards the door. Then, in a stage-whisper, she tells Mrs P: "You should sneak off home."

Mrs P whispers back. "He's still working."

"Ask to leave." Maddie's voice is stronger now. Determined. I know that voice. That tone.

"I will."

My stomach drops to my shoes. At least I can console myself that I was on my way to offer that very thing. Quickly, I scan the corridor, worried someone's creeping up behind me to give away my position, but it's like a ghost ship here.

I miss the beginning of Maddie's sentence but I do catch, "... if you give it to him?"

"As I say, he's still here. He won't mind if you knock. Students bother him all the time."

A scoff. "Let me guess—Gemma?"

Mrs P laughs too hard at that. "She's young and very obvious about it."

There's a notable pause. "We've all been young and obvious about a man."

"Sounds like a story for another time, dear."

A sad laugh. "Mrs P, if you want to swap love stories with me about the devilishly handsome Mr P, gazing at you adoringly in that sweet photo, I'll indulge you."

More laughter. It's the most I've heard Mrs P laugh in all the months I've been here. "Oh, you are a temptation. Now, back to Professor Kit. He's in his office."

"Yeah, I know he's still here! That's why I'm asking if I can give it to you and you can pass it on."

Mrs P is probably mooching her lips together in disappointment. "You don't want to drop it off yourself?"

"Doesn't he have a pigeon hole or something? I'll leave it in there."

Maddie totally avoided the question. I register the sound of paper being handled, rustled. I bet that's the essay I reminded Maddie about this morning. She's ready to hand it in. Early.

"Has he done something to upset you, Maddie? He's one of the best—"

"What, no! I just don't want to see him right now. Again."

At that moment a door opens to my right, so I lurch forward, into the admin office as if I haven't been spying on my student and about to trip over my own feet. My sudden footfalls instantly alert them to my presence. Maddie's arm is reaching forwards, towards my PA, papers clutched in her hand. As she turns to see who's entered the office, her eyes flare, her hand slowly returning to her side as if trying to hide the evidence.

"Oh, Professor, there you are. I was just asking Mrs Pantazis if you were still here." She lifts her hand, her essay thrust towards me. "My essay, due Monday. I've emailed it too."

Mrs P's eyes are bustling between the two of us as we stand statue-still by her desk. She's clearly trying to work out what the hell is going on. And possibly admiring what a smooth little liar Madrigal Devereaux is.

I take the proffered essay. "Thank you."

"Have a great weekend both of you," she trills, zooming past me in a haze of delicate, sweet floral notes.

"You too, dear!"

The sound of Maddie's departing steps holds me captive for a few seconds. When I'm sure they've fully retreated, I look at my assistant. "She calls you Mrs P?"

"*That's* your first question?"

"Yes."

"She called me Mrs Pantazis when you were here, which means you were listening from behind the door."

Well damn. Guess I can't get much past my fifty-eight year-old, valued member of staff. "I thought only I had that privilege."

"No. Maddie does too. She's a poppet."

A *poppet.* I scoff hard at that, noticing a gift-wrapped parcel on my PA's desk. "Did she get Cody a present?"

"Yes. Like I said, a poppet."

I roll my shoulders, suddenly tense. "I was coming to tell you to head on home. It's dead around here and it's been one hell of a first week back."

With the steely gaze only a hardened PA can level at her boss, she must find my offer to be genuine. Before I overheard my student and valued member of staff plotting behind my back, that is.

"That's very kind. I'll head off and see you bright and early Monday morning."

"Have a great time with your grandson."

"Oh, I will. He gives me a lease of life while draining it from me all at the same time."

I nod, the words entirely justified for Madrigal. "Know the feeling."

Leaving her to shut down her computer, I'm about to head back to my office when I stop, a thought returning. "Maddie teaches one class too many. Can you see if we can redistribute it to a keen student?"

Mrs P's gaze softens. "Consider it done."

"Thanks."

"She'll be pleased to know. I'll let you tell her the good news, shall I?"

Quickly, I race through all the ways Maddie will react. Will she be gracious about it, or point out how wrong I was to begin with? However she responds, I'll take it on the chin. "Yes, okay."

"Night."

"Goodnight."

Back in my office, I hastily take a seat on the couch and read Maddie's essay. We didn't settle on a title because she's more than capable of finessing one to suit her argument. To say I'm curious as to what she's chosen is an understatement. Knowing what's going on inside her head and if that translates at all into her heart has been preoccupying me.

It's titled: *Despite the phenomenon of courtly love, conflict of the heart underpinned European medieval literature. Discuss.*

Madrigal references the Arthurian legends of Chrétien de Troyes, and how he extolled honor and chivalry. Through numerous passages she demonstrates a solid knowledge of the themes and motifs. While Guinevere may have been married to King Arthur, she loved Lancelot, their love bringing discord and betrayal.

Relevant quotes pepper her paper from other manuscripts, her focus clearly on the complexities of Tristan and Iseult's famous relationship. We discussed it only a few days ago, at her mock interview and, reading through the meaty essay, it's clearly a passion project of Maddie's.

Love was greatly abased in her, for her heart was given entirely to one man, but her body was shared by two.

The Irish princess Iseult was promised to Mark, King of Cornwall who happened to be Tristan's uncle. Tristan escorted her from Ireland to his king and, after ingesting a potion, the pair fell in love on the way. What followed is a tumultuous affair, with tragedy striking the love-struck couple from numerous angles until Tristan's tragic death by poisoned spear, Iseult dying of a broken heart over his body.

Maddie concludes her argument, intriguingly, with one final quote, demonstrating her point about conflict, destruction, crippling loss, and crucially, adultery: *What the eyes do not see can never pain the heart.*

It leads to one conclusion.

Madrigal has endured a love that goes beyond chivalric literature. That defies the lofty ideals of what love is or should be.

Her heart was broken. Destroyed.

I want to know who did that to her. And I won't rest until I find out.

9

MADDIE

A Tear in Space (Airlock) - Glass Animals

"Dr Hurren shared a really interesting concept with us," Perrie announces as she pours us both a coffee. She's up at dawn this morning, like me. Or rather, she hasn't got into bed yet, her date with Zac turning into one of those nights where you stay up all night, talking and fucking.

Apparently, that's a thing between a new couple which means I missed the memo. Everything with Harrison was hurried, brief, hidden. The illicit nature of our affair was exciting to begin with, but then I realized I was shut off from a large part of his life. Shut out from his thoughts and dreams.

"I don't think I told you about it."

"I'm listening." I say, happy for any distraction from my relationship woes and troubling dreams.

"You know when we talk about being on the same wavelength? Or the energy being sucked from the room? Well, it's all down to frequencies. When two frequencies of equal wavelength meet, the size of the frequency doubles. Basically, you can get energy from conversation—it gives and takes. Constructive or destructive interference it's called." Our eyes hold before she launches into the rest of her tale. "But the really cool part is that talking from a point of authenticity is the most powerful and attractive amplitude. We know," Perrie continues, "when someone's bullshitting us because the frequency of authenticity is *four thousand* times more powerful than love."

"For real?"

"Can't be faked."

"Hmm," I reply, thinking of my recent conversations with Harrison. With Professor Chevalier. "I didn't know you were studying physics."

Tiredly, Perries laughs. Last week she told me about humans being made up of particles of long dead stars, so maybe it's astro-physics she's into.

"How does Zac fit on this scale?"

"We're definitely in sync."

I smile, happy for her. But then my thoughts start dancing all over the place again. Suddenly, I want to meet with my professor, listening to him speak as I wonder about wavelengths and frequencies and if he's being authentic. Apart from our first meeting, which felt off, I've only got positive, genuine vibes from him, even if they leave me confused.

And his voice is a wonder, deep and even-toned.

"I'm so pleased your Dad suggested I apply here. I never thought Jacq U would consider me but I love it here, don't you?"

Like a car crash, the confession comes at me out of nowhere. Disbelief and shock rattle through me. "Dad suggested you apply here? When was this?"

"Um, just about every time your parents took us out for dinner at Princeton? We've wanted to do a doctorate for years and he, well, they were both keen for you to come here."

"Mom too?"

"Yeah."

It's impossible to process her words, my brain buffering as it tries to download the information. Dad's view on this is understandable but Mom always told me to follow my dreams, my heart. Am I here by circumstance, or by choice?

"Sorry, Maddie. I didn't realize you weren't aware of our chats. Though come to think of it," she adds slowly, "he did say you probably wouldn't apply here even if I did, but that it would be a good back up."

"I bet he did," I answer, brushing it off and giving her a big smile. "Well, we're here now and I'm so pleased too."

My words have the desired effect, the troubled expression on Perrie's face smoothing away. There's no time to dwell on the questions this raises; the hectic schedule I signed up to has me rushing off for practice and turning up late again for my Monday meeting. And while the dynamic between the professor today has me on tenterhooks, thanks to the game I accused him of, I'm eager to have my essay back.

I knock and wait for his voice.

Seated at his desk, his eyes are on me the second I open the door. Standing, he greets me with a warm *Good morning.*

"Morning," I murmur noticing some new additions to his office. In the opposite corner to his desk there's a tall, leafy plant. Next to it is a brand new leather armchair in a deep brown. The square shape of it reminds me of the throne in the Club VX video and it turns all my senses upside down and inside out.

Pulling my eyes away from the chair, I drop my racquet bag by his desk. He gestures to the sofas in the middle of the room and leads the way towards them.

"How was your weekend?" he asks with what sounds like genuine interest.

"Productive. Yours?"

"Quiet."

Stopping by the sofas, he looks my way as I amble towards the wall of books by the windows. I'm not ready to be so close to him. When I'm close to him I feel out of control, like I'm outside of myself, a compass needle spinning between north and south.

"How did your inter-squad matches go?"

I shouldn't be surprised that he remembered. His brain is a wonder of facts and deep thought.

"Good. I came second which I'm happy with."

"Second is good. It's a competitive squad."

I tilt my head to read the spines and titles, though really I'm focusing on sound waves. Why did Perrie have to mention them? I'm now analyzing every word choice and sentence more than I was already.

"Was your coach happy?"

Curious, I look up, just as his eyes fall away from my forearm. "He wanted me as first seed but Robyn was too good," I reply, my stomach knotting. Losing doesn't feel good, but with first seed comes enormous pressure and extra training with Harrison.

"I see. Was his confidence warranted?"

"What do you mean?"

"Was it fair of him to be upset?"

"Who said he was upset?"

His gaze flickers to the new bruise on my forearm. Harrison wasn't happy I lost to Robyn. "I'm reading between the lines. I wondered if being late for our meetings is related."

Shit. This man is too perceptive. And honest.

"Respectfully, he can be a dick." I sigh, my eyes drifting around the room. I've been stalling because once I sit down, I might never get back up again. The coaches beasted us in the gym and my legs feel like they weigh five hundred pounds. "I've known him a long time. He wants me to succeed."

Mainly because it reflects well on him and because he's under the deluded impression that tennis will become the most important thing in the world to me again, after him, of course.

"Pretty sure playing Varsity tennis is the definition of success. As is second spot."

This man is playing havoc with my feelings. Being praised makes me feel young again, and I find myself doing that classic girl thing of swaying. It makes my tennis skirt swish, and then, noticing what I'm doing, I stop. "That's kind, thank you."

Kit moves to the table. "Water?"

Bottles of water, glasses, and a bowl of ice stand on the table. Then I notice that the windows are all ajar. My heart skips at the considerate behavior. At the attentiveness.

"Please. How was your quiet weekend?" I ask absently, determined to draw the attention away from myself. "You looked like you picked up an injury playing tiddlywinks."

I can spot a twinge in a knee a mile off. Knee—joint pain in general—was a continual inconvenience for me growing up. When I watched Professor Kit walk across the room, I spotted the tiniest give in his stride. Whatever he was doing *quietly*, it involved some exertion. Maybe there's some carpet burn on those knees.

Disbelief morphs into quiet amusement, his whole face softening, but it doesn't stop him from being any less devastatingly handsome. I like his composed professor face, one that hungers for my thoughts, and this less guarded side of him in equal measure.

"Ice?"

"Please."

Two chunks of ice splash into the glass of water. He passes it to me and I take several grateful sips.

"Your perceptiveness is alarming," he *compliments?* me. "But yes. I am prone to pain in my right knee."

Mentally, I run through all the sports that would put stress on a dominant knee; I know he's right-handed. Even though there are many, I suggest, "Soccer? Squash? Badminton?"

"Nice try."

Seriously? He's not going to tell me?

"So secretive, Professor Chevalier."

And curse me, I shouldn't find it attractive. Shouldn't find him more interesting because of it. Secrets are a red flag. I can thank Harrison for learning that, too.

Smoothing down my skirt, I sink into the couch. After a few seconds I realize the backs of my thighs are sticking to the leather. I jiggle, trying to get comfortable but it's no use.

Noticing my discomfort, I'm asked, "Shall we sit at the table?"

"I think my legs will have to be surgically removed before I can get up so, er, here's fine."

Honey-brown eyes linger on mine for a fraction too long, but I don't look away. "Pretty sure you need those," he says, his tone wry.

"Pretty sure," I confirm, nodding like I didn't just say the most ridiculous thing.

"Best stay right there."

"Yeah," I agree, feeling stupid and wondering if I'm reading too much into the words *stay right there.*

The answer to which is *probably*, because he never once looked at my legs during the entire exchange about them. He either has next-level willpower or no interest in me at all. Which, as my professor, is probably the right and proper response. This man has been bugging me for days and I've come to realize I'm borderline infatuated with him. With his intelligence. With his commanding aura when he teaches. Rarely sitting in class, he prefers to be on his feet, moving around with confident ease, encouraging people to participate. Directing questions at me over and over.

I bring the conversation back to task. "Did you read my essay?"

And then, *there*, just a brief look at my legs. Technically it's a skort, and my knees are pinned together so there's nothing to look at, but it didn't stop the nano second peek. Can he see Harrison's pinch on my thigh is a yellow smudge now?

Casually, he clears his throat. "It was well structured, and the use of comparable judgment in the conclusion meant it was a well deserved A plus."

From a small pile of papers on the neighboring cushion he pulls out my essay and passes it to me. Stuck to the seat, he leans forward, chuckling at my awkwardness and lays it on my knees.

I smack a hand over the top before it slides to the floor.

"An A plus?"

"You sound surprised."

Well, he's got me there. I'm pretty sure I can't call him out for picking on me though. First of all, it sounds immature, and second of all, I don't want to revisit the oddness of last week. Today feels much improved. It's like we've swallowed an honesty pill.

Quietly, he assesses me, waiting for his answer.

"You seem a hard man to please."

Yup, definitely been taking a fuck-ton of honesty pills. Let him interpret that however he chooses.

A muscle in his jaw pulses. "The man or the professor?"

Ah. I was hoping he'd reveal something. Something that would help me understand the game I've no clue of. While I sense we're both attracted to each other, the frisson between us is due to some level of discomfort I cause him. What I don't know is whether it's because I caught him having adult fun in a restroom or if it's for other reasons. Of which, there are many.

"I think the man and the professor are one and the same, aren't they?"

"And if they are?"

"Then you have high standards."

"Expectations," he corrects. "I expect considerable output from my students."

That is not entirely truthful. He expects a lot from *me.* I just don't know why. And crucially, I point out, "That was the professor's answer. What's the man's?"

He does a double take, but just with his eyes. The question surprised him. It kind of surprised me too.

"Men are different. We each want different things, unlike professors, who expect greatness."

I roll my eyes. He totally avoided the question. Doesn't mean I'm going to forget about it though. "Is the *considerable output* you require anything to do with why I was asked twice as many questions as anyone else in the linguistics class?"

A thick, dark brow jumps. "Were you?"

"Oliver and Yves didn't get so much of your attention."

Maybe my teacher noticed how bad I was at the topic and decided to test me over and over. I wouldn't blame him.

"Not all students are worthy of my attention."

I transport to my family's library, looking upon the family tree. *Honneur aulx dignes.*

Honor the worthy.

Boldly, I reply, "Thank you for the compliment." It's how I plan on taking it.

"I'm grateful that's how you chose to take it. The way it was intended."

"It was made clear you have high expectations at our first meeting. Were you hoping for a different student? Did I take someone else's spot?"

A shake of his head. "You deserve to be here, to continue your career in academia."

"You didn't answer my question, Professor."

He drops his head a fraction and looks me squarely in the eye. Not unkindly, just . . . intensely. Like he wants to see inside my soul, or let me see inside his. It's such a notable gesture and it hits me hard because, for some reason, it's familiar.

A memory starts to take shape but disappears before it's barely begun. I've seen that look before, felt eyes on me like this.

"No, you didn't take anyone else's spot," he explains. "I wasn't hoping for anyone else."

The authenticity wavelengths are strong, so I nod, accepting his answer.

Casting a worried look my way, he turns his attention to the pile of papers next to him. "I've amended your timetable. Your class on Wednesday has been picked up elsewhere in the department."

I should give him so much shit for that stunt, but he's trying to be decent, so I just say, "Thanks."

Pausing, as if he's expecting me to say more, I let the matter drop by staring at the paper in my hands. When he looks away, for a second he looks like he's lost his place in a book, his eyes searching the table.

"How are you enjoying your classes so far?"

I'd rather tell him how I'm drowning under all the assignments. The frequency with which they come is relentless. I barely have time to finish one before I'm composing the next. Researching my own project or anything outside of the course seems a dauntless task. At this rate, I'll end up with detentions every week.

"Good. Dr Hurren's seminars are really thought-provoking. Perrie and I get into some heavy debates over the texts. There's lots to think about, especially when compared to what I'm learning in the medieval texts with you."

There's a pleased incline of his head.

"And I'm loving the Machiavelli class with Dr. Lorenzo. It answers so many questions I've had about previous, well, that is to say, men I've known."

My statement lands heavily. His body stills, then he takes a long breath, his head tilting in that oddly familiar way, his eyes burning right to the heart of me when he demands, "How, Maddie?"

The timbre of his voice is commanding, one capable of leading armies.

Wondering how truthful I should be, I turn my attention to the window over his shoulder and take a shallow breath. Two. Earlier, it had rained, and the glass is still covered in droplets of water.

"There was . . . someone. A man. When we parted ways, I told him: *Everyone sees what you appear to be, few experience what you really are.* It was the only quote I knew at the time, but it suited him."

"And his response?"

"Stop quoting book crap at me."

The silence that follows is threaded with anger. Then: "You still see him?"

I nod, self-conscious and cursing the honesty pill and those stupid wavelengths that are four thousand times more powerful than love.

"Do you need my *help* with that?"

Is it my imagination or is my professor offering to 'take care' of Harrison?

I shake my head.

"If you ever wanted to talk about it, I'm here. I'll listen."

This is possibly the first time anyone has truly asked these questions. I've hidden so much of my relationship with Harrison from people who matter to me. Parts of me were ashamed, embarrassed, humiliated, even though everyone understood my only choice was to walk away.

His care weakens my armor further. "If I did want to talk, Professor?"

"Kit," he tells me, his voice a tantalizing blend of cashmere and steel. "I'd treat it with utmost confidence, Maddie. You have my word."

His edict strikes me as believable. Honorable. It lures me in, filling a yawning gap in the center of me. Dark brows crinkle over deep-set eyes, holding me captive as anticipation kindles between us.

"I'm here whenever you need me." A steadfast promise.

I mumble *Thank you,* wondering how the conversation has ended up here, with me giving up personal information to a man I have confusing, complex feelings for.

"Safe-guarding is an important aspect of my job."

Riiiiggghhht. Yeah, that takes the shine away from his impassioned offer from a few seconds ago. "Well, I'd hate to be a statistic."

Sounding pissed, he answers, "That's not what I meant, Maddie. Taking care of you means something to me. On a personal level," he adds with some reluctance, like the last four words came out before he had a chance to swallow them.

Well, okay.

A *personal level.*

I want to interrogate those words. I want to sit and look at my professor and admire him, taunt him, tease him for them. I want to stand and walk slowly towards him, settling on his lap, straddling those strong-looking legs as I grind against him, kissing the ever-loving fuck out of him.

But I can't do any of that.

From a back pocket of his slacks, he pulls out his phone. "I'll send you my number. Any problems, Maddie," he begins in a deceptively calm voice, quickly scanning my legs and then my arms and shoulders as he does, "message me. Or call. I'll take care of it."

And by it, he means *him*. This man I still see but haven't named.

Shakily, I breathe in and out, the lethal threat settling on my skin. All of a sudden I see my professor as not just a man of intellect, but a man of deadly action too. How had I forgotten the dark, dangerous appeal he emitted in the bar?

But I don't feel vulnerable, I feel, weirdly, protected, especially when I notice the fierce light in his eyes as he waits for me to divulge my cell number. To agree to whatever this is.

Silence cocoons us. My body erupts in goosebumps. The book-stacked walls of the office close in on me. I'm only aware of Kit's patient gaze, of my tremulous voice as I submit.

I relay my number.

He inputs the details into his phone and messages me, regarding me in a way that speaks of secrets and crossed lines. "If you need me, I'll come for you," he murmurs.

Relationships with significant age gaps are to be avoided and I briefly regret blurring the lines. Kit needs to know that exchanging digits doesn't commit me to anything. Taking three shallow breaths, each one audible in the pressing quiet, I open my mouth to say something, but the ringing desk phone shocks me from my state of senselessness.

Alert, I shift, or try to at least, a wince sounding as I lift one leg, then another, my skin peeling away from the material underneath as I prepare to fully vacate the couch and this room. A room where my professor is now a potential confidante as well as sometime combatant.

"Here." Kit scoots around my side of the table and extends two hands. "I'll pull you free."

A half-smile tugs free at how ridiculous this is. At how we've crossed yet another divide today. We're not friends exactly, but this is no longer a normal professor/student dynamic. But it's not a neutral space either, it can never be on account of the professional barrier between us.

We're neutral *adjacent,* I guess.

Needing to change the atmosphere to something lighter, my hands lift. I wriggle my fingers at him and he chuffs before gathering them up easily in his firm hold. It's no exaggeration or lie when I say an electric current zips through me as our palms meet. My gaze tangles with his as he lifts me to my feet, both of us transmitting that we both felt that. Whatever *that* was.

Butterflies take flight in my stomach, our hands separating as I settle one over my abdomen as if to control their craziness.

"Thanks."

Perhaps needing a moment to compose himself too, he runs a hand through his hair. "Better check that there's nothing of you left behind," he murmurs, throwing a cursory glance where I was sitting.

I swallow my laughter. "Just my dignity."

"As much as I . . . er, Yves and Oliver and just about every male student in this faculty loves the tennis skirts and dresses, maybe, maybe we don't sit here for our weekly catch ups."

The backs of my thighs no longer sting, but I smooth a hand over my butt, just to be sure the skirt's still hanging where it should.

"You were going to say maybe I shouldn't wear them."

"And awaken the staunch feminist in you?"

"Right. A long-slumbering kraken."

Almost fondly, he answers, "Sounds ferocious."

"Mmm hmm." I agree absently. "So the skirts can stay," I

begin, my voice tentative, wondering how far to push, if I *should* push considering my resolve mere moments ago. But Kit is too appealing, his determined, protective edges too admirable. "You like them too."

Once again his hand smooths down the back of his head and into his nape. If he thinks I didn't catch his small but hugely significant word vomit, he's mistaken. "I should invoke the fifth amendment."

"Lying is against the code of chivalry; so is cowardice." Fuck, maybe that was too honest. "Sorry, you don't have to answer that. I'm gonna go."

Quickly, I pick up my bag by his desk and turn for the door. I'm almost there when I hear Kit's declaration. "You were right to challenge me."

A pause that lasts no longer than two meagre heartbeats is all it takes to drain me of my earlier bravado. What is he going to say? Why did I push? I turn towards him.

"The view from the back is not as good as the view from the front, Maddie, which is *sensational*, tennis skirt or not."

Two metres is all that separates us. Energy of some kind, a palpable force, pulls tight, widening, engulfing us both. My feet want to carry me across that small space right into his arms as a memory knocks against the invisible walls of my memory box, begging for release.

"Says the man or the professor?"

The breath he takes before answering steals the air from my lungs. "They're one and the same, and you know it."

I hold his eye, confirming that I understand.

Whether professor and student or man and woman, Kit thinks I'm sensational. He wants me to be exceptional, in private or in school.

I walk out of his office like I'm Cleopatra, or Boudicca, or Queen Elizabeth I, her reign long and golden. For the rest of the day, I lose too many hours thinking about the encounter. When I see him for class later on in the week he bombards me with endless, difficult questions. In many ways, our interactions are exactly like week one, yet different, too. His confessions—and mine—all thanks to the honesty pill, feel like some glitter-dusted shadow follows me wherever I go, lifting me up, making me feel weightless. Limitless and boundless. Forgetting what he said and how it makes me feel is impossible. But I keep my distance for the rest of the week, and he keeps his, both of us dancing around each other.

Lord knows what week three will bring, but I can't wait to find out.

10

MADDIE

Vampire - Olivia Rodrigo

Torrential rain pelts my umbrella and drenches my feet as I arrive at the tennis center. I shake off the rain and head to the locker room where the girls are talking about their night out and the upcoming matches.

"Hey," I greet collectively, Flora, Yona, Pia and Robyn already here.

There's a chorus of greetings and waves as I find fresh socks and spare plimsoles in my kit bag.

"Two days to go until regionals," Yona remarks, her blunt cut hair looking the bomb despite the weather.

"God, don't remind me," Pia grumbles.

At six one, Pia's the tallest amongst us girls, giving her a huge advantage when it comes to her serve. But her long limbs are less fluid across the court.

Robyn looks up from tying her plimsoles. "You sleep okay, Maddie? You look pale."

"Oh, thanks?" I say on a laugh. "I woke from a really deep sleep."

My dreams have been a continuation of the same theme, or man. But instead of feeling peace and harmony when I woke, I felt devastated. For reasons not yet clear, my future with him looks uncertain. To think my appearance this morning is affected by my dream is curious.

"Hope it was a good dream. Mine have been the weirdest lately," she replies, sliding a racquet from her bag. In many ways, Robyn is a clone of me. We have the same hazel eyes and chestnut hair. Our strengths at playing the game are similar, our builds too.

Details of my dream allude me, but honestly, I'd rather remember it on my own. In private.

"And I didn't mean pale in a negative way," she continues. "I'm just making sure you're alright. Coach will have a fit if you're ill."

Her long look my way tells me she's convinced something is going on between Harrison and I. Something current.

"Sex dreams," Flora begins, admiring the new tattoo of a butterfly on the back of her hand, "are what we want to hear about this morning. You got one to share and I'm all ears."

Laughter sounds, too many hopeful, expectant eyes on me. "Sorry, girls. No sex, just tennis."

"Oof," Flora intones. "Tennis dreams are sex dreams for me, girl."

"Right," Robyn agrees as Pia shakes her head in amusement. "Coach's pep-talks about ball placement feature pretty damn heavy in mine, I tell ya."

Flora laughs out loud. "Oh yeah. Only guy his age I'd do. Jesus. It's hard to concentrate some days." Flora's pale blue eyes drift towards me. "Don't you think, Maddie?"

I've been grinning at them as if I'm like-minded, but her

question that hints at too much knowledge, or suspicion, has me playing dumb. "That Coach is a major distraction? Yeah, he is," I agree for different reasons. "Always yelling at me to move faster."

"I thought he looked good on camera but he's better in the flesh," Flora whispers in case we're overheard. "I only came here because of him."

Pia and I exchange a weighted glance. We both know what Flora is hoping will happen.

"Same." Robyn says. "I think he's into me."

Suddenly, Robyn and Flora are no longer allies in the Harrison Appreciation Club, but enemies. Flora's face is pure threat, giving me chills, and I don't have any skin in this game. Or do I?

"Something happened between you?" Pia asks Robyn.

Robyn shrugs. "It's the way he looks at me. The things he says." Another shrug. "I can tell when a guy wants to fuck."

"Girl," Pia warns with a laugh. "Be careful."

"Don't worry. I carry condoms," she answers with a salacious grin.

Falling into my thoughts, of happier times between Harrison and I, I only catch some of the conversation that continues around me.

"....last year. They were definitely fucking at Christmas."

"See? He'd never go for a freshman," Flora answers, but it's obvious her comment is targeted at Robyn. "Too young."

Here for a master's, Flora obviously thinks her chances are greater, but she doesn't know how young Harrison will go.

He'll go as low as sixteen.

But I'm concerned about what I overheard. That Harrison was screwing a member of the squad, a student, at the same time he came to see me at Princeton.

A couple more girls arrive and I take that as my cue to silently find the coaches and get on with my match. It's hard to concentrate on my surroundings, my thoughts laser-focused on New Year's. The hurt I feel throws me. Does this mean *I do* have skin in the game? Insecurity strikes me hard as I mentally curse Robyn and Flora for oversharing. As we gather around the coaching staff for instructions, I stare at Harrison with new eyes.

Blaming him for screwing other women when we're not together complicates things. Did he make some promises? Sure. But I didn't accept or agree to any of them. Technically, Harrison was only guilty of hedging his bets and possibly holding out for a bigger prize. *If I am* a bigger prize.

Thoughts on prizes brings me to the société d'honneur where the knight wins his lady. Earning a woman's love—romantic or sexual—through honorable deeds, is vastly appealing. I want that for myself.

"Robyn, you're on court one. Maddie, two. Pia on three, Flora and Yona on four. Okay, let's get on court and show Boston why we're the best team in the league," Coach Tait encourages.

Grabbing my bag, I head for the door to the indoor courts, Robyn at my side. In a Jacq U cap and his college athletic wear, Harrison follows.

"Robyn," he begins as we walk past the bleachers where at least three hundred spectators can support. "Make sure you attack the net at every point."

"Yes, Coach."

"Maddie, move those feet."

"Yes, Coach.

"Harrison!" a female voice calls! "Harrison!"

It takes a special kind of willpower I don't possess to ignore the adoring voices that call out to my ex. To not glance towards the women who demand his attention. Usually the fans want an autograph or selfie, but often they're after much more than that.

"Can we have a selfie?"

A couple of young women beam at Harrison, thrusting phones and flashing encouraging looks his way.

"Sure ladies," he immediately answers, giving them his mega-watt, poster-boy smile.

Seeing his attention directed at other women, *all* women pretty much, often made younger me feel like ants were crawling over me. Naïve and insecure, the only way to feel in control was to sacrifice my dignity and make myself available to his demands.

I needed the reassurance. Proof that I was all he needed. These are lies I regularly told myself.

Selfies over, Harrison murmurs smoothly, "Have a great day, ladies."

"Thanks, Harrison! Can I have your number? I'm after some private tuition. You know, something more *personal*."

The double entendre spirals in my thoughts. And even though I have no claim on him or him on me, I start walking for my court because I can't bear to hear his reply. But it reaches me all the same.

"Not right now, but give me your number in case anything changes."

Robyn turns, sad eyes finding mine before she heads for court number one. When she peers over her shoulder to see what's going on I know she's a lost cause.

Harrison catches up to me, a slip of paper in his hands which no doubt holds recently acquired personal details. He folds it up and pops the back cover of his cell case off, slotting the paper inside.

It's a threat. Either get back together or he's looking elsewhere. And I hate that I'm rethinking everything based on that one, stupid interaction.

"Looks like you made some new friends," I say airily, wishing I wasn't so transparent.

His smile is one of victory. "Jealousy suits you, Mads, but you know how to make this right. When you win today, you can celebrate by thanking your coach."

"On my knees?" I say with false sweetness. "That sounds more like a celebration for you."

Mastering vast and inexplicable emotions was hard for me as a teenager, even if in so many ways I felt worldly and wise. I had few close friends at school, everyone acting so young compared to me. They behaved in ways I never understood. Harrison was the opposite of inept and immature and directionless. Whatever I was seeking at that young age, led me straight to him.

He sighs. "Come on, you used to beg for a lick, remember?"

Conveniently, Harrison often mis-remembers, and this conversation is zapping me of all my energy.

At the bench, I dump my racquet bag, Harrison following at my heels. "I was sixteen and willing to tempt you into something you should've had the strength to stay away from."

"You're blaming me? A guy only has so much willpower."

I take the criticism, wondering if I was being unfair.

"As if I could stay away," he rumbles. "You *were* tempting. You still are."

I brush tendrils of hair off my face, tucking them behind my headband. "There's no need to go over this. Especially not here. I was young, the perfect age for making mistakes."

And boy, did we make lots of those.

"Let's give it another try. I want to, Maddie. I really do. I'm ready for you now. For us." Pulling off his cap, he scrubs a hand through his blond hair. "I didn't want to discuss this here but you refuse to have dinner with me. Or talk."

"Sorry," I mumble before regretting it. I don't owe him much but dinner is a compromise. "Dinner can only work if there are no expectations, Harrison. I mean it."

"But you still love me, Mads."

Mads.

There was a time I loved that name too. Now the pet name twists my stomach.

"I will always have love *for* you," I stress.

"I'm not buying that crap. You *love* me," he states.

"Only a conflicted kind, then," I acknowledge, aware of Robyn watching our whispered exchange from the neighboring court. "I'm still hurting, Harrison."

"I know," he says with surprising tenderness. "I know. But love hurts."

And it's such bullshit that those were the first words out of his mouth when he took my virginity. When it had felt like a red hot poker was ramming my insides. When I'd grimaced through every torturous first moment, willing the pain away. And it did subside, sex easier after that first time—until it hurt for different reasons.

Love hurts—it's true. And pain is a reminder to stay away from something. I guess it's apt the college color is barn red—a warning—the logo on his shirt and baseball cap stark reminders.

A humorless laugh escapes as I realize I'm surrounded by warning signs.

I blow out a breath, feeling isolated and stuck, searching for a way through this. And for reasons unknown, my thoughts land on Kit, a man who feels safe. No wonder I tell him everything.

"If you're not committed to us, you need to say. You're leading me on, hanging around me like we're still together."

"What? No, I'm not," I answer, terrified it's true. "You're my coach!"

"I'm not with anyone, honest to God. It's you I want, so let's do this," he insists more calmly, hearing the defensiveness and alarm in my voice.

God, he always manages to get inside my head, setting my emotions off like a mis-firing firework. At times, it feels like I'm still lost in him, wondering what could be. Or maybe I'm lost to the *idea* of him? The idea of us. And yet I know without a doubt that if I wasn't at his side right now he'd have escorted his new fans to the locker room.

What the eyes do not see can never pain the heart.

The problem is I saw too much. Experienced too much hurt. My soul never recovered.

Steel lines my voice. "I'm not doing this. You have to go—I need to get in the zone."

A player's mental strength and pre-game prep is relatable for a former pro player, and recently, I've had lots to process.

Harrison inclines his head. "Then I'll go. Good luck."

11

MADDIE

Mind Still - Sonny Fodera (feat Blythe)

A green, undulating landscape draws my eye towards the horizon. The sun is low in the sky, an orange ball of flame dipping behind a distant hill. Behind, deciduous woods shelter me from a lazy breeze, dappled light reflected on the water tinkling at my feet.

A saddled horse nickers. Another snorts, pawing at the ground. White blankets embroidered with heraldic symbols adorn their bodies.

The cool water of the brook where my feet dangle is relaxing, the skirts of my pale blue dress gathered around my knees to keep dry. The soft exhales of a man deep in sleep has my gaze leaving the narrow stream and dragging along the stretched out body beside me.

I've loved this man since the dawn of time, my feelings vast and endless.

His trousers are dark. The gray overshirt has gold, ornate detailing at the pockets, neck, and wrists. A black doublet lays strewn in the grass. Even in sleep, a sword is clutched in his fist, the metal gleaming. His body is a marvel, lifting with every deep breath, scars lining the thick muscles of his torso and hard stomach. I trail a proprietary hand down his lower abdomen, towards his cock where he's softened.

Happiness, deep and broad fills my heart, my eyes skimming over the beautiful features of the man I love. I can still feel him inside me, his passion finally abated. Leaning in, I kiss him on the mouth and draw myself closer to his comfort and strength. Already I want him again, even as I feel his release smeared across my sex and dripping down my thighs.

Under my hand his cock stirs, my pulse dancing in delight. My lips feel bruised, his taste still lingering on my tongue—a blend of musk, man, and forever.

"I want you again."

A lazy eye opens, his free hand coming to my cheek. "I am here, my love, ready to serve your heart's desire."

I unbutton his trousers and take him in my hand. He's thick and hard, my hand moving over his smooth, hot flesh. "It desires you," I whisper against his lips, his heavy body rolling towards mine and pressing me into the ground.

Voices from the radio station stir me from my dream, leaving me upset and curiously heartbroken. Although it's clear our relationship is sexual, I need this man beyond just the physical.

As I gather my wits, I remember I have the meeting at Club VX later this morning. Nervous for what I'll learn, I'm feeling confident with my decision. With that in mind, I quietly get ready for morning practice and tiptoe past a sleeping Perrie.

Club VX is as exclusive as it gets. The exquisite marble floors, chandelier-decked ceilings, and luxurious, bespoke furnishings smell of old money and secrets. Auburn-haired Sophie, the manager at VX, invites me into an atmospheric office, armor and crossed swords affixed high on the walls and a whole wall of books stacked behind a huge, antique desk.

"Please, have a seat, Miss Devereaux."

"I'm fine with Maddie. Less identifying," I point out.

Sophie nods, gesturing to a sideboard with a host of drink options. Dressed in a killer black pant suit, she looks formidable and impressive.

"You can choose any name, if you wish to proceed. Can I get you some refreshments? Tea? Wine?"

A stiff drink would be welcome, but I ask for water. Before I commit to anything, I need answers. Keeping a clear head when my mind has been far from still these past weeks is paramount.

I can still back out, I remind myself. Signing a document doesn't force my hand, it just means I'll keep quiet about whatever is about to be unveiled. And I have Perrie's number if I need it, Kit's too.

Sophie returns, placing the glass on a table in front of me. I'm perched on a curved banquet seat, the color a blazing red.

"Thank you for meeting with me," Sophie begins, efficient and serious as she sits opposite. "I'm sure you have many questions."

"I do. I've read through the NDA you emailed, so I'm appeased that anonymity is guaranteed."

I had to sign that document in front of Sophie Bouchard's eyes before I was allowed beyond the front lobby of VX. And intriguingly, while the building might be called Club VX, anyone would assume that whatever takes place here is under the umbrella of that name—but it hides a deeper secret.

I am here at the invitation of the société d'honneur. A name behind a name.

"A necessary fundamental of the society's code."

"Aside from the rules about The Duel, I'm interested in who's behind the club."

My internet search found nothing. Not a whisper of the société d'honneur exists. Just who finances this, and with what dirty money?

"That is something I cannot share. What I can tell you," she continues, "is that the money is clean. No drugs, no black market, no arms, no trafficking, no prostitution."

Except what transpires on the dais, I fail to voice, not wishing to put myself off now that I'm feeling more committed to this. "Thank you for clarifying," I begin, my voice turning sharper because I don't want to be made a fool. "If you demand discretion from me, I demand truth from you."

"We are a society based on honor, Maddie. You may put your faith in that."

I accept her edict, Sophie running through the simple rules. The number of members exceeds what a practical tournament can accommodate. To ensure the duels don't last all night, sixteen knights are selected. This group is known as the *détachement*. Each knock-out duel within the tourney whittles the number down to two competitors in the final, which is known as the *conroi,* or duel.

All knights wear white, except the victor of the previous *conroi,* who wears black. He is known as the Black Knight. As Black Knight, he's automatically selected as a member of the *détachement* the following week, save for a few pesky rules. Should he lose the *conroi*, he has to retire from the tournament for a month, giving others a chance to reach the pinnacle of the tournament. I can only deduce that black knights are hard to beat, dominating the event. If they're removed from the tourney for a short period of time, others have a chance of success.

A Black Knight can only win for three consecutive weeks. Again, he has to retire for a month.

"In my opinion, the Black Knight is often penalised. Why is that?"

Sophie smiles like I'm naïve. "We have a large number of highly skilled knights: ex Olympians; World Champions; those tutored from a young age to excel at the épée, foil, or rapier simply because it's family tradition, or because the lure of the chivalric era is strong. Competition is fierce. Blood runs hot and fast."

"Is there discord amongst the knights?"

"The directors are there to oversee that the chevaliers follow the rules, whether they like them or not. And the Grand Master will always have your best interests at heart."

"Who is the Grand Master?"

"Your personal knight."

I like the idea of an escort to keep me safe.

"What if the knights don't follow the rules? There was mention that a white knight can proclaim Ordo Victor."

Sophie uncrosses her legs and then recrosses them the other way. "This is a rare occurrence, but the Black Knight, whether a new champion or as a returning champion, can be challenged. Whoever unsuccessfully challenges the Black Knight—during or after the *conroi*—is exiled from the society for a calendar year, with immediate effect."

It's a high risk, but is the reward worth it? Other than getting their rocks off with the lady on the throne, what else do the knights win? It's then I realize I've been looking at this all wrong.

Membership here is worth so much more.

This isn't some role-playing kink fest. This is the real deal. This is legitimate chivalry for the twenty-first century, where gentlemen participate within a series of strict rules, proving themselves through heroic deeds. The woman on the throne is of high value, whatever that means to each individual knight in the *détachement*. Only they can decide if she's worth proclaiming Ordo Victor for. Only they can put their name in the ballot, hoping to be one of sixteen.

"Exile is a high risk."

"True, but to be worthy, Miss Devereaux, by what other code can a chevalier live by? *Honneur aulx dignes*, is our motto, and while many of the members are traditionalists, swearing fealty to the guiding principles of the society, a small number see their victory differently."

So it is a role-playing kink fest for some.

Each to their own. I know why I'm beyond interested, determination coursing through me. The motto, and the existence of this society are signs, some serendipitous happenstance that has brought me here, a place where I might live out a fantasy I haven't properly identified. But it's there, in my dreams. I know it.

"Could you explain how the sixteen are selected?"

"Of course." Sophie flicks imaginary dust off her pants. "Anonymity only goes so far. Once you have confirmed a date, as lady, your picture will be circulated—using the most secure system available—amongst the members. Anyone who wishes to win the lady's grace and admiration—"

Just say pussy.

"—enters the ballot. At the deadline, usually four days after the lady's details are circulated, the *détachement* is selected at random, the Black Knight automatically advancing."

"What if less than sixteen enter the ballot?"

"That is more rare than announcing Ordo Victor, and will certainly not be an issue for *you*." Almost fondly, Sophie smiles.

"What's the average age of your members?"

"Forty-three."

I consider that age gap for a moment. A spike of nerves hits and I reach for my drink. Why didn't I ask for something stronger?

"How many members do you have?"

"One hundred and forty seven. The younger members are more successful, if that allays any fears on age."

Yeah, that definitely helps. I open my mouth to ask a question I'm unsure how to phrase, but Sophie must take pity on me, this question voiced by many in my position.

"At the end, if you become uncomfortable with what comes next, you do not have to proceed. Just let the Grand Master know and you will be excused."

"Will he be watching?"

"No, and the Grand Master is a dame. She will ensure your wishes are upheld."

I'm reassured, and I'd rather lose out on twenty grand than feel pressure to sleep with the Black Knight if I change my mind.

"A blindfold is mandatory. You will never see the face of the Black Knight."

"Why?"

"Occasionally, the Black Knight and the lady are known to each other. Over the years, we've had a large number of college students from neighboring states. Social media means our friendships are not limited to just one school or state. But more concerning for some of our members who hold positions of status and power, is that they are recognizable, and to protect everyone, a blindfold is required."

Holy fuck. Famous people are members here? I knew this place was exclusive. And even though I'd rather see what was going on and who I'm *with,* maybe a blindfold will be a Godsend.

"Can I refuse the blindfold?"

"No. That would mean you forfeit your role as lady. Anonymity is sacrosanct here."

"For the men," I point out.

"Oui," she agrees. "But it is intended to avoid awkward situations."

"What if it falls off? Sex can be rigorous."

Serious Sophie actually laughs, her face soft and carefree for a moment. "Keep your eyes closed."

Fine.

"What can you tell me about the ladies?"

"They are educated, well-mannered, beautiful, inside and out. As for attire, you choose what you wear. We do have an excellent masseuse, beautician, and hair stylist for you to make use of."

Sounds like a good night out.

Discussing the forthcoming opening, and what time I'd need to be here, are questions I should only ask if I'm serious about this. But there are two further questions I need answers to before I commit to this wild experience.

"Two final points," I venture. "Do the women enjoy this?"

"Oh yes. I should've said this before. Many ladies return, but they are limited to six occasions within twelve months. The compensation is helpful, but they return because they're well treated, as is fitting for our members ascribing to the society's code. I must stress that this is not a dating opportunity though, Miss Devereaux."

What happens in Vegas, stays in Vegas.

"I understand."

"Anything more permanent is not encouraged. Some members are married."

I deflate, deeply disappointed. It had all been looking so promising. "I don't want to participate if there's a chance the knight will be married."

Sophie holds out a placating hand. "We have ways of ensuring your wishes can be met, on this point only."

In other words, don't ask for them to be under thirty, or handsome, or fit. Just unmarried.

"I can work with that," I agree.

She inclines her head.

"One last question: How did you come by my name and details?"

More imaginary dust on Sophie's leg is brushed away, keeping me on tenterhooks. "I can only tell you that you were nominated."

"Nominated?"

"Recommended to us."

Someone gave her my name. It's hard to find breath as I flick through a mental rolodex, scrutinizing and dismissing name after name at breakneck speed. "Who?"

"I'm unable to say. You should be extremely flattered by this," Sophie informs me. "It does mean the chance of you knowing the Black Knight increases fractionally."

"Why? If there are over a hundred members—"

Like a lightning bolt, understanding strikes me.

"Oui," she answers, aware I've worked it out. "They are automatically selected for the ballot as one of the *détachment.* Married or not."

12

KIT

Lose Control - Teddy Swims

With a Chinese take-out in hand, Josh knocks at the door of my new apartment. Conveniently, we live ten minutes apart, a host of restaurants and food joints lining the route, which is why he's offered to bring dinner. He's been here before, but after describing his apartment as *box city*, it was easier to host.

Josh follows me into the open plan kitchen/living room. He checks out the antique chest of drawers, the new black L-shaped couch, the modern art and prints on the walls that I spent way too long choosing.

The apartment's pretty standard but it was the balcony that won me over. With the lights switched off, some nights I gaze out beyond its small confines, looking up at the stars and criss-crossing planes. On those nights, a restlessness consumes me, this feeling that I've forgotten or lost something.

"Did I ever tell you I like your stuff? I need to max out my card soon on new furniture."

"The salary jump will take care of that," I remind him.

"Too fucking right."

In the dove gray kitchen, I sort us out with a beer as Josh unpacks the food cartons. Taking a seat on the island stools, we tuck in.

Thinking of Josh's boxes, I offer, "I can help you unpack, you know."

"I know. But with your track record, I think you'll end up making it worse."

He'll never let me live down the story about the woman and her suitcases. "Maybe I won't give you the chance to find out."

"Small blessings. I'll host dinner next time," he confirms. "When it's less bare and more lived-in. Finally, it feels like I'm where I'm meant to be."

"I'll drink to that," I agree, feeling settled and with purpose. And while I'm in dangerous territory, I'm not pulling back from Maddie. Not only do I not have the willpower, whatever is brewing between us is beyond my control.

We catch up on the usual departmental politics: which colleagues aren't pulling their weight; students at risk of dropping out; and suspected hazing.

"So, three times this week, my trash can has been used to catch projectile vomit."

"Jesus," I commiserate, glad I finished my food. "Does he do sports? Could be hazing."

"Hazing's not allowed."

"It still happens," I remind him. "Even if it's low level stuff."

I hope Maddie hasn't had to deal with any of that. If so, I'm locking that shit down by whatever means necessary.

After tidying up, we head to the couch to watch the game.

Any game. We don't care if it's European soccer on cable or the NFL.

"So, you been back to Midnight Blue?" Josh teases.

"Without you? Not a chance."

"Jesus. It was a total ambush."

I scrub a hand through my hair. "I'm done with bar staff."

I didn't think the announcement was all that interesting but Josh stops watching TV and looks at me like he's confused.

"What?" I ask when he doesn't look away.

"You've got someone in mind. Who is it? Where's she from?"

Looking back on my various, casual dates, I can't help but think now, with the benefit of hindsight, that I was searching for someone. Someone standout. Someone in particular. Focusing on work, my research, and wasting time in the gym or at fencing tournaments suited me just fine. But now it's like the sand has emptied from the egg timer. The hands of time have stopped. I'm here, present in the moment but feeling like I'm missing a huge chunk of myself. A whole pocket of time.

I must pause too long as I mull over this yet again, deliberating on how to continue with my sharpening thoughts, but it only sends Josh into more of a blood frenzy. He's like a fucking piranha.

"Oh god, I knew it. I knew it when you called up asking why anyone would redact a Declaration of Emancipation."

"It's nothing to worry about."

Josh mutes the TV, the stadium chants of English soccer fans suddenly cut off. "What's been going on?"

The next twenty minutes are spent retelling him in precise detail every. single. moment. I've spent with Maddie. With far too much clarity, I recount her defiant, blazing looks when I skirted around her questions on Brownlow, or the low, challenging voice she uses when questioning me - *me*, her professor! And I can recall in 4K UHD color every fleck of amber in her hazel eyes, every caramel strand in her chestnut hair that makes it glimmer like gold when the light shines on it, and every way she fidgets like a sixteen-year-old high schooler, fighting her attraction to her teacher. I might also recap her essay, our frank conversations on love, courtly or otherwise, and my deductions about her devastated heart.

"Jesus, Kit. You're fucked."

"I know."

"Considering your view on her a few months ago, this is some next level paradigm shift."

I shrug, unsure how to answer. Hopeful he had a solution, he's reiterating what I already know, and that's sweet fuck all.

"Is this because she's your student?" I shake my head but he's not actually wanting an answer. "Is your position of authority influencing you in some way?"

"No," I instantly dismiss.

He raises his hand to placate me. "I'm not saying that's what you're doing, I'm just questioning everything right now and trying to be your voice of reason."

"Yeah, okay." I don't plan on telling him I gave her my cell number. I dread what his response would be.

"She sounds like a firebrand," he says, frowning and smiling at the same time. "A suitable challenge for the impossibly hard to please Christophe Tristan St Pierre Chevalier."

"I'm not that hard to please." His laughter makes me grin. It's infectious like that. "What?"

"We're both masters of casual," he begins. "And from what you've told me about her attitude to courtly love, I get the impression Maddie would never settle for anything less than a love that transcends the boundaries of time."

I nod because he's making perfect sense. Wasn't I just talking about egg timers? And he might've phrased it better than me but that's exactly what I was thinking.

"She's a challenge, and you want to rise to it."

"Something's been rising," I mutter under my breath, too fucking aware of how often I shove my hands in my pockets to hide how aroused she makes me.

"TMI, asshole."

I laugh tiredly, trying to work out how to move on from here, because I know that I do. I *shouldn't*, but I do. "Fuck. How do I make peace with the fact that I want my student? This has never happened to me before, Josh. I'm in unknown territory." And it's why he's giving me advice rather than the other way around.

"Moral compass pointing due north," he teases, following it with a sigh like he ought to make better choices. "God, I've fucked loads of undergrads. Upperclassmen mainly."

"I've got to let you best me at something."

"Dick," he says with a smile.

He hops up to retrieve more beer, so I flip channels and concentrate on the women's soccer match from yesterday. With the volume off, I can't hear the commentary, but I can at least read the names on the backs of shirts.

"She's young," I tell him when he returns, handing me a perfectly chilled bottle. "Still twenty-two. She's a baby of the year."

I catch his raised brow.

"Yeah, I looked it up." I'm *that* guy.

"So what's got you so hard for her? I mean, it's not like you've not been with smart women before. Beautiful women who ran triathlons, raced."

"She's the full package, the gold standard in a way the others weren't. And to me, she's not just beautiful but *fucking* beautiful. Her questions makes me respond in a way that feels necessary. Every guy in class has a boner for her and I want to punch them right in the face," I say aggressively, making Josh crow with laughter.

I knock back half the bottle in three long swallows, refusing to see how territorial I'm feeling. When she spends time with her friends, away from me, it feels like she's slipping away. Like I'm losing her. It's madness. "I'm either going crazy or I'm a complete pussy."

"A total loser. Utterly pathetic. But I've got your back," Josh tells me with a shit-eating grin before turning more serious. "You've got two choices: ask her out, or we hit a club and you take home a girl and see if it fixes the problem. How long since you got laid?"

We're four weeks in to the semester, about a month since I saw her in the bar. "Before I met her."

"Could be why," he leads.

I shake my head, knowing there is only one outcome from this, not that I deserve any of it, and especially not her.

Sheepishly, I snag my best friend's eye. "I really fucked up before I left Brownlow. I shouldn't have ruined her college aspirations. I don't know what possessed me."

The thing is, if I could take it back, I'm not sure I would. Because if I hadn't turned down Maddie's application, then she wouldn't be my student. She wouldn't be at Jacquard, making me lose my mind, wondering when our paths will cross again. And I wouldn't be desperately trying to impress her, skirting around the wafer-thin boundary of seducer and educator.

"That's not ever coming up."

Despite Josh's reassuring words, a burst of nervous energy races through me. If Maddie does find out, will she think I've done her a favor, or a huge disservice? Christ, it doesn't bear thinking about. Part of me knows I didn't convince her when she asked me a direct question about it. And even though I've been trying to make up for my misaligned attitude, I doubt she'll care that I lied.

For a painful moment, I think about all the ways Maddie

could and *does* find out. All it would take is a conversation with her father. Or mother. When she hears the truth, she'll know why I rejected her application, while at the same time wondering why I took the job at Jacquard if I hated the Devereaux family so badly. The family ties to the college go back generations, their money funding half the buildings, and it was why I didn't apply as an undergrad. Why I turned down a job here five years ago. But my career aspirations finally replaced any misgivings I had. They were a luxury I couldn't indulge. And with Josh here, why wouldn't I want to come too?

"Playing devil's advocate, do you think she's leading you on?"

"The thought crossed my mind," I admit. Seducing your professor and getting him kicked out of his job, disgraced and ruined, would be a slick maneuver from an old foe. "She's some next level actress if that's the case," I lead. Shaking my head, I add, "She's honest to a fault. You can't be that open-hearted without coming across as insincere. She's dealt with something messy and seems willing to confide in me."

Leaving me to my musings, Josh eventually asks, "Are you going to ask her out?"

I point at my head. "Professor."

"I know that's normally an impasse for you. Let's look at this another way: are you hot for her because of your own vendetta?"

"That's not my agenda here."

Josh knew that would be my answer so we sit in silence for a moment, neither of us sure how to proceed.

"Officially, staff-student relationships are prohibited," Josh begins. "But it's not like she's eighteen and fresh out of high school, an inexperienced cliché. Don't let it bother you. You're one of the most integrity-stubborn people I know—huge aforementioned lie aside." He takes a breath, eying me carefully. "You got this job under unusual circumstances. No interview, just a shoe-in. I think that means you can get away with an awful lot here."

My appointment at Jacq U was seriously cloak and dagger. Not to mention The Duel and all that the club entails. Neither Josh nor I know why I've been given such an easy ride, but maybe he has a point. To say I've benefitted from a type of leniency here is an understatement.

"There's no way people—if they ever found out—would see you two as anything but in a typical relationship brought about by a shared love of an academic specialty. It won't be exploitative, corrupt, or nefarious. If anything, with you being you, you'll be a much harder critic of her work than if you weren't fucking."

He's not telling me anything I haven't already considered and internally debated a million times over, and I'm not worried Maddie would be influenced by my position. Authority doesn't seem to bother her. Besides, she's in a complicated place and I owe her space to solve the dilemma of her heart.

"I bet there have been dozens of relationships like this at Ivy League schools. Everyone is more cautious, necessarily so. But as long as there's no competitive advantage, as long as it's mutually consensual, you're golden." When I don't respond, he taps me on the shoulder with the back of his hand. "You good? When can I meet her?"

"There's the whole department drinks mixer soon."

Posters decorate the hallways across all language departments. Emails have gone out reminding students—and staff. I even mentioned it to my medieval literature class, making significant eye-contact with Maddie to convey I wanted her there.

"Riiight. Cool. I've seen her, of course, but I'd like to chat to her and understand why she has you frothing at the mouth."

"Thanks."

"You're welcome. What do you think her thoughts are on this? On you?"

I blow out a tense breath, considering every way I make it obvious that I'm interested. "Hard to say. She's been badly burned but she still loves him. She's taking her time to make her assessment."

"Smart woman. I've never seen you so animated about a girl before, or looking so dejected."

A mournful laugh tumbles from my chest. "Sorry, I'm being a miserable bastard."

"I get it. So how are you going to play it from here?"

I have some plans underfoot, but I've yet to voice them. Automatically, I think of Evan. They know each other—I've seen them talking. He's on the fencing circuit, a cocky little prick because, frustratingly, he knows what he's doing.

"I'll leave you to ponder on that. I need to take a leak."

Absently, I rub a hand across my chin stubble, a rasp sounding. I need to shave before work tomorrow.

Eager for an update on what's going on with the club, I unlock my cell. Keeping this secret has been hard, and keeping it from Josh harder still. We share a lot. We're like brothers. When he returns, I'll clue him in.

Sunday night is when the details of the ladies are available. Two weeks prior to the tournament is the earliest a knight can enter the ballot for a particular lady or week, depending on what motivates you. Usually the app is updated at 8PM which leaves two minutes to go.

My encrypted VX app has several new notifications. I tap the icon. Once my face has been recognized and I've inputted an eight digit alpha-numeric code, I click on Ballot. Since my inauguration as knight, I've only put my name forward three times. Considering I've had eight opportunities, it means I'm not making the most of my position. But work just before the semester started was manic, and the ballot is over-subscribed anyway. And while the ladies so far have been worth the effort of competing, none of them capture my attention as much as the ensnaring beauty sitting in my class. None of them have made me want to show the members of VX just how skilled a swordsman I really am.

Returners, as denoted by the R in the top right corner of their picture, are often scheduled in the calendar weeks in advance. One is a Californian-looking babe, but I scroll down to the box that asks if I want to be included in the ballot and hit *No.*

From down the hall, just as Josh returns, his phone rings. "I got to get this."

"No problem," I murmur, refreshing my app now it's 8PM.

The face that smiles back at me sends me over the edge of my restraint. It's who I hoped and feared. Hoped for obvious reasons, and feared for the consequences I can't predict.

Madrigal's photograph takes up my entire screen, which is fitting because she's become my entire sphere of existence. The photogenic image looms like a 3D picture, jutting beyond the limitations of my screen. Her smile is broad, natural, the picture taken in high summer as she sits happily on a bench in jean shorts, sand dunes and beach behind her.

Sophie Bouchard likes to have a more serious face shot, one full length, and then a candid. Interestingly, Madrigal put her beach-scene candid first. The full-length photo of her has me sucking in a breath. Wearing a cranberry-hued, form-fitting dress, she looks stunning. Her athletic shape is there for all to see, a beautiful hourglass of curved hips and defined thighs.

The final photograph is a black and white close-up. Maddie looks exactly like the Hollywood movie stars from the 30s and 40s, her skin flawless and smooth, her eyes beckoning. Studying Maddie in class is something I can't do for long—it's one reason why I ask her endless questions, just so I can admire her legitimately. Still, I indulge my inner beast now, glutting on her image.

I take screenshots of the photos and save them to my cell.

Satisfied, I relax, letting the couch take all my weight. Counting down the next two weeks has just got a lot more exciting. My chances at winning Maddie's admiration as lady is a sure thing. Entering the ballot is unnecessary, my position in the *détachement* guaranteed. To prove that, the app doesn't even give me the option to add my name to the ballot.

It doesn't need to if you nominated the lady.

13

MADDIE

Stargazing - Myles Smith

My entire vision is made up of black tuxedos and glittering dresses. Waiters balance glasses of champagne on silver salvers, my ears bombarded by the low, rumbling din of two hundred people mid-conversation. To my side, Mom and Dad converse with a famous news anchor, one of many guests at the thousand dollar plate charity dinner for a cause close to Mom's heart: CanTRA, the Canadian Therapeutic Riding Association.

Mom looks lit-up, happy. Watching how her and Dad interact makes my heart glow.

The day, however, has not been as successful. Earlier, I participated in a mixed doubles tournament, combining retired pros, wannabe pros, and the general public with a flare for tennis. Harrison convinced me we should double up for the charity efforts, so I agreed. Playing alongside him wasn't as fun as I remember, even though I've grown as a player. We couldn't read each other as well as we used to, our play off balance. Our intuition was trash.

Harrison hid his displeasure well but I saw the cracks in the polished exterior.

I sigh, acutely aware of which old flames he's been catching up with today. I thought this level of paranoia was behind me; I hate that I still clock his movements. Hate that my attention is piqued whenever someone mentions his name.

Perrie was supposed to be here to distract me. To run interference if Harrison got too clingy. But Hank offered her a job at Midnight Blue and she couldn't swap her shift.

When I catch Mom's eye she takes pity on me. Excusing ourselves from the conversation, we link arms and amble away. In a floor-length, silver dress, she strikes a beautiful figure.

"There's someone here, a guest tonight. I think you would enjoy meeting him."

Him. "Oh?"

Her head swivels in all directions, scouting the room.

"Who is he?"

She taps her nose, giving me a chiding look.

"Why can't you tell me? Is it another TV personality?"

Her focus returns to the room, her brows knitting. "Where is he?"

The strange sensation of eyes dragging up and down my back has me turning to look behind me. A pulse of heat turns everything bright and hot when I realize those eyes belong to Kit.

Kit is here.

He stands to one side, an empty glass of champagne dangling from his hand. For a suspended moment it's like I've returned to Midnight Blue, our gazes tangling across the bar. Wearing the hell out of his tuxedo, I start to form a smile when a brunette in a gorgeous pale blue dress approaches him. His eyes flick from me to her, the woman capturing all of his attention. So I turn away, back to my mother, something inside tightening to the point of pain.

"Ah, there he is," Mom smiles, leaving me mute and rigid as she heads behind me towards . . . oh fuck, my professor.

"Hélène, Kit, I hope you're enjoying the evening."

Hélène answers kindly, "Thank you for the invitation. We've had a lovely evening."

"My absolute pleasure. And I'm so sorry about the table plan mix up."

"Oh please, don't worry."

Mom turns to me, whispering loud enough for our circle of four to hear. "Kit and Hélène were meant to be on our table as my guests; I could hardly change arrangements once everyone had taken their seats."

Personally, I think not sitting near Kit and his date at dinner is a blessing. It's saved me from hiding the quiet devastation that is slowly taking over my body.

"We enjoyed meeting the Duvals and the Rodrigues'," Hélène stresses.

"I'm glad, but it means I didn't get to introduce you to my daughter, Madrigal," Mom says, smiling brightly.

I copy her smile, putting on a brave face. "I generally go by Maddie," I tease Mom, unable to not look at Kit. Does he remember me correcting him—repeatedly—about my name? "Hélène, lovely to meet you. Professor Kit."

Kit's voice is like a tender embrace. "*Madrigal.*"

"Maddie, it's lovely to meet you. Kit mentioned you're his student."

I nod, fighting a scream of horror. To disappear in a cloud of mist so that I don't have to be around this beautiful couple because she is stunning, her bright blue eyes contrasting with her luscious hair and enviable black lashes. Similarly aged to him, she has the comportment of someone more his style. Erica needs-a-bigger-shirt has got nothing on this sophisticated woman.

I dislike Hélène intensely.

"Yes, my doctorate is in medieval literature," I reply.

"Are you enjoying your studies so far?"

I take a breath. "I am, it's been five demanding and challenging weeks," I say, my eyes flicking in Kit's direction. His attention hasn't left mine as I chat with his date, my insides shriveling to husks. "And I've long been an admirer of Professor Kit's work. His knowledge is inspiring."

A smile brushes her mouth, her eyes flying to Kit's with questions in them. Or is that confirmation of something?

"Thank you," he says, a little surprised. "Professors do have a knack of professing knowledge, amongst other things," he adds. Turning to Mom, he reveals, "Maddie is a bright and capable student. I enjoy our discussions very much."

My cheeks feel warm and tingly. I begin to sway but stop myself.

Stuck on what else people profess, I'm distracted when Harrison appears at my side, and for the first time in forever, I'm grateful for his attention. Looking handsome, if not a little uncomfortable in his tux, he carries two glasses of bubbles in his hands, offering one to me.

"Excuse us," he tells the small group, whisking me away with a hand wrapped around my upper arm.

"That was rude," I hiss, throwing an apologetic glance over my shoulder to Kit and Hélène who are getting further and further away from me. And to my Mom, though she's well aware of Harrison's flaws. "And embarrassing."

"You looked like you needed saving."

"Did I?"

He dings his glass against mine, smiling his easy smile that still packs a punch. He takes a long sip suggesting, "Let's get a little sloppy on booze and find a cloakroom. It'll be like the good old days."

A familiar gleam in his eye brings thrills and trepidation. It's drowned out by the insistent voice in my head to turn around, to see if Kit is still there.

"What are you looking at?" Harrison asks. "Or who?"

Kit and Hélène have disappeared from view. Maybe *they're* in the restrooms, up to no good. After all, my professor has form.

"Nothing."

"I enjoyed playing with you today—it's been a while. The losses we had proved it."

I smile through his criticism, passing my untouched champagne to a waiter; I need a clear head around Harrison. "It was a lot of fun."

Not buying my lie, he laughs quietly before sipping from his flute. "We should play some more and iron out those kinks. I hope I wasn't too much. Old habits."

Old habits.

The phrasing has me doubting, spiraling into memories of locker rooms and a deceptive kind of love. And then I remember the beautiful dream I keep having, interrupting my thoughts like a clarion call. Each time I wake, echoes of a grand love affair settle in my bones. It's a reason, a cause that has me preoccupied, wondering when I'll figure out what it all means and who the man is. Often, we exchange love tokens: small embroidered scenes; the shape of a horse made from grasses and bull rushes; flower chains and flower pressings.

Is it Harrison, my subconscious directing me back to him? Do I want to rekindle our romance once and for all?

"You still want to do this doctorate?"

"Yes," I say, but it comes out more like a question.

Harrison pulls a face and I realize my arm is still smarting from his touch. "It's a long fucking time. All that studying and researching. It seems like such a waste of your talents. You're young, you should be out there living your life."

"I am living my life."

"You know what I mean. You could do something meaningful. I know you want to earn your own wage—why prolong it?"

Swallowing the hurt his words cause, my face becomes a blank mask. "The doctorate is everything right now, Harrison. It makes me happy."

It's not a lie. Year one is always tough, a stretch, but as I drop classes and teaching from next year, things will improve. Finding time to research my field will become easier.

"Seems like a colossal effort to me." A shrug. "Come on, let's get out of here."

Dinner finished an hour ago, the eight-piece band that kept us entertained through the four-course meal altering the mood with some up-tempo music to lure us to the dance floor. The night won't end for another three hours.

Several couples move to the center of the grand, chandelier-decked room to dance as a new song starts. The joy on everyone's faces makes me mourn Perrie's absence tonight. We would've been unstoppable out there.

"You go if you like," I suggest, catching sight of the Duvals, friends of the family. "I've got people to meet."

"Ditch the party," he urges. "We'll find somewhere to talk then. About us. It's long overdue."

"I'm not in the mood to talk," I respond. "Soon," I promise, wanting to delay the inevitable. "I haven't had time to think."

"What's there to think about?" he genuinely asks, his hand catching up mine. His touch is irksome. His touch is beautiful. "It's a no-brainer."

"If you push me, if we rush this, Harrison," I begin, "then I'll call it now."

His chest expands on a deep inhale as he releases my palm. "Then I'm out of here. Maybe you'll miss me," he says with heavy irony, a small smile transforming his hurt features into something infinitely more desirable.

I whisper, "Goodnight, then."

He kisses me softly on the cheek before leaving, the imprint of his grip fading as he walks towards the nearest doors. Wanting space and quiet, I walk the opposite direction, bumping into Dad on the way.

"Maddie." His eyes track someone behind me. "Harrison leaving?"

"Yeah."

His eyes crawl over my face, looking for clues. "He's not for you," he surmises.

As always, my answer is *no*, even though I'm cursing my indecision, hating that I feel so stuck.

"He was never right for you, was he? You can do better."

"What?" I ask, baffled. "I thought you were gunning for our reunion."

Wearily, he shakes his head. "Only because I hoped it would bring you to Jacquard. I let you follow your heart at sixteen because I wanted to be supportive. And I thought it was a fling, a teenage rebellion. When I suggested you wait until college, that you might meet someone there, you were adamant Harrison was for you. You always defended him because . . . you loved him." He looks around the room as I stand there, drinking in his admissions. "You always did the opposite of what I suggested." There's a sad smile. "Find someone worthy of you, Maddie."

He pecks me on the cheek and heads straight to Mom. Either through motherly intuition, or because Dad says something to her, she looks my way, offering an encouraging smile.

Lungs tight, I head for the doors, processing the night. Passing down a long hallway, I exit into the formal gardens. I walk until I think I've walked far enough away from the crowds and that room which has me all twisted up.

Giving myself a mental slap, I look up, into the night sky. A meteor zips across the velvet black and I remember that the annual meteor shower is peaking tonight. I head north. Away from the patios and flower-filled borders, the white bulb lights peter out. Using the vast sky of stars as my guide, I wander to the edge of the boundary where the view is uninterrupted.

A bird calls, the blackness above me illuminated by endless pinpricks of winking silver. Peace envelops me, the stillness of the cool night welcoming. Gazing at the horizon, I let the majesty of the night awe me. Celestial events often leave me feeling insignificant, a propensity to ponder my existence, my life and my goals often at the forefront of my thoughts.

Movement to my right has me turning. Amongst the shadows stands a man, his black silhouette blending into the night around him.

"Maddie."

The voice is mellow and sensual. There's a familiarity to the outline of the shoulders, to the tall frame and the head of dark hair.

"Professor?" I ask, my pulse spluttering.

Slowly, he walks towards me, the light playing tricks on my vision. Shadows give way to moonlight as he stops in front of me. Features sharpen, and even though I saw him ten minutes ago, an agonisingly handsome face regards me with dark temptation.

"Kit," he corrects.

He cuts an impeccable figure, a physicality that makes a woman breathless and wanting. Appreciative eyes roam my face, my body, my dress, each glide a physical touch that brands my skin. My floor-length dress is midnight blue, tiny sequins catching starlight, echoing on earth what captivates me above. Right now, I'm grateful for Mom's extravagant gift.

"You look—" There's a puff of air. "Beautiful is too simple. Incredible is not enough." He takes a breath. "You look like ruination."

The description lands like a bomb. I can't breathe, my chest tight. It takes me a moment to gather my wits after his devastatingly honest compliment.

"Thank you. You look—" *Divine, fucking gorgeous, like heartbreak*, "—very handsome tonight."

He smiles his thanks, but after his compliment, my words seem like empty platitudes.

"Are you cold?" He shrugs out of his jacket, offering it to me.

Although I'm not cold, I take it because it feels like the right thing to do and throw it around my shoulders. "Thanks."

Subtly, I inhale his timeworn scent, tingles spreading along my skin: mint, pine forests, something spicy, and a scent like metal and fire. A forge?

I glance behind him, wondering where Hélène is. "Are you here to see the meteorites?"

"Yes," he answers. "There are—" he twists, a thumb pointing over his shoulder. "There are chairs," he trails off, inviting me but also immediately regretting it by the sound of his voice.

I peek towards these chairs I cannot see. Maybe his date is over there. Maybe that's why he regrets mentioning them.

"Are you meeting—is your date there?"

Cursing Harrison for making me doubt every man, it's too late to take back my intrusive question. And curiously, I've realized the tight sensation I felt earlier is jealousy. The thought of Kit with another woman makes me mad. I'm not overjoyed at meeting her again, knowing she's his, and he hers.

"Come with me."

Kit starts to walk away so I follow, my heels sinking into the grass as the eight-piece band play a new tune, its fast beat faintly discernible all the way out here.

Two black and white deck chairs greet me. They face due north, perfectly positioned for the meteor show.

"I came across them by accident," Kit reveals, the night absorbing his voice, turning it velvet soft. "Though I must confess, I did appropriate the bottle and glass."

The items are propped on the lawn, in between the two chairs. I sit in the nearest one, Kit catching me by my left hand to lower me down. Sparks scatter from my palm all the way up to my shoulder.

I flash him a smile. "I promise not to rat on you."

His mouth curves as he sits in the chair beside me. "Only fair, seeing as I promised not to tell on you to Perrie," he rebuffs.

Smiling, he lowers himself into the chair, taking up all available space.

"How new are your shoes?"

"Why?"

"I'm trying to work out who needs to drink out of a shoe tonight."

He lifts up the one glass with a commiserating look on his face.

My smile is automatic. "Part of my initiation involved drinking out of everyone's shoes. I've got this."

"As if," he objects. "You can have the glass and I'll take the bottle."

I laugh off his reasoning and accept the glass he pours me, taking a sip. "Got lots to ruminate over tonight?"

There's a notable pause, the stillness of the moment feeling weighted as he quietly looks across at me, assessing with a soft, almost worried expression.

"Lots to think about," he confirms. "And I'm not with someone," he clarifies, answering my earlier question. "My sister was my date tonight, or rather, I was hers, and she's turned in for the night."

Ohhh. A sister. I never knew. And I can see it now, the stunning resemblance. Relief, swift and sharp hits me right in the solar plexus. "I'm sorry about the way I left."

Leashed anger slices the air between us, and I think I understand what made the atmosphere so heavy a moment ago. "Didn't look like you had much choice."

Acknowledging his statement is pointless. "Please pass on my apologies to Hélène."

"Your mother did on your behalf."

Grateful for her tact, I take a fortifying breath as Kit puts the bottle to his mouth and tips the end, swallowing. When he speaks, his voice is cold calm. "My offer still stands if you need help with a difficult situation."

"I'm managing it," I tell him, Kit searching my eyes and accepting my answer. He won't interfere. Won't overstep. His support and faith in me are like building blocks, raising me up.

"How bad was the hazing?"

"For tennis?" I ask, to his nod. "Nothing too terrible. The captains aren't fans of it."

"Good," he says approvingly. "Let me know if it changes."

His enquiries have me smiling to myself. "What is the connection between you and my mother?"

It was never referred to at our introduction. Nor was the relationship between Kit and Hélène. Surely my mother knew, so why didn't she reveal it? And why does it feel like my mother was playing with me tonight. Weeks ago, she referenced that I had to meet someone at this event and then she introduces me to my own professor. What's going on?

"My sister uses the funds your mother raises—amongst others at CanTRA—to support her work and people with physical disabilities to access horse riding."

My heart melts. "An extremely worthwhile cause. Mom is passionate about it."

"It appears so. It was the first time either of us had met her." He looks across at me, as if his statement is important. "She seems like a good woman."

"She is," I agree fondly. "She's a great mother." I change the subject. "It makes sense you have a sister."

"Does it?"

I nod, considering every facet of his character that he's shown me so far. And it's interesting that I note in this exact moment that Harrison's an only child. Like me. But we don't speak about who tore me away from our conversation. If he's the man who broke my heart and who dislikes quotes. It's obvious.

In contemplative silence, we turn in unison and look up at the sky, at the North Star hanging directly above. Feelings of home and direction and time-weary distance assault me. Seeing that bright star shining down upon me, us, feels like a talisman. There's something pleasingly familiar about tonight. About sitting here under the stars. I sense happy endorphins mirrored in my soul. Being in Kit's company makes me comforted, happy beyond measure. And his proximity, the pulsating energy of the air, makes me dizzy. Maybe it's the champagne that's fuzzing my thoughts but I sip down the bubbles as Kit drinks from the bottle, the fizz and slosh of liquid audible in the still night.

Reaching under his chair, Kit brings out a book, angling the cover towards me. Moonlight reflecting off the cover reveals it's a collection of works by Oscar Wilde.

"Turns out I was meeting you—and Oscar Wilde tonight. He got me thinking."

His answer coaxes a smile. And he was *reading.* I love that. "*I can resist everything except temptation.*"

I don't exactly regret the Wilde quotation but my cheeks

burn as I offer an insight into my state of mind. At how he makes me feel.

His voice is a double-bass, making me feel drunk to my bones. "Are you tempted by something?"

Blood roars through my veins. I clutch my glass like it's a life raft, our eyes connecting over the rim. I can't answer. Daren't.

"*You don't love someone for their looks...but because they sing a song only you can hear.*"

My heart slows. Stalls. He's quoting Wilde back to me.

Sounding annoyed, he continues, "I always thought it a lie."

And I can't tell if he's cross at Wilde for suggesting such a stupid thing, or if he meant to say *I always thought it a lie, until I met you.* Which is nonsensical and vain but a small part of me was hoping. So, I ask, "Do you hear music?"

There's a long pause as I become aware of the *lack* of music from the band. At how quiet it is.

A seductive smile tugs at his mouth, his golden brown eyes undressing me as I recline in the deck chair, hopelessly, thoroughly turned on. The alcohol has warmed my blood so I can't blame the cool night for my peaked nipples or the goosebumps that run along my arm at the intimacy of this moment.

"What do you think, Madrigal?"

I think he's teasing me for my name, one he's a little fascinated with. But the look on his face is one of pursuit. Of want. And I want him inside me, on top of me. I want him *everywhere.* But I drop the glass to the ground and his jacket to my seat, walking a few paces away where I turn my face skywards.

Meteors burn across the sky, their fiery tails blazing streaks into the dark heavens.

"There," I say, pointing, feeling his eyes on my back, at the deep vee of the dress that goes beyond my back dimples. Standing, he walks up behind me, the heat of him absorbed into my bare skin.

It's like he's born of a star, eclipsing every thought and sense. Why I ever felt overlooked by him, I can't think. I'm consumed by his orbit.

"Do you think love transcends time?" I whisper.

Some days, I feel like I'm at page zero of my own creation. That I have the memory of the world contained in my soul and in my heart. Recently, I've been chasing my own tail, seeking, hunting for this great love from which I was forged. I'm close to understanding it, on the precipice of a font of knowledge.

"I think there are powers greater than we can imagine."

I'm lost to indecision. Torn from staying where I am, my back to him, or turning and welcoming what we're on the cusp of exploring. Worries about repeating the same mistakes with a man of authority rise. My instincts about Kit are strong but I don't want a love forged in the dark again. Hiding who I love was a torment I don't want to relive.

And my involvement with Club VX approaches at pace. There are answers I need, about myself. Would it be dishonest to start something here and not explain myself? Is it best to have a conversation, clarifying what I'm doing and why? Owning this for myself has to take priority, even though I want Kit too.

But not yet.

Not Kit, not yet.

A hand brushes my waist, resting gently as thudding drum beats of a new tune in the ballroom mirror my heart. "Maddie."

Involuntarily my eyes close, wanting to give in to that voice. To the night, the man. The steady press of his palm against my waist stirs a deep, barely moving breeze until it builds and grows, roaring against my skin, tearing at my flesh with hurricane force until I'm on the cusp of exploding apart.

He's a compulsion I can't deny. A gravity I can't fight.

So I open my eyes and turn. Give in.

I obliterate as his mouth meets mine in a blistering kiss, one that lights up my soul and turns me into nothing more than vapour. Everything, *everything* narrows to this moment, to his warmth that wraps around me, the masculine strength as he hauls me close. Thoughts empty from my head as my hands skim around his neck, our bodies pressed tight together. I feel him *everywhere,* a hard, thick bulge wedged between us which has my breath catching. With an arm around my back and a hand threaded through my hair, I let myself fall, become consumed.

His deep groan of male interest, of pure want, is my undoing. I can't fathom where I begin or end. I just know that he devours me, little tremors and vibrations racing through my limbs at how perfect he feels. A strong heartbeat pounds against my chest, resonating into my rejoicing heart.

His kiss is oxygen. Life-giving. I feel lit up like the sun.

A low, needy moan climbs up my throat as our mouths chase and explore, his lips pulling and savoring. Large hands roam across my back, bare to the night and to his electrifying touch. A roughened fingertip, two, dip beyond the low vee of my dress, exploring my skin. Shivers scatter, nerve endings blaze, my pulse frenzied as we stand under a sky of portent and time. As I melt into his arms and addictive scent of mint and vetiver and forest and fire.

Time disconnects, and I'm unsure how long we stand in this spot, entangled, kissing away the night as I deconstruct at his touch. I'm only aware of the slow, thorough kisses, of his warmth and strength that makes me feel lost and found.

I end the kiss, my words spoken against his mouth as our foreheads dip and meet. "I'm sorry."

His breathing is ragged. "What for?"

I don't get the chance to answer. Involuntarily, my mouth

finds his again, my fingertips running through his hair as time dissolves. I cling to him like the world is ending, our bodies joined at hip and chest and mouth. His tongue is wicked as I grind against his cock, his breath fast and hot as he claims my neck and throat with clever, dexterous lips, stubble scratching my skin.

"Kit," I whisper. Hating myself, I pull away, and with reluctance, he lets me.

Starlight shines in his eyes. His thumbs trace my cheekbones. "I want this, Maddie. This isn't—I'm not playing games here."

I accused him of playing a game I didn't understand. Now I do. Every point of contact these past few weeks, every conversation makes believing him easy.

"I know. And I want to be invested, but I can't. Not yet. There are . . . things I need to resolve. And until they are, I can't confuse myself. Can't take this further. It's not fair to you."

His eyes trace mine, longing mixed with disappointment, then acceptance. "I understand. Take what time you need."

The band plays Muse's *Starlight,* recognizable all the way out here. Neither of us step away; we just hold tight as the chorus arrives, my body held against Kit's, his white dress shirt soft against my cheek.

Allowing myself five more seconds, I take a step back, his heat leaching from my skin. "I should go."

"Let me walk you." The register of his voice is no longer seductive but insistent, commanding. "I don't like the idea of you walking around here alone."

"I'll be fine."

I lurch for the lights of the country hotel. Taking those steps hurt me in a way I can't process; my soul feels like it's torn in two, my heart buried under a boulder.

Looking over my shoulder as I leave, his outline fades into the night. "Goodnight, Kit."

A disembodied voice sounds from the dark. "Goodnight, Madrigal."

14

KIT

Balance - Wilkinson & NORTH

A notification from Gramps flashes up on my phone.

This girl you seeing got a name?

Whilst I'm not strictly seeing Maddie, I was fed up with Gramps' passive aggressive comments about time waiting for no man and that I needed to lock down a sweet-hearted, pretty girl. So I told him I was seeing someone, mostly to get him off my back, but also because I wanted it to be true.

Yes, I reply, being a dick.

For the next few minutes, I receive a dozen or more messages, each one offering up five girls' names. He can be one stubborn bastard sometimes and so I decide to give up on account of his uncommon persistence.

Maddie. Now stop being nosy.

I don't hear anything from him after that, so I get ready for class. Usually, we lose students a few weeks in, but there's been a recent surge for my medieval literature class and we exceed the capacity of my office. The only option is to teach in the lecture theatre. Still, it's too big a space for twenty students, so I make them sit in the first four rows.

"Come closer," I encourage Maddie and the others, my eyes unable to leave her.

I think about her all the time. About her day, her happiness, and what she's working on. Today, she's wearing black leggings and her red hoodie with Jacquard University Tennis written on the back. Going by the cardboard cups clamped in her hand and the hands of her friends, they've stopped at a campus coffee shop on the way to class. Feelings of envy rise; I want to be able to do mundane, ordinary things with her, like cooking dinner together, or grocery shopping, or just sitting next to her while we read. "There are spaces down here."

Since our kiss at the ball, our weekly meeting and regular classes have continued unabated. I'm thankful that she still stops to chat after class, resolutely not avoiding me. The kiss meant something to her; I'm sure of it. But we've reset to our earlier dynamic, questioning each other, inviting and assessing.

I have to proceed carefully. In two days' time, her participation in a secret club will have an impact I can't predict. Concentrating on the here and now, I drag a chair closer to the bank of seats, hoping it will allow for a more intimate, collaborative discussion.

Quietly, Maddie watches my every movement. Holding her eye for longer than I would normally for any student, I let her know I still want her. Her answering inhale, and her appreciative gaze tell me I'm not imagining this.

Once everyone settles, I begin. "We have new starters so, for their benefit, and as a useful reminder for all, who can recap the core principles of courtly love?"

No one raises their hand so I pick on someone, purely because he annoys me by sitting next to Maddie. "Oliver."

Looking resigned he recounts, "Out of the courts of medieval Europe came a highly ritualized form of love between a knight and a lady, a so called chivalric romance."

"What else?" I point to Maddie, next to him, just because I can't wait any longer to hear her voice. The absence of her between classes is a toll on my sanity I wasn't expecting. I miss her. And yet somehow, she's under my skin, living there alongside me like a second soul.

"Different to medieval marriages—which focused on possession of a woman, her sexuality, and ability to produce heirs—chivalric romances were a highly idealized portrayal of courtly love," she replies, "characterised by restraint, devotion, and discretion. It was a spiritual love, not necessarily physical."

A perfect answer.

"It was always outside the marriage bond," I stress. "An impossible love. What are the core values of chivalry?" I ask Yves.

"Piety, honor, and prowess."

"Who springs to mind?" I ask. "Anyone you know?"

Laughter fills the lecture theatre but no one offers up many options except the usual favorites. "No more suggestions than a couple athletes?" I probe as Maddie finishes the last of her coffee.

"I did say it was *highly idealized*," Maddie points out. "Knights pursued love for love's sake. It was the means as well as the end."

While Maddie is an enthusiast for this topic, she's always dissecting and dismissing. It's as if she wants someone to contradict the well established themes of the literature. To prove that the rules were impossible to follow.

"Explain."

She blows out a breath. "Courtly love encourages a knight to do everything he can to bring honor to his lady. Love for her spurned him towards ever greater trials, desperate to prove himself. I've said it before, but what man can live up to such expectations?"

"Are you saying that not all knights lived by such a stringent code?" I can't look away from her. Maddie challenges the texts regularly, and I'm keen for her insights. "There's little evidence to contradict the common themes."

A sigh. "I know but there must've been one knight out of a hundred who struggled. Who fell foul of the high standards."

"It would mean banishment. Loss of status and his place at court, his lands and staff, his income and credibility," I say for the benefit of the new undergrads. "All men are fallible and it's why the literature was cautionary, highlighting a knight's balance—his *mésure.* It was up to a knight to determine which side of the line he was comfortable with."

For a moment, a wistful expression settles on her face. "But what of *true love*? It couldn't have been real if the knight didn't throw all those rules to one side and love freely. You should love someone with your *whole soul.*"

Silence settles in the lecture hall, Maddie shifting in her seat as students exchange glances, or nod quietly, feeling represented in that passionate statement.

God, I feel Maddie's pain. I can see the anguish on her face and her it in her voice. She's tortured by the idea of love and her experiences of it. What the hell happened to her? What idiotic fuck ruined her heart, her soul?

Softening my voice, I remind her, "Loving fiercely was, unfortunately, not a knight's, or a lady's prerogative. Remember, the love was outside the marriage bond. And therein lies the constant dilemma of a knight at court," I declare to the wider class, refocusing them on what's important. There were always choices but the knight had to make the right ones to be worthy of his position. To feel moral pride for his behaviors and deeds. "It wasn't meant to be true love. It was essentially pretend."

"Who wants pretend?" Maddie argues.

Jade, whose hair is a different shade of the rainbow every week mutters, "Yeah, that blows. I'm with Maddie on this. I want to meet a man who embodies all those ideals, but for real."

"Get in line," Sylvie mutters to chuckles, whose monstrously fake eyelashes must make blinking difficult. "Men like that don't exist anymore."

"Some do," Maddie answers quietly, her gaze running over me before she swiftly looks down at her notebook.

Oliver offers, "Chivalry denied is why chivalry died."

Fluffing her blue hair, Jade responds, "It needs to make a come-back."

I allow the discussion to continue for a few minutes, several students joining in with new options on positive male role models.

"Okay. Let's bring it back to task. Questions? Any points that aren't clear?"

With a crumpled coffee cup in hand, Oliver asks, "Professor, what if a knight kills himself trying to show how worthy he is? Seems a bit pointless."

"That's not in keeping with the spirit of chivalry," Maddie rebuffs, and I'm glad it's not just me she argues with. "The knight is determined to prove himself."

"So is chivalric love blind?" I ask the class.

There are murmurs of agreement and mumbles of dissent. No guesses for which camp Maddie stands in.

When I give my answer, I plan on drowning any doubt in her mind. "The lady is a knight's *sworn love.* The mistress of his heart. Everything he does is out of honor for her, regardless of the cost to him."

"Doesn't that just portray him as having no agency?"

"In which texts does it state that?" I challenge Maddie, the class too.

There are a few suggestions but none of them hold water. On the board, I reference relevant quotations that disprove Maddie's thoughts.

When she raises her hand, I nod for her to make her point. "I still think love is portrayed as an inherently unreasonable thing."

"Go on," I encourage.

There's a frustrated shrug. "Loving someone and being unable to express it, to be open about it, must've been . . . difficult."

Ahh. Like a magic trick, the hows and whys unveil themselves before my eyes. And I know without a doubt that she has lived this, experienced this. Naturally, Maddie is cautious about finding herself in this situation again.

"We heard today that chivalric love was based on restraint. On devotion. An unconsummated love," I remind her, of the words she spoke a few minutes ago. "And De Troyes shows us that love and reason are powerful influences on a knight. *Mésure* is a knight's agency," I tell Maddie. "There's *conflict* but the knight must find his restraint. His honor.

"Court politics demanded it. Defying your king, your orders, your code, was to commit social suicide. To act beyond acceptable norms was rare, but we are witness to those struggles and desires through the literary works of the medieval era." For Maddie's ears especially, I say, "For a small few, defiance of those laws and codes was worth everything."

"But not without cost," she replies softly. "And love shouldn't cost us a thing."

My heart feels heavy—for her, for what could still be entirely lost to me if she weighs the cost of *us* to be too great. Teaching my favorite medieval texts for over a decade has shown me the full spectrum of thoughts and explanations from my students. But Maddie seems to *feel* it, her depth of understanding not limited to her recent experiences of love. She displays an empathy that goes beyond that of critic and student.

And it must be why one of the things she has to resolve before committing to me, if she ever does, is to go to Club VX and experience a fraction of what it is to be idolized and revered.

To quell any last doubts, I tell her, "A good thing that we are afforded freedoms that did not exist in the French medieval courts."

The quiet hope in her eyes calms the rising anxiety in mine.

Jade begins, "So basically it's a choice between, like, a guy holding a lady's hand one second, but the next, he's bending her into a pretzel and showing her a good time?"

Hoots of laughter fill the lecture theatre.

"Thanks for the clarification," I murmur in her direction, noticing Maddie has blushed to her ears. And damn, she makes blushing sexy.

"To be clear," I add, drilling home my point, "the knight will find balance with his sworn love *only*. The other ladies at court *do not factor*. And he'll do all he can, however small or grand, to win her high regard."

With a contemplative expression, Maddie stares at a point behind me. As a collective, hopefully we're reinforcing the many positives of courtly love, and despite gaining some insights today, there's more to know. I want to learn why she's so resistant to the merits of love. It's clear she's been hurt, and while my suspicions of who that was have been confirmed, I need to know how Tait hurt her. And I'm not referring to the little bruises I saw on her body—for which he needs to die, painfully and slowly. I need to know how because I need to make sure I never fuck up as badly as he did. The past few assignments I've given her have been helpful, and while I need her to think and interrogate the texts, she needs to get out of her head and listen to her heart.

I hope my next questions unearth more.

"Let's bring this to life by referencing music that corresponds to a knight's view of his lady love," I suggest to amusement. "What've you got?"

Confused faces greet me, but thankfully, the irrepressible Jade has an option. "*Adore You* by Harry Styles."

There are a few nods of agreement.

"Good. What else? And let's keep it PG 13."

Snorted giggles ripple among the students, but I heard Sylvie whisper *WAP* to the student in the neighboring chair.

"*Be The One*, Dua Lipa."

It's not quite right, but I let the students decide, each of them shouting out suggestions that are met with groans of disagreement, or murmurs of assent.

"*Into You*, Ariana Grande."

"Bonnie Tyler and *Holding Out for a Hero!*"

"For the Swifties—*Lover.*"

Yves offers, "*Sweet But Psycho* by Ava Max. I mean, the knight *is* slaying people left, right and center. He's got problems."

Maddie laughs, Yves grinning across at her. Yeah, I definitely want to kill him. Also slowly.

"Right?" he asks her.

"A bit psycho is good. Five percent tops."

He gifts her a questioning look, but she's already turning away. But to answer his query, she says, "Courting a married woman is the definition of psycho."

Just about everyone has contributed in some way, everyone but Maddie. When the class quiets, I look directly at her, wanting—needing—her answer. "Maddie," I press, when she averts her eyes. "Anything spring to mind?"

She shakes her head and my world dissolves. I can't let the momentum slip away, so in a code she may or may not interpret,

I ask, "How does a knight's sworn love, his lady, want to be treated by her chevalier?"

Lips parting, she takes a breath. Is she thinking of our kiss? Does she understand what I really want to know: how does she want her knight—me—to love her?

Softly, reverently, she tells me. "I think she'd want to be Rihanna's *Only Girl in the World*."

15

MADDIE

One Night - Griff

My love cuts a lock of my golden hair, tying it together with a lace ribbon before pocketing it.

"I will be worthy of your favor," he promises, dark hair falling into his eyes before his mouth is on mine, hungry and hot.

"Be careful," I stress, the grass underneath me tickling my ears and neck, the sensation intertwining with his soft breaths as his lips dance along my throat.

"Always," he answers, his persistent mouth slipping lower and lower until it covers a breast. My back bows off the ground, chasing more as he sucks my nipple, flicking it with his tongue, working me to boiling point. Quickly, he gives up all pretence of patience and tugs my skirts up my thighs, his hands running up my bare legs until he finds the heart of me.

Aching with desire, a cry escapes as his fingers move languidly inside me, his head lowering to seek the silken heat between my thighs.

"I love you. I live for seeing you, for hearing your song, for tasting you. For having you as mine, Iseult, even for a moment."

Curling my fingers through his hair, I whisper, "I love you, Tristan."

A wet, hot tongue teases my flesh, his hand and mouth and soft beard wringing every drop of pleasure from me until I give in to it all, breaking underneath him.

"Maddie. I've brought you coffee."

No! Perrie's voice has me rising from the welcoming black as I scramble to hold onto distinguishing features. The face . . . bearded, his jaw hidden beneath. His hair. What colour is it? Dark, to match the beard. I catch the final, blissful moments of a dream that's repeated on a loop since the ball. It feels like I'm drifting through layers, flying towards the sky as I return to consciousness.

Waking fully, feelings of loss overcome me. Tears leak from my eyes. I don't know why this dream has such a crippling hold on me but leaving this faceless, unknown man behind leaves me devastated. Recently, it has only intensified, events and details clearer, sharper.

"Did you get some sleep?"

Rubbing any evidence from my eyes, I throw the covers off and shuffle until I'm sitting against my headboard. "Thanks," I murmur as I check the time on my cell and accept the mug of coffee. "Yeah, I got a good hour."

"That's good."

Emotionally, I'm wired, my thoughts scattered everywhere as I think about tonight and what to expect.

Still in my hand, my phone pings. The supportive message from my mother comes at just the moment I really needed to hear from her.

Thinking of you, dear Maddie. We're so proud of you and all that you're achieving at Jacquard. Keep learning, living, loving. Open up to new opportunities, don't dwell too much on your studies. College is meant to be fun too!

With my departure for Club VX within the hour, Mom's message came at just the right moment. I punch out a quick text, grinning to myself. Sounds like Mom is telling me to get laid. If all goes to plan, that is what I'll be doing tonight.

To a *knight.*

Ha!

Okay. Calm down, Maddie.

"I've had too many late nights," Perrie grumbles, sitting on her bed, her back to the wall. "Having a boyfriend is bad for studying and bad for beauty sleep."

Her downer has me laughing. Seeing less of her was to be expected now that her and Zac are going steady.

"Who needs beauty sleep when you're glowing all the time," I tease.

"The post sex glow?"

"Don't tell Gemma about it. She'll find your body's coping mechanisms disgusting and disown you."

Perrie's eyes bug out. "Right, you told me about her. Jeez, she's a piece of work. Before the semester is out, I bet you ten bucks she makes a pass at Professor Kit."

"Ooohh, ten bucks."

She throws her beloved teddy bear, Marly at me. He's small and care-worn and has been her bed-buddy since she was three. "Ten bucks is a lot of money!"

I consider how much money I'll be making tonight and the lie I've told my friend. It has never sat well with me, so I confess, "Perrie, the job I've got tonight at Club VX isn't to wait tables and serve drinks, but something else."

Looking puzzled, Perrie crosses her legs.

"I signed a really tight NDA with hefty financial penalties, ones I cannot afford. I need you to promise not to tell a soul. Not

Zac, not your folks, not even discussing it with me after tonight."

"Okay. I'm worried. What's going on?"

I explain what I can about the process, stressing that I'm doing this to feel empowered. That this is, in part, to fulfil a fantasy but mainly because it feels like a calling.

"You have sex with the knight at the end? Maddie, are you sure?"

"No. I mean, it could be awful. But I've had awful sex before."

She screws up her face. "Who was that?"

"Sophomore year. A guy called Eduardo."

She snorts, "Oh yeah, I remember now." We share a commiserating look. "So, the sex might be bad, and it's probably best you go in knowing it will be disappointing and terrible, but what if it's *unsafe*. You know, aggressive psycho unsafe. Or what if you feel icky afterwards? Like—and I'm sorry to say this—like you gave away a piece of your soul?"

I take a deep breath, Perrie's words striking a chord; unwittingly, she's describing my relationship with Harrison.

"I can't predict how I'll feel, Perrie. I just know this is something I want to do. It feels necessary. Could be fun, could be awful. But this is the closest I'll ever get to living like Iseult, surrounded by knights. Feeling protected, admired, and put high on that pedestal."

Perrie blinks. "Harrison really fucked you up."

My good mood deflates. Harrison's general douchebaggery has had a toll on me, it's true. "Yeah."

"Fair enough. You have to do what feels right for you. And you can back out at the end?"

I nod.

"Is this anything to do about your weird dreams?"

The dreams come nightly, confirming what I suspected about living in a different time period. Dismissing them would be easy, pointing out that the events and landscapes, the buildings and scenarios are all taken from the texts I'm reading. I'm so immersed in my studies that it's unsurprising they're manifesting in my sleep. But I know it's more than that.

"I've never experienced this much déjà vu before. The memories are numerous," I say, knocking the side of my head with the heel of my palm "and stuck in here. They flutter about, near the surface and tempt me with their knowledge, only to fall away, back inside the box they escaped from." It's maddening. "I can't describe it to you. But sometimes—" I falter, regretting my honesty. "Sometimes I wonder if I'm really here."

"In reality? Or at Jacquard?"

"This life."

Perrie hops over to my bed, throwing an arm around my waist. "Babe, I think you're working too hard. All these assignment and quizzes are bad for us. Especially with your tennis schedule."

Recently, I've wondered the same.

"And let's not forget Harrison's bugging you for another try. I know he takes up a lot of head space."

"Yeah," I reply, knowing he and I have to resolve things soon. I return Perrie's embrace, saying in to her shoulder, "I'd better get going."

She releases me, and I shuffle off the bed.

"Okay. I hope it's good. All of it. The ambience, the theater of it, the sex at the end . . ."

I snort. *Me too.*

"Keep in touch. Let me know you're safe."

"Will do. Have you decided if you're staying in yet?"

"Zac can hang here until you're home."

I make my bed and grab a few last things. "He can stay. Don't kick him out out of concern for me."

"Let's see. You might need support," she says quietly.

Fair point. I'm trying not to dwell on this being a disappointing experience, but one that helps answer everything going on with me right now.

"Well, there's a car on standby, so however long it takes, I'll have a ride home."

"Good. I was wondering about that."

I hug Perrie goodbye, her *good luck* following me out of the door.

THE SUITE I've been assigned has everything I could need: closets for my clothes; huge mirrors; a ton of refreshments, and a massive tub in the en-suite.

The masseuse, Lia, might be worth all the angst and nerves tonight has brought. While Natalie, the tennis physical therapist, took care of my achey legs after my match this morning, Lia has smoothed out every knot in my back and shoulders. I feel like I could float, and after I get out of the deep, warm bath, various salts and gorgeous smelling liquids drizzled in the water, I feel relaxed but energized.

Gino offers me several good suggestions on my hair. In the end, we decide that wearing my hair loose, with strands of gold woven in for added effect, will combine iconography of Iseult's fair-haired lineage with the medieval court of today.

Stella, the beautician, agrees that looking as natural as possible will work with my dress and hair. She uses a light base and powder. My eyes are kept dark and dramatic. Gold highlighter is dusted on my cheekbones and décolletage, catching the gold in my hair.

"Let's get you dressed."

Locating this dress was one of the most stressful parts of preparing for tonight. Needing something in keeping with the era felt important, so I spent hours scouring the internet for a stylist, boutique, or online fashion brand that matched my ideas. Dresses were worn long and loose. They were simple, a belt at the waist for definition. But modern taste demands more glimmer and glitz, some crystals or sequins sewn into the fabric to give it a boost. And to be honest, I need the boost of feeling glamorous. The dress needs to feel like my own special armor.

In the end, I found a rose gold dress, more blush pink than gold, but the icing on the cake is the sheer gold over-layer that shimmers with every movement. The sleeves droop in triangles at my wrists, the neckline is a vee of simple bows. Wearing gold slip-ons, the heel no more than an inch, all I need to add is the thin gold belt I got for six dollars in a thrift shop.

Gino helps secure the simple, unadorned tiara. Stella touches up my make-up. Lia demands my cell. Earlier, I rambled on about needing at least twenty photos, knowing Perrie would want to see. And I want a permanent memory of today.

"For courage," Gino says, offering me a cool glass of white wine.

The alcohol hits my stomach like liquid lava, warming me, chasing out the cold and nerves that are returning with a vengeance now Sophie has entered my suite.

Surprised by my transformation, her eyes widen, her lips part in shock. "You look *parfait*. The *détachement* will do everything they can to win your favor tonight."

"Is it time?" I ask, sipping quickly.

"Yes. They are ready for you."

Earlier, when Sophie escorted me to this room, she explained more about tonight's expectations. With those front of mind, I take a final look in the mirror and mentally prepare.

Kit's rough-voiced compliment from a week ago rattles my memory as I look at my reflection. Am I ruination in a dress? A woman men would do anything for?

Escaping reenactments of our kiss last week is futile; he's all

I think about when my concentration slips, my thoughts deviating to the most perfect moment. Classes this week have been the same but there's an invisible connection between us now that didn't exist before. Every time our eyes connect I feel it. And I can't look away from him. Can't stop myself from wanting to hear his voice, to feel his presence.

Leaving the security of the room, I follow Sophie down the hall towards the stairs. The polished bannisters curve majestically towards the first floor, and I hold on tightly. At the bottom of the staircase we turn right towards a lobby, off which several doors lead. The Grand Master, dressed in a silver tabard over black trousers, waits for our approach at two oversized double doors, a plaque on the wall reading *salle de banquet.*

"Lady Iseult," the Grand Master greets. "I trust you are well."

In a bid to protect my identity, I chose my middle name as my pseudonym tonight. But I also chose Iseult because Iseult's life was tragic, her body and mind torn apart by the men she loved in different ways. I hope I can give her a happier experience tonight.

"Merci, Grand Master."

The blade at her hip is slim and sharp.

"I am at your service. Refreshments, questions, *anything*," she stresses, "I await your instructions."

Nodding my thanks, she throws the doors open and walks through them with purpose. I follow, my heart pounding. The banquet room is a long rectangle which we enter from one end. The first things I notice are two raised fencing pistes in the middle of the vast room. No expense has been spared—there are lights, lasers, and lines demarcating positions.

The seriousness of this hits home.

I give the pistes a wide berth as I enter deeper into the salle. Four chandeliers hang on the panelled ceiling, the lights dim; ornate coving runs around the perimeter; the walls are papered in a blue and gold pattern. The temperature of the room feels cool, vents at ankle level circulating air. My heels clack softly across the parquet floor as I follow the Grand Master to the dais where my throne waits, an ornate, double wide wooden chair with a padded, chocolate brown leather seat.

The Grand Master stands at attention to the side and I sit, two unused fireplaces behind me, suits of armor fixed to the length of the wall. Opposite are four deep windows, shutters fixed across the glass and obscuring any light. The logo of the société d'honneur is directly in front of me, a shield with a sword running through it, black stallions rearing either side.

Tentatively, I wait for what comes next. Ten manic breaths later, the doors to my right open. In single file, the knights enter, the sound of their boots soft on the floor as they march in sync. The Black Knight, last week's winner of the *conroi* leads them.

None of them wear chain mail. Instead, they wear fitted, modern day kevlar fencing jackets, but there are nods to the traditional doublet in the design. Padding is visible in appropriate areas, the conductive lamé allowing the jacket to record hits from the foil which each knight holds in a gloved hand. The Black Knight wears all black, the white knights in something that's closer to silver in color.

With fencing masks covering their faces, it's hard to make out any features. Clearly, the Black Knight is one to watch tonight, his chances of winning again high. Did he nominate me?

He comes to the bottom of the dais and kneels, bowing his head.

"My Lady Iseult," he says, his voice muffled by his mask which is entirely black to match his pants and jacket.

"Good luck, knight. What name do you go by?"

"Zorro, my lady."

"How many *conrois* have you won to wear black tonight?"

"Two."

This is his third *détachement*. An automatic right to be here based on his previous win. And if he wins again, he will have to retire for a month.

Straight-backed, I watch him leave. The first white knight approaches, kneels and bows his head. He tells me his name is King Arthur and I wish him good luck, watching him take position on the right hand side of the room.

Another fourteen follow, names half-remembered. Rikard is one, Hector another. Only occasionally do I notice a distinguishing feature like a bald spot, or longer hair, or possible ethnicity. In the end, I start to name them based on their mask designs.

Crusader's mask is a black cross. Captain America wears the star spangled banner, the colours of the flag sharp and well defined. Another wears an eagle's face, in reference to the famous Eagle of Brittany I assume. A fourth wears a mask with the detailed cross guard of a sword. His name I do recall: Ronin.

When the last knight joins those who have already bent the knee, I'm invited by the Grand Master to offer my favor.

On shaky legs, I stand and walk towards the center of the room where the *détachement* waits in a line. It's hard to pick out a favorite, especially as I can't remember all their names. I liked the voice of the eagle-masked knight, but it's Ronin, his mask depicting a sword that calls to me most.

The pre-prepared strip of material that I fashioned out of the hem is tied at my wrist. As I make my choice, I loosen it and move towards Ronin. "Chevalier Ronin," I say. "Good luck tonight."

He bows his head in gratitude while I tie the small strip of my dress to a loop on his jacket. Against the pale jacket the rose gold stands out.

The Grand Master escorts me back to my throne. When I sit

down, two pairs of knights are already moving to the fencing strips, or *pistes.* Their fencing pants are 3/4 length, with long socks to just below the knee. In their back pockets, each knight wears a wireless device to connect them to the scoring machine.

"Who oversees the bout, Grand Master?"

"The directors act as referees, Lady Iseult. Members of the club who did not make the *détachement* but know the rules back to front. There are always two, one for each strip until we reach the *conroi.*"

I study the directors, both of them wearing navy equivalents of the knights' attire. One looks my age, the other twice that. I move my focus to the knights, considering how each of them varies in their preparations. Some sit on available benches, some stand. Nearly all of them throw long looks my way. Several talk in whispers.

"Is it my imagination, or does it feel tense."

The Grand Master nods. "The chevaliers wish to win. They wish to prove themselves to the lady."

I've spent some time thinking about the purpose of this tournament, trying to see it from the perspective of each of the members of the club. I think of the southern states and their passion for battle reenactments. I think of my love for period dramas set in the UK or the French court. Dressing as Iseult offers me a taste of what it is to be her, bringing me closer to her life's experiences, and to her love, a victorious, worthy knight who earns the right to be at her side through his heroic deeds.

This is my identity tonight, that of a lady at court, and these knights each play to the strength of theirs. Dismissing their endeavors as mere sexual gratification is unkind. Thoughtless. This means so much more than that, and I know that because it means so much more to me.

They expect the pay-off to be worth it; it's important to live up to their high standards too.

I swallow. "May I have a drink please? Water if you have it."

"Of course."

The Grand Master turns to a large oak table laden with refreshments. She brings me a glass of water and I sip as the older director calls out the names of the knights on his strip.

"To my left," he throws out his left arm, "the defending Black Knight, Zorro. On my right," he throws out his right arm to indicate the opponent, "King Arthur."

The younger director steps forward. "Yves and Geralt, my lady." He sketches a bow which brings a hesitant smile to my lips. I hope it breaks the ice a little, because I can cut the tension in the air with a knife.

Each knight calls *en garde* before they commence. Some, I note, lift their mask when they face each other, though they are careful to use the hand that blocks my view. For the next few minutes, my focus is split between each duel. Sophie explained it's the first to five points, and the scoring machines allow me a view of the scores as each bout plays out.

The match between the Black Knight and King Arthur is over first, Zorro winning convincingly at 5-2. As soon as they leave the piste, the next two knights take their positions.

I'm in awe of the quality of the swordsmanship and with how far they advance down the rectangular piste to score. The speed of each knight is breathtaking, their movements at times subtle, but always precise and fast and highly strategized. At times the director calls out a decision; I often miss how a point is won but the LED masks are a robust way of understanding who got hit by their opponent.

It doesn't take long for there to be a commiserating group of knights, eight bouts already over, the winning eight now through to the next stage. Happily, wearing my favor, Ronin has been successful. Tall, solid and dark-haired, he moves like lightning along the piste. He beat his opponent 5-1.

The evening moves on apace. Sadly, Geralt is knocked out by Zorro, leaving Saint, a knight named Cruz, and Ronin. At this stage of the tournament, only one bout takes place at a time.

First up are Zorro and Cruz, their contest a flurry of lunges and thrusts, parries and counter attacks that are so fast, several points are contested with the director. Ultimately, the Black Knight wins 5-4.

So close.

The bout between Saint and Ronin is less close. It is no less entertaining to watch though, Ronin impressing me with his whip fast skills. In the end, it's an easy win for him.

"Remind me, Grand Master—is Ronin from real life or a film character?"

"Real life, my lady. A renowned swordsman."

"And Zorro?"

"Based on an outlaw, I believe."

The final is between an outlaw and a renowned swordsman. It makes me happy to see a knight with my favor has made it to the end.

Sitting in a state of anxious wonder, I note amendments made to the floor space. The pistes are moved, then abandoned. Lanterns are brought closer, into a circle roughly four meters in diameter.

The directors unlock a wire-fronted wooden cabinet embedded in the wall, bringing out chainmail, metal helmets, and swords that aren't cosplay friendly. The items are distributed, chainmail is carefully adorned—silver for Ronin, black for Zorro.

The long, deadly-looking swords have hilts with ornate shapes, protecting their fingers.

"Rapiers, my lady," the Grand Master explains. "Swift, nasty blades."

The atmosphere turns thick with expectation and excitement, those who were unsuccessful tonight murmuring between themselves as the last two knights prepare.

The *conroi* is about to start.

As one, both of the knights turn towards me and bow before the older director invites them to take their positions. Briefly, they flip up their helmets in acknowledgement, but I can't see any distinguishing features from this angle.

After a determined *en garde*, they begin.

16

MADDIE

Life - Jamie xx & Robyn

Muscles in my body feel tight, my nerves shot, as the two men stalk each other with steel blades in their grip.

"What are the rules?" I whisper quickly.

"First to three strikes," the Grand Master whispers back. "When the armor is struck it emits a black or white dust. We will know who is victor."

Both knights look at ease, familiar with the sword in their grasp. To begin with they assess one another, looking for opportunities as they move slowly around the circle. Their swords meet, each strike terrifyingly loud and swift before the knights break apart, but Ronin is first to attack successfully, lunging at Zorro and striking him on the shoulder that we can hear as well as see.

Black dust percolates between them, much to the anger of Zorro if the disgusted shout he makes is anything to go by.

After re-setting, they more around the circle for ten stressful heartbeats before Zorro lunges. Ronin parries and counter attacks. He appears to hit the Black Knight in the exact same spot.

2 - 0 to Ronin.

I don't think I've ever been more invested in a sport—apart from anything tennis related. Engrossed, the rest of the *détachement* watch from the sidelines. Every now and then I catch one of them turn and look my way, wondering what I make of it all.

I'm a little turned on. A lot apprehensive. After this, it's all about me.

"Who do you want to win?" I whisper to the Grand Master.

With a chastising look, she asks, "Who do *you*?"

"Ronin," I whisper, worried my words have carried too far, to the ears of the *conroi*. The Black Knight looked a bit cocky when he faced off against Ronin. His posture has changed since he's been losing; this isn't going the way he expected.

In direct contrast to Zorro's frustrated demeanor, Ronin looks seriously cool and calm. Is he one of the Olympians or World Champions Sophie mentioned?

The two knights stare each other down from opposite sides of the candle-strewn space. Ronin makes his move, flicking his rapier towards Zorro's chest. Zorro parries the sword away, attacking strongly, but Ronin manages to deflect his riposte, hitting him right in the belly.

Yes!

In a cloud of black-dusted disgust, Zorro hurls his helmet to the floor. It bounces into the wall, the clattering sound swallowed by respectful applause from the watching *détachement*. The director moves to escort Zorro out, picking up his heavy helmet as he does and handing it to the knight who promptly puts it back on.

Amused chuckles sound from the small audience, some shaking their heads. But Zorro is turning around.

And then, in an angry shout: *"Je proclame Ordo Victor!"*

Total, utter silence descends.

"Ordo Victor!" he shouts again, his sword pointed towards his opponent.

My heart cannot take any more suspense. It's pounding in my rib cage, blood roaring in my veins.

Everyone looks from Zorro to Ronin. Then me.

I hold my breath, waiting for his answer, because that is what everyone else is doing, aren't they?

Confidently, in French, Ronin replies: "J'accepte le défi."

I accept the challenge.

The other members erupt into heated debate.

Sounding completely out of character, the Grand Master tells me, "I knew things would get spicy tonight."

The younger director retrieves the rapiers, replacing them with a different sword. "What now?"

"An arming sword, my lady. A knightly sword."

"New rules too?"

"First to strike, or first blood."

While Zorro's passion is evident, I'm not sure he's one of the traditionalists, here in the spirit of the club's founding ethos. Ronin must win. I practically chant it in my head.

The metal helmets they wear have a long nose guard and slits for eyes; I've no idea how they see out of them, but they meet in the centre of the circle again, taking up defensive positions. This time, there is no traditional greeting. As soon as the older director retreats beyond the lanterns, Zorro goes on the attack. The sound of these swords meeting is three times as shocking and thrilling as the rapiers. Just how accomplished are these men with these instruments of death and injury? How deep will they cut or slice to make their opponent bleed?

And why do I feel like the emergency room is where tonight ends for one of the chevaliers?

In reality, I know nothing about fighting, but Ronin looks more confident. He parries Zorro's attacks easily, his arm and sword moving swiftly and decisively to meet and block over and over. The chainmail rustles and gleams in the candlelight, undoubtedly heavy and slowing their movements, but Ronin looks steady on his feet, advancing and retreating, moving around the circle like this is child's play.

Encouraged, my heart steadies a little. Unable to look away for a breath, a blink, I watch Ronin's muscles strain and flex as he forces Zorro back and back towards those lanterns.

"How much blood?" I ask quickly.

"A trickle. No loss of limbs."

"And if the knight's opinion of their skill is inflated?"

"Only those with skill would ever declare Ordo Victor. To lose means injury. To lose means banishment."

Ronin steps to the right, attacking with vicious strokes and flurries. He moves effortlessly, quickly, his heavy sword striking Zorro's torso, arm, torso, shoulder. I'm so sure there must be blood but it's never called by the director. But he does call, "Hit! Hit! Hit! Hit!"

Zorro's roar of frustration tells me Ronin's playing with him. And even though it's clear from the black dust that he's defeated, that the director has called it, he's not relinquishing his grip.

"Why haven't they stopped?"

"Arrogance," the Grand Master says with disgust. "An ugly quality."

Ronin isn't letting his guard down, his blade aloft and ready. Then he feints, Zorro lunging. Their swords tangle, circling, metal scraping metal until Zorro's is ripped from his hands with a vicious, powerful flick. It clatters across the floor, spinning until it hits the lanterns. A director quickly scoops it up.

What follows takes me a moment to process. Disarmed, stunned, Zorro still doesn't retire or admit defeat. So, wrist snapping, Ronin cuts Zorro's chin with the tip of his sword, a trickle of blood seeping from the thin wound.

The precision and skill is breathtaking and the resounding cheer from the *détachement* fills my lungs with relief.

"Victory to Knight Ronin! Our new Black Knight!" declares the older director.

"Hell's teeth," I murmur. *That was insane.*

"Sensational swordsman," the Grand Master returns. "Reminds me of someone I used to know."

Zorro departs, escorted by both directors out of the *salle*. Ronin disrobes his chainmail, the clinking sound of the metal folding over and over like a slinky as it hits the floor.

Knights congratulate Ronin, clapping him on the back. Then he's walking steadily towards me, his face hidden by his helmet. But I can see a hint of shadow at his chin, the jawline sharp. Bright eyes fix on me. How he can see from the confines of its structure is baffling.

In awe of his prowess, I'm also feeling trepidation, alongside a deep feeling of want. Want and need. We both know what comes next and his skilled display has me impressed.

At the bottom of the dais, the new Black Knight takes a knee and bows his head. To my surprise, he removes his helmet partway, offering me the top of his head which pleasingly reveals a full head of rich, dark brown hair, damp with exertion. I rise, and descend the two steps, laying a hand on the crown of his head. It lasts all of a second, and I'm not sure why I do this other than to get some kind of sense of him. It's not as if I can tell if he's married or not, though my preference is not. But weirdly, it felt normal to touch him like that.

"Congratulations Champion. Your skill with a sword is

exemplary, the defeat of Zorro breathtaking to watch. You have acquitted yourself very well."

He bobs his head, letting me know he heard and answers in French. "Merci, ma dame."

I follow his lead. "Levez-vous, Chevalier Noir."

Rise, Black Knight.

Adjusting his helmet, he stands to his full height. He's got to be six four easily in his boots. Looking into his eyes through the helmet slits has my pulse rushing. It's intimate. Clandestine.

As per the protocol, Ronin departs to freshen up and change. When the doors behind him close, the Grand Master escorts me back to my suite where I drink more wine for courage. Trying to keep busy, I pat my neck and chest with cool water and make sure my make-up hasn't run. Studying my reflection in the mirror I ask, *Ready?* Now that I've seen the chevalier in question, my decision feels more secure. He has a good aura about him. Strong and worthy.

"Do you wish to proceed?" I'm asked.

The night races on—it's already close to 11PM. I nod agreement, the Grand Master returning it with a satisfied nod of her own before she escorts me back to the *salle de banquet*. The chandelier lights are dark. A dozen hurricane lanterns with fat pillar candles inside provide ambient light. Shortly after I sit on the throne, one of the directors checks inside the room. Seeing me there, he holds open the door for the newly crowned Black Knight, who slowly makes his way towards me.

Shielded by his fencing mask of a sword's cross-guard, and dressed head to toe in black, he looks like night itself. It thrills and terrifies in equal measure, but mostly his strong posture, the steady, long strides he takes towards me, and his overall commanding appearance has me nervously excited. The sword hangs at his waist. Underneath his black surcoat, the words Honneur Aulx Dignes written underneath the club's shield, he wears a black, long-sleeved shirt. A belt at his waist, fitted pants, and leather boots complete his attire.

Hands clasped before me, I descend the dais. I catch my protector's questioning gaze, prompting me to say, "Merci, Grand Master. You have been a great support to me tonight. You may take your leave."

She bows, "It has been my honor, Lady Iseult. I will ensure you are not disturbed."

Her footsteps pick up where the Black Knight's stop, until she heaves open the big doors and exits. The room feels darker now. With the benefit of insubstantial candlelight, I look fully at my chevalier.

"Black Knight," I greet shakily.

"My lady."

His muffled voice rings of authority and I'm reminded that he's a man who's comfortable with mortal combat and dangerous liaisons.

Why am I drawn to the forbidden?

When he steps closer, the front of his surcoat divides, flowing either side of his legs. I can't deny he has a good physique. I've watched him parry, thrust and lunge, his stature strong, his movements fluid.

I take a shaky breath.

The knight walks past me, behind me. I twist my head to follow him, but he places his hands on my shoulders and gently presses.

Face forward.

My breathing turns rapid. I can feel my pulse everywhere.

In French, he tells me, "Be at ease, lady. Nothing happens that you don't want to."

I nod, grateful for his reassurance and that he understands it's what I, crucially, need to hear.

"Thank you."

"A knight honors his sworn love."

His words are sweet. I can almost picture that pedestal, me sitting atop it. And understanding is threaded through his words, knowing that giving over all my trust to a man in a mask isn't easy.

Confident hands come to my waist. Every inch of me is hyper-aware of every movement, of his hands as they slide over my abdomen. Our positions remind me of how Kit approached me at the ball. Of his measured hands at my waist as he towered over me from behind. This week, I've allowed myself to dwell in an alternate reality of that night. A fantasy where I let Kit nibble kisses into my skin, encouraging more, demanding all of him right there on the grassy lawns as I let go of everything and welcome him into my pliant body.

The knight murmurs, "Close your eyes. Keep them closed."

Heart stuttering, I do as commanded, marveling at the implicit trust I'm giving him. A hand lifts. The sound of his mask being removed and dropped to his feet follows. That hand runs down my arm before returning to my waist. It settles there, warm and heavy.

It's grounding. I need him to lead this.

Heady notes of mint and vetiver come off his skin, my head foggy from his freshly-showered scent. His presence behind me becomes more soothing than daunting as I get more accustomed with his body so close to mine. It's hard to process everything, and it's no wonder I can't think properly when his lips find my shoulder over the fabric of my dress. Warm kisses press into my skin, my hair gently scooped out of the way as his lips trail a path to my nape. When his lips first meet my skin, a breath whooshes out of me.

A pause comes, his lips lifting free. Although he doesn't comment, the fact that he's making sure I know this is a choice earns him major points.

"Don't stop," I whisper.

Gently, his mouth nuzzles and nips at my neck, right at the perfect spot that has my head lolling and my body tingling. At the same time, his hands caress my waist, his touch assured and welcome. Switching to the other side of my neck, his lips light a path across my skin, week-old stubble scraping along that same path. Restless, his hands roam over my dress, but never higher than my ribcage. Never lower than my stomach. But I'm melting into his touch, wanting more of it.

"You can touch me."

There's no pause of restraint this time. His hand glides over a braless breast. In the end I decided against one—it felt more authentic. And I benefit from the lack of layers when he cups me, my breast weighed in his hand. When he cups my other breast, a thumb runs over my nipple which is hard and stiff. Each time I lift into his touch, pressing into his questing hands that have turned me silken and languid. Sensing my arousal, his mouth becomes more insistent, his hands greedier, his thumbs rubbing and rubbing until I burn as hot as a flame.

A groan rumbles from his throat, sparking something inside me. Wanting his mouth, I turn my head . . .

Movement tells me he pulls away, ducks his head behind me. Fabric rustles by my ears as a blindfold covers my eyes, the tie tight and secure. I suck in a breath; I'm not upset. I knew this was likely. All the unsuccessful knights, bar four, kept their masks on today.

His hands caress my hair and the straw-blonde strands in homage to Iseult. "Beautiful," he says before taking off my tiara and placing it somewhere.

The Black Knight steps around me until he's directly in front of me. He lifts my hands and places them on his chest—an invitation. A tentative smile creases my face, his torso like steel under my fingers.

I sense him moving closer, his lips pressing a kiss to each eyelid covered by the blindfold.

Thank you.

Lifting my chin and parting my lips, I let him know he can have my mouth, but he makes me wait, kissing along my jawline and throat. Stubble rasps against my skin. I want other kinds of friction so, frustrated, my hands curl through his thick hair, urging him.

There's a breath of laughter before he murmurs, "So beautiful."

Finally, his mouth closes over mine. It's a careful kiss, another following quickly, his lips molding to mine before pulling free to kiss me again. Again. Each kiss is distinct and slow, and I feel the warmth of them travel to my bones. Moaning softly, I pull him closer. Wherever his hands trail, fire blazes across my hyper-sensitive skin, a sweeping path of heat as they slide up my neck to hold my face, gently angling me as his lips pull at my mouth. Fingers slide into my hair. I expect pulling, but it doesn't come. He's gentle and careful and respectful.

At last, his tongue slides against mine. Shivers scatter and I hunger for more, all but throwing myself at him, this man that can kiss as well as he fights. I give up all inhibitions. My core has liquified, my body craving his as I kiss him hungrily, my breasts pressing into his chest, his erection a long solid bar. And my God, I want it. Want him.

"Chevalier," I murmur as we break our kiss for air, his body stilling momentarily before he's back to kissing me to within an inch of my life. We're lashing tongues and ravenous lips, hot breath and grabbing hands. He pulls at my outer thigh, lifting my knee to his hip and grinds his swollen cock against my pussy. My back bows, but he has me firmly in his hold, his strength evident as I slide my hands over his chest wall, his back, his shoulders, relishing every hard muscle group.

With the blindfold on, all I can do is follow the knight's lead. But I'm happy to, his touch making me feel treasured and wanted. Adored.

A heaviness slicks my core, a burning, pounding ache building. Hands skim over my ass, his thumbs brushing the space between my butt cheeks. Even over my clothes the thrill of that illicit touch has my blood spiking.

"Please," I beg, my hands reaching for the zipper at the back.

I'm turned, the knight unzipping me in a breathless second. The dress slumps to the floor, leaving me exposed and naked except for my black lace panties. Our mouths crash together again, both of us inhaling deeply. My panties get tugged down to my hips. A hand slips between my legs. Languidly, a finger glides through the dizzying ache there. When he feels how wet I am, he releases a tense, punchy exhale.

"Lady Iseult is too generous."

All we've spoken is French, his accent from Brittany.

"I will give my champion everything tonight," I promise.

"Thank you, my lady."

I hear the sword drop to the dais, muffled by the scattered soft furnishings: cushions, rugs and blankets. Hands support me as he smoothly takes me to the floor which has my heart rocketing out of my chest in momentary alarm. His body follows me down until he's stretched out over me, his mouth nuzzling at my breast. Then he sucks, hard. It has my hips bucking against his, nerve endings exploding, my body white hot as I slink back and forth against the promising, impressive bulge in his pants.

"Yes," I mumble, my body craving him inside me already.

I'm barely aware of a single thought except how good I feel. Hands and fingers tease, pulling moans and yeses from me. His attention is an aphrodisiac all of its own and I arch into his touch, silently begging.

Moving down my body, he kisses my inner thighs as he tugs

my panties down to my knees. I help as much as I can, desperate for his cock. I'm burning, throbbing, losing my mind.

"Hurry."

But he doesn't give it to me yet. Instead, his mouth sips at my center, soft flicks and licks that turn into long drags and generous suckles. His tongue slides inside my pussy, thrusting deep, my pleasure his only focus. I suck in breath after breath, my sight blinded, every touch and point of pressure feeling double, triple. A thumb circles my clit as I build towards the peak, climbing until I'm flying, cresting at the very edge of my sanity until I fall.

I call out to God as I come undone. Everything washes away. My knight drinks in my quivers, kissing my thighs as my trembles slowly cease.

I want more.

Clothes rustle, dropping to the floor. I hear the crinkle of a condom packet. I hear the soft roll of latex over his cock, smell it.

"Do you want this?"

The rough quality to his voice tells me I get this one chance to stop because he's incapable of making that decision himself.

I wish I could see him and if he matches the image I have in my head. Of someone who's a fantasy, forbidden, but someone I want all the same. I try not to think of kissing Kit as the knight climbs over my body, his lips securing mine and stealing the *yes* from my lips. Our groins align, his knee pushing against mine, my legs opening wide for him. Cool air kisses my sex, my hands tracing each flexing back muscle as he settles his weight on me. He slicks his crown through my drenched slit and notches himself at my entrance. With a slow, inexorable push, he cleaves me apart.

I luxuriate in the feel of him inside me, filling me, the knight letting me get accustomed to his size. Then, a noise beyond the doors has me stilling.

"You're safe," he murmurs. "Protected by my sword."

The Black Knight has a sense of humor.

"This sword, chevalier?" He was *so* implying his cock.

There's a deep chuckle that has the hairs rising on the back of my neck. Have I heard this in real life or is it another dream memory?

I make a satisfied noise as he gets comfortable, sliding out slowly and pushing back in. I barely register his answering grunt of satisfaction, thinking of his familiar laugh. Of his voice that sounds close to one I know, though this one is higher in pitch, its cadence faster and melodic.

"Do I know you?"

There are similarities, but then I reason there are many tall, dark-haired men. And the facial hair is confusing; some days Kit is clean shaven, other days it's short or longer.

I give up thinking about it when skin meets fevered skin, my pebbled nipples brushing against firm pecs. His mouth secures mine, drugging me with a devouring kiss as he slides his cock all the way out before thrusting back inside, hitting me with an intensity I feel in every cell. There's no room to breathe, no air in my lungs.

"You know me intimately, lady."

It's not an answer, but I also don't want one, even though I asked. Anonymity is king here, permitting freedom to be who we want to be. To live in the moment. To take from this experience what we want.

Every thought flies out of my head, the question forgotten as he stokes a fire inside me, his hips sinking into mine with unhurried skill. If I thought he'd climb over me and fuck me like a conquest, I'm mistaken. Instead, I'm kissed, slowly and thoroughly as our bodies grind together. Quickly, friction builds where we join, my breaths shallow. I tear my mouth away from his, sucking in air as his head falls beside mine. Bit by slow bit, the blindfold dislodges with our energetic movements. I screw my eyes shut, Ronin tugging it up again before his pace quickens. My knees are up by his shoulders, my feet by his hips as he surges inside, every muscle under my fingertips coiled and ready to unleash as my body races towards the finishing line.

Heat consumes me. I obliterate around him, his shoulder absorbing my cries. Gradually, his movements slow as I catch my breath. Pressing a kiss to each eyelid, he pulls out, gathering up my hand. "Up you get."

I'm pulled to my feet. Keeping a tight hold of me, he guides me to the throne. I can tell by the pressure on my hand that he sits, pulling me in front of him.

"Does Lady Iseult like to ride?"

Even though I can't see him, I smile down at him. Then I'm clambering onto the throne, straddling his thighs and the wet, hard cock between his legs. Wet from me. He kisses my neck as I get situated, as I grab him by the root and angle him where I need him. Sinking down, I feel every satisfying inch again as I rock into him.

"Like that," he praises. "Look at you," he adds, fitting the tiara to my head.

My fingers run down his torso, bumping over scars incurred from his sport. Closing the gap, I wrap my arms around his neck. Assured, callused hands run up and down my bare back. He feels too good, whether at the mercy of his tongue or slotted over his beautiful cock.

Using my core, I undulate against him, slicking up and down his shaft and hitting a perfect angle that has my back arcing. Taking hold of my hips, he slams me against him, the sounds of sex echoing in the vast room. His harsh breaths and my exhales mingle as I adjust my legs for a better angle, the Black Knight hissing out *oui* and *parfait*.

I don't want this to end, even as pressure heats and bubbles, expanding until I blow apart, his name expelled from my lips. "Chevalier."

His cock swells, everything stretched and tight. With a gasped groan he comes, throbbing inside me as his roughened hand trails between my breasts where my skin is dewy with sweat.

The timbre of his voice is pure male satisfaction. "Comme ça, beauté."

Beauty. The endearment makes me smile, as does the couched praise. Compliments were not Harrison's strength, and anyway, I'm trying not to think of him. I want to bask in my lover's kindness and affection, the pet name striking me hard.

This is such a different sexual experience to any I've had before. Any barriers existing between us melt away as I slump against him.

"Thank you," I whisper. "For making it so good."

"Do I fuck as well as I fight, my lady?"

A laugh escapes at his dirty talk. "The mouth on you," I respond, a little shocked at this other side of him whilst simultaneously liking the sound of his arrogance.

"It was on *you*. Everywhere."

Okay, he's definitely not only the courtly gentleman. And damn him for becoming even more appealing because of it.

"But it's me who must thank you, beauty, for your bravery."

Our hearts regulate. In the large space, my naked body feels chilled, even though we're sharing body heat. Wanting to ask if he nominated me burns a hole on my tongue. But knowing is not up for discussion. Nor is dating.

I let my fingers touch his face, tracing the thick brows, the straight nose, the curves of his clever mouth and his jaw which is strong and sharp. He can't be more than a decade older than me, two tops, his body showcasing he's in his prime.

Aware of him softening, I pull up, letting him secure the

condom as I lift off his legs and the throne. Reaching out with a hand, I steady myself on the arm, wondering if he'd notice if I peeked at him from under my blindfold. Wondering when I can take it off. The cool air has me turning in the direction of where I think my dress idles, and I think about texting Perrie and letting her know I'm safe. About how I'm feeling.

In some ways, Perrie was right. But I haven't given away a piece of my soul; in contrast, it feels like something fundamental has been returned to me. Like I've been remade or made whole again.

"Don't go far, chérie," a rumbling voice warns. "I'm not done with you yet."

17

KIT

Into You - Ariana Grande

The departmental drinks mixer started at 5PM, and so far I've suffered Gemma's effusive conversation, Keira's fake eye-lash fluttering awkwardness, and Jade's outlandish questions. Josh is deep in conversation with a few senior year students but I don't want to leave my spot facing the door to join them.

Not once this week has my path crossed with Maddie's. Our Monday meeting was cancelled, leaving me restless and frustrated.

My phone buzzes. I pull it out to see Gramps is harassing me about Maddie. I *did* tell him we were going on another date, my plans at Club VX firmly in my mind. There was no way I wasn't winning the *conroi.*

How did the date go?

Quickly, I reply: *Not to get your hopes up, or mine, but she's the one.*

He replies with several encouraging emojis, followed by a gif featuring multiple hearts and fireworks.

The old romantic.

I'll keep everything crossed for you, he offers.

I'm going to need every drop of luck, so I like his message, going over the night on the dais again. While I wanted it to be good for Maddie, I didn't want it to be *too* good. And that's partly because I want to save the best for us, in real life, without the blindfold. And it's also because I didn't want her signing up at the club for another night, hoping to meet Ronin again.

Thankfully, I can park those worries to one side because the evening takes a turn for the better and I can finally relax. Forty minutes late, Maddie walks in with Perrie. Unable to look away from her, I watch as her eyes sweep across the room as if looking for someone. They skip over Yves and Oliver and keep going until—

Our eyes catch and hold.

Keeping her in my eye-line, I drink in every physical attribute I can before the moment is broken, someone passing in front of her and disconnecting our link.

Maddie needs answers to her questions, her doubts. As Lady Iseult I hope she found some. I hope they lead her to more resolutions, and quickly. While she gave in to my advances at the ball, a beginning for *us*, Maddie and Kit, there was a huge development for us as participants at Club VX. Despite the monumental physical connection between us, I'm certain she doesn't suspect who bent her over the arm of that throne and fucked her like a man on the brink of his sanity. Recognizing my voice was a potential pitfall, and she asked if she knew me, but the dialect I chose changed the rhythm of my voice considerably.

I've replayed our first kiss in my head several times, but I've indulged in the hours I spent with Iseult on the dais every spare moment since. She, our time together, was everything I could've hoped for.

The lady's virtue at Club VX is not a God-given right, a thing to be won, but to be *earned*. Winning the lady's regard and treating her well when he's won it, are core components of a knight's character. Of his honor. This is what love between a man and woman can look like.

But it's not all there is. And a man has his limits. That's when he tells her he's not done with her yet, showing her the other ways he likes to fuck.

Aware of Maddie's exact position, I ask Sylvie, "Another drink?" I head towards the table laden with glasses, wine, beer, and soft drinks. "What will you have?" I call over my shoulder.

"White wine, thanks."

I pass her a glass that the catering staff have already poured, and then pick up two spares. With a hurried *Excuse me*, my feet carry me towards Maddie of their own accord. And although I'm acting like a complete simp, I don't care. With any luck, I can carry off the over-attentiveness by acting the host—which I am tonight, one of several staff from the languages faculty.

Already, Maddie's surrounded by a small group of boys—no surprise there—which includes the faintly-scarred Oliver and the big-eyed Yves who've been here at least twenty minutes.

"Welcome," I greet. "Can I offer either of you a glass of wine?"

Maddie regards it with suspicion while Perrie eagerly accepts. "Thanks, Professor Chevalier. It's a good turn out." She nods to the room, the glass already at her mouth.

"Yes," I agree, looking at Maddie and waiting for her to either dismiss the wine or request something else. "Would you prefer something different?" Because I'd get it for her. That way, I know no one's spiking her drinks.

As much as I'm used to seeing her with slicked-back hair, a

thin black hairband adorning her scalp like a simple crown keeping flyaways out of her eyes, I get a kick out of seeing her made up too. Loose hair gleams under the lights. Soft, rosy skin emits a healthy glow. Her lashes are long and black, not fake. And a red slogan of *chérie* on a black t-shirt, paired with tight denim jeans has my blood rushing for personal reasons.

My body remembers hers. But I wonder: Is this her figuring it out? Does she know my preference for terms of endearment?

Since the age of five I was trained with a wooden sword, followed by the foil and épée, the sabre and rapier after that. Fencing only interested my sister for so long, but it was my father's life's work. I took to fencing like a duck to water, beating the best instructors Dad could afford by the time I was sixteen. And although my father was good, I was better.

Only now, after my invitation to The Duel where my skills were assessed, do I understand why I was forced to spend so many hours practicing. Books and other sports had to wait. Girls too. If I wanted to immerse myself in literature, in history, then I had to know how to defend myself first and beat every man who opposed me.

Father was playing a long game, I fear. Why else was his name written in gold letters on commemorative wooden boards at the club? Something else is going on here.

"I should pass, but what Coach doesn't know won't hurt him, right?" Maddie says to Perrie. "Thanks," she whispers, taking the glass from me and flashing me a quick grin like I'm in on her prison break. "I didn't realize you moonlighted as a waiter after class."

I shake my head, because. This. Woman. She's never treated me as her superior, and while I love it, I can't get over the familiarity. Like there was never any barrier between us to begin with. It allows me to reconsider Josh's advice, lending weight to the argument that there wouldn't be an unequal dynamic between us. She doesn't see it. It doesn't exist.

Not that it was going to stop me, but it's reassuring. It promises so much.

Perrie appraises us both before getting accosted by a student I don't recognize.

Passing her bottles of water in my office, or champagne under a meteor shower aside, I know I'd do anything for her. "Early morning, during the day, or late at night, meeting your needs is my wish, chérie."

Her eyes pop, but I'm already turning towards two guys who I feel like I'm competing with. Striking up conversation with Oliver and Yves who have moved to the bar, I try and distract myself, to prevent myself from returning to Maddie to see what answer she's got for me.

Ignoring her is fruitless. She's in my line of sight and I can tell I've completely blindsided her. While I might've been prepared to give her time, my patience is wearing thin now I've had her body.

For a few minutes, her and Perrie speak in close quarters. Twice Maddie's eyes drift towards me before returning to her friend who tries to look at me without me noticing. Eventually, they seek out Dr Hurren, so I bid the guys a pleasant evening and do my best to avoid the Chair of the Department who's keen for me to be interviewed for an internal fluff piece.

Reaching for two more beers at the drinks table, I stroll up to Josh and pass him a bottle.

"Those guys," he says, referencing the three guys and girls he'd just been chatting to, "want to plan a department trip to Berlin for spring break. What d'ya think?"

"I think it's a great idea, but I'm not going."

"Same. They also want to know who you're looking at?"

"What?"

Josh elbows me. "Like I can't work it out. Athletic, addictive, chestnut-haired bombshell. One you know intimately," he murmurs.

It goes without saying I filled him in on my reign as Black Knight. And the kiss before that.

"Well, well, well. And she has a hot friend," he adds quietly, knowing he's being highly unprofessional.

"Perrie Secker," I murmur, holding the beer to my mouth to try and thwart any lip readers. "Best friend to Maddie."

"Let's go and speak to Delphine."

AKA Dr Hurren, who Perrie and Maddie are both happily chatting to.

Josh squeezes through the milling crowd and I join him half a minute later.

"I'm being challenged," he says as soon as I'm within earshot. "Perrie wants to know if I can name any female soccer players. I managed two, which she says isn't good enough."

Delphine laughs, her caramel blonde hair falling into her eyes before she brushes it away. "Because we know you can easily name thirty male football or soccer players."

"It's not my fault they don't air as much women sport," he protests to Perrie's look of absolute horror.

"Well, Professor Kit. You're obviously in a charitable mood tonight, assisting at all hours. Want to help your colleague here?" Maddie asks coyly. And fuck me, the underlying challenge in her eyes sets my heart aflame.

"Careful," Delphine warns. "These two go back over a decade, right from freshman year as undergrads."

"Really?" Perrie asks. "Snap."

I pocket that piece of information and glance at Maddie, who's looking at me as if she's delving deep inside my brain, stealing information directly from it like some wizard. So, disregarding everything else that's happened tonight, I put her out of her misery and list eight names from the soccer match I watched with Josh.

"Dude," my friend murmurs my way, his eyebrows raised.

"You could've made those up," Maddie offers.

"You don't know who they are?" I mock. "They're legit players."

"And that right there is why I'm friends with the man."

Maddie's eyes narrow. "It's good to know he has a friend," she says quietly, almost as if she's talking just to me. "I didn't think professional tiddlywinks players had many of those."

"Even killer tiddlywinks players need an opponent, Madrigal. Luckily for me, Josh wears protective eyewear."

She dissolves into a fit of giggles and it makes me so fucking proud to have caused that reaction that I can't help but share a smile with her. She's compelling and bewitching and all I want to do is hang around her.

But then the humor vanishes, a frown replacing her joy. Lifting the glass of wine to her mouth, Maddie takes a tiny sip. "I'm going to get a juice." To Perrie, she asks, "Want anything?"

"Aren't you going to drink that?"

Maddie shakes her head.

"Pass it here. I'll finish it."

Maddie hands her glass to Perrie and I offer, "Let me get it. What will you have?"

"Um, OJ, if you have it. Thank you."

"Be right back."

I head to the drinks station, going over what just happened. Did I expose the fact that I listen to her carefully? That I pay attention to the little jokes and jibes we share? *Yeah, sure did.* Did I expose my underbelly by straddling the boundary of professional and flirtatious with her? *Yup.* But it's not like I haven't done that before. Or has something jogged her memory from Club VX?

I return with an OJ for Maddie and a beer for Delphine because hers looked close to empty. Maddie takes the glass I offer, her mood quiet. Delphine is regaling an eager Perrie on her professional career to date, Josh quietly listening in. He raises his brows at me in question and, because I have nothing to give him, ask Maddie, "Everything all right?"

She nods.

"You literally went from happy to sad in about a second."

"Is this you wearing your safe-guarding hat?"

Dropping my voice low, I tell her, "I wasn't lying that taking care of you means something to me." In many ways, I repeated that claim, here, in this room mere minutes ago. *Chérie.* She's dear to me. "I hoped our kiss proved how I feel about you."

There, I said it.

She blinks several times, her demeanor turning inwards. And fuck, did I push too soon?

"I do know," she whispers. "It was special to me too."

Reaching out to her is all I want to do, cocooned like this in our own personal bubble, sounds of everyone else drowned out. God, if only I could drag her into my office and have her.

"Okay," I say, inhaling, trying to rectify my mistake. "No pressure to talk until you're ready. But is everything all right?"

Her eyes bounce to the people around us before coming back to me. She nods as if steeling herself. "I wasn't sad, it's just I had a really bad case of déjà vu. It's been happening a lot lately. It just . . . shocked me, I guess. I was trying to place it."

"What exactly? The tiddlywinks reference?" Because I can explain *that.*

"No," she takes a deep breath, clearly reluctant to say it. "It was a feeling. A deep sense of laughing like that with you before and seeing you smile that way at me."

Relieved, my face softens, but I'm a little lost as to how to move forward. Keep on acknowledging the intimacy we shared, or go back to how things were? Deciding to retrace my steps, to linger in territory that was less complicated, before our kiss, I say, "Pretty sure I smile from time to time. Even with you glowering at me."

Her smile widens. "I do not glower."

"You used to. Maybe you've forgiven me."

"Not a chance! You gave me a hard time for a reason, I'm just not sure I know what that reason is yet."

"You know why."

Her eyes turn softer. "Things might have changed between us lately, but when we first met—Were you embarrassed about that night at Midnight Blue?" she whispers.

"No, and that's not—"

"Then why? Is it Brownlow?"

Vehemently, I reject that suggestion, my pulse hiking. "Of course not."

"Then what?"

I want to promise *One day I'll tell you* because I know I will. That I'll *have to.* This family secret will eat me alive otherwise, and already I know it's not worth the effort to hide it. Despite my best endeavors, Maddie is becoming the center of everything. And in a perverse way, getting her opinion on it all might be refreshing.

And although I don't need to tell her I'm Ronin, I want her to know, to work it out. Worried she might return to the club will eat me alive unless I get this all straightened out. Hopefully, when she learns who I am, she won't want to sit on that throne again because I'm going to be everything she could ever need.

"What's going on, Tristan?"

She called me *Tristan.*

If anything, I was expecting Ronin, or Black Knight. But not a random name, even if it's a middle name.

With a dismissive shake of her head, she confirms, "Kit. I mean *Kit*. Sorry, I don't know where that came from."

Truthfully, I don't care what she calls me. Without the faff of my title I like the sound of my name coming from her mouth, the shape of which is committed to memory. From experience I know her lips are soft to the touch, their color a rich pink. A sharp cupid's bow on the top lip captures my attention often in class, the shape of her lower lip pillowy and tempting.

For a suspended moment, everything fades to black and white. All I see is a highly memorable woman standing before me, her strength and arresting beauty drawing me in until I feel consumed. The red, stylized *chérie* on her black top broadcasts so brightly in my monochrome world, it's like I'm standing before a car's headlights on full beam.

Sound disappears and I murmur, "I want you so fucking badly."

Her breathing stutters, her eyes grow as big as saucers. I'm about to ask her to come over tonight, at the weekend too, to talk, to do more if she'll let me, I don't care, but then the Chair of the Department clamps a hand on my shoulder. He's lucky I don't chop it off.

"Any thoughts on who we should ask to interview you?"

Curse his *awful* fucking timing. Taking a breath to compose myself, I ask, "Patrick, have you met Maddie Devereaux? Maddie, this is the Chair of the Department, Patrick Byrne."

They exchange greetings. Naturally he knows her, her name listed on several buildings thanks to the generosity of her forefathers. I scramble for words, wanting him away from here. From her. So I blurt out, "I was thinking of asking Maddie, actually."

"Excellent," Patrick enthuses, taking a longer look at her than is acceptable. "Yes, good idea."

"What's this?" Maddie enquires sceptically.

In a single breath, I summarize the article the department wants, Josh joining our group of three.

"I'm already slammed," she tells Patrick. "I don't have time." She looks to me, mouthing, *Sorry.*

"Nonsense," Patrick begins. "If you want something doing, ask a busy person."

"True," Josh agrees and I kind of love him for it because it makes three against one. Maddie will go berserk but it's worth it.

"Genuinely, I've got away games the next two weekends. I have assignments coming out of my ears. Three of them are due to Professor Chevalier," she points out.

Patrick chortles, the buttons on his shirt straining against his rotund belly. "Consider it a personal favor to me," he suggests with a thick undertone that has my muscles tensing. "It might be useful for the Chair of the Department to owe you one."

I glare at the odious man, on the precipice of saying something, anything, but then Josh slaps me on the back. Helpfully, it knocks some sense into me and I glance at Maddie to see she's smiling politely.

"If *quid pro quo* has currency here, I'll do it as a personal favor to the professor. And he can give me an extension on my essays." Playful eyes find mine. "Right, Professor?"

Beside me, Josh chuckles, murmuring, "Outstanding negotiation skills," before sliding his eyes my way. *She's got you by the fucking balls* they say.

"Sounds like a fair trade," I tell her. "We can negotiate on Monday at our weekly meeting. It would be unfortunate to give you a detention."

She knows me well enough to hear the underlying message, but I don't want any ambiguity. So, I quirk a solicitous brow, letting her know she'll spend it bent over my desk, my cock deep inside her.

"Wonderful," Patrick rejoices. "I look forward to reading it."

When he wanders off, I blow out a tense breath, admitting, "You're the only person I trust to do the piece."

Looking unconvinced, she finishes her drink. "Really? Aren't there some other capable students? Ones studying, I don't know —journalism. A subject which requires they write articles for magazines."

I ignore her sarcastic rebuttal. "You'd prefer the detention in my office? Noted."

Her slow, broad smile hits me hard. "Worth it, are they?"

"Yours would be. Two hours well spent."

Biting her lip, she looks towards Josh who pretends to be engrossed in his phone.

"I've got several meetings coming up, some out of town. I won't have much spare time for at least two to three weeks. It'll work," I press.

She sighs, casting another glance at Josh who's ditched his phone now our conversation is more PG. "I'll still be slammed in three weeks. And your friend is impossible," she tells him, but there's a lightness to her voice that I recognize as invitation. "High maintenance, confusing, exacting."

Hmm, I was hoping for something a little kinder, but she's not wrong.

"Don't forget meticulous," Josh joins in.

Even though I have no qualms being labeled as such, I throw him a look. *WTF?*

"Otherwise known as painstaking," Maddie adds, still holding the proverbial door wide open.

"Thorough," I suggest.

Maddie listens to my counter offer and obviously disapproves. "Mmm. Pedantic."

"I much prefer diligent, conscientious," I state, aware of Josh's eyes pinging between us like he's spectating a tennis match.

"Just synonyms for fastidious and particular."

"I'm rigorous, maybe a perfectionist. But detailed works too," I suggest, the register of my voice dropping. "Giving my undivided attention to what's right in front of me is really important."

Maddie's pupils dilate, her breathing hiccups. And maybe I'm the asshole for the double entendre, for what it implies to my colleague, but she needs to know I'll pursue her until the last breath in my body. That whether her boss, professor, or lover, I am all in, and we're not hiding.

When I throw Josh a grateful look for not interrupting our verbal sparring, he pulses his eyebrows at me. But Maddie appears lost for words. A first, so I tease, "Anything more complimentary to say about me?"

Hazel eyes flick to Josh. He winks at her. *Fucking winks.* I think it says *Your secret is safe with me.* Knowing Maddie, she's probably looking at him to rally him to her cause. To collude further. I wouldn't expect anything less from her; her backstory requires I prove myself, and I'm fucking ready and willing.

She aims a serene smile my way, a gorgeous eyebrow quirking at me now. "Hmm, compliments," she muses, tapping a finger against her lips as if thinking hard. "You'll have to wait for my article to find out, Professor Chevalier." And then she's stepping towards Perrie and wrapping her arm around her friend's waist, calling my way, "Enjoy the rest of your night!"

Watching her disappear towards the door leaves me deflated. Calling her back is an impulse I struggle to fight off. But I console myself by taking in the rear view, the one that's also spectacular, no matter what I said to her. Just before she disappears she looks over her shoulder. Her eyes find mine, full of promise.

"You are such a swat," Josh goads as he, also, follows her out of the room with his eyes. Or is it Perrie he's so focused on? "Now I know why we were watching women's soccer."

"All part of the strategy," I divulge.

"The strategy that pertains to Operation Devereaux?"

Making Maddie mine, especially in light of her romantic history, will require a precarious blend of dexterity, charm, and perseverance. "Yeah. My battle plans."

"Does it involve killing Patrick Byrne?" he asks wryly.

"Maybe." Followed by Yves, Oliver and her ex, not necessarily in that order.

"Thought so. You looked a second away from running him through." Josh blows out a breath. "This sounds serious."

"It is," I agree.

He clinks his beer against mine. "I like her."

"Yeah," I murmur. "Me too."

18

MADDIE

Kiss it Better - Rihanna

The bright yellow ball whips past my outstretched racquet, my opponent delivering an ace that would probably register an eye-wateringly high MPH on the scoreboard.

It was *the. moment* to serve an ace; it's leveled the score to deuce.

I return to the baseline, bouncing on the balls of my feet as I wait for her serve. It whistles right for me and I turn to the right, jumping as I hammer it down the line with a forehand that felt perfect off the strings. My opponent races for the T, hoping to volley it past me, but this time, I have the speed and angle. She misses the ball entirely, her grunt of effort music to my ears.

Cheers from the crowd dressed in college colors rally my mood.

"Advantage Devereaux," the umpire announces. "Set point. Match point."

Pulling in a breath, I tune out the shouts of support and concentrate on the Boston University opponent as I swap to the other side of the court and get into the ready position. The ball gets tossed high before it rockets towards me. But it's too low, the net snagging it.

Yes.

"Fault. Second serve."

I take a short step forward, bouncing, muscles primed and eyes ever watchful as the ball launches up from her cupped palm. Simultaneously, her racquet swings behind her, then up to meet the ball as it descends. The loud pop of the ball being struck registers. It flies towards the tramline so I turn left, stepping to connect cleanly with the ball. My return cross-court is met by Irina's deep backhand. We battle it out for five more shots, cross-court, backhand to backhand. Then, she slices the ball. It takes all the speed, the angle acute as it drops over the net. I race for it, just getting my racquet underneath it before it bounces for the second time and that's when my ankle pops.

With a frustrated cry, I pull up, hobbling to the net as Irina races for the shot. I pulled all power from it, just letting it bounce off the strings and skim over the net. If she reaches it, she'll likely win the shot, game, and match. I need to retire; I'm in no fit state to continue.

Luckily, she isn't fast enough.

"Game, set, match, Devereaux," the umpire announces. "Devereaux wins 6-2, 6-3."

Relief and euphoria flood my system but so does a dull, throbbing pain.

After shaking my opponent's hand and thanking the umpire, I turn for the refuge of the bench, and hopefully some assistance from the coaches or physical therapy team. I'm momentarily startled when a tall man in a charcoal shirt and black jeans appears at my side and throws a steadying arm around my waist.

Kit is here, materializing right in front of me.

"Did you twist it? A sprain?"

Shock plasters my face as I limp to the bench, though Kit is practically lifting me off the ground. "What are you doing here?"

"I've been watching. Great win by the way." He aims that crippling smile my way. "You were phenomenal out there. Fucking fast to the ball."

Giving praise is effortless for Kit. In many ways I'm getting used to hearing his encouragements and compliments, all of them a bellows on the smoldering coals that ignite into a roaring bonfire at his presence. So I mumble *Thanks* as he lowers me carefully to the seat. Gently, he picks up my throbbing foot, resting it on his knee as he squats in front of me. Carefully, he unties my laces and slides off my shoe.

"I heard a pop."

"You can't weight bear."

"No." Still in disbelief that he sprinted on court to help me while the coaching staff are still nowhere to be seen, I stare at his bowed head as he studies my foot and ankle. "I can't believe you're here."

Humor flashes in his eyes before he returns his attention to my ankle. "We'll get you to the emergency room to see what's going on." Then he picks up my other foot and pulls off the other shoe. "Where are your pants?"

I motion to my bag. Kit wastes no time in pulling out some black athletic pants. They're tight, but he manages to get my feet in the legs and pull them up to my knees. Wriggling them up my thighs, I can't get them over my butt unless I stand. Wise to my predicament, Kit helps me to my feet. Automatically, I steady myself by putting my hands on his shoulders. It means he has to pull my pants up, his eyes searching mine briefly before he grabs the waistband and gently fits them over my ass.

I'm unsure why letting him dress me, touch me, feels so

normal, but whatever the reason, he doesn't make a big thing about it. And he didn't overstep the boundaries that I've stupidly kept in place while I've tried to find time to end things with Harrison.

It's time to do that. I'm so ready.

Pants on, I sit down, Kit tossing my shoes into my bag. He holds out my water bottle. "Drink? Do you have pain relief?"

"Front pocket."

After rummaging in my bag, he drops two tablets in my palm and I swallow them down. Then he helps me to my feet, supporting me as I tug the pants up a little higher over my tennis skort. The material bunches up but I can't be bothered to straighten it out.

"Put this on before you get a chill," he suggests, grabbing my tennis hoodie.

Like I'm a child, he helps pull it over my head, stretching out the neck first to make certain there's enough room for my head. Then he tugs the material down my body, his nearness and the intimacy of every small interaction making my heart *thump*.

Suddenly, Harrison hovers at my side. Either ignorant of Harrison's arrival, or refusing to acknowledge him, Kit gathers up my bag and slings it over a shoulder.

"Jesus, this is heavy," he murmurs.

"What the fuck's going on?" Harrison directs his question at Kit, his eyes narrowed.

"I'm taking Maddie to the hospital."

"I'll take her."

Putting an arm around my lower back, Kit scoops me into his arms with surprising ease and speed. Swallowing my yelp, my arms thread around his neck, my body instinctively curling around his as if honed by muscle memory. Our faces are barely inches apart, making me hyper aware of his heady scent, his strong heart beat, his utter beauty.

"I've got her," Kit tells him, walking towards the court exit.

But Harrison speeds up, prowling at my side. "Mads, who's this?"

"Kit," I answer and nothing more, maybe because it's hard to define what we are. "I won, by the way."

The fact that I still need his mediocre praise frustrates me, but his tone is flat when he answers. "Good job. Let's get you to the locker room where Natalie can check you over. The others are still playing."

So he's not taking me to the hospital?

Natalie is the team's physical therapist and while I love her, I'm perfectly happy where I am, cradled in Kit's arms, snuggled up against his tempting masculinity.

Threading innuendo into his voice, Kit answers for me. "I'll take good care of her." And then he cuts Harrison a look that tells him to go and get fucked. Harrison's answering look gleams with a competitiveness only serious athletes can convey. It shouldn't thrill me to see Harrison so bewildered by Kit's presence. By the way he treats me. Harrison thought me in love with him still, and I'm one hundred percent sure I'm not.

"Maddie," Harrison grits.

"Bye, Coach."

But he can't let me go that easily. "I've booked De la Croix for dinner next Saturday."

Mortified, my heart weighs as much as the world. And I dread Kit's questions. Dread him asking about Harrison and why we're dining at Boston's fanciest restaurant. So I'm mildly relieved when silence, not questions follows us out of the sports center to the lot, despite feeling sick to my soul. My arms lose their strength, my grip slipping, so I tighten my hold around Kit's neck which brings me fractionally closer to his face.

He looks at me then, really looks at me. His eyes drift over my features, cataloging, lingering on my mouth. All it would take is for him to drop his chin a few inches and our lips would meet.

If he kissed me, so help me God, I would kiss him back. Kit and I seem inevitable in a way that's different to how I knew I'd end up with Harrison.

Kit's chest expands as he takes a deep breath. My tongue darts out to lick my lips.

He rumbles, "Okay?"

Faint from his proximity, all I can do is nod. As we near his car, realization strikes. That wasn't a casual question. Kit was asking me if I'm okay after being near Harrison. If I'm hurt in other ways.

Could this man be any more perfect?

Once inside his Mustang, Kit checks my seat belt is on tight. When he's behind the wheel, the door shutting us both inside, I'm hyper aware it's just the two of us, alone, together.

Like his presence, thoughts crowd me. Two weeks ago, we kissed. Last weekend, I spent in the arms of a stranger, the night more than I could've hoped for. Despite the loss I felt after the Black Knight and I parted ways, I knew it was only ever meant to be a temporary moment. A chance to live, to put things in perspective. But I'm glad for my treasured experience as Iseult, a woman I needed to embody to help me understand how, and with whom, my future would unfold.

Whether my encounter with Kit or the Black Knight, they showed me what passionate reverence looks like. I want that for myself. For always. So it's Kit's mouth and hands and touch I've been daydreaming about these past days. It's his undivided attention I want. And I have it, the departmental drinks evening proof of his intent. My guard always seems down when I'm around him, his presence a safe space. It must be why I called him Tristan. I'm not entirely sure why, other than becoming aware that every night since my debauched night at Club VX, the faceless man in my dreams has a name.

Tristan.

Consciously or not, my heart wants him to be Kit, and Kit, Tristan. It's time to be brave and tell him. I want my parallel life, the one where I wake every morning aching, longing for him, longing for the night when I can experience our golden life all over again.

After the club, I fell into bed, exhausted but confident. Happy. Closing my eyes, reliving what had got to be the most memorable night of my life, it wasn't long before the welcoming comfort of my dreams found me.

My throat is sore from reciting Latin psalms and reading Gospels, the verses long memorized. Placing the texts on the small table, I look out of the window to see the sun is long into its descent. Anticipation and impatience accompany me every day as I dutifully follow my lessons, waiting for the day to unfold.

Turning to my friend and long-time companion, Béatrice, we head downstairs. A servant brings us a small glass of wine and we take two apples from the bowl on the table and a few other provisions.

My father sees us leaving. "Where are you going?"

"For a ride," I answer.

He studies me closely. "Do not leave the boundaries of the estate," he warns.

Agreeing, I kiss him on the cheek and take Béatrice's hand. Together, we make our way to the stables where the stablehand has our horses saddled and waiting. Hope is a gray mare of five and she happily accepts the fruit I offer her.

We ride out into the countryside towards the woods that take us away from our lands. Atop his black stallion, Tristan waits for me, chain mail covering his torso, a sword at his hip. At the sight of him, my heart is full, my belly in somersaults. Slowly, we pick our way through the trails and paths, Béatrice following. When we reach the vale where the brook runs, Tristan dismounts and reaches for me. I don't need his assistance but I allow him to help me from my saddle, my hands on his shoulders as I'm lifted, weightless to the ground.

Our horses graze in the long grass as my friend keeps watch nearby. Entwined in his arms, we speak of our day. On occasion, he asks me to sing to him, but mostly we talk of court politics, of our commitment and duty to God, of love and honor, of our hopes for the future.

Our discovery would be ruinous. Keeping Tristan safe is my priority, the risk to myself irrelevant.

"I would never want to be parted from you," I vow. Both of us fear separation; our destinies diverge.

"We have eternity," he promises, though we both know it is a lie. I have overheard my father's plans for me. "We are forever tied," he explains, pressing a palm to my heart. "Here."

Briefly, I consider my mother and father, of how I would bring shame to the family, to our name. Of God's wrath instead of His glory. But neither of us think of God as we join together until the sun sinks beyond the hills, the sky ablaze with stars. Even God must recognize the futility of forbidding a love as pure as ours. Even God must grace His children with the strength to face adversity.

Soon, it will come for us.

I cannot bear the pain of giving him up.

Shaking the emotional memories from my head, I focus on how right everything seems *now*. I feel resolute and happy as I turn to Kit and say, "Thanks for the ride."

"Of course."

"You say that like this is no inconvenience to you, and I think you would do the same for anyone." His attention flicks my direction, letting me know he's listening. "In all the years I've got injured under his watch, he's never offered to take me to a doctor."

Kit clenches his jaw. I know what he's thinking: *Of course, you needed a fucking doctor*, but he's not going to tell me that. He'd rather make me write five hundred words on why I loved a man like Harrison, drawing all the necessary conclusions myself.

"Sounds like he had other priorities."

Harrison's priorities aren't my concern anymore. Rebuilding something with Harrison is no longer on my radar. That option is so far beyond my realm of thought that he might as well be on Saturn.

I drop my head to the headrest, hoping my injury is superficial. Temporary. I hate being injured. "I'm sure you must be busy, too."

"Not too busy to take you to see a doctor, Maddie. Besides," he begins, gifting me a half smile that has warmth leaching into my soul. "The sooner you get looked at, the sooner you can get back to your studies and complete the two essays you owe me."

"Oh my God," I mutter. "Kit, do you ever take a compliment, or do you just like to give me a hard time?"

His low chuckle makes my blood drunk. "Isn't it *you* who likes to give *me* a hard time?" He doesn't give me a chance to answer. "Maybe I just want to look good, knowing you're about to write a horrifyingly honest article about me."

I plan on writing the article over winter break. I haven't got time to do it justice and I want it to be excellent. Negotiating that extension will come later. "Nice try, but this isn't some ploy to look good."

We stop at a red light and he takes the opportunity to look me over. I must look a state, but I'm stupidly happy. Finally, my mind is clear of all the clutter.

"No?"

I shake my head. "I know you too well."

The assured comment makes his eyebrows rise. Then he nods, like he actually believes me.

Deciding I need to take a stand, to show my intentions, I say, "It's over, with Harrison. He just doesn't know it yet."

His eyes swirl with questions, ones he decides not to voice. "Good."

"I'll tell him soon."

Almost immediately a lightness to the space between us grows. If I expected him to ask what that means for us, I'm left wondering. Maybe he's doesn't need to ask, my next steps obvious. As the light turns green, he repeats: "Good."

So I ask, "Why did you want to become a professor?"

A wry smile. "Learning is a consequence of thinking—it's why I give so many written tasks. The most important thing any one of us can do is *think*. To challenge. If you can interrogate and argue a point of view, it will make you deadly."

"Hmm. So maybe you *do* think De Troyes et al portray love as inherently implausible? The texts prove it."

Changing lanes, he murmurs, "Surely it matters how a man, how I, would treat a woman today, no?"

Our eyes catch and I have to look away. And as I seem to have swallowed honesty pills court-side, instead of pain relief, I answer, "I think a woman would be very lucky to have you."

Hope glimmers in his voice. "Do you."

I nod, focusing on the traffic. Kit is an educator, the definition of someone who's devoted to a cause, who lives to serve. If a woman could keep him, she'd be the luckiest girl in the world. I couldn't keep Harrison. Could I keep Kit?

Feeling hot, I slide the window down a fraction.

Kit asks, "How come Robyn beat you at the inter-squad matches?"

My stomach sinks. "What do you mean?"

"You're a much better player than her. Did you throw the match?"

There's no escape from this car, from his scrutiny. "Yeah. It hurt to lose, but I didn't want to be number one."

Kit doesn't ask me why. Harrison's possessiveness earlier was hardly subtle, and I bet Kit knows being number one seed requires too much of Harrison's time and attention, both of which I've been trying to avoid.

"I understand," he murmurs. "You looked really good out there, Maddie. Watching you is—you're incredible."

Shyly, I answer, "Thank you."

At the hospital, Kit insists on carrying me inside. Once we're triaged, we wait to see the radiologist who turns out to be a young, pretty bi-racial woman, her hair dyed a sophisticated dark blonde. After greeting Kit, her eyes never stray very far. And here I am, sweat drying in my hair and my fashionable skirt-caught-in-pants look adding twenty pounds to my butt.

Kit clears his throat and looks at me, which prompts Dr Rosen to ask me a series of questions.

"And you were there?" Dr Rosen asks Kit, like that's important.

"Yes." Throwing an arm around my chair, he gazes down at me as if I'm the center of his world.

"Right, and you are?"

"Kit."

The doctor flutters her lashes at him. "Brother, husband, friend?"

It's not my imagination when she stresses the word *friend*, hoping against all hope.

"Friend," he confirms, looking at me as if I'll correct him. Although we're not just friends anymore, I think Kit defined us as such to make me object. To force me into action.

Ignorant to our silent conversation, Dr Rosen's answering smile is serene, her eyes full of invitation that would have most men undressing, knowing a sure thing when they see one.

Resigned as to how the next twenty minutes will go, I enter a state of mild distress. It's like I'm holding my breath, waiting for him to flirt his way through the appointment. But Kit acts as if oblivious to her interest, assisting in every way he can: taking me to X-ray; helping me on and off tables; getting me drinks and snacks and making sure I'm not in pain.

He tends to me much more than Dr Rosen.

When he pops outside to answer a call from *Gramps*, the doctor tells me, "You have a good friend. Very attentive. I'm surprised he's single."

I tell her, "He's not single. He's taken," just as Kit returns through the open door.

An eyebrow cocks in my direction which makes me think he overheard, a smile growing which only confirms my suspicion.

"Can you help me with my pants?" I ask him. "It's hot in here."

He doesn't look at Dr Rosen, he doesn't need to; he knows exactly what I'm doing because the air is cool thanks to the A/C.

"Sure."

Rising to my feet, our eyes lock as his hands come to my waistband, the space between us feeling charged and non-existent. Slowly, he slides the material over my butt, his palms skimming slowly over my cheeks. Thumbs run over the crease of my ass, my breath hitching.

Kit's gaze rakes over my features as he smooths down the tennis skirt. And then he's kneeling at my feet, dragging the material down my legs. Seeing him there, kneeling, has me automatically placing a hand on his head, his hair soft and thick and this scenario so familiar to me, that I blink away the déjà vu.

A gentle hand wraps around my bad ankle. "Lift."

I raise my foot, the pant leg pulled over my shoeless foot. We repeat the action for the other foot, Kit holding me secure at the waist as he undresses me. Time and again his heated gaze dances down the length of my body, his face inches away from my pussy.

Can he scent me? The pheromones I'm emitting must be insane. It's as if my body knows him. Craves him. Wants his mouth on me.

"Better?" he murmurs, his hands steady on the backs of my thighs. As if he can't help himself, a thumb curves along the underside of my butt cheek. And damn, but he makes me feel like I'm the only girl in this room.

"So much better," I murmur.

Eyes bouncing between us, we take our seats as Dr Rosen returns to her computer and the X-ray visible on the screen. "Good news. You rolled your ankle and should be back to light tennis duties in a few days."

The smile Kit gives me all but shatters my heart. It's Tristan's smile, direct from my dream. "That's great news," he says quietly.

"Looks like you won't need your friend's assistance for much longer."

"Happy to help," he answers, pulling me to my feet and helping me with my sneakers.

We're just about to leave the doc's office when she hands Kit a piece of pink paper. "My cell. Call me if there are any questions, about anything."

He takes it from her without a word, my mood plummeting. This scene has played out in front of me countless times before, just with a different man.

In silence we walk down the hall, Kit supporting me at the waist, the pink slip of paper in his free hand. Feeling petulant, I consider shrugging off his arm but that would only demonstrate my insecurity. My immaturity.

Kit's next move happens before I can commit to any one

thought, balling up the paper and lobbing it towards the nearest trash can.

My heart squeezes. "Not going to call the hot doctor?"

The hand at my waist tightens. "No, Maddie, I'm not."

"But she's a doctor. And beautiful."

His mouth quirks. "I think we've established that. And for the record, I work with beautiful women who are doctors."

Immediately my thoughts skip to Dr Hurren and her impressive brain. Maybe hot academic doctors are more his thing. The brief buoyancy I was feeling deflates like a week-old balloon. Dr Hurren is right there, in the faculty. He must bump into her every day, have departmental meetings with her. Chat about nonsense and what they got up to at the weekend.

Voice deepening, he adds, "I also work with *aspiring* doctors. There's one who I can't stop thinking about. An exceptional, incredibly talented, spirited woman who steals my breath every time I look at her."

Butterflies take flight in my stomach. They dive straight for my brain and make me light-headed. And the way he's looking at me voids all my stupid worries because he's talking about me.

Our pace slows. "I'm not him," he stresses, his features earnest.

"I know."

"And I'm *not* your friend."

He's so much more than that. "I know."

"I'm taken, remember?"

A puff of laughter escapes, embarrassed that he overheard. Despite his infinite patience, it's coming to an end. If I don't act soon, then he will.

The exit is just ahead. The doors act as a demarcation line, this moment, this place giving freedoms that need to be voiced quickly. "I think about you, about our kiss, all the time."

The automatic doors slide open, effortless and welcoming,

green-lighting our future path. I look to that rosy horizon with determination, certain I'm not making the same mistakes. Kit is different. *We* are different.

Just outside the doors, we stop. Neither of us wants to walk away from this moment without marking it more permanently.

"I just needed to be sure."

"And now you are?"

100 percent. "I needed to know you'd catch me. Catch me, keep me, only me."

Gently, Kit's hands cradle my face, his mouth descending to mine where he lays the most perfect kiss. It's a promise, sealing our fate.

"I'm falling headlong with you," he whispers before pressing another kiss to my mouth. It's achingly tender, my mouth parting for more. I pull him in closer, our mouths meeting again and again until I feel weak-kneed and boneless. Around me, the world could be burning down but I wouldn't know it, his tongue dragging against mine until I'm molten lava, ready to erupt.

With a long inhale, Kit pulls away. "Better stop," he says shakily. "Whilst I can." He presses a kiss to my temple. "Still got my number?"

I nod against his shoulder.

"Are you ready to jump?"

"Yes."

"Then I'll be waiting to catch."

19

MADDIE

A Question of You - Inhaler

Harrison's penthouse Brownstone is the sort of apartment that I imagined myself living in—at one time, at any rate. Aside from the open-plan living area, fabulous, luxury kitchen, sophisticated bedrooms, and to-die-for bathrooms, he has a study where he keeps his trophies from the court and memorabilia from presenting.

He points out a new photograph of him interviewing the female winner of this year's US Open.

"Unreal," I compliment. "I'd love to meet her."

We head back to the hand-crafted kitchen and collect our drinks. Arriving early, I suggested pre-drinks before dinner. The reason is entirely selfish—I can't have this conversation in a crowded restaurant with Boston's high net-worth individuals watching the ensuing drama unfold. I owe Harrison the dignity of a private breakup.

A whole week has passed since Kit took me to the hospital.

Earlier, I texted Kit, forewarning him that I would be calling. He didn't reply and I'm trying not to be worried.

Clearing my mind of all thoughts, I retreat to the sofa where I nurse my wine. Harrison tugs on a beer.

"You had a successful year last year, your first for Jacquard," I point out. "Do you enjoy coaching here?"

He half nods, half shrugs. "I pulled back on the TV opportunities to be here, near you," he amends, throwing an arm along the back of the sofa. "Thank fuck you saw sense and applied, else it would've all been for nothing."

The smile he gifts me is endearing. The sweeter sides of Harrison felt few and far between but when they came, boy did they make me feel good.

"I am grateful, Harrison, but I've never asked anything of you. I'd never want you to miss out on doing what you love most."

It's the honest truth because I want him to be happy. And after losing his title as *King of the Court*, being adored on TV gave him a measure of worth, attaching value to the compliments and accolades of a different kind. Sometimes I forget how much of a prodigy he was. His injury makes me sad for what he had to give up.

Deep blue eyes study me. "It was pretty clear you wanted something extraordinary from me." He lifts his hand. "So here I am, waiting patiently for you."

His tone is irritated. I was hoping that we could talk like adults, but the underlying criticism blackens my good mood. When I hit eighteen, I started to wonder if ending our relationship was for the best. Since that momentous birthday, I've spent years wondering what Harrison was to me, getting back together for a night at a time. But we're unable to be around each other without acrimony and hurt surfacing. So while letting him go had been hard, getting back together in the intervening years has been *harder.*

They say the first time you do something wrong, it's a mistake. The second time you do it, it's a choice. Well, I hate to count the number of times I've made shitty, ruinous choices. Keeping my distance from him by attending a different college was meant to help me. Fortify me. But returning to our roles as coach and player has made me feel powerless.

Confident about my feelings and how I want this to play out, I tell him, "I came here to end things, officially."

"No you haven't."

His over-confidence, his dismissal was expected. "We're not having a re-do. I'll always be your friend—and tennis partner if you ask—but I don't want to resurrect anything."

"Seriously? Why not?"

"We don't work, Mark."

There's a burst of shocked laughter. "*Mark?* Jesus, I must be in the dog house."

"We keep going over old ground but nothing's changed."

"That's because you keep pushing me away. Just take me back and it'll be plain sailing. It's been months already. You've had plenty of time to work things out."

I consider pulling out my phone to call Kit now but I need to resolve this once and for all.

"Is this about Kit?"

"Yes."

Harrison asked me about Kit as soon as I was physically fit to train again after rolling my ankle, even though he messaged me several times when I got back from the ER.

"Are you fucking?"

Harrison doesn't deserve an answer to that, but he needs to know how serious I am about the end of our situationship. "He's someone I can see a future with."

As expected, Harrison doesn't give up easily. "You saw yourself with me and you've known me longer." I nod, unable to deny that. "And your parents like me."

Whilst not strictly true, especially after Dad's recent admission, I nod again.

"He's your professor," Harrison stresses. "The college won't like it."

"The college won't like what's going on with you and Robyn, Harrison. Don't be difficult," I warn him.

He's unable to hide his surprise, but he shrugs, pretending not to care. "It's casual. I'm just waiting on you to take me back. You used to put me first, but recently, you've made me feel like second place."

The recrimination in his voice reflects his misplaced entitlement but I don't rise to it. I've made my decision and there's no way I'm backtracking.

Placing my glass of wine on the coffee table in front of me, I ask, "Unlike Robyn?"

"Yeah, unlike Robyn."

"If you want someone else, move on. I'm not stopping you."

"But you are! You want me devoted to you. It's fucking hard to be devoted to someone that doesn't trust me."

Stressed, I stand. "And whose fault is that?"

"Mine," he growls, his beer slamming onto the table top as frustration rides him hard. "But it was years ago! A man's priorities can change."

Once, at the beginning, I remember Harrison telling me, *You want me to treat you softly and touch you cruelly, don't you?* The thing is, I was never treated softly. Every word and touch was cruel, starving me of affection as he fed my skin bruises and welts. My protests of being tired from a match or training were ignored, Harrison demanding things from me that I wasn't in the mood for.

I wanted to be *loved*. Cherished. Adored. I want to sit on that pedestal, feeling like Lady Iseult every day. And the way I feel about Kit far eclipses any feelings I had for Harrison. He's shown me what a relationship could and should look like. And I've experienced a slice of it for myself, with a stranger dressed as a knight. It's spurned me to find that for myself in the real world.

On his feet now, Harrison closes the gap between us, brushing a hand over the side of my face. It's a fleeting moment of affection; in the next breath he's cupping my jaw to hold me still, his fingers digging into the bone. We're so close our breath mingles. "You don't want me, and yet, you don't want me with anyone else."

"Let go."

His hold loosens enough that I lift out of his touch, but we stand nose to nose, my anger rising, ready to spew like dragon's fire. "The girls talk, Harrison. I know you were with team members last year. The year you came to Princeton and promised me the world." Again.

"Well, I realized it was pointless giving it to you. You always throw it back in my face."

"I'm not the one who broke our wedding vows."

It's strange how long we've avoided talking about our mini-marriage. Ironically, it was shorter than the average honeymoon, though not ours, which was a three week vacation to the Bahamas. Harrison caught up with a few of his tennis pals. Then he fucked a few of the wives and girlfriends.

At the time, my holiday reads weren't the popular chic-lit novels but epic tales about chivalric love. I'd spend the days lounging by the pool and beach, reading, researching, figuring out what I could do after Princeton. A doctorate at Brownlow felt right, papers the college professors had published tempting me to apply when the time came.

Harrison was with other women several times on honeymoon. Even married, he was never going to stop the side-fucks. Never love me right. Thanks to a heart to heart with my friend and badass lawyer, Jo, I even managed to video his infidelity. The judge annulled our marriage on our return and I, a free, emancipated young woman, got a summer job and headed to Princeton, meeting Perrie at orientation.

At seventeen I was a divorcee. *God*, what was I thinking? What possessed Harrison to agree!

I blow out a relieved breath, thankful this relationship is behind me. That I have the strength to let go. Kit has given me that. He's given me knowledge, forcing me to interrogate what is and isn't true.

Just as he predicted, I became deadly.

"I regret that more than I can say. And the annulment—"

He trails off, the truth of the aftermath never spoken between us. But the annulment was important. It prevented access to his money and property, and it meant my inheritance was protected. Harrison offered me an allowance but pride wouldn't let me accept. Independence was all I needed. It's why I couldn't return home and live off my parents. I had to stand by my decisions, my code.

"I know," I agree kindly, because I sense his guilt about my lack of funds, but I won't be misdirected by his guilt. "But you didn't just stray when married."

Anger and frustration are etched into the smile lines at the corner of his eyes. At the frown between his brows. "What do I need to say or do to make you understand you're all I want?"

The list is endless, but the most obvious one gleams like a shiny coin in a pan of dirt. Professing I'm not interested in him anymore won't cut it. I need a demonstration. Evidence. "Let me see your phone."

His reaction is telling. Immediate. *He. Freezes.*

"You play unfair."

"How is it unfair to ask for proof of your words?"

"You've made it clear we're not together. I'm just scratching an itch until you take me back."

Knowing how silver-tongued he is doesn't stop his lies from hurting. "You told me you weren't seeing anyone." Twice.

"I wouldn't be if we were back together. If you don't like it, then it's your own fault."

Silently, I scream. I will my heart to play dead. Command my emotions to wither and die. To not let his touch or words hurt me any longer.

I. Am. Done.

A spurious thought catches my attention, some awareness that it feels like I've lived a hundred lifetimes trying to get over Harrison. At trying to find some semblance of this once in a lifetime, expansive love between us.

But it's just not there.

I've no idea what my dreams were directing me towards, but it's not this, a dynamic built on a complete misconception of love. That anticipation I felt on arriving at Jacquard wasn't pointing me towards my ex, but to Kit. Suddenly, it all makes sense, my thoughts and emotions caught up inside each other so tightly the night I was at Midnight Blue that I couldn't tell what I was feeling for who.

"Surviving you is too hard, Harrison. This is the end."

"It ends when I say it ends."

To think I had the courage to walk away from him aged seventeen seems impossible. Looking back, I'm not sure how I managed.

Closing the gap between us, he presses his mouth against mine. The kiss tastes of hate and passion, hurt and desperation. It's an exploding memory of all the tears I cried, wanting wanting wanting him. Watching him seduce his way across the room.

Age and distance might not have been the cure I hoped for, but I've learnt how to protect myself. So I channel all that resolve and resilience now. And then I recite Kit's cell number in my head until Harrison ends the kiss, his eyes alight with what he thinks is my surrender. Our breathing is quick, his familiar taste absorbed into my bloodstream.

But I know it for what it is—a poison.

Nothing simmers inside, nothing ignites. Unlike with Kit, there's no sense of falling, of soaring. It's just stagnant, unhealthy waters infecting me. And I need the antidote.

"Say it," he demands, holding my head. "Take me back and mean it."

"Why do you want to get back together?"

He blinks, the question surprising him. "We're meant to be."

"No we're not. It's obvious we're not. So why?"

His eyes ping so quickly between mine I fear I'll get dizzy.

"You understand me, even if you can't stand me," he says on a deprecating laugh. "Our families are tight. Everyone expects this. It's—we're just good together, baby."

Pulling against his hands, he releases me, allowing me to take a step back. "What's your happiest memory of us?"

Harrison shrugs. A bewildered expression crosses his face. "Our first night on honeymoon was pretty nice. You'd bought blue lingerie. You looked good, Maddie. You always do."

I hate his answer; it's an empty platitude and a reminder of my terrible decision. Plus my lingerie was red, so he's remembering another woman.

"What's the nicest thing I've ever done for you?"

He throws his arms wide, exasperated. "How many of these do I have to answer?"

"Last one."

He sighs, thinking. "Nicest thing is probably asking me to marry you."

"Why is that *nice*?"

"I don't know. I can't think on the spot like this. But being asked to marry someone is pretty special, Mads."

"Okay, but what else?" I push. "A small thing that stuck with you."

I'll take anything: handing him a tennis ball that I kissed for good luck and which earned him a match-winning ace in one of our earlier doubles matches; surprising him by turning up at Flushing Meadows to see him play a veterans game; buying him a birthday card so that he wouldn't miss his mom's birthday; getting him a stupid vintage t-shirt that he couldn't be bothered to look for himself.

"Nothing has stuck with me. You're just there, being you. We don't all have elephant memories, able to bring up shit from years ago."

Memories are all I have. I overflow with them; old memories of Harrison, old memories of a life I think I lived. Each memory brings depth to my life, to my meaning. To be so forgotten by Harrison only solidifies what I already know.

We're so over.

"You never told me that you loved me."

As realization hits, his face slackens. "It didn't need to be said when it was obvious to everyone that knew us."

"It wasn't obvious to *me!*"

For a taut second we just stare at each other, breathing hard.

"Of course, I loved you," he says sadly. "Of course, I do now. But before you had the wedding annulled and I told you how much I loved you, how much regret I felt, you told me to stop telling you. So I have."

While it's true I told him to stop saying those three words, sick to death of hearing the empty lie over and over, now, it's just a convenient excuse.

Sighing, he says tiredly, "I can't win with you. It's like you expect so much from me, things I can't give and never could."

The words land with impact. Have I always expected more from him because I had knowledge of a different experience of love? A different lover?

"You're so pretty, Harrison," I tell him, my eyes tender as I catalog for the last time all the physical ways he's a feast for the eyes. He's America's golden boy with the billboard good looks. The deceptive, heartbreaker smile hides the villain from the world, making me question myself a hundred times over the years. Age and distance couldn't change him, but I can change how my life looks from here on out. "So pretty," I murmur, just for him. "But so are your lies. And the biggest lie you tell is to yourself."

Sadness washes over me, but it doesn't linger. Instead, I feel resolve. Cleansed. It's taken some time to get to this point, to process, but coming to Jacquard University has been a profoundly positive experience. I'm no longer off-kilter or confused. My path feels right, a series of circumstances leading me to a man who has turned my world upside down but now feels like my true North Star.

Grabbing my coat, I head for the front door. Behind me, Harrison follows like a rogue wave, furious, snatching at my heels, threatening to drown me until I give in. Give up.

"What lie?"

"Your regret," I point out, turning to face him. "The guilt, this idea that making amends and getting back together will work. Will put things right."

He's speechless. I can practically see his thoughts churning in his eyes. I head for the door, his footsteps hurrying behind me.

"Wait."

"We're over. For good. Forever. I mean it, Harrison. Go and

live your life with someone who loves you back. You deserve more than the half-assed feelings I have for you, and I deserve something better too."

I know how it feels to be valued, to be treated like a princess. And while I don't need a man to kneel at my feet, knowing he's prepared to worship me even once in a while is enough for me.

The growling fury inside him subsides. If he looked at this objectively, he'd know I'm right. He *does* deserve more than I could give him. But now that Kit is in my life, Harrison hasn't a hope in hell.

"Mads, come on. Give it another month. Don't rush your decision."

"There's nothing here for us, Harrison. Go commentate. Or just go and be part of the circuit. You're happy on tour. And you're good at it. And you're good at it because you love it."

He stares at me, fighting his thoughts. Losing is not in his arsenal, his competitive spirit struggles with anything but victory. So I encourage, "I'm sorry this is how it ends for us, but let's not be strangers, okay? Let me know how you are." Knowing this might be the last time I see him for a while, softly, I kiss him on the cheek. "Bye."

Head high, I leave him behind. And while I'm proud of myself and happy with the outcome, tears threaten. Sorrow floods my system—for him, for us, but mostly for all the time and energy I wasted on him. And I'm borderline crying because I hope I'm not too late for a man who deserves to be loved, strongly, fiercely. And the person who should shower that man with love, needs to be me.

Kit is out there waiting to catch me up in his arms.

All I need to do is call him.

20

KIT

Where have you been? - Rihanna

Concentrating on my driving skills and not Maddie's dinner with Harrison Tait at De la Croix tonight is beyond my capabilities. Twice, I nearly rear-end other vehicles. Earlier, I called in on Josh, eager to check out his new furniture and distract myself from Maddie's evening plans. If she's to be believed, Tait is getting his marching orders *tonight.* I have to trust that everything is resolved as she promised it would be.

Pushing people into corners never really pans out. Maddie needed time and I gave it to her. After all, it's what she asked for. But a part of me wonders if I'm getting ahead of myself. What if every bad thing my father had to say about her family is true? What if Harrison sweet talks her into giving it another try? In my pity party for one, I try not to remember all the times we were *so close* to igniting the touch paper all over again, willing to welcome the ensuing fire. Perhaps her encouraging words, her expressions of interest are all part of my wild imagination. Old flames can be reluctant to extinguish.

My phone buzzes, the caller's name illuminated on the touch-screen display.

Madrigal.

I hit accept, my voice thick with relief. "Maddie."

"Hi."

My brain picks apart her voice, seeking clues. Just because she promised to call and has, doesn't mean it's for the reasons we agreed. So I say, "You okay?"

"It's done. I'm ready."

A breath I've been holding for what feels like my entire life is expelled from my lungs. I've always appreciated Maddie's honesty—she's not one for games or manipulations. Walking away from Harrison cleanly was important to her; it was the least I could give.

After giving me an address on Commonwealth Avenue, I tell her, "Hold tight. I'm on my way."

Thankfully, my route was as close to serendipitous as can be, and I'm pulling up alongside the sidewalk five minutes later.

I call her cell, and even though she knows my car, I tell her, "I'm here. Black Mustang."

At that moment, she moves from whatever doorway or corner she's been hiding out in and my pulse finally slows. "I see you."

We disconnect, our eyes latching as she looks at me through the car window. Pushing open the door, I exit the car and take a couple of steps towards her. A new intelligence dwells in her eyes as I open up my arms and we step into each other's embrace. Her arms tighten, and I stand there, wondering how this can feel so natural and right.

Our lips connect for a drawn out, euphoric moment where comet tails brighten behind my eyelids in remembrance. I sway on my feet, my head in free fall as I go deeper, that one kiss not enough. Never enough. Again and again, my lips return to hers, pulling, nipping, tasting. Soft mewling noises in her throat has my dick responding, rising to meet whatever she needs from me. Fingers rake through the hair at my nape, our bodies fully aligned, my hard-on pressing insistently against her. When the tip of her tongue strokes against mine, all restraint leaves me. My body craves more. Her addictive taste has want streaming through my veins. It has me groaning and growling as I drown her with my love and affection.

She pulls back, a flash of devastation marring her face. "I was worried I was too late. Didn't you get my text?"

Underneath her question is a different one: why didn't I reply?

I palm her face. "I did, but I made myself wait for your call. And no, Maddie, you're not too late. I'd wait an eternity for you."

"Take me home," she breathes.

Home.

I open the door for her and she clambers in. I will my cock to get down as I slide in behind the wheel and drive Maddie to my apartment. I run every light I can get away with, the short drive a blessing. We barely make it inside before we're on each other, but then she's grinning into the kiss, pulling away.

"I want to see where you live."

Her eyes drift behind me, to the bedroom, the door ajar. For a moment, I think about dragging her in there, but she backs away, to the kitchen and living room behind her. I follow, letting her look, but she's got about ten seconds before my patience hits zero. There's just enough outside light to see by, so I don't switch on any lamps. Almost affectionately she runs her palm over the island, and that's when she spies the balcony to her left. She diverts towards it, striding past the couch and windows until she's at the sliding doors looking out through the glass.

Coming to her side I unlock them, sliding the main door so that she can step out and view the city skyline, office lights and the dark, moody sky in juxtaposition.

Looking out and up, she takes it all in. "I love this view. Your balcony." Then she turns for me, resting her hands at the base of my throat.

My thumbs trace her high cheekbones, her skin satin smooth. Hazel eyes drown in mine, her hands sliding down my chest appreciatively. I lean in that final couple of inches, our lips meeting in a suspended moment of perfection until I overflow with some unnameable, unfathomable emotion. And it's not love, because I know I am already in love. With her. It's something else, intangible and monumental, clawing inside my chest with a desperate kind of hunger.

I draw in a breath, our lips reconnecting. My hands thread through her long hair, her tongue teasing mine as our mouths move together in slow exploration. A whimper sounds in her throat, transmitting into my lungs where I inhale it deep, locking it away. Hands clutch at my shoulders, dragging me even closer until the soft lines of her body meld to the solid planes of mine.

From experience, I know she fits well, slotting against my chest and groin like she was made simply to be held by me. Without a doubt, I know she's who I've been looking for and I'm not letting her go.

Catch me, keep me, love me, she asked. It's done. She has me.

Dropping an inch or two, my hands slide down her outer thighs. Understanding my intentions she jumps up, just as I lift, her legs wrapping around my hips. A tattered breath sounds as

Maddie rubs against my erection. Walking us back inside, I take her down to the rug and pull her onto my lap.

A groan of approval rumbles up my throat, my tongue gliding against hers as we fall into a rhythm as old as time itself. Back arching, Maddie rides the length of my cock, heat from her pussy scorching through my clothes.

I never want to let her go. Staying wrapped up in her arms like this all night seems necessary, despite the heaviness in my balls and the energy trembling through my body. I pull back, smoothing my palms down her face, checking in.

Her eyes are dilated with lust. But she looks fucking happy, smiling at me in a way that pierces my heart.

Nimble fingers fall to my belt, threading the leather through the buckle and tugging it free of the prong. Metal clinks, the zipper lowers slowly. The sound of the teeth unclipping has me on the precipice, like the anticipatory wait for the pop of a starter gun before a race.

"I want you. I've thought about this for so long," Maddie declares, her warm hand delving inside my boxers, wrapping around my cock and pulling me out.

Sucking in a breath, I reach for the buttons at the front of her dress. One by one, I unpick those tiny, fiddly buttons. I sense Maddie's impatience, but when it comes to undressing this woman tonight, I have all the time in the world. When I reach the very last button, I peel the material aside, revealing two pert, plump breasts.

"Kit," she begs, pulling me in for a kiss.

Reaching under her dress, I tug her panties down her body, Maddie lifting a knee, then another as she wriggles out of them. I slip the fabric from her shoulders until it pools by her knees, her hair tumbling about her bare shoulders.

I take a moment to admire her body, to reacquaint myself with her gorgeous curves.

"I called it," I murmur. "Total fucking ruination."

Her bra is pale pink, dusky rose nipples pointing through the sheer material. I run my thumbs over them in tandem, Maddie moaning *yes* and *more*. Quickly, I unsnap her bra and let it fall from her shoulders before tossing all her clothes aside.

In my palms, her breasts feel full. I pinch her peaked nipples before leaning in to flick my tongue over each one. Small encouragements urge me as I close my mouth around them, sucking hard, gorging myself. My cock pounds in her tight, steady grip, her pace slowing to run a thumb over the head and smear a bead of pre-cum.

Unable to wait any longer, with my hands on her hips I urge her to lift. Positioning me where she needs me, she slowly sinks all the way down to the base, flooding me in wet heat. Fully seated, Maddie throws her head back, her face slack with lust, her teeth biting into her lower lip in ecstasy. Then she refocuses, lifting my sweatshirt over my head before falling on my lips again.

Briefly, I consider the power dynamic. I'm her academic, reporting professor, as well as her class teacher. She's my favorite student over whom I have a filthy, unhealthy obsession. And while I will be a gentleman from time to time, cherishing her trust in me and enjoying all the tender moments, it will be hard to find restraint. To not turn feral. So yes, the sex will also be dirty. I'll feed her my cock and watch as she drinks down everything I give her, watch her take my dick like a good girl until she can't take any more.

Maddie lifts my shirt over my head, soft fingers trailing over my pecs and across my abs. Her expression changes when they scoot over a long scar, but she doesn't say anything as I wriggle out of my jeans, kicking them off my feet.

Upright, Maddie rocks into my body with fluid hips and feminine strength. I hold her tight, her tits flattened against my chest, her arms wrapped around my neck. The grinding pressure on my cock has my body heating, our lips locked in devouring kisses as I thrust my hips up, meeting every long, deep stroke.

Maddie falls first, her body stiffening as she crests the peak and tumbles down the other side. Her moans and sighs of pleasure have me at the edge, but I hold off, rolling us until Maddie's back hits the rug.

Bright eyes find mine, my cock still lodged inside her. With my knee, I push hers up and out, my dick comfortably deep. She looks as beautiful as I remember surging inside her, our bodies flush and her skin dewy. Faster, we rock together, heat gathering in my groin, my body desperate to be unleashed. Hands clutch me tightly, urging me on as the beauty of the moment gathers us up and triggers her release. Picking up the pace, I adjust my knees and fuck her harder. My balls tighten. The base of my cock burns. And Maddie is still coming, clawing at my cock, dragging me deeper into oblivion until I'm throbbing inside her tight walls and shuddering out an orgasm so strong and intense I think it'll be tattooed on my soul.

"Oh God," she mumbles. "That was—that was—" she smiles, eyes drowsy as our lips drag together. "We need to do that again."

She felt perfect. Better than at Club VX where the barriers of masks and blindfolds and strangers lingered between us that first time.

Pushing her hair from her rosy face, I check her over. No regret lingers in her eyes, so I kiss her mouth. "You felt like heaven."

Throwing a look to the balcony doors, she asks, "Do you think anyone can see us?"

"Unlikely." Aside from the occasional gleam of lights from

nearby buildings catching her face as she moved against me, the apartment is dark. "We can move to the bedroom."

"Here's good," she breathes, palming my face and studying me with vulnerable intensity.

"Okay?"

"Very okay," she laughs.

Rolling off her, I pull her against my chest.

Softly she asks, "Do you follow a faith?"

"Not really. I sometimes go to church at Christmas. You?"

"Same."

"Why do you ask?"

"Just a thought."

Idly, we chat about God and chivalry while I rub a thumb over her shoulder, Maddie tracing patterns on my torso, licking at my nipples and nibbling at my neck between discussions. Naturally, my body begins to stir. So I cup her face, kissing her until our thirst becomes too much. Until our craving consumes us.

Under the light of the city and the shrouded stars, I flip Maddie to her stomach, grip her hips and raise her ass. On my knees behind her, I tilt her to my waiting cock and impale her all over again, rutting into her like a crazed man, a feasting animal who's not eaten in a month and can finally have his fill.

With the rough pads of my fingers, I circle her clit, dancing over and over that tight little nub of nerves, Maddie's *Oh God, yes, right there* music to my ears. I thrust deep, hands gripping her hips as I let loose on her, finally able to sate this constant need. When she plummets to her desire, when I unload inside her, bareback for the second time, I grit out, "There's your again, Madrigal. Now let me hear you fucking sing."

I didn't know I could love a woman's voice as much as I do hers. Didn't know that the rich tones, the clear clarity of her cries and mewls and sobs of pleasure would make my cock swell to the point of pain. Would make me harder. Make me come harder than I've ever known. I am damned and doomed by this need to hear it. Live it, over and over.

Exhausted, she slumps to the rug as our breathing evens out. After sucking her taste from my fingers, I trace lines and circles along her back and ass, her muscles jumping.

"Maddie, are you on birth control?"

There's a gasp as she turns towards me. Her face journey jumps from shock to horror to concentration as she recaps the night. "I am. Yes, sorry, I totally forgot."

"It's okay."

I don't give any thought to STDs. We get tested at Club VX and there's been no one since.

Maddie bites at her bottom lip, the watermelon pink colour ingrained in my memory. I want that mouth on mine again, on my chest, my abs, my cock. I want it puffy and swollen, cum-stained. And if it begs for more, for me, my name sighed, whispered, and murmured, how could I deny her?

Reaching for a blanket, I lay it over our bodies as we stretch out on the floor. Across the balcony, we gaze up at the stars and let the night hold us captive.

"I want to tell you about Harrison."

Naturally, I want to hear everything.

"Got any liquor while I do?"

Pulling on my jeans to find what she needs, Maddie wanders to the guest bathroom with her underwear in one hand and the ends of the blanket held together in the other. When she returns, sitting on my couch with the blanket secured around her, there's a bottle of vodka from the freezer and a bottle of water waiting in exchange for her secrets.

I throw on my sweater and sit next to her, fixing our drinks.

She downs a shot, wincing slightly. "You'll get the full story.

A story Perrie doesn't entirely know. That no one really knows," she confirms sadly, as if burdened with the cold hard facts.

I accept her gift of trust with both hands and a full heart. "I will treat that knowledge with great respect, Maddie. You have my word."

She nods. And then she begins her tale, weaving in a shot of vodka or a slug of water throughout the next thirty minutes. She accepts my questions, my clarifications, but soon I learn Maddie's formative years were spent getting groomed by a sick fuck, a rapist, a man who mistreated her, abused her, and blamed her for all his faults and cretinous, depraved behavior.

I'm so angry, I'm trembling. The first shot chased away my curiosity and replaced it with one thought only—annihilation. And to think all I was focused on was the Chevalier agenda concerning the Devereaux family. I never imagined they suffered in any shape or form.

Maddie shouldn't be the one who hurts.

"I realize it wasn't a good relationship. He abused his position and gaslit me over everything."

Already gathered against my side, I hold her more tightly. "I'm so sorry."

"There's something else," Maddie begins. I try and focus on her face, her words, but I'm struggling with what that cockroach did to her. That she excused it by somehow *tolerating* it. All I can do is be grateful she's survived him. "The last thing you need to know about him and then I never want to discuss him again."

She's five vodkas in. I should probably cut her off but she's a grown-ass woman getting some heavy shit off her chest. Tonight, she gave Tait his marching orders and is fucking serious about it. It's everything I've been waiting to hear.

I nod, fortifying myself.

She looks up, drawing back a little to see my reaction. "I was married to him."

I can't look away from her, wondering if she's joking. *Married?* Searching her face for signs she's messing with me, all I see is worry. She's worried about my reaction and if I'm put off.

I'm not, but it explains her reluctance to entirely give up on him. And Christ, it's a blow, I'm not going to lie. I pull her back against me. "I wasn't expecting that but it changes nothing about you and me."

Maddie watches my reaction, then nods. "I was seventeen. It was my idea." She shakes her head, disappointed. "Such a ridiculous idea, but a few weeks later we got hitched and then we were on honeymoon."

Well, fuck. But at least she *was* married. And it doesn't matter because I still want her. "How long were you married for?"

"Less than four weeks. Luckily, thanks to Joséphine, my lawyer extraordinaire, I managed to avoid a divorce. Makes things simpler with regards to assets—not that I have any," she says, throwing a hand wide, vodka sloshing over the side of the glass. "No," she says, her demeanour reflective. "It was annulled, like it never happened. Which is good because that's how I want to view it. And it means I'm back to being a virgin. A wedding virgin."

Despite the serious subject, a laugh rumbles out of me.

Maddie throws back what remains of her shot and blows out a *Whoo!* "Just to be clear, I'm not commiserating but celebrating. It's taken me a long time to move on, but being here," she says, her eyes steadfast and clear, "with you. Meeting you has given me clarity."

The compliment surprises me, even though Maddie reaching her own conclusions has been a goal of mine for months. "Me?"

"Yup."

That's all she says, not elaborating one bit.

Confessions hover on the tip of my tongue, my conscience yearning for me to rid it of this disquiet and heavy guilt. Tonight would be a good time to get it all out there, but I don't want to diminish what she's shared today by hijacking this moment of honesty with my own.

She sighs contentedly, her head lolling on the cushions at her back, her face turned to mine. Despite her day, the booze, and her emotional struggles, she looks surprisingly lucid.

"After our kiss at the ball, it was a battle every time I saw you not to jump your bones," she murmurs.

I crack a smile. "Why didn't you?"

"I needed to be certain."

"And now you are." It's not a question. Outside the hospital it was, but not now.

A determined, genuine nod. "Very. Totally."

As if sharing her backstory has worn her out, Maddie leans into my side and throws an arm around my waist. The truth I should be offering up is not getting more than a half-second's thought. For weeks I've ached to hold her. And while I jump-started things by inviting her to the club, this is the only way we can have a proper relationship. I'm not ready to jeopardize that yet.

The fact that she was married, is my student, is the daughter of a family I dislike for countless reasons should warn me away. Yet here we are, holding each other like we've done it all our young lives.

A tiny sigh escapes as she softly exhales.

"Maddie," I murmur, not wanting to break this moment. "Are you staying or should I take you home?"

"Am hoooome," she murmurs, nuzzling into my neck.

My arms tighten around her, partly because getting close to Maddie will always be high on my agenda, but also because she's drooping, slipping down my shoulder.

"Don't fall asleep on me, will you?"

There's no answer, just deep, slow breaths.

"Maddie?"

Still no answer. Long lashes curve towards me, her cheek is squished into my upper chest, her face slightly upturned and—oh. Drool . . .

"Oh my God," I whisper to no one. "Drool aside, you're too beautiful."

Lifting her into my arms, I carry her bridal-style into my bedroom. I shove the bedding aside, then lay her down on the mattress. I regard the lingerie-clad beauty lying beside me. "I was hoping getting you into my bed was going to involve you being awake, Maddie." Making sure she's on her side, I drag the duvet over her body and adjust the pillow under her head. "Sweet dreams."

I watch her chest rise and lower for a full minute before I head back to the kitchen to see what I can rustle up for dinner. There's a chance she'll wake and I want to provide for her. Once I've got some options organized, I grab a bottle of water from the refrigerator and head back to check on her. When I enter the hallway off the kitchen, she's standing at my bedroom door in her bra and panties, the blanket held loosely in her hand. Her quiet, still presence startles me, but it's Maddie who says, "Holy crap."

"You fell asleep."

She nods, looking at her surroundings and then back at me with the most bewildered, confused expression. But it's quickly replaced with a breathtaking smile. "Sorry!"

"It's fine." I take a step towards her, wondering if she's woken with doubts or regret. The easier mood from earlier has slipped a little on the dial. There are jitters in the air, some hyper-sensitivity coming from somewhere. "I thought you were out for the night."

A huff of laughter. "That's never happened to me before."

"It's not a problem," I dismiss softly, something pressing down on us. "I can drive you home if you'd like," I offer, though I'd much prefer she stayed put. "I wasn't sure where you wanted or needed to be."

A blink. "O-okay."

She turns on the spot, disorientated, wondering where her clothes are. The lightness in her features has turned heavier, so I say, "I want you to stay."

She sways side to side before stopping. "I want to stay, too."

"Good. And while I'm a big fan of you standing in my apartment with next to no clothes on, let's find you something to wear."

Once she's dressed in some sweatpants and a t-shirt of mine, I offer, "Coffee? Hot chocolate? Bed?"

Her eyebrow quirks, and I'm about to suggest *bed* again when she says, "You have hot chocolate?"

Going by the expression on her face, it's a favorite. I'm not sure what possessed me to buy it in the grocery store, but I'll chalk it down to gut instinct. Gathering up her hand like it's perfectly normal for us, I lead her back into the kitchen.

"Your apartment is really nice. Immaculate. But then your office is spick and span."

"I like a tidy space."

"Tidy doesn't look like this," she rejects kindly.

In the grey-toned kitchen, I direct her to a stool at the island. "Don't fall asleep. I might not catch you if you slide off."

"Funny," she dismisses, her eyes dragging down my body. "Actually, I fall asleep where I'm comfortable, so, obviously, you have the nicest sweater."

When she was cuddling into me she said she was *home*. "Sure. It was the sweater. Are you hungry?"

"A little."

Having heated some risotto while she slept, I spoon a decent helping into two bowls and lay one in front of Maddie.

"Oh wow, thanks."

She digs in, clearly starving as I bring over our drinks. All the while Maddie peers at my furnishings, the art on my walls, the antique chest of drawers that I inherited from Gramps, even though he's still alive. She eyes the lamps and plants and books dotted around in small piles on side tables.

"Office?"

"I converted the second bedroom. Got a wall of books in there, too." Affording a home with two bedrooms is thanks to the generosity of the department. To the affluence of the college. In a weird way, it's thanks to Maddie and her family.

She chuckles. "Of course you did."

I shrug, playing with my food and dwelling on my worrying thoughts. "My predictability is nothing to be ashamed of."

"I love your predictability."

I analyze her answer, realizing that a dependable male has been missing from Maddie's life.

In companionable silence, we sip and eat. Maddie looks so lovely in this soft light I want to kiss her until the dawn comes screaming through the balcony windows. And yet something is there, between us. "Is everything ok?"

Her nod is too enthusiastic.

"What's up? Something's changed."

"Nothing's changed. Well, everything has changed," she corrects, "but it's nothing bad."

I deflate. Something's definitely off. Quickly, I rattle through my memories of the night, of our conversations. But apart from her waking up disorientated, nothing sticks out. I offer a noble compromise. "Perhaps you need some time to work out if this is what you really want. In light of your recent break-up."

Maddie groans, putting her head in her hands. She pins me

with her trademark look, one that's fearsome and tender all at once. "I know it might look like I only broke up with Harrison today, but we've been over for four years. Being honest with you, we've hooked up since, three times in total," she admits. "But not since I've been here. Last time was New Year's," she stresses. "Well, actually there was a brief kiss when college started but it was meaningless. Each time was due to weakness and my confused feelings. It was nostalgia, to some degree, an idea that we were an epic love that hadn't turned epic yet." She stops to reinforce her words. "I know for certain he's not in my future. It's a decision I've been working towards for some time and it's why I ended it. And besides, tonight, coming home with you, has confirmed *everything*. The grand love I've been waiting for is *right here*."

Her bravery renders me incapable of speech. I'm her grand love? Honesty shines from her eyes. I hear it in her voice. And as much as those words bring me comfort—she hasn't been with Tait for almost a year—I don't want any part of a love triangle. I don't share, and I will never share Maddie with another man.

But I must acknowledge her properly. "I'm your grand love?"

She winces. "You can pretend I didn't say that."

"Not gonna happen," I state emphatically. "I'm flattered, Maddie. That you're so sure about us . . . "

My voice sounds questioning and maybe I am asking for proof because Maddie blinks several times. Suddenly, she looks uncertain. I prepare myself for a shrug, or a half-assed *I just know*.

"Don't be weirded out," she begins softly which has my attention piqued. She takes a breath. Two. "I never dream. Or, I never really remember them. *Feel* them. But since meeting you, since coming here, I dream about you, every night. I dream like I've known you forever—in a past life."

Okay, I wasn't expecting that. That's sweet and a little freaky, to be honest. A teeny bit freaky, but in a good way. And dreaming about me can only be a good thing, right? But I'm also wondering if Maddie is dehydrated, or drunk…

"And I dream about you, and me, in a particular place. And I know it's you with me now. I see you in my memories. And I know it's you because there's a painting of the place in my dream on your bedroom wall."

21

MADDIE

Make You Mine - Madison Beer

Kit frowns, expressive eyes tracking across my face as he absorbs my words.

Waking up in a strange bed was a freaky moment. For a second, I was confused, wondering where I was. Then the memories came full and fast, setting me straight. I shoved the duvet aside and stood, my head a little woolly as I checked out my surroundings.

There was a large closet, another door that led to an en-suite. Plants and books and lamps and frames holding family photos. Everything had a place.

Walking to the photo frames, I picked one up, seeing Kit and a woman in jodhpurs atop two saddled horses. Thanks to the charity ball, I knew the woman was his sister. But the sight of Kit shirtless, in *just* black jodphurs—tight ones that showed off his physique—was a particular feast for the eyes.

Bare chested, he looked fit and happy.

So this is what he does as a sport? How fitting.

Replacing the frame, wishing I had my phone so that I could take a snap of it as a memento, I glanced around the room again. And then I saw it. The oil painting on the wall depicting the scene that had made me feel so warm and loved. It was the place from my dreams. It had to be. The distant slopes and hills looked remarkably similar in formation, the babbling brook in the foreground, and a hint of woodland to the side, were the same.

And then Kit's face came into view, hovering above me as we made love in the long grass in that very same scene.

Holy crap, I thought.

Mind reeling, I walked to the bedroom threshold. Kit appeared from the kitchen, stopping opposite me, a bottle of water in his hand as I just stared at him.

It was impossible to feel happier. To finally feel utterly at peace. This man *is* and *was* everything to me. Completely thrown by the revelations, I didn't know what to do with myself. How to act. I wanted to tell him everything but thought better of it. I would sound insane.

Fast forward twenty minutes and it was clear I had to convince him that I wanted him and only him, for real. So here we are in his bedroom, both of us staring at the painting.

"Where is this place, Kit?"

His hand rakes through his hair making it sexily dishevelled but his rough, sad voice focuses me. "It was in our family once. A long time ago. A farm. If we ever got it back, my mother, then my sister, had dreams of building stables there, of training horses for riders with physical disabilities."

My heart breaks. I think of his beautiful sister. Of her ambitions and how my mother helps how she can. Softly I ask,"Is it in Canada?"

"Yeah, close to the border. A place called Sherbrooke."

"What happened to it?"

Kit's expression fades, his tone resigned. "It was lost. A stupid, reckless disagreement years ago."

"I'm sorry. I didn't realize it caused sadness. It's a beautiful painting. I thought it was a place you know."

He walks to the console table and straightens the books until the edges have moved exactly one millimetre. Then he turns the orchid by forty-five degrees.

"My grandfather lives next door. It was ours, now it isn't."

Fuck. Me and my big mouth. I was so sure it represented something significant for me. For Kit. Feeling dreadful for bringing it up, I apologize again.

"It's not your fault," he says quietly, resolutely. "Don't feel bad for things outside of your control."

The words register and then I let them go. I know I'm not to blame for his family losing the farm, but I feel guilt for my questions about it.

Quietly, I approach him, cuddling into him from behind. Immediately, he responds, twisting until his arms enclose me. We stay like this for a long minute, Kit's gaze far off and fathomless.

When he takes a deep breath, when he releases me after a long squeeze, I whisper, "Where did you go?"

"I'm right here." He cups my face. "And so are you, Madrigal Devereaux." He kisses me softly. It lasts all of a second but it seemed to give so much in its brevity. "I'm sorry if I ever made you think I wouldn't put you first. I'll fight for you, Maddie. With you, for you, against you if needs be. I'll make this work."

More confusing words, but I brush them aside as his head bends, his lips finding mine for a drawn out moment. It shouldn't be possible to want him again, so soon. But then I remember that this is what couples do, staying up all night talking, loving, fucking.

Each slow exploration of his mouth has me building, yearning for more. His masculine scent surrounds me, his body heat recharging me like a battery. Strong hands sweep up my back and into my nape, guiding me, leading the kiss and where I should follow.

A palm comes to my hip, pressing me against his thick cock.

A low moan whispers from me. "Yes," I mumble, trying to convey where I want this to go. Again. Grinding against him, his breathing quickens, his hands roaming over my body.

I jump into his embrace, his hands securing my thighs around his waist. Turning, he pins me against the wall, right next to the painting. Slow hands glide up my ribcage, a banked fire smoldering in Kit's eyes. A thumb brushes over my peaked nipples, gusts of air leaving my lungs as those small, soft caresses turn me craven. It all feels too good and my eyes flutter closed, my body no longer my own but his. His to drive mad with every blistering touch. With every sip at my lips that has me chasing more.

"Kit," I demand.

"I know," he answers, his mouth moving against mine with more urgency now. He's still savoring, but his tongue licks against mine with slow, deep, sensual strokes, a ragged *Maddie* torn from his throat.

My hands roam his neck and scalp, lost to the intensity of his kiss. He reads my body and wants like he knows it. This, this is what I dream of. This incendiary heat, this obsessive need for Kit's body. For his cock.

A groan rumbles from his chest, his hands pulling me closer, kneading my flesh. Soft lips caress mine with such painstaking skill my legs tremble. He devours me, an unending hunger crawling along my blood. I feel hot like a sun, desire exploding out of me like destructive solar flares.

Breathless, he pulls us away from the wall, takes three long strides and throws me backwards onto the bed.

A yelp escapes.

"I want to taste you."

There's no chance to respond. Kit is on me, his gaze dark and restless as he climbs over me, peeling me out of his clothes and leaving me in my pink underwear. Dexterous lips trail kisses down my throat. Little bites have goosebumps prickling, his mouth teasing my breasts in turn and leaving me a horny mess. As he travels further down the bed, he peels back the elastic of my panties.

They're destroyed, wet through.

With unhurried movements he strips them down my legs, kissing the inside of my thighs as he peels them from me, his eyes finding mine for a long, heart-stopping second. He's too handsome. Too much to look at in his black sweater and jeans that show off gorgeous thigh muscles and impressive bulges.

"I don't want to go over the edge alone," I plead.

The warm, powerful tones of his voice have me ready to do anything he asks of me. "I'm eating this pussy, Maddie. Several times. And when I've had my fill, when you're an incoherent mess on the bed and crying out for me to stop, that's when you get my cock."

Chest heaving, desire pooling between my thighs, I lie back, watching him slowly peruse my body, debating where to begin. Deft fingertips trail patterns across my thighs and calves. Then Kit puts his hands on my knees and pushes them out wide, revealing me fully under the lights of his bedroom.

He looks and looks and looks his fill. "So this is what's hiding under those tennis skirts."

"Did you wonder?"

"All the fucking time."

"Did you want a taste too?"

Only now does he find my eyes, a sternness coating his voice. "You drove me wild, flashing these legs at me. At all the boys."

Callused fingertips skim down my legs, pressing them out further. Wider. I suck in a sharp breath at how exposed I am to his intent gaze.

"Yeah, I want to taste this."

Grabbing a fistful of his sweater, he pulls it over the back of his head and drops it the floor. Strong rounded shoulders cap a chunky bicep, his arms long and muscular. His chest is a marvel of muscle and strength, his abs and ribs sharply defined.

Eyes on me, he slides between my legs with predatory intent. Taking hold of my legs, he throws them over his shoulders and I wrap my thighs around his head. Kisses are planted on my inner thighs as he works his way higher and higher. Stubble scratches as he licks my clit, just once, that first touch sending bolts of pleasure through me. He returns to the same spot, licking, flicking his tongue over and over as my thigh muscles shudder. Parting me wider, he strokes me from back to front in a long, sensual slide.

His tongue is a tool of precise, expert pressure and rhythm. The slick, light pace has me building, every glide and stroke leaving me in a manic state of overwhelming pleasure. I'm not sure I can take much more as a thumb rubs tiny torturous circles over my clit, his tongue thrusting deep where it throbs and hurts, where I'm right on the cusp and desperate for release.

I cry out, my body clenching around his probing tongue as I spasm, Kit lapping from me as keening noises fill the room.

When I come down from the high, I sigh long and slow.

He nudges my clit with his nose. "That was one—say it."

I don't think he's messing around so I say, "One."

Soft licks and flickers of his tongue continue. I'm not sure I can go again so quickly but I watch him feast on me as two long fingers push inside, curling, rubbing against my G-spot.

He's too good. Too much. "I'm so, so hot for you right now."

Sinful eyes flick up to mine. "Hot for your professor?"

His arms curl under and around my legs, securing me exactly where he wants me—on his face. His tongue circles my clit in endless torture, and oh God, the sensations are mind-blowing, teasing me until my toes are pointing, my nipples straining into the air desperate for more of his touch. Moaning, I grind against his hungry mouth, his face buried in my sex as I seek all and any friction until I break apart again.

"Two," Kit says, his tone that warm, authoritative one I love so much.

"Two," I repeat.

Panting, feeling overly sensitive down there, I murmur, "He's gorgeous. Have you seen him?"

He chuckles, hot breath fluttering across my pussy before he blows across my heated flesh. "Gorgeous, huh? What do you want to do to your professor?"

"Everything."

"And what would you do for your professor?" he asks.

"Anything. But I can't go again, Kit. I don't have it in me."

"Let's see, shall we? Tell me to stop and I will."

For the third time, he works me with the flat of his tongue, his fingers pushed deep. Slowly, I build and climb, reaching the peak in a series of gasps, the winding, twisting pleasure wringing every breath from me until I drop off the ledge. As I judder, he pumps his fingers inside me as I writhe against the heel of his hand, wrenching every last drop of bliss.

"There, good girl, Maddie."

I exhale into the air above me, memories coming. "When you said you were rigorous, that paying close attention to the detail was important . . . "

Kit's warm laughter ties me up in knots, playing havoc with

my heart. "Yeah? Got something more complimentary to tell me now?"

I laugh, catching his eye. "So many good things. We're going to need a thesaurus."

Totally relaxed, I make grabby hands at him. He understands, climbing up against me and folding me into his chest.

He kisses me, his back soft and warm and, is that another scar?

"You did well." Kiss. "Sometimes, it will be like that." Another kiss as he kneads a breast, pinching the nipple. "Because I will need you. Often. And right now, you need to take more of me."

Shifting, tugging down his jeans, his stiff cock pushes against my entrance, sliding in to the hilt.

"And I know you can handle it. Handle me. All that training in the gym is going to pay off."

It feels rougher this time, my body swollen and tight. And he's back to dominating me, his fingers threaded through mine as he pins my hands to the bed above our heads and fucks me hard. I'm immobile, restrained by his body weight as he attacks my body and my mouth, his physical strength consuming.

Feeling out of it from so many orgasms, I weather his passion and hard thrusts, listening to his choked breaths that tell me he's close. But welcoming him into my body again ignites something deep. My body awakens, running alongside him as he drags his cock against every sensitive spot I own, pleasure ratcheting until I'm crying into his shoulder and shaking underneath him.

His body trembles, his cock jerking with the final pulses of his release. Letting go of my hands, I run them through his hair, the texture thick and soft. Thoughts tangle, mixing up memories of earlier with memories from my time with the Black Knight.

For a second I can't breathe. I blink away the fog, trying to separate the facts, the occasions, but I can't. Everything's a blur. Familiar.

Kit pulls out, the backs of his fingers brushing against my cheek affectionately. He kisses me hard, his tongue sweeping against mine briefly before he pulls back and regards me with erudite scrutiny.

"I'll never have enough of you."

He slumps to the bed, both of us breathing hard.

"Not sure I'm sorry about that."

Chuckling, he pulls me into his side, my breasts squished against his chest and ribs.

"I didn't like it when you told Dr Rosen that I was your friend."

It takes me a moment for my brain to catch up, remembering the consultant radiologist who assessed my ankle. "You said that, not me."

"Took you long enough to set her straight," he chides softly.

Ah, so it was a test. Reflecting on his words, on my actions, and mindful I said I never wanted to talk about Harrison again, I confirm, "You're worth fighting for."

"Good to know," he murmurs as I pull the duvet over our cooling bodies.

"You said your schedule was busy," I venture. "When are you away?"

I know he's around for some of my classes but not all, and each week is different.

"I'll be away until Wednesday morning. I'll miss our literature class that day, but Wednesday's *Chanson de geste* will take place. Then I'm away again until Monday afternoon. By the way, can we have our weekly meeting at 5PM?"

"What are all these meetings for?" I ask sleepily, unable to keep up.

"Discussions about foreign languages and education, some

in the US, some in Canada. They're international meetings." He nudges my nose with his. "Can you bunk off that Friday? Have you got any matches that weekend?"

"I'm sorry, is my academic professor suggesting I miss class to fuck my academic professor? Dr Hurren will be scandalized."

A large, confident hand smooths down my back and rests on my ass. "Maddie, I'm serious."

Right, *think* Maddie.

Trying to mentally calculate what weekend he's talking about while trying to remember what my tennis schedule looks like, has me staring off into the near distance. "I think it's a free weekend."

He looks far too pleased. "Dinner then—Thursday night. Spend a long weekend here."

It's hard to hide my excitement. That's at least three nights!

"Ok."

Kit gets up to use the bathroom. He comes back minty-breathed, so I decide to find my underwear and do the same, taking him up on his offer to use a spare toothbrush.

When I return, he's sitting up in bed. With the covers gathered at his waist I get the best view. "Tiddlywinks sure has honed your body into a weapon to woo women."

"Glad you're finally appreciating the merits of my sport."

I huff a laugh, but don't bring up the pulse-jumping image of him on the dresser. It might make him think of the farm he lost.

"Have you messaged Perrie?"

"Fuck. No."

Perrie's well aware that something's been brewing between Kit and I; we've spoken about it at length. When I locate my phone, I find to my horror that it's 12AM and she's texted me several times to ask if I was all right.

We share our location with each other but I write: *Sorry for being a crap friend. All good. Staying over at a friend's. Not Harrison. Lots to tell you.*

I litter the message with relevant emojis and hit *send.*

Done, I look towards Kit who regards me with a deep intensity. "Come to bed."

I clamber up beside him, deciding to lie on my back and stare at the ceiling; I'm not sure which way to turn or how much space to give him. Ideally, I'm a clinger.

Kit scoots down beside me, angled towards me. "I love these expressive brows," he murmurs, running a finger over one, then the other. "And these pretty eyes—I wanted them on me all the time." The honesty in his voice threatens to break me apart. "And as for this mouth . . . " Reflexively, I smile, his lips finding mine for a soft kiss. "I want this everywhere."

"I want it on you too," I point out.

"I'm saving some of you for another time."

"As long as it's soon."

"It will be." Kit urges me onto my left side. "I want to hold you."

An arm comes underneath my head, his forearm and hand resting precariously close to my boobs. His other arm is draped over my waist and then I'm tugged, backwards, into his chest, his groin, his heat. "Good?"

I nod, a huge smile on my face that he can't see. The night suddenly catches up with me and my eyes close, my body sinking into the mattress. Sleepily, I tell him, "For the record, if you're ever wondering what I want or need, just put me in this apartment, your arms, this bed."

Strong arms tighten around me, my body heavy and on the cusp of sleep. Right as I drift off I hear a whispered, "Oui, chérie."

22

KIT

Make You Mine - Billie Eilish

Sunday is always an alarm-free day if I can help it, but I've been wide awake for ages. Maddie is secured in my arms, her ankle hooked over mine. Her ass is cradled against my groin, causing my dick all kinds of maddening discomfort.

Not being truthful with her is hounding me, especially when she's been so gut-wrenchingly honest about Tait. As I lie here, incapable of comprehending the past twelve hours, I'm undecided how to broach telling her of my role at the club. Would a slow realization with dropped clues be better, or should I just lay it all out there in a grand reveal?

Fear of Maddie walking away is staying my hand.

After she called, I couldn't foresee that the evening would take us here, to my apartment and bed, though I hoped. But after *her* confessions, of which there were many, I'm certain of the following things: I'm in love with my student; she ended things with her coach before she saw the painting on my wall; I've featured in her dreams since our first meeting; she thinks we were lovers in a past life.

In the kitchen, before we moved back to my room to look at this painting that seems to hold a special place in her heart, she told me about these dreams. About the people in them. Her dreams are hard to make sense of, but that is the nature of dreams. Add to that her déjà vu, and calling me Tristan, I'm not sure what to believe. In the end, I have few options: dismiss her by saying she's simply fantasizing about me, her professor, or I make allowances for her creative, clever mind. Effectively, are these dreams some kind of memory, prediction, or wishful thinking?

My attention turns to Maddie when I notice a change in her breathing. Indiscernible sounds fall from her lips. There's a jolt, then another, violent enough to wake her. In my arms, she stiffens, her breathing fast and loud.

"Maddie?"

Her body bows forward, followed by a muffled cry.

"What's wrong?"

There's a sniffle. "I—you. My dream continued. Our story." Twisting, her amber-flecked eyes look imploringly into mine as if I can fix this. Tremulously, she reveals, "I have to marry a lord. I have to give you up and marry him. I'm wealthy. My parents are nobles too."

I tug her closer as she weeps and convulses against me as if this is all real. And then I remember that this is her *memory*. It's not just a bad dream, or a story. If I'm to believe her, this *happened* and she's just relived her reaction to it.

"It's okay, Maddie. I'm here, You're here. We're together."

A sniff. "He's your lord too. God, this is so weird," she says, trying to get a handle on her thoughts and emotions. "And you're his best swordsman. He wants you at his side, protecting me as we wed."

Brides were often taken and ransomed. The best knights, the most accomplished swordsmen, were always on hand to protect. The tradition has continued, grooms appointing a best man to this day.

Maddie's cheek rests against my bare chest, our breathing in sync. "Eleven days," she says. "That's how long we have until . . ." She blows out a breath. "We're worried he'll know I'm no maiden."

I detect a glimmer of a smile and it's like sunshine after a month of rain.

"I took your cherry?"

"Mm hmm."

I drop a kiss to her brow. "Was I considerate?"

She turns contemplative. "I don't know. I just know we're very compatible."

A dark chuckle looses, one born of wicked delight. "Do I fuck as well as I fight?"

Maddie appears to stop breathing. Eyes wide open, she stares at a fixed point in front of her. Is she considering how and when she last heard those words, by me, even though they were spoken in French?

While now might not be the most opportune moment to discover my secret, at least I wouldn't need to carry this burden any longer. Not wanting to be a coward, I vow to myself that when she's here for the long weekend, I'll reveal all.

Maddie nestles into my shoulder. We hold each other as her sniffles and trembles subside. As her memory slowly fades. "God, that felt rough."

"Thank God you're not an heiress to a dynasty, daughter of Canadian royalty who's of marrying age."

It's the first time we've broached this topic. And I'm only

stating facts, her life mirroring her former life in strange parallels.

Her voice is fearful. "Kit. That's not funny."

"But it's true."

"I decide who I marry, not my parents."

"Thank fuck for that. Though do better next time."

She peers up at me from her shoulder-pillow. "I plan on it."

I lean down to kiss her. An apology for my harsh comment. God, I hate her ex with a vengeance that eclipses all others. "Feeling better?"

A nod. "How long have you known about my family?"

I stall. "A while. And with my connection to the college, I'm aware of the Devereaux links."

"Did Pete Gallagher give me a spot because of them?"

I hate her question for what it might lead to, but at least I can be honest. "On paper you are exemplary, and I expect that's why you're so hardworking, unwilling to rest on your family name. Any college would want you on their program. I can't account for his motives other than you deserve to be here."

I anticipate the comment before it comes. "Any college except Brownlow."

Smoothing my hand down her waist and hip, I let time gather up her words and bury them in the past; feeding oxygen to that conversation isn't part of my strategy. Not yet.

"My dream felt so real. I don't want to leave just yet. Is that okay?"

Her honesty has my heart melting. I'm meant to drive to Montréal today. I have early meetings tomorrow and family to see. Parting from her today has spikes of anxiety blooming; I need her near so that I can watch over her. "Stay as long as you like."

"Just for another hour or two. I have essays to write," she says wryly, turning to press kisses into my chest, her tongue flicking over every intercostal and abdominal muscle. My cock kicks in desire, blood rushing, filling. "Getting lost in you will help me get over my dream."

Little liar, but she doesn't need to convince me. "I will accept all and any excuse," I admit, lifting her chin so that I can have her mouth.

The next hour dissolves away as we fuck, twice. The first time is slow and tender, her orgasms teased from her one by one. The second time is a claiming, Maddie on all fours as I take her hard and fast. As her final orgasm barrels out of her, I tell myself this kind of rough passion is the perfect reminder that we're alive and breathing. That nothing can harm us or separate us. In a blur of sensation we unspool together, my body roaring as I empty inside her. Collapsing to the mattress underneath her, Maddie takes every shuddering inch as she gasps into the sheet for air.

Wrapping myself around her, we wake a little later, both of us taking an unexpected nap. Then we gradually get ready for the day, Maddie padding about my apartment like she's lived alongside me for months already.

"What do you think? Shall I own the walk of shame and wear my heels and dress, or can I borrow your clothes?"

I'd rather she wear me instead, so I suggest she hangs onto the gray sweatpants and white t-shirt. When she spots a black hoodie she likes, she throws that on over her head and inhales, her nose stuffed in the fleecy material. "Your clothes smell good. Vetiver and mint and something like fire." Her brow crumples. "It reminds me of—"

She never tells me what it reminds her of, so I leave her to her thoughts and pack what I need for the next few days. Maddie sits on the edge of the bed. Often, her eyes drift to the painting of Sherbrooke, but mostly she watches me as if she can't believe I'm here. Or real.

As we drive back to her dorm, I marvel at how capable she proves herself to be. The Declaration of Emancipation is something I want to talk about, and the annulment of her teenage marriage. Growing up, it felt like I only knew hard times and heartbreak. But Maddie has lived too much for a twenty-two year-old.

"Your student record says you were offered a full scholarship to Jacq U." Maddie nods, making me ask the question. "Why'd you turn it down?"

"I wasn't certain I deserved it. I was worried Pete Gallagher offered it because he was friends with Dad."

"You deserved it," I state. "Why think otherwise?"

A shrug. "Brownlow rejected me. I wasn't that special."

Fuck. Me. Could I feel any worse?

"And your excuse for not accepting one at Princeton?" I push, curious.

"I had some assistance," she protests half-heartedly. "But I can't coast around on my parents' good fortune."

"What about your good brain?" I object. "Isn't that worth it?"

She peers up at me. "I was emancipated, Kit. I had to go it alone, and for me, taking a full scholarship felt like cheating."

"That's ridiculous, Maddie," I tell her, searching her face. "Why make it harder on yourself?"

"Not having anything keeps me honest. Hard working."

Suddenly, I understand. She's such a fucking fighter, rising to every challenge, knocking them down as each one rears up.

"Yeah, I get it," I say softly. She's self-reliant. Any other way, she'd be selling out.

"Does your car have a name?"

I give her a curious look. There's not a stitch of make up on her face. It's how she arrives to our Monday morning meeting every week, bare and beautiful. Often rosy-cheeked, her eyes are bright and alert and destructive in all the ways a woman's beauty is when all you want to do is look and admire and hope. "No."

"When you think about your car, does it have a gender?"

"What's this about?"

"Humor me."

I think on it for all of two seconds. "Probably a guy, because the car gets me out of trouble."

"Are you saying girls can't be helpful?"

"No, Maddie, I'm saying that girls get me *into* trouble, as is pretty fucking obvious right now. The car is my wing man." I glance across at her. "Do I pass the test?"

She nods, giving me nothing more. But then she murmurs, "I like the symmetry that a chevalier chose a Mustang to rescue damsels in."

Knights were called *chevalier* because they rode a horse—a *cheval.* "I really am predictable," I agree belatedly.

A few minutes later, we turn down her street. We stop a little past the main doors, away from prying eyes. The sidewalk is quiet.

"I guess we need to be careful."

Feeling downcast at the reality of our situation, I murmur agreement. The constraints of our fledgling relationship are frustrating, so I venture, "I'd rather we didn't have to be. Hiding you away like you're not important to me feels disingenuous. The biggest lie."

She studies me quietly, almost expectantly.

"I've tried not to pursue you at school, Maddie. What we have is real. I wanted this to be legit and—" *Fuck, romantic sounds sappy.* I take a breath. "This isn't some tawdry, time-wasting, power-hungry move to fuck your brains out because I get a kick out of manipulating my students. I'm not here to coerce you for my own sexual gratification."

Her eyes are soft. "I know. But detention with you sounds like an experience I need."

"Does it now," I ask, beyond intrigued and loving the need in her voice. Jesus, I couldn't want her any harder. "We'll explore your expectations, but what I'm asking is: would you object if I made the faculty aware?"

Keeping silent about our relationship just gives the impression that this *is* some tawdry affair. One built on secrets and lust and power dynamics. And while there are secrets, I don't want Maddie and me to be one of them. Claiming her as robustly as I can reassures not only me but her, too.

Understanding all those unvoiced thoughts, Maddie's eyes turn warm and glinting. "You don't want to take advantage."

"Oh, I will," I tell her, my voice deep with want and determination. "There will be times I will absolutely take full fucking advantage, but it's not where I wanted us to start."

Maddie's soft breaths fill my ears. "I'm in."

"Good. Good," I repeat, unable to express how happy I am. "But back to task," I direct. "What I was saying, is—"

"You'd risk your career for me."

When she puts it like that my brain tells me to reconsider. But I won't. I can't. And we both know it would be me that would lose everything if our relationship was revealed. Getting on top of the rumors is my priority, but mainly, Maddie is my priority.

"I'd risk everything for you." As is also pretty fucking obvious.

"Kit," she murmurs, awed. "If you're certain, then yes, let's make it official."

At her happy agreement, the restless dragon inside curls up and gets comfortable. And yes, official. I like that. "Yeah?"

"Yeah."

I link our hands together on the console. "Leave it with me."

She looks at me like she wants to say more. Do more than

just reach for the door handle and get out like the last sixteen hours haven't meant something monumental. Soon, we won't have to hide.

"Does this make you my boyfriend?"

Somehow, the term doesn't seem grand enough. But I chuckle, Maddie tightening her fingers around mine as she grins at me.

"I'll never break your heart, Maddie. Treat you callously. I give you my word that I'll be faithful and true and loyal as long as I live."

Laying out my heart at her feet takes me by surprise, but I'm not embarrassed by my proclamation.

"I know. I trust you."

"You do, huh?"

Cupping my face, she runs her fingers along my jaw. "I'm in. All the way. Completely invested. I've told you things most men would run away from and you're still here, somehow believing me."

Loving Maddie means loving everything about her, including this complex, crazy idea about past life regression. Of our past life and love. "I like the idea of knowing and loving you in a past life. Of having had that time together. And that I got your V card."

She shoves my shoulder, laughing.

"As your boyfriend, if you need help with anything, financially or otherwise, you can lean on me, right?"

"That's sweet but I'm all set."

"When you're ready to accept my help, let me know," I backtrack, aware I'm pushing hard and that she's an independent woman who doesn't need to be rescued—she's managing just fine on her own. "Can I have your cell?"

She passes me her phone, curious, but probably safe in the

knowledge that she can always undo whatever it is I'm about to do.

"I'm going to suffer hard the next two weeks, snatching just a few moments with you. I'm sending myself an invite to follow you. You can follow me too. It goes both ways."

Before my eyes, her face transforms from dubious to quiet understanding. A message pops up on her phone—one from *Dad*, asking her to call him.

I finish the phone admin, making sure she can follow me too and adding read receipts to my contact details. "This will help me know you're safe."

"I'll be fine."

"I'm sure. Any problems when I'm gone, call Josh."

"Um, I don't have his number."

"Right." I toggle to his name and forward his details on.

"Got it," she confirms, checking her messages.

I can see she's humoring me, but I'm grateful she's willing to.

"Have a safe trip. I'll keep an eye out for you."

"Same. Be good."

She laughs softly. "And if I'm not?"

I know she's joking, but I've seen the line of guys hoping to make it with her. "I hold all the cards in this relationship."

"Is that so?"

Despite my arrogant words and expression, she thinks I'm teasing, but I don't point out all the ways I plan on proving that I have the upper hand. But for reasons outside of those plans, I'm going to count down the days, hours, and fucking minutes until I see her again.

Side by side like this, I'm aware of her every breath. Of every tiny movement she makes. Soon, I'll be able to reach out for her whenever I want.

A breath whooshes out of her. "This feels like a dream. I can't believe we're doing this."

Earlier this year, as I shuffled through the doctorate applications to Brownlow, too focused on the past, there's no way I foresaw this. Us. Maddie has had a transformational impact on every aspect of my existence. I can't believe we're doing this either.

"For weeks, all I've been able to do is think about all the places and ways I wanted to touch you. I thought about all the discussions we'd have over texts; rating the passages we liked, or arguing over the interpretations. And before all of that, in between, and after, I thought about all the ways I wanted you in my arms, in my bed, wherever you'd fucking have me, quite frankly."

Maddie looses a tremulous breath. Her eyes dip to my mouth. "If you don't kiss me now I'll hate you forever."

"No, you won't."

"I will." Her adamant response has me smiling which pisses her off by the look on her face. "Kit! What about the noble sacrifice? What about keeping your lady happy?"

I swallow back laughter, telling myself she's not worked out that I'm the Black Knight. That is a whole world of trouble yet to be discussed. "Are you trying to shame me?"

"Will it work?"

"No. I want to take you on a date. Several. And we need to do the interview and see where the evening takes us."

"To bed, hopefully. Together, in case that wasn't clear."

I laugh at her thought process. She's fucking priceless. "Why do you think I want a long weekend with you?"

I want a solid seventy-two hours with Maddie. More. Snatches of time won't do. We have important things to discuss and pieces of time will make it feel like I've lost her, waiting for the next break in our schedules. We're both busy, but if she's willing to cut practice, maybe I have a chance to apologize.

"Sold," she agrees, looking at me with such clarity it's like a punch to the heart.

With a whispered *See you Wednesday*, she exits the car in my clothes, winking. It's then that I spot Erica, sitting in an Uber on the opposite side of the road, looking right at me, then Maddie, as she walks into her building.

After my meeting in Montréal, I drive out to Gramps' cabin just outside Sherbrooke and pull up on his dirt drive. Having checked in on Maddie's location far too many times today already, I tap into the app to see she's in her dorm.

Reassured, my eyes look beyond the windscreen, cataloging Gramps' place. As long as I can remember, he's lived here on his one acre plot. How he's stomached living next to the farm that was once ours never ceases to amaze me, but he was always more level-headed than my dad, his eldest son. Firstborn of three children, Dad died when I was twenty-seven, killed in a multi-vehicle pile up on a freeway thanks to a drunk driver. Only Gramps' middle child has survived, Dad's younger sister dying at the unforgivable age of just five.

The yard looks more run down with each passing year. The grass needs cutting and weeds plague the paths and drive. From the trunk, I grab the bags of groceries and walk up the four steps to his wraparound deck. I drop them by the door as Gramps emerges from inside, a thick parka coat on.

"How's that odd job man working out?" I ask, giving his fragile body a gentle squeeze. His strength wanes with each passing year.

White-haired and a little hunched with age, everyone in the family tells me I took after Gramps more than I did my own father. It's not so noticeable now, but my smile is the same. Grandma loved to tell me all he had to do was smile at the young ladies in town and they'd be putty in his hands. She could never quite believe that he loved her and her only, a faithful man all his life.

Dad wasn't so minded.

But more importantly, I have Gramps' temperament. His good qualities.

"I hope you didn't drive all the way out here just to give me a hard time."

I chuckle at the familiar joke, his voice thinner than I remember. "Who else will?"

Sadly, my extended family don't make it out here as much as we should. Aside from the one remaining uncle, it's basically me and my sister who visit. Gramps' other grandchildren don't bother, which makes me mad, but the plus point is that I have a good relationship with him and I can reliably say I'm his favorite.

Probably. Aside from Hélène.

Despite wrapping up in my coat, it feels cool as we survey the overgrown lawns, birds tweeting and cawing in the background.

"Seriously, Gramps. What happened to Ronnie?"

"He stopped coming."

"When? Why didn't you say anything?"

"You have a good job now, Kit. One that gives you more time to research. Don't worry about me."

I'll always worry about him. One day, I'm going to knock this eyesore to the ground and rebuild a new one because he sure as shit isn't keen on moving anywhere else. God knows why. But until I can afford to do that, a construction crew are due in ten days to remodel some of the worst of it. With a new kitchen, bathroom and full paint job inside, this place will look brand new—once the outside is tidied up.

"Well, with all the construction about to start, the yard will take a hit. I'll appoint a new Ronnie for when the work's done."

"Yeah, okay."

"I put some money in your account." It was only fourteen hundred dollars but it'll cover some ad hoc bills. "There's cash in the bag, too."

"Keep it for yourself. Save up for an impressive engagement ring. I haven't been to a wedding in too long."

"Listen here, old man," I tease. "None of that crazy talk."

Chuckling at how funny he is, he murmurs a *thank you* as I head indoors to make coffee, taking the groceries with me. Trying not to imagine Maddie walking down the aisle towards me as I wait by the altar consumes my thoughts for a dizzying minute.

Eventually, I become aware of Gramps putting away the groceries. Knowing I can improve his situation, even if it's with Devereaux money, money I have somehow earned, feels good.

When the coffee is ready, we sit outside on old chairs, the sun slowly emerging from behind a bank of cloud.

"I assume you want to talk about the Devereaux girl."

"Maddie," I tell him, disliking her being referenced that way. "She's a woman now."

"I meant no disrespect," he murmurs.

"I know. Nor did I," I say remorsefully.

"What does Hélène think?"

Last night was spent at my sister's house. I always stay with her if I have meetings up here. She wasn't surprised to learn of our relationship, sensing something between us at the ball. But like me, she couldn't find anything negative to say about Maddie, or her parents, other than the tales and feud our father spoke of. We both met Pippa and John Devereaux at the ball for the first time. They were kind and generous and I couldn't fault them. And Maddie—I don't know how I existed before she burst into my life.

"She was worried Maddie might report me to the college, but I trust her. Trust what we have. And anyway, I plan on telling college. And Hélène trusts me to know what I want for myself."

Gramps nods. "So—Maddie?"

Despite covering a lot of this on the phone with him a few days ago, I briefly recap everything I can about my initial meetings and interactions with her. About my feelings for her. Then I tell him about her dreams, and that I've featured in them. That she called me Tristan and complains of déjà vu.

"She's dreamt about Sherbrooke, Gramps. She dreams about me and her, down by the brook." I point west, where the brook lies, the hills rolling away into the distance. "The other night, she dreamt she had to marry a lord and give me up. We were lovers. In love."

Sharp eyes study me, Gramps looking more alert than I've seen him in ages.

"It's strange but loving her feels like there was never any choice in it. I can't explain it."

Gramps lets the silence wrap around us. He was always good like that. Dad pushed, drilling my sister and I until we were sore, our muscles cramping. Gramps gave me time to read and think and process.

"I hoped this day would come, when a Chevalier fell in love with a Devereaux."

I don't correct him because he's entirely right. I am hopelessly in love with Maddie. But why does the old man sound like this is such a profound, ordained event?

"Considering our history, it's a little fucked up."

"Considering our history, it's entirely plausible and long-awaited."

The only sound is the soft wind at my ears beckoning whatever secrets he holds closer. "Go on."

There's a head shake that speaks of regret. "Some folks, without feuds they've got nothing going on, nothing to feed their tired existence. I never had time for that. But Mom, your Granny Hettie, used to tell me a story. A year or so before she passed, she told me to commit it to memory. To write it down and pass it on. A tale, a fable, family lore—call it what you will, one to share with my children and grandchildren."

"What lore?"

He drains the last of his coffee and stands. "I have something for you." Heading indoors, his footsteps sound strong and purposeful. Hooked, I follow. He removes a thick cardboard tube from a sideboard and extends it towards me.

I take it. "What's in here?"

"Family tree. It's yours now."

I prise off the end of the 9 cm diameter tube and carefully remove the scroll of paper inside. Together we lay it out on the kitchen table, but it's unwieldy, coiled for so long all it wants to do is return to its natural state.

"This is fucking huge."

"As you know, we can trace our ancestors back to the Normans of the eleventh century, when your grandsires were knights in the noble courts. This copy of a master family tree which the Devereaux family keep, details an alliance that was denied at the time. A love between a knight and a lady."

Using coffee mugs, we pin the corners of the thick paper scroll to the table. It's not an ancient document, the writing legible in black biro. But it is made up of multiple *trees*, taped or stapled together. Names and dates that go back centuries run down the paper, which has to be nearly two metres in length.

"Here is where the line could be traced. To 1156." Gramps points to the top of the scroll. "Tristan Chevalier was a knight to

Lord Devereaux, whose wife, Iseult, was already a lady of high birth in the Norman French courts."

Gramps points to the name on the scroll. Nine hundred years of births and deaths lie in front of me, the names written in tiny block capitals. Gramps points out my direct family—uncles, siblings, parents—as I absorb as much information as I can. He retells a few tales I have vague recollection of from my youth, of family members in the preceding generations who were struck with tragedy: murder of a great grandparent; cardiac arrest that killed Mom before she made old bones; Dad killed in a tragic accident. And crucially, I discover that Tristan and Iseult died young, their love immortalized.

It's odd that the Chevalier line is listed when Tristan and Iseult were never married. Why would his line be adjacent to hers, running the length of the extended paper? Why not just focus on my family tree?

I ponder my name for a second. Tristan is derived from *triste*—sad—so it doesn't surprise me that this love was doomed, names put to paper to show how fucking unlucky we were.

The information weighs me down and I rub the back of my head. In some ways, my life has felt cursed for as long as I can remember. Is this why? I laugh bitterly. "To be a Chevalier is a double-edged sword."

"One you know how to wield. But there is more."

I look up into his old wise eyes as he pulls something from his pants pocket. It's gold in color, and as he lays it in my hand I realize it's a key. A heavy, solid gold key. Battered and scratched, the bow is a hollow oval shape, though it looks like a squashed heart. The shank is seven centimetres in length, ending in a small post and several knobbly bits and wards. Initials are etched above the point of the heart. *ADC.*

"There's an Auric Degas Chevalier in the tree," Gramps

explains, pointing to the name. "Could be him. It would date the key about six hundred years old."

I whistle, impressed. "What does this unlock?"

"We've never known, or we did and that knowledge got lost."

I turn it over in my hand and see the image of a horse and rider scratched into the bow. A knight.

The purpose of this key occupies my thoughts. I study the family tree, counting back roughly six hundred years, trying to determine what transpired and who was involved. By all accounts, as Gramps mumbles bits of information at me, this is the family lore he's referring to. This key will unlock a mystery, one we have never been able to fully understand.

"Have you heard of the Honor Society?"

"The Société d'Honneur," Gramps corrects. "Founded over two hundred years ago by a group of wealthy businessmen, I'd wager."

"Like the Devereaux?"

He nods, shrugging.

"For what purpose?"

Gramps shakes his head. "I don't know for sure." His eyes lift, pinning me. "Were you invited?"

With all that I've learnt, I should've expected the question. That whatever *this* is, that I'd be involved up to my neck in it as well. "Yes." I take a breath. "I was Black Knight."

Unsure whether he knows what that means, he offers me a proud smile. "Naturally. The years of lessons paid off. The scars too," he adds wryly.

I chuckle half-heartedly. Many of the scars earned were no more than an uncomfortable throb or sting, but several from ill-judged opponents wielding rapiers needed stitches and time.

The silence screams the question I know Gramps would never ask. He must be familiar with the inner workings of the club but he's too much of a gentleman.

"I only wanted to win once, when Maddie was the lady. As Iseult," I confess. "At my invitation."

"You won her in the *conroi*."

I nod. "Technically, at Ordo Victor." Gramps' jaw drops. "It was the only way I could see us moving forward. A complicated relationship has already been her curse. At the time, I wasn't sure she wanted another."

"And now she does?"

I nod. "We're not hiding it from the college."

"Good." A careful look my way. "But she doesn't know it was you."

My exhale is long and deep. "No."

Looking at him requires a brand of bravery I don't possess. "I *will* tell her. Soon." My honor demands it.

Affectionately, he pats my shoulder. "I know."

Gramps has always been the verdant, life-giving oasis on the horizon, his calm demeanor the cool waters I need to dislodge so much from my shoulders. But there are more uncomfortable points to discuss. "Dad was a member. I saw his name and pseudonym etched onto a board on the wall. He was a champion."

Gramps looks off into the distance. "He was an outstanding swordsman."

For a moment, the memory of him cuts so deeply, it takes my breath away. I miss the hard-hearted bastard, but for all his faults, I realize he was leading me to this point in my life. It's a shame he's not here to see me succeed, as professor, as a man, as Black Knight. It only makes me more determined to uncover what's going on here. To finally win this family quest and put it to rest for good.

"Were you part of the society?"

"I had met Dorothy. She was all I wanted. And picking up a sword again didn't interest me after Gilbert's death."

Gilbert was Gramps' father, making Hettie a widow. His

tragic death still haunts this family. It's another reason why the Devereaux name is anathema. I grip his shoulder and give it a squeeze of solidarity, letting our sorrow linger in a pocket of time.

I ask, "But you can fight?"

"Yes. All first born Chevalier males fight."

Unsurprised, I'm pleased my sister at least had the chance to learn as well. "Dad was Black Knight several times over the years. Years when he was married."

Sadly: "Yes, my boy, he was."

Dad's disloyalty comes as no surprise. And considering Tristan Chevalier had an affair with a married woman, a lady of the court, tells me his morals weren't exactly down the line either. Yet, Tristan's behavior is excusable. She was always meant to be his, and he hers. She was always his *first.*

I bounce the key in my palm, wondering how it all connects —because there must be a reason behind all this. Somehow, Maddie, me, an antique gold key, possibly so old it should be deemed treasure and kept in a museum, and then this family tree that presumably I have to add to with the names of my own children, are all interlinked.

I just need to solve how and why.

"Young men need purpose, Kit. Adventure not comfort. A cause designed of honorable endeavors, of responsibility, not complacency." He places an age-spotted hand over mine. "Just be careful, my boy, that whatever noble quest this key leads you to, it doesn't kill you too."

WHATEVER I DO or don't know about the next few days, weeks, and months about Maddie and I, I know that I want to see her tonight. Under the guise of a meeting to discuss her assignments, I send an email asking her to come to my office.

It's only when I make a gas stop halfway back to Boston that I see she's responded, able to meet me. It's the injection of adrenaline I need right now because everything else is just too hard to work out.

It's pitch black when I pull into the staff lot, my breath fogging the air. The faculty appears deserted, the hallways quiet. In my office, I lower the blinds and switch on a desk lamp. The overhead lights are too garish for the mood I want to set.

The knock at my office door has me shoving aside everything I've learnt over the past few days. In many respects, I'm none the wiser, so I reset to the day I dropped her off at her dorm.

"Come in."

Maddie enters with a tentative smile, no doubt wondering how we're going to charter the new territory we're in. I'll happily show her.

Expressive eyes dart from my empty desk to the corner armchair where I currently sit. Waiting for her. Seeing her again after the enforced separation, after that night in my apartment when I got to taste her again, is a relief I've never felt before. She looks the same, but better. And she looks better because I know she's mine, or as much mine as she'll let me.

Stepping further inside, the door shuts behind her.

"Professor," she greets.

Her appreciative gaze sets my blood pumping as she takes in my posture. My right forearm rests on the arm of the chair. My right leg is bent at ninety degrees, my foot flat to the floor, my left leg stretched out before me. My thighs tighten as her eyes fall over me, flicking to my chest, my groin, my face, and returning to my growing cock.

"You look comfortable."

Hardly. I'll be comfortable when she kneels between my spread thighs and my aching cock is stuffed in her mouth.

Setting the tone for the meeting right off the bat, I school my voice to one that's low and authoritative. "Madrigal. Thank you for meeting with me. Will you get the lock please so we're not disturbed?"

Turning for the door, I can see she flicks the switch as required, stopping anyone entering from the hallway. When she faces me again, there's a sly grin.

In my office, when I'm reclining in this chair with fantasies and lewd wants running through my head, she'll always be Madrigal. She'll quickly learn that I bought this armchair with her, and only her, in mind.

"Unfortunately, we need to discuss your recent assignments for Historical Linguistics 101. While you are an exceptionally talented student, your essays of a very high standard, the last two papers haven't been as polished."

Madrigal is an A+ student, except for this class where she hovers around the B+ mark.

The happy expression on her face slowly disappears. Shrugging out of her winter jacket to reveal a tight t-shirt with the words *coeur et âme* across the front, she tosses it towards the couch.

"Right, I got your email. As you know, this isn't my favorite class and I struggle with it."

I nod, watching her take a tentative step closer, her eyes falling over the relaxed frame of my body.

"How bad are they really?"

"Average," I admit softly. "But don't be downhearted; I can help," I offer. "You can earn extra credit."

"I'd like to avoid more assignments," she points out, completely missing *my* point. "I've no spare time."

"These assignments are non-negotiable if you plan on passing." I let her absorb that piece of information before reminding her, "As you know, I'm guest speaker at a conference in London soon. The department is funding a student's place. At the minute, you're slipping behind in the race for that spot, which I'd really like to offer you."

"Really? I'd love to go," she says breathlessly, looking so fucking earnest and naïve it almost has me re-thinking my goal for today.

"That's good to hear. Your friends and peers are prepared to go to *any length* to attend."

Her focus dips to my cock, straining against the zipper of my pants. "Any length?" she murmurs.

"Gemma offered me no end of sucking up."

Madrigal's eyebrow lifts. She's definitely bothered by this news.

"I trust you told her that wasn't necessary."

"Correct."

I know she's onboard and willing to play when she tugs an elastic hairband off her wrist and hastily ties her hair back. Fine tendrils escape and frame her features, her tongue darts out to wet her lips. Her voice curls. "And what can I do to ensure my assignments meet your expectations, Professor Chevalier?"

I love it when she uses my surname. As Lady Iseult, it made me so hard for her when she called me *knight,* unknowing she called me by my name.

She takes those final three steps towards my chair until she's standing right where I need her.

"I'm prepared to give extra credit if you can prove your knowledge of the topic via robust oral presentations over the coming weeks."

Madrigal squashes down her smile, but her eyes are depthless pools of fire and sin as she sinks to her knees and reaches for my belt. I'm so hard, my body desperate for her mouth, that it's difficult to remain still and let her come for me. Because while I'll happily invite her, in here she needs to be the one to make the move.

"What if my schedule can't meet your many demands, Professor?"

"I'm sure we'll find a way to make them fit."

Making quick work of my belt, Maddie opens up my fly and releases me from my boxers, my cock proud as a fucking missile.

A whisper of *Professor* is just audible before she wets her lips and rubs them together. Leaning forward, she licks me from root to crown. A tattered groan slices the air, her touch ripping my sanity apart. She repeats the action, the flat of her tongue gliding sensuously along my shaft.

"Eyes on me, beautiful."

They lock on, hazy with desire as she runs the pointed tip of her tongue along my shaft.

"Like that," I praise.

A palm rubs my thigh as her tongue works me harder, slicking up and down my cock. Then she burrows her face in my groin, swallowing me deep before dragging back up slowly and so goddamn tight, I might misfire.

"Fuck," I groan, running the backs of my fingers down her cheek and into the hollow she creates as she sucks.

The wet suction of her mouth has me tipping back my head in ecstasy, my eyes losing focus. Her mouth is extraordinary, her tongue lashing at the underside of my cock, along the prominent vein. She swirls it over the crown, any pre-cum licked away, swallowed into her belly. Little moans and hums from her throat vibrate through me, every sound and sensation sending me deeper into a pit of dark pleasure.

"Good girl. Just like that."

Madrigal is an eager lover, her mouth and tongue constantly moving, stoking the fire in my loins until I'm a restless, foaming beast. With an open throat, she sinks down onto my cock, every sensation tight and wet and impossibly warm. Every few seconds she takes a breath, her hand jacking my cock with a tight twisting action. In the end, my orgasm is too hard to fight off when she concentrates on the flared head, stroking stroking stroking with her tongue, her hand firm and fast on my shaft.

I crest that wave of release, a guttural sound torn from my chest. Maddie doesn't immediately pull away; she swallows every pulse and kick, her hands snaking over my abs as she laves my flesh and drinks down every drop.

Watching her slowly worship my dick has the primal part of me thrashing to be set free. I want to claim her, bent over my desk, marking her as mine. Tearing my eyes away from her is impossible, her ponytail swishing, her head moving restlessly in my lap as she finishes me.

When she releases my dick with a slow slide and a wet pop, I murmur, "Come here."

She rises and I lower, our mouths somehow meeting as I haul her up until she's stretched out against the entire length of my body.

"I've missed you," I tell her, ravishing her mouth despite the taste of me on her tongue.

"I've missed you too," she manages between harsh pants. "But this was worth the wait."

"That was." Kiss. "An incredible." Kiss. "Blow job," I praise.

Her breasts push into my chest and I'd love to take care of her too, but we can only ever snatch at snippets of time together here. My apartment is safer, but the added thrill of letting her suck me off in my study has been more than I imagined.

Ending the kiss, I press my forehead against hers as I breathe her in. "Have you had any more bad dreams?"

Memories?

"Just the same one."

"Okay." That's good, I think. I didn't want her remembering

her wedding night, married to a man who isn't me and who takes his due from her body. I hate that I can't protect her from her memories.

"I thought we were waiting until Wednesday."

Suggesting that was my fault, determined to be patient. "I'm readjusting my *mésure*. Risking everything because I'm in deep, Maddie." Wide eyes find mine. Unwilling to have a conversation about love right now, I tell her, "And you should go."

"What? Already?"

"This is to protect you. I'd rather flip your feet up to your ears and eat you out in this special chair, but that will have to wait. It's late," I stress. "Staff rarely meet students at this hour and HR are being obtuse."

"About us?"

I nod. "Nothing to worry about," I murmur. "But if you're willing, an email would help."

She presses a kiss to my mouth. "I'll do it tonight. And I'll courier a signed copy to the HR Director so they know I'm not messing around."

Her sense of righteousness, her fight, will always raise a smile to my lips. "Thank you," I say, tucking myself back in.

"Why ask to meet me here if we can't enjoy the moment?"

"Because I did need to speak to you about your assignments. And because I've been thinking about your lips wrapped around my dick for a long time."

This was the part of her I was saving. Now I've had her mouth, I'm going to be making up all sorts of reasons to have it again.

Reluctantly, she gets to her feet, a playful pout on her face while I straighten my clothes.

"What did Patrick Byrne have to say?"

The head of the department could assign her a different

professor, though it's unlikely; I'm the most qualified. "He'll give me a decision by the end of the week."

Momentarily, Maddie looks worried. So I gather her against me and breathe in her beautiful floral scent.

"It won't stop me," she asserts. "And seeing you tonight is better than waiting until class tomorrow."

I needed to see her too, for many reasons. Gramps' words have left me shaken, trying to understand many unfathomable things. And denying the attraction I have for Maddie is pointless. Everything I know is narrowing towards a moment of truth.

She presses another kiss to my mouth, readying to leave. "When can I expect the assignment, because I'm pretty sure sexual favors don't count?"

I'm glad Maddie understands that can't happen; it saves a difficult conversation. Besides, she'd never settle for anything less than excellence.

"Give me two evenings a week and I'll make sure your essays are worth an A plus."

"Okay," she beams my way. "Walk me out though? We had a legitimate reason to meet. The email confirms it."

It's why I sent it, so I nod. And then, because I can, because she's here and invested and just about all mine, I hold her, kissing her for a small eternity.

Breaking apart, I make sure I have everything before nodding to Maddie to unlock the door. I switch off my desk lamp. The only light entering my office is that from the hallway, or whatever light Dr Hurren doesn't block with her body as she stands at the threshold, her fist raised as she prepares to knock at a now open door.

23

MADDIE

Hot To Go - Chappel Roan

A bolt of horror flashes through me. "Hello, Dr. Hurren," I greet with what I hope is perfect pitch and poise.

Hiding a relationship with my coach honed my mis-direction skills and I try and look bored and upset due to my low grades. In many ways I am upset: Byrne might switch out my professor which I'm not in favor of. And HR are—admirably, rightly—being cautious.

However, if they threaten me, or take this man away from me, I'll threaten right back.

"Maddie, Professor Kit," she returns slightly surprised. Her eyes flick between us, trying to work out the situation. And when I realize her eyes find the windows, with the shutters curiously closed, a sting of unease darts though my veins. "I wasn't sure if anyone was in, it was so quiet."

"How can I help, Dr. Hurren?" Kit asks, and I take that as my cue to leave. Hanging around and involving myself just looks suspicious.

Calling out *Goodnight*, I head down the hallway as their voices fade. I descend the creaking wooden stairs and walk out of the main doors into light rain and a cold wind. I put my jacket on and pull the hood up over my head, hoping Delphine doesn't read anything into the late night meeting.

That was close!

In contrast to the cool temperature, my cheeks feel warm, my body running on adrenaline and lust. I can still taste him. Smell him. Feel him. He surrounds me, even when we're apart.

Students walk the lamp-lit paths across the quad, heading to or from the library and dining halls. Perrie messages me to say that tonight's theme is Spanish cuisine and I need to get there stat. That's when I see Evan walking on a nearby path. It feels like I haven't seen him for weeks.

Under the light of a lamppost our paths collide. "Hey, stranger," I greet, noticing a livid pink scar on the tip of his chin. "What happened to you?"

"Oh, this?" he asks, pointing to his chin. "Sliced it open."

"Huh. Frat party adventures, or fencing?"

He seems to evade my gaze when he answers, "A bread knife."

"How'd you manage that?"

"Was drunk. Usual tale of narrow escape of more serious injury."

I chuckle, wondering why it feels weird between us. According to Perrie he was interested in me after our chat at Midnight Blue, but any positive thoughts I had that night were fleeting. "Well, I'm meeting Perrie for dinner. You eaten yet?"

"No, but I could eat."

Although Professor Chevalier was a delicious hunk of man meat, I need proper sustenance. Reflexively, my eyes lift to the back corner of the faculty, to the second floor where Kit's office is situated. The lights are off. Maybe his conversation with Delphine is over.

Evan looks towards the same building. "What are you looking at?"

"Nothing much."

"That your professor's office?"

"Chevalier's?" I reply, feigning annoyance. "He just gave me another essay with an insane deadline and I'm not happy."

Quietly, Evan looks away, his mouth curling. "Heard he's a real tyrant."

I scrunch up my face, disliking the description. "He's no different to all my other professors. Or yours," I point out, knowing all students here have similar complaints.

The dining hall is packed, Evan and I getting lost and separated in a sea of hungry students. Thankfully, Perrie snags my arm and drags me towards the line for the paella. But my mind is stuck on Evan, his scar forcing me to consider coincidences. It might've been a blade that cut him, but it wasn't a bread knife.

Perrie knows *everything,* whispering, "How was your chat with the hot professor?"

My stomach somersaults with feminine awareness as I think about our meeting. I want to do that again, and soon. And while Perrie knows about the night I spent at his, about our conversations and that my relationship with Kit is no longer that of just student, I want to keep what happened tonight all to myself for a while longer.

"Not great. I'm failing linguistics."

"What?!"

"Well, I'm averaging a B plus and I need to do better if I want the London conference gig."

"What are you going to do?"

We shuffle forwards in the line and I whisper, "I'm getting some private tuition."

Her eyebrows hike. "For real?"

I nod, transmitting several things to her as our eyes latch: *This is different to the private tuition I had with Harrison, because Kit is different; I'm older and wiser and know what I'm doing; I don't have a choice—he's in my dreams, he's everywhere.*

"Okay. Just be careful," she agrees, grabbing my hand and clasping it between hers. "I know you've completely fallen for him, but stay frosty, as they say."

"Sure," I say chuckling.

"I'm so happy for you. Worried, but happy."

Perrie is protective of me. And while I've loved that side of her, her voice one of sense and logic, even she can tell, that with Kit, it's different.

"Sorry to spoil the good mood," she ventures, "but I've got bad news to dispel those love endorphins floating around your body right now."

"Nothing can ruin this cloud I'm on."

"The boiler's failed. There's no hot water or heating. But the good news is that the Estates team is at Parker House right now, trying to fix it."

The nights are cooling quickly. Already the news channels are predicting storms and bad weather systems this side of Thanksgiving. "Crap. Let's hope they get it back on by the time we've eaten."

With our plates loaded with a variety of Spanish dishes, the fragrant aromas making my mouth water, we squeeze onto a table with Dylan and Mimi who's getting regular heating updates from the Resident Assistant. All the while my mind stirs, wondering if I can text Kit and ask if Delphine confronted him. Knowing I'll have to wait is a chore.

When Kit asked if I objected to the college knowing about

our relationship, all I felt was a huge sense of relief. Hiding our relationship made me anxious, the fear of revisiting past mistakes leaving a bitter taste. I needed it all out in the open. Knowing Kit understands and wants the same as me, makes me feel incredibly valued and respected. But I hate that I only got to see him for fifteen minutes. That tomorrow we'll be constrained by our conflicting timetables and his off-campus meetings.

Distracted by the evening's events, dinner drags.

"Where's Zac?" Mimi asks Perrie.

"Not sure. He was hanging out with Giorgia in the library."

Mimi's eyes find mine, both of us flicking our gaze towards Perrie. The other week, I heard that Giorgia and Zac's timetables were identical and they spend a lot of time together.

"Everything good between you?" Mimi presses. I want to tell her to back off and mind her own business but I want to know, too. And while I would've asked Perrie in our dorm room, privately, I no longer have that option.

Under the table, I lay a comforting hand on Perrie's leg.

"Yeah," she professes, but her hand wrapping around mine tells me otherwise.

Thankfully, a text comes in alerting us that the heating is fixed and we head back to the dorms. In our room, Perrie confesses, "I'm thinking of calling time with Zac."

I nod. "Because of Giorgia?"

She shakes her head. "I've been avoiding him a little lately. I'm not sure I want to be with him anymore."

"Might be why he's spending more time with Giorgia."

A shrug. "Could be." She smiles pensively. "It's fine. I'm gonna have a shower and get into bed."

I wrap her up in a hug. "Okay. I've got an email to write."

I compose my response to the HR contact Kit gave me and hit send, letting them know in no uncertain terms that this is a consensual relationship, based on mutual love and respect.

Because even though Kit hasn't mentioned love to me, or vice versa, he's demonstrated ways in which he fiercely loves me. No man would jeopardize his career for anyone undeserving of their heart.

I think.

Despite the night's excitement, I'm tired, and when Perrie crawls into bed, I do the same. I'm eager to see if my dream evolves tonight; spending time with Kit seems to be a catalyst. Considering my early starts, which find me with a wave of melancholy, my favorite part of the day is bedtime.

Almost immediately I fall asleep, my mind opening to a new chapter in my dream-story.

A fire burns in a huge stone fireplace, though my skin, my body feels chilled. Large colourful tapestries, swords and shields and other weaponry hang from the gray stone walls of the Great Room. My hair is long and loose, my ornately detailed dress crimson in color.

Just then, Sir Tristan Chevalier enters the room, his black surcoat fluttering with each steadfast stride, the sound of his sword clinking at his hip. My breathing turns shallow. It's only been a day since I last saw him, had him, but the sight of him makes my heart soar. He makes my miserable existence as Marc's wife survivable.

He stops a few feet away and drops to a knee. "My lord. My lady."

My brave knight looks up at me intently when Marc commands, "Rise."

When Marc turns for his chair, Tristan smiles conspiratorially at me. How deeply I've missed him. He's in touching distance, but I must abide by the constraints of our situation. When he straightens, the golden key hanging from a strip of leather tied around his neck catches my eye.

"Chevalier," my husband greets as he sits.

They discuss unrest in a nearby village, plans for a small party of knights to ride out in the morning to restore peace. As always, Tristan will ride Virtue, his black stallion.

Soon, it's the early hours of the morning when the sky is pitch and the stars burn bright. On quiet feet, I steal from my chambers to those of my love, my faithful attendant, Lady Béatrice Floquet, checking the hallways are empty.

She's my accomplice, caught up in my grand love.

Tristan greets me just beyond the door to his rooms. Light from the full moon floods the private balcony but we stand in the shadows.

"Are you well?" he asks, assessing my expression before gathering me into his strong arms.

I nod into his shoulder. My marriage to Marc is young, three months old, but he doesn't mistreat me. He wants an heir, as expected, but I don't love him. Don't enjoy his visits to my bedchamber. But we don't discuss my duties as Marc's wife. I tolerate it because I must, and because Tristan cannot shield or protect me from this alliance my father made.

Tristan leads me to the bed, positioned by the balcony doors. Here, we talk softly as the sky spins above. In his arms, we find solace, our risky desire too strong to deny. Panting his name, I fly apart. And even though dread stalks me that night, fear of the coming morning and what awaits the man I love with all my heart a constant worry, I cannot leave him. Cannot stop this.

"Beauté," he husks in my ear as he falls, his hands tangled in my long hair.

All too soon, the first light of dawn limns the horizon. Reluctantly, I dress, Tristan's goodbye kiss a kind of life-giving destruction. Before I leave, he passes me the small, gold key around his neck.

"Keep this safe."

I look towards the small chest it opens. At the treasured possessions we keep in there. "When will you be back?"

"A week."

"Come back to me," I urge.

He kisses me hard on the mouth, his confirmation. Then he drops to a knee, and bows his head, "My lady."

When he looks up at me, his expression one of blistering loyalty, love, and undaunted devotion, it's hard to keep the tears at bay.

With a whispered "I love you," I rush from his suite of rooms and creep back to mine, hopeful both of us can find sleep before morning has fully broken.

WITH MY LIFE admin long overdue, I delete a bunch of emails, replying to Sophie Bouchard to decline her invitation to return to Club VX. As much as my experience was exceptional, Kit is the only man I'm interested in, one who embodies all the positive characteristics I was looking for but never expected to find.

Various European Opens and Masters have lured Harrison away from his coaching commitments, making my schedule a little easier. The move was unexpected, Sam pretending Coach Tait would be back soon.

I'm glad he took my advice, but I don't know how Robyn feels about his absence. Still, I hope I've done her a favor. Tennis was his life, and while I'm flattered by his willingness to give it up to try again, I realized that this great love I thought he and I were missing out on, that I was prepared to keep pursuing, hoping to find again, was actually not for him at all.

My heart sought a man I hadn't even met yet—in this century at least.

Eight days later, it's finally the long weekend, one that promises a blank match schedule, bunking off class, and a lot of sex with my professor if my work output matches his expectations.

Bring your books he messaged me this morning. *And the linguistics essay you owe me.*

Kit delivered on his promise and started tutoring me, either at his apartment, or via an online meeting around his appointments. We only got an hour together, but it was enough to go over some of the more intricate elements that I was missing from my essays.

He followed that message with: *And bring something to celebrate in. I'll book us a table for Saturday night.*

HR caved. As did Patrick Byrne. My work will be moderated by Kit's colleagues but it's a small price to pay. Neither of us has anything to hide. When I travel to London it will be with my head held high and my grades even higher.

But there is one thought hounding me. Counting the days, I think it's eleven since my dream-memory, the one I had after I woke up in his bed, knowing I—as Iseult—had to marry a lord and be irrevocably torn away from Tristan.

Knowing that dwelling on these things does me no good, I glance at my packed bags stashed next to the door and text Kit that I'm ready. That's when Perrie returns from the library, announcing as she walks through the door, "I've broken up with Zac."

Despite knowing this was imminent, my stomach sinks. "For real?"

"Yup. It's no biggie. It was coming."

I pull her in for a hug, squeezing her tight. As much as I'd rather not delay my time with Kit, I murmur, "I'm sorry. Shall we get a takeout? We can watch a movie."

She pulls back, her face stern. "There's no way you're staying here with me when you've got a hot weekend planned. As I said, it's no biggie. I'm fine with it," she stresses. "Seriously."

"You sure?"

"One hundred percent." She kisses me on the cheek. "I won't miss your early alarms, and having the room to myself will be kinda nice, so go!"

We pull apart, Perrie flopping to my bed and stealing one of my cashmere-soft blankets, wrapping it around her.

"How'd he take it?"

"He told me *Actually, I was thinking the same*. Bearing in mind how often he hangs out with Giorgia, it's possible."

"That sucks, but at least you can walk away guilt-free."

"Right. He's already forgotten!" she trills.

Her demeanor is one of quiet contentment, and I think she's going to be okay. Which is good because while I want to be a good friend, I'd much rather be a good girl for my professor.

"Kit's on his way," I say, checking my cell before joining her on my bed. "What are you going to do with yourself all weekend long?"

"Watch any film with good eye candy."

"I'm definitely staying."

She laughs but I'm genuinely a little sad not to be here for her.

A sharp rap at the door has me calling out, "It's open!"

Expecting to see any number of the girls from Parker House entering, I'm pretty shocked to see Kit walk in like he owns the place.

My stomach tumbles in that nervous, girlie way it always seems to when he's near. He just looks too good.

"You're already here!" I exclaim, my mind unable to think of anything except, Oh My God, My Professor Is In My Bedroom! I haven't seen him since yesterday's class but he still takes my breath away.

"I was waiting in the lot."

He was? My heart melts.

He steps forwards, the door swinging closed behind him as he regards us both on the bed. "Hello, Perrie."

She can't hide her amusement. "Hi, Professor Kit."

Intelligent eyes swivel between the two single beds either side of the room. "Which one is yours?" he asks.

Perrie clears her throat. "Uh, do I need to leave?"

"No!" I all but shout, turning to look at Kit to make sure *that's* not why he asked. Surely, he's just curious.

He shakes his head, a rueful smile on his face that has me sharing a grin with Perrie.

"Guess," I demand, his eyes crawling over the wall art, neon hearts, and desks looking for clues.

Perrie's taste is different to mine. I prefer a floral, vintage decor compared to her modern, bold interiors. And the posters on my side of the room are all black and white, previous favorites of sophisticated couples kissing in Paris, or of tennis balls stuffed under panties elastic.

So even though Perrie looks super cozy on my bed, Kit sees all of those clues and points right at my bed. "This one."

"That was too easy," Perrie remarks with resignation.

"Yeah," I agree to Kit's warm laughter.

He nods to the bags stacked by the door. "I'll take these. Come when you're ready."

I'm ready, so I hug Perrie goodbye as Kit calls out a goodbye of his own and heads out. A few moments later, I've caught him up and we walk outside to the small lot over the road and load up the trunk of his car. We can't stop looking at each other, grinning like idiots because this casualness is something I thought I'd never experience. Instead of hiding, we can act openly and it's a joyous feeling.

Back at his apartment, at his insistence, I hang my clothes in his closet as he cooks. Over dinner we talk non-stop about his trips and meetings, about what I'm learning in my other classes and the events of my latest dream.

"We were desperately in love," I announce. "It's so strange."

"Strange because it's the exact parallel of now?"

Talking about love is easy with Kit. We discuss the concept in just about every class. Every essay. I'm surrounded by it. And while our relationship is in its infancy—in this decade—I know

Kit's soul, learning and relearning it all over again, lesson by lesson, week by week.

So I nod. "Yes. It's exactly how greatly I love you now."

Swallowing, he reaches for my hands across the table. "Honestly, at times I'm worried you're only into me because of us knowing each other in a past life." His easy acceptance of my dream memories lifts my spirits. At times, I've felt like I'm falling apart at the seams, but he gathers me up and fits me back together. "But that's not why I'm in love with you."

My heart thunders and roars. A smile creeps over my face until I think it will split apart. Gently, his fingers which are still wrapped around mine, squeeze. I squeeze back, giddy. Dizzy.

"I love you, Maddie. You know that, right?"

"Loving you in any life is easy, Kit. I know who the man sitting opposite me is; he's loyal and honest and has the strength of his convictions." He blinks, briefly looking down at our interlaced fingers before capturing me in his intense gaze. "You make me feel strong."

Harrison made me feel weak.

Kit's voice is sincere. "I've never had a relationship with a student before, or one with an age gap like ours. I never expected to feel this way about you, to have this with you. To feel anything close to this in *any* lifetime."

"We get it twice," I assure him.

Scrubbing a hand through his hair, he smiles with incredulity. "Yeah, we do." Lifting a hand towards me, I'm immediately on my feet and moving to him as he murmurs, "Come here."

We hold each other for long seconds, my ass in his lap as time ticks on. Eventually, we tidy up and retire to the couch, Kit ready to crack on with my intellectual advancement. And it's necessary, the announcement of who's joining him for the conference due next week.

The idea of London, of England in November all decked out for Christmas, has me unimaginably happy. So, nervous, I hand over the essay he's been waiting for. I try and read a few pages of my book but my eyes can't focus. My brain won't settle. And when I remember that in my latest dream Tristan called Iseult, *beauté,* just like the Black Knight called me, my heart stutters.

What does that mean?

Kit turns to the second sheet of paper, drinking in my words and distracting me from my thoughts. Finished, he returns to the first sheet, his eyes flashing across the paper. Tucking the second page behind the first, Kit places them carefully on the seat cushion and looks across at me.

"That's a very good essay," he rumbles, his glimmering eyes settling on mine. "I'm very pleased, Madrigal. *Very* pleased," he stresses, cupping my cheek and bringing my mouth to his. He kisses me once, twice, each kiss distinct and ardent and thorough. "Do you know what good girls get from their professor?"

And *good Lord*, the way his voice deepened on that question has my core liquefying. "Kissed?" I croak, my throat dry.

Huffed laughter brushes against my tingling lips. "Good girls get my cock."

Oh Jesus. I can't even . . .

He drops to his knees, right before me. Grabbing underneath my knees, he tugs my ass to the edge of the cushions, spreading my legs either side of his hips.

"But smart girls get my mouth first, and I can't wait to eat this pussy again."

Somehow, I'm out of my loose-fitting jeans in record time, my panties following. With my heels digging into his broad shoulders, Kit feasts on my clit and core until I haven't a coherent thought in my head. I lose count of the number of times he brings me to climax, his fingers rubbing inside me, those calluses working their fucking magic. And his tongue is a constant menace, dragging through my sex, licking at me as he drives those fingers deep inside over and over until I split apart again. His double bass voice declaring me his *clever, clever girl* as I flood his tongue, everything hyper sensitive down there, is my complete and utter undoing.

There's no time to catch my breath as he rips the t-shirt I'm still wearing over my head and slots his cock home, pushing all the way in with a long, solid flex of his hips.

"Very pleased," he murmurs onto my lips, rotating his hips until he hits my cervix. My insides must be so swollen because he feels thicker and longer than ever.

In just my bra, I'm maneuvered until I'm flat to the couch cushions, my hair fanning out around my shoulders. Kit's slacks and briefs are long gone, his shirt too. Wrapping my feet around his lower back, I clutch him against me as he fucks me fast, the leather cushions squeaking with every thrust. A hand grabs my left knee, pushing it higher, pressing it into the seat and opening me up wider. It brings us even closer, his demands of me rough and hard and so fucking good, I know I'm going to suffer for it.

"You make me so proud," he purrs in my ear, his hot breath causing goosebumps to rise across my skin. And I know this is a real moment amongst the dirty little fantasy we've got going on here. I know this is a truth, and that I am at the center of his existence, just as he is at the very heart of mine.

"Kit," I answer, unable to convey more than one word as he fucks every drop of oxygen from my lungs.

It doesn't feel possible to be happier. More empowered. To know I loved this man in another lifetime and that I've found him again. The solid beat of his heart kicks against my sternum and I feel a whip-fast sense of loss, that one day this heart won't be so steady or strong or beating at all.

My lungs collapse but I fight that terrifying doubt. Clutching at his skin, those raised scars I'm aware of on his back focus me, bringing me back to the moment. With jagged, rough strokes, Kit and I unravel together, my body combusting as I break apart and bring him with me.

Deep masculine groans of pleasure mingle with the soft, escalating cries of mine. I convulse around his thickening cock as he feathers out the last strains of my release. Into the confines of my neck and shoulder he murmurs, "Beauté, chante pour moi."

Beauty, sing for me.

Beauty—don't go far; I want you again.

Do I fuck as well as I fight?

The words, the memories following, clang through me.

Kit and I have never spoken French; we study the medieval texts in Old French, often referencing relevant sentences by line number. But I know this voice, this accent. Intimately. It ricochets through me like a bullet.

And I know the calluses and scars, the potent strength of this body that knows mine so thoroughly. That knew mine dressed as a victorious knight as I bared my soul and body to him.

Ice floods my skin.

Pushing at his shoulders, I demand, "Get off me."

No longer slumping against me, Kit pulls away, his still heavy cock dragging from my body.

"Maddie."

Scrambling to the side, I find my panties on the floor and pull them on. It hurts to look at him, to face what I know to be true. Where does this leave us?

Kit's face is solemn so I know I'm not imagining this. Wrapping my name in regret and fear was his one-word confession and the look of guilt that follows is a sledgehammer to my heart. I stare at him, unable to comprehend, trying to align everything in my head as I determine what's a dream or déjà vu or reality.

"Let me get dressed. Then I'll tell you everything."

24

KIT

Waiting All Night - Rudimental ft. Ella Eyre

I knew it would be while I was buried inside Maddie, speaking a shared language that would be either the ruination of us, or the chance to assuage myself of the colossal guilt I've been carrying.

There's a lot to go through. But above all, I wish I had her memories. I wish I can remember loving her in our past life, showing my devotion. Over dinner she described to me in minute detail her latest dream. When she revealed a detail about a gold key at my neck I almost confessed everything there and then.

I'm the only one who knew we'd fucked in this life too. That it was perfect and crazy and cemented my obsession with her. What, if anything, did she feel for Ronin, the Black Knight? My enquiries tell me that Maddie rejected an invitation to return to the club. Did the Black Knight not mean anything to her? Was she not won over with his sword, skill, or passion?

Plucking her t-shirt from the floor, Maddie shoves it over her head, leaving her jeans on the floor. Her eyes are wary, her scent of delicate meadow flowers still lingering on my skin as I redo my belt.

Worries that she'll walk away when she learns what happened between us has stayed my tongue until now, but I hoped memories of our night together might be an easier route. Memories are a path she favors.

Arms crossed, Maddie waits until my belt is secure before she demands, "Speak."

Causing this reaction, this fear, worry, and sense of betrayal feels catastrophic. "I'm sorry I lied to you." Because lying by omission is still lying.

"So, it's not horse riding but fencing—fighting—that keeps you so strong," she remarks, her eyes flitting from my feet to my face. "That stresses your knee. That gives you scars and calluses."

Concern for my joints and injuries is not the starting point I expected for this unveiling. "I learnt as a boy. It was all I knew for a long time."

Her arms drop to her sides, but then she shivers, not from cold but because she's terrified. Knowing I'm the cause of her acute discomfort makes me feel like shit. Watching her struggle with the cataclysmic knowledge of who I am to her and what I did, hurts more than I could've imagined.

"Why?"

"Because," is the only answer I've got. "Because I was falling for you. Because I needed you to know that love can be better than your experiences of it. That men can be worthy of earning your love." She scoffs, but I carry on. "Because you're a melody, matching an internal rhythm that feels like it's finally woken, wanting to play right alongside you."

She stops staring daggers at me and frowns instead.

"Because I wanted to love you, even for a moment, fearing that is all I'd ever get from a woman as invincible yet as damaged as you."

"Damaged?" She blows out a breath. "Fuck you."

"Through no fault of your own, Maddie. You've been made to believe you were never enough, and yet you are. You're more than I deserve."

"You fooled me."

"Not to purposefully hurt you."

She strides to the other side of the room, pacing around erratically. "In fact, you fooled me several times, taking me to *that* floor, *that* bed!" she shouts, pointing towards the balcony and then in the direction of my bedroom, "while I was still none the wiser about your identity. So much for honor."

I hang my head because I have no good answer for my actions. "What would you have done if I'd removed my mask as I bowed at your feet?"

Her pacing slows. "I don't know. I didn't get the chance to find out."

"I feared you'd reject me," I say quietly, because it was a valid worry. "That I'd embarrass you. Anonymity is intended to make it easier." Maddie blinks several times. "At this stage you'd called me a coward, a liar, and made it clear I was no hero of yours."

A look of horror crosses her face before she wipes it away. "I wasn't certain of your character at first. You busted my ass! So I might've pushed, wondering how you'd respond."

"How did I respond?"

Her gaze drops. "You were—" A sigh. "You were charismatic and smart and fun and dependable. You became everything I ever wanted."

Allowing myself a moment, I marinade in her softly spoken compliments, her endorsements, but I push back, letting her know why I continued to hide the details from her. "At the ball, after our kiss, you walked away. I thought you didn't reciprocate my feelings."

"My feelings for you were vast. Frightening. I didn't want to make the same mistakes." She takes a deep breath. "I explained why it couldn't go any further. That I wanted to but couldn't. I —" she laughs sadly. "I wanted to go to the club and experience a night that felt important to me for reasons I couldn't comprehend. From that night on, many things started to make sense."

"Did *I* make sense?"

"As *who?*"

The word hits like a truck at 70mph. "As Kit or as Black Knight."

Sadness flashes in her steely gaze, the tension in her muscles loosening. "Yes, Kit. Of course, you did." She hesitates. "As Black Knight you were exactly what I needed. You reinforced everything I knew I deserved in real life."

I fought for her, shaping myself into someone she needed. And while I'm certain I was always that person, waiting for Maddie to walk into my life, to look hard enough in my direction and away from the temptation of an old, quiet flame burning in the background, I need her validation. I need to know that I'm enough.

I'll always be a Chevalier and she, a Devereaux. And despite the power dynamics of our professor-student relationship, outside of her doctorate, I didn't know how things would evolve for us. It's clear she's never been informed of the strife between our families. Aside from rightly calling me out for my behavior, not once has she made me feel inferior. Less.

"And as Kit?" I ask, the question hard to form.

Her back straightens. She opens her mouth to respond before closing it again. "The Black Knight was unattainable. After that night he could only be a figment of my imagination.

You existed in reality. You demonstrated that a man like him existed in real life. You played me, tricked me into wanting you."

"There was no trick."

"Feels like one," she insists.

My hands rake through my hair. "Fuck," I grind out, furious at myself, trying to work this through. "You wanted me before you met him. Sounds like a convenient lie to me."

"There's nothing convenient about this."

"You wanted me before you met him," I repeat. "*Deny it.*"

"I can't deny it," she responds irritatedly. "And you nominated me. You wanted me there."

"Yes."

"Why?"

"For reasons I've already explained. So many reasons," I begin. "Taking a doctorate in medieval literature is pretty niche, Maddie. In its simplest terms I thought you'd get a kick out of the experience. Within a few days of meeting you I was desperate to learn your take on things, your essays baring your soul in a way that had me demanding more and more from you. My feelings for you grew, and as I slowly discovered that your ex was a piece of shit who didn't deserve you, I knew I wanted to show you how a man should treat you: with respect, devotion, with patience, standing at your side as you flourish. And I wanted to have one moment with you, just in case I was never enough, just in case I was undeserving despite all the ways I'd shown you how much I wanted you. When our paths crossed at the ball I thought that was our time, and while I understood that you needed space to work out what you wanted, you still walked away. I respected that decision but it wasn't going to stop me from pursuing you any way I could. As a finalist in the *conroi*, I didn't know I would win. I expected that I could, though."

That fucking delectable brow rises in challenge. "You are an incredible swordsman. You annihilated Evan. Don't play innocent."

"How did you guess it was Evan?"

"He's been weird with me, asking questions about you. And he has a gash on his chin from your sword."

Agitated, she fluffs her hair away from her neck. She dressed so quickly some of it was still tucked down the back of her t-shirt.

When she walks away, I command, "Don't go. We need to talk about this."

A cushion flies for my face. "You could've died!"

Hesitating, it allows me to absorb the worry in her voice. The terror. "But I didn't," I soothe, dropping the caught cushion to the floor.

"You could've! If Evan had miscalculated," she accuses, her voice trembling. Turning, her face in her hands and agony in her voice she says, "Thank God you didn't. And thank fuck you beat him."

"You didn't want him as an option?"

"No." Taking a long breath, she explains, "I'm getting a sweater," before walking away.

I follow her into the closet and sit on the bed as she throws on my black hoodie she commandeered a couple of weeks ago. Not that I care; I take it as a good sign.

She sits on the bed and stares at the painting of Sherbrooke.

"I know exactly what you're thinking," I begin. "That I was selfish. That I taught you for weeks, all the while knowing that I had explicit, intimate knowledge of how to make you come, and at how beautiful you look when you do. That I know how you cried out my name as I kissed you, worshipping your body with my mouth and tongue and cock. That you know the sounds I make when I come inside you. At how hard you make me, how desperate I was to have you again and again before the night was over."

"You're twisting this to your benefit."

Dropping to my knees before her, I look up into eyes that have the power to destroy me or breathe life back into me. "I knew for weeks how stunning you looked as Iseult. That you bought into the ideals of a courtly love, rewarding a man for his skill and honor."

"Kit—"

Slowly, I place my hands just above her knees, sensing those still present trembles. "That I want to hold you in my arms for an eternity. That I want to worship at the altar of your body as strongly as any knight did for his sworn love, because you are mine, Maddie, and I am yours." I take a breath. "I've been waiting a lifetime for you, as you have for me. Without knowing it, we were lovers in a past life and the universe has brought us back together. There is nothing I won't do for you. I'll fight for you, die for you—in this life or the next. I'll always put you first. I've found you and I won't stop until you're entirely mine."

Out of breath, all I can do is stare at Maddie as my chest heaves. Her breathing is fast, but she's not shouting at me. Instead, she looks conflicted, lost to her thoughts.

"Deny our destiny," I challenge again. "But you know you can't."

Tears drip down her face and she hurriedly wipes them away. "I can't deny it," she whispers. "It's what I've been telling you for weeks."

I reach for her hand and she lets me hold it, so I scoot a little closer. The small gesture makes me feel victorious but I give Maddie a chance to consolidate her thoughts.

"It would be a lie to say I didn't . . . picture you when I was with the Black Knight. He reminded me of you in many ways." She sniffles. "Your voice—I knew it but wasn't certain. Didn't dare dwell on if it could be you and what that would mean." She swipes at her nose. "You gave me something that night. Remade me." She looks into my eyes, and my heart gives out at the grief I've created. At the fear and mistrust that's replaced the love and joy. "It sounds weird to say this aloud but I've felt embodied in the pages of the texts, like I'm living them. But I can't deny that since meeting you, I've learnt more about myself. About—" She considers for a moment. "About what love can look like. About what it could look like for us."

A hesitant sense of relief has me relaxing slightly. While it might be hard to convince her on my own, I hope her memories of us from another life will weigh heavily in my favor.

"But I'm mad that you hid this from me. I accept keeping silent at the club was probably best, but you should've told me sooner."

"I know. I wasn't sure if you'd ever give in to me. I sensed you'd never trust a man in a position of authority again. There was reluctance alongside the attraction."

Tucking hair behind her ears, softly, Maddie agrees with me. "Once bitten, twice shy." She huffs a laugh. "You were too tempting, even before my dreams made things clear about what you meant to me."

"And what was that?" I ask, ensuring I use the past tense.

"Everything."

My soul relaxes back into my body. "And now?" I ask.

She straightens, inhaling. "I'm disappointed, but I understand. I went to Club VX with one goal in mind; to make sense of what was happening to me. My dreams, the déjà vu, these memories that never quite formed—that night confirmed so much for me. That it was you as my champion, surely that only reinforces everything, proving the point."

I hope it does, but I don't voice it. That's her conclusion to come to.

"And now that we're together, the dreams are progressing," she reminds me. "And it's because it's you and me."

You and me. I like that. "Can you forgive me?"

"Yes. Eventually," she tacks on with a wry smile.

Still on my knees, I drag my eyes over her body suggestively and ask roughly, "Do I need to make you forget everything for a while?"

She fights a smile. "Are you saying you can put that mouth of yours to better use?"

"I love you," I tell her plainly. "On my life."

"Don't say that," she whispers fearfully, leaning forward to kiss me quickly. And I'm reminded of where her last dream ended. Of Tristan's journey to a nearby village to quell unrest.

I rise, cupping her face, our mouths meeting. "You take pictures of you as Iseult that night?"

"Yes. You want them?"

Steadying her against me, I nod. "You bet I do."

Safe in the knowledge that we'll get through this test in our relationship, I move onto everything else that stands between us. Not least because I'm dying to hear her thoughts on it, but because it's a good distraction. "I have something to show you. There's more to tell."

Leaving Maddie and her questioning expression behind, I go to my closet and grab the two items Gramps gave me. I return, saying, "Hold out your hand."

She does, and I place the gold key on her palm.

"What's this?"

"Possibly Tristan's key."

Her other hand flies to her mouth. "Oh my God. Where did you get this?"

"Does it look like the one in your dream?"

"I, no, it was smaller. I think." She sucks in a breath. "Look at the engravings!"

Eyes wide, she studies the horse and knight, then the initials on the opposite side.

"Why do you have it, and why do you think it was yours? *Tristan's*," she amends.

I explain everything I discussed with Gramps, and, when I unroll the family tree and point to my name, to hers, to Auric's, Maddie starts crying.

"What's wrong?"

"You don't understand," she says through teary eyes. "I used to look at this for hours, wondering about the names, about the origin. There was a small signature in the bottom of what I think is the original at home. And there were some words, a phrase, that was ripped in half. I think it reads *âme du coeur.*"

Soul of the heart. It's more common to read *coeur et âme*, heart and soul, but Maddie would know what she saw so I don't question it. And I'm in no way surprised to hear she has the original at home.

"The initials, Kit—are you sure they're for him and not âme du coeur?"

"I have no idea. It was all Gramps and I had to go on."

"And this key must fit a piece of furniture, one like the old chest of drawers in your lounge, Kit."

"I've already tried," I admit. "There's no keyhole, only handles either end of each drawer. It must be for something else. Any clues from your memories?"

She shakes her head, leaning into my side and I gratefully wrap an arm around her. "I can't picture the chest Tristan referred to. What's going on?" she asks. "What does all of this mean?"

"I'm not sure, but it's something that we have to work out together. Our two families are intertwined in extraordinary ways, and this key could solve why."

A loud knock at the door to my apartment has us startling.

We pull apart, eyes wide with curiosity. It's late, close to eleven. Unless it's a neighbor, you have to buzz from the first floor entry door. Checking my phone, I can see there's nothing from Josh.

"Stay here," I whisper as another knock sounds.

Quietly, I walk across the hall to the door, peering through the peephole. Knowing I have a sword in the closet next to me brings me little comfort when I see who's on the other side. Reaching for a weapon is the last thing I should do.

Two uniformed police officers wait for me beyond the door.

"Christophe Chevalier? It's the police. Open up."

My heart thumps, wondering what this is about. Firstly, my thoughts dart to Gramps, or my sister, hoping they're okay. Please don't let it be a car crash, some tragic accident where yet again I don't get to say goodbye before they're gone.

With one last look at Maddie, and while hoping it's none of the above, I open the door.

25

MADDIE

I Will Wait - Mumford & Sons

The police are at the door, their authoritative, loud voices easily discernible from the relative safety of Kit's bedroom. Worried, I head his way as he opens the front door with his hands in the air.

"Can you confirm your name please?"

Kit does, asking, "What's this about?"

That's when I see Officer Fresh Out Of The Academy reach for his cuffs. "You're under arrest for the sexual assault of Erica Reid."

The world falls from under my feet. Fog fills my head as Officer Too Many Stakeout Steaks reads Kit his rights, his finger pointing at me and telling me at the same time to keep my hands up high.

I do as asked, angry at this intrusion but worried there's any truth to the accusation. Kit turns to me, drinking in every one of my expressions. No doubt he's wondering exactly what I remember. If I will condemn him with my testimony.

"On what evidence?" Kit asks as the officers jostle him forwards, towards the door. "This is a fabrication. I never assaulted her, sexually or otherwise."

"CCTV says otherwise," one of them replies, causing my stomach to turn.

I hurry towards him. "Wait," I yell to the one closest—Officer Steak. "Where are you taking him?"

"Ma'am step back."

I check his badge number. "I'm asking you a question, Officer 722. Which precinct are you taking him to?"

He eyes me up and down, noticing my tear-stained cheeks and my dishevelled, tired appearance. Also my lack of clothes. "Ma'am, do you have a complaint to make against this man? Are you okay?"

"I have no complaint, no. Please, just tell me."

He confirms the destination and I lock eyes with Kit. "I'll call Josh. Kit, don't worry."

"On my honor, Maddie, I didn't do this."

His honor has been in question tonight, and I think he realizes the poor choice of words as soon as they leave his mouth. But nothing I've seen of him, either as Kit or the Black Knight, causes me concern.

With a final, reassuring smile, I nod. "I know."

As soon as the door closes, I rush about looking for my phone.

Where the fuck is it?

There, in the pocket of my jeans that have been tossed halfway across the lounge. Hands shaking, I toggle to my Photos app and find a video that was already in my recently deleted folder. For weeks it sat on my phone, biding its time. Until now,

I've thought it harmless, a lusty moment caught between two consenting adults. And even though I'm secure in that thought, I wonder if I've come full circle. If a man I love has twisted me so far inside out and upside down, that I can't see the wood for the trees. Now, with my finger hovering over the small white arrow, it feels like a portal, one that will transport me to hell.

Watching video of Harrison with other women made me reluctant to watch this one. But it also made me reluctant to delete it. In the end, I knew I had no right to look at it, so it got trashed. But it's proof of his actions—good or bad—and with no choice anymore, I press play.

The first minute or two is my frustrated voice and attempts to get my cell back. It's funny listening to myself, but I can't indulge in the humor. A short while later, I leave the bathroom. My heart gallops when I hear Erica and Kit enter roughly ten seconds later.

There's some indistinguishable words shared as the door slams shut. I catch something about the light not working.

"Erica," Kit says in a serious voice. "Come on. I thought you were taking me to an office."

"We can talk in here."

"No we can't. Let's go."

"No. I've missed you. Haven't you missed me? Missed this?"

There are sounds I can't clearly make out, but I presume they're bodies moving. Then: "Erica, stop. I'm not here for that." Fumbling noises come through the speaker. Of clothes or fabric.

"Move away from the door so that I can leave."

"In a minute," Erica whines.

I can hear lips against skin, kissing sounds. My breathing speeds up wondering if this is it. If this is the moment the portal takes me to the depths of despair.

"Erica," Kit grits out, clearly cross. "Stop touching me like that."

"Please, Kit. I need you. I've moved to Boston to be near you. It's what you wanted!"

"I never said anything remotely close. We were casual. We were stop-gaps."

"No, we were *more* than that. You love me, I know you do."

"I don't—Erica, I'm sorry but I don't feel that way."

I hear the jangle of a belt. I hear Erica giggling, a muffled, "Come on. It'll be good."

Indistinguishable sounds can be heard; I imagine hands pushing hands.

"Stop. Erica, I'm not having sex with you. I need to go."

I hear the door handle jiggle and I wonder if that's Kit, Erica, or me on the other side of the door. I'm certain I tried the door when I returned after seeing Hank.

A sob comes through on the video, then the sound of the door opening, of Erica exiting and sobbing again as she hurries down the hallway.

Vaguely, I can hear my voice, apologizing. Of Kit murmuring *Excuse me.*

I don't need to hear the rest but I listen to the entire thing, even as Hank helps me rescue my cell.

Like clouds parting after a torrential storm, relief hits me hard and I collapse sideways to the couch cushions. Tears gush, so many emotions pouring from me that I feel wiped out. But one thought lingers: if I see Erica, I'm going to punch her right in the face for assaulting Kit like that. He should press charges against *her.*

Feeling optimistic, I dry my eyes. Needing to call Joséphine, I dread seeing how late it is but I'll beg for forgiveness. With bated breath, I call her number. When she doesn't answer, my heart cries. I redial, whispering a prayer over and over. When I think the dial tone is finally going to kick into the message service, she picks up.

"You okay, Maddie?"

"Oh thank God," I answer, so happy to hear her calm, strong voice as an image of her pops into my head. With her gray hair cut into a sharp bob, she always looked so formidable. "Yes and no. I'm so sorry for calling late but I need your legal help, Jo. And this time I can pay." I have twenty Gs to my name, which should be enough to get Kit off. There's no way the police can demand a high bail. "Can you come to Boston, like, now?"

Please don't be on vacation. Please don't be on the other side of the country. Please don't be busy with some huge case in New York right now.

"I'm actually in New Haven tonight." She's closer than I could've hoped for. "Is this about Mark? What's going on?"

She hated Harrison, always calling him by his legal name. "No, it's about my boyfriend, and to some degree about me. I'm going to have to make a statement."

"Maddie, I'll do anything I can for you, you know that. And it'll still be pro bono. Tell me everything."

I relay everything as succinctly as possible, Jo asking relevant questions until she has the main facts. When I tell her that my boyfriend is also my professor she's quiet for an extra long moment.

"Does the administration team know?"

"Yes."

"I'll speak with him. Do I have your approval to confirm the relationship with the police?"

"If it keeps him out of jail." Then I warn, "The officer said something about CCTV proves the assault. I know it was getting fixed that night so I don't know when it started recording."

Jo assures me she'll look into it. With a promise to arrive in the next three hours, and after I send her the video that will exonerate him, we hang up.

Next, I call Josh and rehash everything. After several minutes of cursing Erica's name, it's clear he's outraged at the injustice for his friend. "I know this is bullshit because I was also there; he told me about it afterwards. I'll get going ASAP."

"Pick me up first?"

"He wouldn't want you getting caught up in this, even though you are. And to some degree, thank fuck that you are. That you were with him tonight. That you were that night, too, vandalizing bathrooms."

I can tell he's aiming for a playful tone, so I reply, "It's a side hobby."

He laughs softly and I'm grateful for the lighter moment. Tension grips my body, stress chemicals coursing through my veins.

"He's crazy about you, Maddie."

With my energy depleted from a night of various dramatic revelations, the words hollow me. I don't have the strength to be stoic, to stop the sobs that eject from my mouth. I just want to hold Kit and forget any of this happened.

"Shit, I'm sorry. I didn't mean to make you sad, but I've never seen him so devoted to anyone, and I've known him all his adult life."

I murmur, "I know."

"Do you? You're it for him. He's been a restless man the past ten years, and now I know why. He's been waiting for you, and now that he's found you, he's keeping you, Maddie. He'll fight to the death for you."

I don't know if Kit has told Josh about my dreams or past life theory, but I know without a doubt that he's more than capable of killing a man, as Tristan or as the Black Knight. And despite the violence, tears prickle, Josh's voice so vehement that I wish I could hold Kit right now. Wish I could kiss away all the anguish and hurt he's going through. "I know, Josh."

"Okay, good. I'll keep you updated."

"If you don't come and pick me up in ten minutes, I'm calling a cab."

He sighs down the phone. "Okay. Ten minutes." A soft laugh sounds. "When this is over, remind me to tell you a story about him and this old lady with two really heavy suitcases."

And then he hangs up.

I take a moment to catch my breath. Then I move to the bedroom, finding appropriate clothes. I change as quickly as I can, my phone right by my side. That's when I see the gold key, tossed to the bed. I pick it up, marveling at its existence. That the Chevaliers kept it, passing it down for endless generations until it came into Kit's hands. Then I go back to the lounge, directly to the mahogany-colored chest of drawers. Just as Kit said, there's no keyhole, so I leave it on the surface and count down the minutes.

The mystery distracts me, but a deep sense of dread has me checking the time again. Minutes feel like years, the distance and separation I feared in my dream now a reality.

After shrugging on my coat, I pull on my sneakers. Texting Perrie in case the cops come looking for her to corroborate my story, I find a coat for Kit and wait by the door for Josh to arrive.

Processing the night is beyond me. Am I shocked and hurt by Kit's admission about his role at the club? Yes, but deep down I wished it were him. Wanted it to be him. My choice was to either let it destroy me or accept it for what it was. Considering how tightly our paths are bound, it was inevitable. Evan would've been with me on that platform otherwise. It might've been a very different experience, one where I lost that piece of my soul Perrie warned me about. Kit was respectful. His actions were selfish, but in winning me, he showed me exactly what I needed to see.

Teaching, education, is his perfect calling. I didn't expect such a hands-on experience from my professor but I can't say I'm disappointed.

Now, it's my turn to fight for him, and I won't give-up until his enemies are dead and buried.

THE SMALL HOURS of the morning—night?—drag when all you want is progress, a just resolution, and have crap coffee to keep you company. In between, Josh and I pass the time with chit-chat and stories. Despite the awful situation, there is plenty to smile about, Kit our common ground. I soak up every tale and fact Josh shares about his long-time friend, Kit taking up every bit of space I have left.

Being kept from him hurts more than I could've predicted.

Thankfully, Joséphine arrives around 3AM and that's when things really start to kick off. After a quick greeting where she lays out how this will go, she makes demands to see Detective Trammel with the officer at the front desk.

Detective Trammel, a petite woman in her mid-thirties, collects Jo almost immediately. From their introduction, it's clear they spoke on the phone earlier. With a nod my way, Jo disappears through a door to my right.

Josh murmurs, "She seems good."

"She is."

"How do you know her?"

I swallow the last of my cold coffee. "She got my marriage annulled when I was seventeen and arranged my emancipation from my parents."

Josh sits in stunned silence after that and I'm grateful for the quiet. It helps me concentrate. These next few minutes feel especially critical.

Some time later, Detective Trammel comes to collect us. We're brought to an office where Jo is waiting for us.

"Where's Kit?" I ask, hugging her again in thanks.

"Holding room, just for a bit longer."

"That sounds hopeful," I hedge.

We sit on plastic chairs and accept the offer of coffee, my heavy mood lifting slightly at the positive news.

Detective Trammel has a strong Boston accent when she informs us, "We just need to fill in a few gaps. It's why we're not formally interviewing you."

I glance at Jo who nods reassuringly.

We confirm our names when asked, our addresses, our professions.

"Professor Cusack. Can you explain your connection to Professor Chevalier, and how he knows Miss Erica Reid."

Josh summarizes the past ten years, then goes on to explain that Kit and Erica hooked up every now and then in Providence at a bar she worked at. It hurts to hear he was with her several times. It hurts to think of her having him, touching him, kissing him. Irrational feelings flood my head, my heart sick with jealousy.

Josh is asked about events that night which he relays. About Erica serving them. About her asking Kit to speak in private.

"When he returned to the table he was agitated. Cross. He said Erica had all but locked him in a bathroom, keeping him hostage while she tried to get inside his pants. I didn't ask for more detail than that really. He was never emotionally into Erica. It was a casual thing. He only agreed to talk to her at Midnight Blue because it allowed him the chance to make it clear that nothing was going to happen. He was a gent like that."

"How do you know that was what he intended to say?"

Josh hesitates. "Because he left Providence without a backwards glance. Erica was just one of a number of women he had casual sex with. There was no relationship. If he'd wanted one, he would've invited her to Boston."

Josh's apologetic blue eyes cut to me before returning to Detective Trammel.

"But Erica *was* there. And they had history. How can you be so sure he had no intention to have sex with her once they were alone?"

"He'd never hurt a woman. And besides, he'd just seen the love of his life across the bar, not that he knew it at the time."

Wait. Is he talking about me?

"Is that so," Detective Trammel says absently.

"Maddie's video proves everything."

"Yes, Madrigal Devereaux." Detective Trammel locks gray eyes on me. "Anything to do with the Devereaux Museum?"

"Not personally, but yes."

"Your video has been crucial. The bar was having problems with CCTV that night and only shows them leaving the cubicle, Erica visibly upset. Did you know Erica Reid before that evening?"

"No. I had spoken to her about my drink order, and my friend had asked about jobs at the bar. That was all."

"What is your relationship with Professor Chevalier?"

"I'm studying for a doctorate in medieval literature. He's my assigned professor."

Quickly, her eyes dart to Josh before focusing on me. "Are you the love of his life that he saw across the bar?"

"I hope so."

Mild amusement transforms her professional gaze into something more human as Jo interjects, "How is this relevant, Detective Trammel? Madrigal isn't facing charges, and Professor Chevalier has all but been discharged."

The detective stands, anxiety blooming as I wait for her next words. "Even hardened detectives like to hear a happy story now and then, Ms DuBois. Thanks for coming in and assisting with our enquiries." She opens the door. "We'll have Professor

Chevalier brought to you; all charges are dismissed. You're free to go."

26

KIT

Never Tear Us Apart - INXS

When I walk through the station door to see Maddie, Josh, and Jo waiting for me in the lobby, the exhaustion and fear I've been wearing like an oversized cloak lifts away in an instant.

Freedom awaits, but also Madrigal Devereaux.

After the night we've had, I was scared to death she'd walk, sick of the lies and drama. But it was clear she had evidence to help me, *was* helping me. And the smile she gives me rivals the dawn breaking outside the windows. Wrapping her up in my arms, I'm all at once grateful, relieved, and so fucking in love with her I need to invent new words for how I feel.

"Thank you," I murmur in her ear. "Without you, I'd be lost on so many levels." This woman has saved me from exile, from career-suicide. "Turns out girls *can* be super helpful."

"Told you," she teases.

Her arms tighten around me and then I'm pulling her in for

a desperate kiss that speaks of the many hours of worry we've lived through. I forget about everyone else, Maddie's mouth on mine all I care about. We're rudely interrupted by Josh throwing his arms around us both and giving us a gentle shake. "Guys, go home. Get into bed and sleep or whatever else you've got the energy for."

Maddie grins against my mouth, our kiss over as she hides her face in my shoulder. Keeping an arm around her, I pull Josh in for a hug. "Thanks, man." That's all he needs from me and all he'd ever expect.

"You bet. Glad it's over."

I walk to Jo and extend my hand. "Thank you for everything."

"You're welcome. Look after this one," she says, as Maddie leaves my side to hug her friend, breathing a heartfelt *thank you* down her friend's ear. "She's one of the best people I know."

My eyes drink Maddie in as I drown in emotion. "She is."

"I'll be in Montréal at Christmas. Let's catch up," Jo tells Maddie as they part ways.

A blast of cold air hits us squarely where we stand as Jo exits the building, only for Perrie to walk in right at that moment.

"What's going on?" she asks. "I came as soon as I got your message," she directs to Maddie.

Maddie throws her arms around Perrie. "Thank you for coming. And I'm sorry, maybe not sorry, that it's a wasted journey. It's over. Kit has been released without charge."

Over Maddie's shoulder, Perrie's eyes lift to mine. She nods, smiling. "That's great. So, we can go?"

Hands in his pockets, Josh nods. "Yeah. All done." He looks my way, winking.

Disbelief wars with relief. I struggle to make sense of events. I'm not even sure what day of the week it is. Friday, I realize, as

Maddie hands me a coat, one she's thought to bring from my closet.

"So, what's next? Home and into bed, the waffle house round the corner, or shall we hit the Irish pub down the street and celebrate with a pint or two. They're bound to be open at—"Josh checks his cell, "—seven—oh—three in the morning."

Maddie laughs tiredly, shrugging, looking at me to make a decision. Snagging her hand, I hold it tight. I've got everything I need right here, but I don't voice it. Maddie looks like she needs something more sustaining than my declarations of love.

So I suggest, "Waffles, beer, then pub," to happy agreement from the others.

WE'RE ABOUT to leave the warmth of the pub when Maddie turns to Josh, saying, "Wait. You haven't told me the story about the lady with the heavy suitcases."

Josh laughs, snagging my gaze as I roll my eyes. "I think you should tell her," he explains.

"Only because it means I can't blame you," I point out, though clearly he's mentioned it at some stage tonight.

Maddie looks between us both. "I don't mind who."

Clearing his throat, Josh begins. "Picture this." His hands are in front of his face, separating theatrically. "It was the year we were both in England. I was at Cambridge," Josh tells Perrie. Kit was at Oxford," he tells Maddie. "We met up one Saturday in London, hitting up all the museums near Kensington. The Underground platforms were packed, a delay causing huge crowds to gather. Some passengers are walking back up the stairs, trying different options. That's when Kit spots this old lady, two suitcases at her side at the bottom of the stairs. She's looking up them, to the top, debating what to do. These suitcases are as big as her," Josh continues. "Old-looking, easily from the seventies, with zips holding everything inside, fit to burst. Kit taps me on the chest and walks up this lady. She's gotta be in her late seventies, granny dress, beige overcoat, pink headscarf."

Josh takes a breath. "*Can I help you carry those?* Kit asks her. She shakes her head. *No thank you. I'll just wait.*

"The stairs are choking up with people. *Nonsense!* he replies. *It would be my pleasure.* He picks up the suitcases by the handles. They're fucking heavy, his arm muscles tensed, his legs powering him up the stairs, knocking into people either side of him."

Maddie hasn't stopped grinning, turning to me every few seconds for my reaction.

"The old lady chases him—at her slower speed. Kit has almost got to the top when the handle snaps off one of the suitcases. The type that had flimsy metal loops attached to the fake leather handle, you know the ones."

Maddie nods. Perrie grins.

"So the handle snaps, the bottom half dropping to the step. The weight of it pulls the other half of the handle off, and then the suitcase is sliding down the stairs, out of control, bumping and spinning until it hits the lady in the knees, completely knocking her over. It somersaults to the bottom of the stairs. The zip splits, bras and granny pants jettisoned in all directions, contents littered fucking everywhere."

Maddie squeals in delight. Enraptured, Perrie watches Josh.

"Mortified, Kit races down the stairs to help her, but then the second handle snaps off too! Momentum, gravity, who the fuck knows, has it skidding across the steps where it slides between the railings, bouncing off someone's shoulder before falling to the platform."

Maddie gasps, loving Josh's theatrics.

"The suitcase explodes on impact, toiletries and clothes showering everyone in a meter-wide radius. Desperate to pick everything up, to help the woman get to her feet, it's utter chaos. The train is coming into the station, people are jostling for position, clothes are getting blown around by the wind in the tunnel."

Taking pity on me, Maddie nestles into my side, pressing a kiss to my chest.

"With some help from other passengers, we get the lady to a bench and her contents and destroyed suitcases by her side. The zips are busted, nothing fits. Kit apologizes profusely, offering to go the nearest department store and replace them immediately. The old lady tells him. *I didn't even want to go up the bleedin' stairs. I'd just got down them!*"

"No!" Maddie yells. "No!"

"Yup," I say. "She was joining the platform, not leaving it."

Perrie's sniggers set off Maddie, who elbows her in the ribs. "Stop, you'll get me started."

That properly sets off Perrie, who snorts, Maddie covering her mouth as a snort erupts from her, too. In a heartbeat they're rolling around the bench seats as uncontrollable laughter takes them in its grip. The infectious, happy sounds have Josh and I joining in, overtired bodies and brains no longer under our control.

Eventually, the giggles turn to tired sighs. To complaints about achey stomach muscles.

"My jaw aches," Maddie says, making Perrie snort again.

"Which is better?" her friend asks. "A sore jaw from laughing too hard or from sucking a fat cock all night?"

Maddie explodes into laughter again. "I can't even," she struggles to say. "Stop."

Despite the toll of the sleepless night, Josh is watching the girls—Perrie, in particular—with smitten eyes.

"Time for bed," I announce, helping Maddie to her tired feet. She's like spaghetti in my arms.

"I'll drop you all home. You too," Josh offers Perrie.

She loops her arm through his, dragging her eyes up his six foot three frame. "Thanks, Professor Cusack. That would be awesome."

As I surface from a deep sleep, the space next to me where Maddie should be, lies cold and empty. Fatigue makes itself known in every muscle group, as I turn, looking for signs of her. From somewhere, I hear her voice, so I pull on some sweatpants and a t-shirt, finding Maddie stretched out on my couch, her legs dangling over the arm. In her hand is the key, her cell to her ear.

"Thanks, Dad. Yeah, we'll meet you there tomorrow at 10AM."

I drop to the sofa at her side and unfurl the family tree a few centimetres, reading the earliest listed names of my ancestors as Maddie signs off with a *bye*. The cell, along with the key, gets tossed to the seat and then she's crawling into my lap, warm and happy and somehow, still mine.

"How did you sleep?"

I lay the document to the side and run my hands over her hips and ass. "Like the dead. You?"

"Good, but my mind woke up before my body and I couldn't settle. I want Erica charged with whatever crimes we can make stick, and I was also wondering if Perrie went home with Josh."

"Yeah."

"What does *yeaaahhhhh* mean? Did you sense it too? I thought it was tiredness clouding my spider senses, but she's into him, I know it. I checked our GPS app and she's in the dorm. Do you think they spent the night together?"

"Let me get my cell."

Maddie disentangles herself from my lap and I wander back to my room, unplug my phone from the wall and check for messages. There are none from Josh about how he spent his night. But I write: *Thanks for taking Perrie back. All good?*

As soon as I'm within earshot, Maddie asks, "Anything?"

"No. Who were you talking to?"

"I remembered I texted my parents last night, or rather, this morning, when we got home. I had questions about the Collection."

Flopping to the couch, I ask, "You think they have something that matches the key?"

"I'm hopeful," she answers, lifting up my arm and putting it around her. "We're going to meet at the museum tomorrow and go through the digital catalogs."

As much as I want to find out what this key fits and how it might be important, I'm not sure I trust Maddie's extended family. But before I acknowledge the deadly quarrel that my father shared with me when he was alive, this unshakeable enmity that Maddie doesn't appear to be aware of, I enjoy the fact that I'm home, a free man, and Maddie is still at my side.

When we got in this morning, we undressed, showered, and tumbled happily into bed and straight to sleep. And while I'd like to make use of the half chub of morning wood, I can't keep delaying. "Maddie, as I understand it, our families were not on good terms. Are probably still not on good terms."

"What do you mean?"

"Well, aside from the family tree that gets handed down the generations for some spurious reason, I was told that Sherbrooke was taken from us by, presumably, your great-grandparents. Maybe the generation before."

"Yeah, I've been wondering why our families' names are on the tree and what that means." She offers me a sad smile. "Was there a house with the land?"

"A cottage. Now in ruins." A bit like Gramps' cabin, I think to myself, before the mini revamp currently underway. "I was told it was all lost in a disagreement."

"What kind of disagreement?"

"The kind that ends in a duel. To the death."

Her hand covers her mouth. "No."

"I think it was all to do with honor, or what felt like a sleight to someone's honor."

"Who was killed?"

I hesitate. "Gramp's father—Gilbert. I think he strayed, involving himself with someone that was forbidden to him. A Devereaux." Maddie's lungs deflate in a whoosh. "He accepted the challenge from her father and was killed."

Maddie struggles with this knowledge. "Are you sure?"

"According to my father. Gramps confirmed it."

Looking ashamed, Maddie bows her head. "I'm so sorry. I don't know how you can stand to look at me."

"It's not your fault, remember?" I told her the same thing the night she woke in my bedroom and saw the painting of Sherbrooke on the wall. "And you're beautiful, so it helps."

My grim humor tugs a chastizing smile from her lips. "Our families dueled? To the death? This is—this is *unbelievable*."

"Does your father fence?"

A shake of her head. "He swims, plays tennis." Suddenly, she looks at me with a fierceness that has me recalibrating the softer side of her. "Don't put yourself in jeopardy."

I run my hands over her shoulders, soothing her as best I can. "Never."

"Promise me."

I don't hesitate. "I promise."

Satisfied, after seeing the truth in my eyes, Maddie gathers the scrolled tree in her hand and heads to the kitchen. On the counter, she rolls it out, cans and coffee mugs holding the corners down.

Following, I point to Gilbert and Hetty Chevalier on the document. "My paternal great-grandparents. Their son, Gramps, otherwise known as Fred, still lives near to the farm at Sherbrooke. He gave me this document and the key." Maddie gives me all of her attention and it feels like we're back in class. "His mother, Hettie"—we find her on the tree—"Gilbert's widow, gave it to Fred with some tale about a family lore."

"What lore?"

"That this key would provide the answers."

"Answers to what?"

Disillusioned laughter tumbles from my chest; this is some stupid fucking riddle. "No one knows. It's a ruse designed to make us all go crazy."

"It's not crazy though," Maddie dismisses. "This spurious reason, is a reason. Think about it—Iseult and Tristan loved each other. That's a fact. That fact, I live out every night I dream of them. Of us. That fact, we get to live out *now*, Kit. We're meant to solve this, together."

Her ambition never ceases to amaze me but it's hard to feel motivated, despite all the valid points she's making. To believe her, means believing in some higher power. I've not had much reason to believe in anything besides rotten luck, and life bending you over and asking you to call it Daddy.

"We're the point of connection, Kit," she pushes. "Your line and my line." She traces a finger from each hand down each corresponding line of the family tree to emphasize her point. "Besides, you know the direction of my intended thesis. What if I'm right? What if there are other manuscripts?" she asks with wonder in her voice.

"That's a big if."

"But what *if?*" she stresses, "this inkling, or hope—whatever—is based on some memory hidden inside me?" Reaching for my shoulders, she jumps up and down like a sugar-laden five-year-old. "There's a chest and a key, Kit! There's something to find!"

Trying not to get accidentally chinned, I gather her up against my chest. "Let's save all the excitement for tomorrow, shall we? Let's see what the catalogs divulge." Then a thought occurs. "When we fly to England—because you'd better be coming with me—we'll spend a couple of days in Oxford first and search the Bodleian Library. I'll reach out to my contacts and ask them to find anything relevant." I smooth a hand down her cheek. "Did you know I've seen the earliest surviving manuscript of *Chanson de Roland* at the Bodleian?"

Maddie sighs in appreciation, her eyes glazing over briefly. "Can you ask if I can see it?"

"Already have."

"And?"

"Done deal."

Her lush mouth is on mine in the next breath, her lips devouring, her hands skimming up the inside of my t-shirt and tracing the muscles of my torso.

"All this talk of old manuscripts gets me hot," she murmurs against my lips. Then she grabs me by the hand and leads me back to the couch. "And you are too thoughtful, Professor."

Playfully, she pushes me so that I fall backwards onto the seat. The ever-present hair tie at her wrist gets twisted around her hair, keeping it away from her face.

I shouldn't mourn the fact that we're not using my special office chair because I'll never turn down Maddie's mouth, no matter where we are. Need punches the thought out of my head when she tugs the navy sweatpants away from my waist and pulls out my leaking cock. Sunlight makes her eyes glint, her head lowering, the flat of her tongue licking me from root to tip. I suck in a taut breath, her tongue swirling over the head, her mouth molding to each ridge and line as she tastes every goddamn inch.

I'm as hard for her as I've ever been, my blood molten, my heart bursting into fire for the love I have for her.

Her hand wraps around me like a vise. Another drop of precum leaks from the head, her thumb smearing it, rubbing it around and around in soft circles. She strokes my cock a few times, nice and tight and then swallows me, her tongue lashing my flesh and forcing a curse from my lips.

"Think I know how you prefer to get jaw ache," I quip.

Laughter consumes her, and because it should be me kneeling at her feet after my confession and last night's trauma, I scoop her up off the floor and take her to my bed.

There, I bury myself inside her slick pussy, Maddie driving me full throttle towards oblivion, my hands threaded through her silken hair as I come undone, her name forever on my lips.

WHEN SATURDAY MORNING ARRIVES, we head to Berkeley Street to meet Maddie's parents. Despite meeting them both at the ball and having at least two pleasant conversations with Pippa, I'm reluctant to share such a big piece of Chevalier history. But, as I plan on being a part of this family for evermore, I'm going to kill with kindness.

Maddie told me everything there was to know about them over breakfast. In a nutshell, due to a regrettable but possibly non-sexual affair, and due to the fact that Maddie is an only child, her dad will do anything for her. He expects compliance in return which Maddie is not inclined to give. Her mother is charitable, of a more timid disposition, and has suffered great loss in her attempts to have a family. She treasures Maddie and has always told her to follow her heart, though she wasn't thrilled it led to Harrison.

Maddie alluded to some underlying conflict, the details of which are unclear, even to her.

"Come on," I encourage, snatching up her gloved hand as we stroll towards our destination in a head-wind, the temperature hovering around a chilly 37 degrees.

Pulling on my hand to slow me down, Maddie murmurs, "I don't know if my parents know, you know? They haven't said, and didn't say anything when we spoke. And they knew—well, Dad knew—that you were going to be my professor at Jacq U."

"I'm sure he knows," I suggest. He seems to be a man in control of his destiny. "But again, not his fault."

"Now I'm worried how this will go. About what else they've been hiding from me."

A calculating look in her eyes has me second-guessing her thoughts. "I'd rather you didn't raise it, Maddie. I might have doubts about the Devereaux family's honor—present generation excluded—but we can't alter the past. I'm not here for anything except answers to this key, which considering what little information we have, appears to be tied to your family line."

"Okay, if that's what you want. Personally, I'd find it hard to hold my tongue."

"There's a surprise," I say, flashing a smile.

The Devereaux Museum is one of the oldest buildings in Boston, following a neo-classical design. It houses close to a million books that can be loaned to the public, art by European and American painters, sculpture, furniture, and other highly collectible artefacts and treasures. Having bought our tickets online, we show them to a member of staff who scans us inside and offers us a map of the museum.

"Thanks," Maddie says, turning to grin at me.

"How many times have you been here?"

"As an adult—twice?"

"No wonder you disappoint your dad," I tease.

She glowers at me before urging me to follow her to the specified meeting point. Her parents are easy to identify. For starters, they're dressed like they've stepped out of a movie, with their cashmere coats, designer scarves, and impeccable auras.

A brunette, her mother is slender and striking, like her daughter. Graying but impressively handsome and lithe for his age, John looks as astute and sharp as I remember him.

Two steps ahead of me, Maddie greets her parents with warm hugs and kisses.

"You remember Kit," she introduces. "Kit, this is Pippa and John."

Pippa kisses me on both cheeks, her hands resting on my upper arms. "Lovely to meet you again, Kit. We're so happy you're together. Maddie has told us good things."

I glance at Maddie. "Thank you."

John extends his hand and I clasp it without pause, remembering how this was a show of faith in olden days that neither man was armed.

"Kit. Good to see you again. Welcome to the family."

My chest feels like it's been struck by Thor's hammer. *Welcome to the family*. Is this flattery, some kind of deception, or could they really mean their kind words?

Grabbing Maddie's hand, who sparkles like a star next to me, I say, "The pleasure's mine; I'm honored your daughter's in my life."

Pippa looks delighted. "We're thrilled for you. And we're so happy that we had a rare free day to meet."

"Yes, very happy to help. We can't wait to see what you've found. Shall we?"

John lifts a hand, directing us towards a staff door. After flashing an ID card, we go through to find a corridor, off which several offices can be found. In one of them we meet Margaret Mann, a senior curator, who offers to take us through the catalogs and either give me hope, or ruin all my dreams. Maddie's dreams too.

As we huddle around a computer screen, Margaret, with her red hair and pale green eyes, tells me, "Now, Mr Devereaux did outline a few places for our search to start, so I've selected all items of furniture: credenzas, trunks, trousseau, chests, wardrobes—that kind of thing."

"Yes," I agree. "Anything that this key," I say, pulling it from an inside pocket of my coat, "could fit."

Margaret's eyes light up. "May I?"

She examines it carefully, murmuring words such as *exquisite* and *condition* and *so very rare*. According to Maddie's dream, the key was smaller. If Maddie's right, this key may not yield anything useful, but we have to start somewhere.

"Would you mind if we dated it?"

I hesitate, unwilling to let it leave my sight. "I'd like to wait until we've tried a few locks first. Do you have any idea of the date by sight?"

"Hard to say for sure. Most definitely from the seventeenth century or earlier."

Maddie, who's not moved from my side, slides her arm around my waist and glances at me encouragingly. Maybe this *was* Auric's keepsake. But who was he, and what did it keep safe?

Pippa edges closer. "Might I see?" Margaret passes it over, Pippa holding it close to her eyes. "Look, John. A knight and his horse. How marvelous."

John peers closer. "Incredible," he answers. "And it was your grandfather's?" he asks directly.

"Yes. It's been handed down the generations." I explain the hypothesis regarding the initials, John looking genuinely intrigued and borderline avaricious.

"Thank goodness it's been kept safe."

I shouldn't be surprised he covets it; it's a rare collectable, of potential cultural significance, let alone what it could mean for my family. And more importantly, it's a clue to a secret, hidden within his vast collection. I'm prepared to bet my life on it.

Pippa passes it to John, Maddie piping up, "We'd better keep a close eye on Dad, otherwise it'll end up as an exhibit."

John indulges his daughter as her mother laughs softly. "And there I was, hoping no one would notice if it ended up in my pocket."

"I think the rough heart shape of the bow might have been fashioned, so to speak, at a later date," Margaret suggests as John returns the key to her. "Hearts were not the symbols they are today."

"The artefacts that the search will find," I begin. "Are pieces listed even if they've not been examined yet? That remain unlocked, the items inside undetected or impossible to access?"

"Good question," Margaret replies. "Occasionally, an item will be listed if its contents are unobtainable for reasons that can be numerous, mostly because opening the container might damage it irrevocably, and/or damage the contents."

Makes sense. "But you have them listed until new technology allows further investigation, or let's say, a key turns up?"

"Yes. The search will list anything worth investigating. Known or unknown items." Margaret turns to her computer. "Good, the search has concluded."

A quick glance at the screen reveals there are twenty-nine items this key could fit, which sounds not enough and far too many. She begins to count. "Fourteen are in the Collection, two of which are in storage. Eight are on loan to museums in the US. Three are in London, two more in Oxford. Two are in private collections."

"Private collections?" I ask, my eyes pinging to John as my heart sinks. "Accessible ones?"

"We can enquire," he replies. "Just a formality."

Bright-voiced, Maddie asks, “Where in Oxford?”

Margaret returns to her screen, reading the detail I can’t make out from my position. My heart races, knowing what Maddie is hoping. “Bodleian Library.”

“Any on that list stand out? Keyless, locked, yet to be analyzed?”

Margaret purses her lips. “No.”

My heart sinks to my toes.

“Wait, there’s a note here that says one item has been lost in the Oxford archives. It was first cataloged in 1738 but couldn’t be located five years later or since.”

Wide-eyed, Maddie nudges me. This has potential. “What type of artefact?”

Margaret returns to the screen, reading, “Chest box of unknown date. Forty centimetres long by twenty centimetres deep and twenty four centimetres high. Material: metal. Double padlock without keys. Legacy gift by—” Margaret pauses. “Mr Henri Vaudeville.”

27

MADDIE

A Thousand Years - Christina Perri

Beyond the train window, late fall foliage decks the trees of Oxfordshire's countryside, the sky a brilliant blue, and the temperature a few degrees above freezing. Beside me, Kit preps for the conference in two days' time where he's a keynote speaker. As he works, I toy with the idea I'm becoming more convinced of.

"I think we need to get the key scanned as well as dated." Dating it in Boston wasn't an option when we needed to take it with us to Oxford.

Looking up from his computer slides, Kit nods. "I thought we'd ask Rob."

Professor Rob Langley is the man who's providing me with access to *Chanson de Roland*. Needless to say, I cannot wait.

"He's someone you trust." Unlike my parents, or specifically, my ancestors who stole from his ancestors.

Kit fails to meet my eye. "Yes, I've always had a good working relationship with him. I spent eight months with him while working on my doctorate and we became close friends."

This isn't news to me. Over the past two weeks, my nights often spent in Kit's apartment as he tutors me, fucks me, and shares the story of his formative years with me, Kit has divulged many reasons why Rob Langley is a man to be trusted. Kit has already asked him to find this missing artefact but I don't think it's going to be easy. Frustratingly, the Bodleian Library has over 150 miles of shelving, and while those shelves mostly house books and manuscripts, locating the chest is a daunting task. There are hundreds of instances about miscataloged books, about them being randomly found decades later in a completely irrelevant archive, or people's attics. Considering it was last cataloged in the 1700s and hasn't been seen since, we might never find it.

"Did you see that article about fragments of a Spanish chivalric romance being found under Tudor floorboards in Norfolk, England?"

"How do you know these things?"

"I read about it. I just remember."

Kit stops clicking through his slides and scoops up my hand as we pull into a station. This quest we're on is important to both of us for slightly different reasons. Undoubtedly, we both feel this key will right wrongs the Chevaliers have endured by my ancestors, but I'm also really interested in this on a personal level. Dreaming is how I gather information for us.

I think Tristan gave these items to me, presumably because he loved me. And I sense that somehow, some of my ancestors have tried to address the imbalance. Why else record our family trees? Why else was Gramps—Fred—so adamant about this family lore that would rectify injustices?

After testing the key in all possible locks in the Devereaux Museum, Kit and I went straight to his apartment to consult the family tree. There was no Henri Vaudeville. And searching ancestry sites has revealed nothing to connect either family to this name.

When the train pulls out from the station, I murmur, "I have a theory I'd like Rob to help us with."

"What's that?"

"I think there's a key inside the key."

Kit absorbs my idea like a sip of fine wine, sinking into his seat as he toys with my idea. "It's a great theory. I know your dream key is smaller."

"What if we're distracted by coincidental initials—ADC? What if it's not Auric but Âme du Coeur. What if inside the key, this key with a heart added to its design, lurks the real treasure."

"I like it. It's clever."

I glow under his praise. "It would be clever, right?"

He nods, lost in thought, but his eyes are bright. He knows this is worth investigating.

At Oxford we gather our suitcases and hop in a taxi. During the journey, I greedily take note of the spires and towers and domes, the ancient buildings and classical designs. Kit points out places he's familiar with as we get out of the car and head towards the impressively beautiful Bodleian Library.

Inside, Kit asks for Rob Langley.

Awed by the interior, I whisper, "Are we really staying in your old college room tonight?"

His eyes darken from whiskey to decadent chocolate. "Yes."

"In a single bed?"

"Double. Postdocs got an upgrade."

I grin. "Does Rob know about us?"

"Yes. Made sleeping arrangements easier."

"But there won't be much sleeping?" I enquire with an arched brow.

Kit's chest inflates on a deep inhale, his expression one of sensual promise as he looks down at me from his considerable height. "I've been waiting close to a thousand years for you, so fuck sleep, beautiful, if you're in my bed."

We're interrupted by Rob's arrival, Kit and his effusive greeting a joyous occasion. They hug, take stock of each other in overlapping soundbites and then Kit introduces me. "This is Madrigal Devereaux, my brightest doctorate student. Maddie, this is Professor Langley, but he'll ask you to call him Rob."

"I most certainly will," Rob declares as I smile broadly at him. "Maddie, it's a pleasure to meet you. Kit has spoken very highly of you." Turning to Kit, he says, "It's been too long."

In his late forties, with light brown hair that was probably blond as a boy, and turquoise-hued eyes, Rob has a similar aura to Kit. It's a sense that he's academic and erudite. He assesses me, cataloging a million pieces of information in a blink and remembering it in a rolodex of relevancy.

"I'm so happy to be here. What an amazing place to work." The grandeur of the building exceeds Jacq U by a million percent.

"I have to pinch myself sometimes," he says amiably. "Right, come with me. Let's get you some refreshments, store your bags, and then we can talk about the plan for today."

Kit says, "We have an addition to the plan."

"Sure," Rob concedes.

"We need access to a 3D scanner and a carbon dating machine."

Rob's pale blue eyes sparkle with curiosity. "Leave it with me."

A SHORT WHILE LATER, we meet Rob's colleague who assists us in our pursuit of information. Lakshmi, who has a long black bob and wears a white lab coat, suggests we also make a copy of it with a 3D printer. It's a good suggestion. As the item is small, we do that first. It doesn't take long to complete, which is good—no-one seems to have much patience today.

Afterwards, we get it scanned. Bit by slow bit, second by second, the structure of the key is revealed as we gather around the computer screen linked to the scanner. In a state of nervous tension, I'm unable to look away, staring at the image until my eyes hurt. And just like that, we see what looks like a hollow in the center of the key where something else hides.

"There," Kit exclaims. "My god, you were right!"

The excited expression on his face swells my heart, as does the emerging picture of a key floating lengthwise in the middle of the inch wide shank, secured to the solid gold interior by little arms at either end.

Rob grins. "Good spot."

"How do we get it out?" I ask.

"I have all the necessary tools," Lakshmi offers.

"I can't believe it," Kit murmurs as the image unfolds. "Does it look familiar?"

"Yes," I confirm, peering closer, a tingle running down my back. This is proof of everything I've been reliving. It's been in my hand, in Kit's, both of us pulled into a time-spanning mystery that's slowly unraveling.

The next ten minutes are spent taking photographs with a professional camera as we discuss next steps. And then Lakshmi takes the key to a laser machine.

"There's no going back once I make the first cut."

"Do it," Kit tells her, his tone purposeful.

With the key pre-marked, she guides the laser along the lines, cutting off either end. Thankfully, neither the initials, nor the engraved images are affected. After checking the interior and the arms the key is soldered to, she makes a series of tiny movements with the laser until each end is smooth. When the machine is turned off, Lakshmi slides the key out of the shank, all of us crowding around the protective cabinet to get a glimpse of it. Just like my dream, it's gold but more dull in color. The shape is identical, a plain, simple round shaft.

Carefully, Lakshmi passes it to Kit. "All yours."

He takes it from her, stunned into silence. When he turns it over, he sucks in a surprised breath. "Another knight! And there's script."

"What does it say?" Rob presses.

Angling it to the light, Kit tries to decipher the tiny writing. Once Lakshmi hands him a magnifying glass, it becomes legible.

"Honneur aulx dignes."

I scream with excitement, Kit hugging me, the others too, overcome with elation. We're on the right track, but I'm going crazy not knowing where this is leading us.

The atmosphere in the lab is purely celebratory, all of us animated, chatting happily about what this message means. When the moment seems to end and we look ahead to the next steps, Kit gathers up the remains of the outer key, securing them in a sample bag.

At some point, Lakshmi will carbon date the fragments of gold, but the date of the keys isn't crucial information. We'd rather know what it opens.

"Wait, should we scan this key too, whilst we're here?"

"Hmm, might be worth doing," Kit agrees. "A copy too. The box was double padlocked, remember."

Lakshmi's hand is already reaching for the key, nodding her agreement.

Smaller, but with a quantifiable weight to it, this key is scanned in a matter of moments. With answers already revealing themselves from the original key, I don't think any of us expected there to be further developments, but I'm still crestfallen when nothing new comes to light.

The anticipation is killing me, and I know it's the same for Kit. Despite our success, there's still a long way to go.

Beyond the lead-lined windows of Rob's study, the sky darkens into late afternoon. With tummies full of English breakfast tea and Victoria sponge cake, we discuss how to find this missing chest. Prior to our arrival, Rob requested it brought from the archives, but it's still unable to be located. No staff members can recall the item, long since disappeared from memories.

"It's like no one wants us to find it."

Rob smiles grimly at Kit. There are no words of comfort. And if we're not careful we might lose ourselves to this hunt.

"What about an anagram? What about anything linked to honor or worthy or Club VX," I suggest, mainly for Kit. "Sophie wouldn't tell me who funded the club, but there's got to be a clue there."

"What's Club VX?"

I let Kit handle what he can or can't say to his friend, and he simply explains, "A fencing community where winning a duel is really important."

"Get a good prize, do you?"

Honeyed eyes settle on mine, Kit's mouth curling. "You do."

Any upset over his role on that dais is behind me. I have much more important things to put my energy into. "So," I interject, "is there any point in looking through the inventory? How can we find this missing item?"

"Yes, what's the process?"

Rob's explanation leaves us with little hope. Short of an employee coming across it accidentally, this chest has been lost for a very long time and might never be recovered. Likely shelved to a different identifying number, or stolen out of the archives long ago, the only thing we can do is search every inch of the 150 miles of shelves in vain hope.

Which is a hard no.

"Short of anyone remembering pertinent details," Kit offers in reference to my dream-memories, "we will have to enquire at the club."

"This is proper *Indiana Jones* stuff," Rob says wryly, frowning at the momentous task ahead of us.

Smiling coyly at Kit, I ask, "Does that make me Marion, off on wild adventures with the hot professor?"

Rob chortles, eyes swinging between us both.

Meanwhile, Kit looks far too happy with himself. "I'm good with that."

28

KIT

About You - The 1975

A strong current of hot water blasts my back and shoulders, the shower invigorating me. I tried not to pin too much hope on finding this lost item in Oxford, but my mood's swinging around like a misfiring compass. Reminding myself there's been progress, it's hard to feel settled when there's still so much to discover. Both Maddie and I feel dejected at the lack of a physical item, but the new key provides another clue. And I'm pinning all my hopes on Sophie Bouchard to provide more of them.

Yesterday, Maddie and I spent hours in the Bodleian looking at old manuscripts. Providing her with these once-in-a-lifetime opportunities has felt good but I'm hoping they'll also rectify past mistakes.

Jet-lag beat the elation, and after hours of admiring Oxford's resources, we took the train back to London and checked in to our hotel. The past twenty-four hours have been spent on us;

mooching around London; window shopping; sitting at cafes and drinking hot chocolate has been the kind of normal *couple stuff* I wanted to experience with her.

With a final pep-talk in the privacy of the shower, I exit the bathroom with a towel wrapped around my waist. Maddie is stretched out on the bed, face down. Reading. Every now and then, she writes on a sticky note and attaches it to the page of her book. Watching her study is fascinating. Watching her do it while naked, fully clothed, or in just her tennis dress, is a view that's become another norm these past few weeks.

Tossing the towel to the carpet, I crawl up behind her on the bed and tunnel under the duvet alongside her. The sound of her happy giggles has me smiling. Pressing a kiss to her shoulder, I ask, "Where are your clothes?"

"I couldn't dress fast enough after my shower. I got cold and hid under the covers."

Every day I discover more of her endearing ways, all of them the hottest thing on earth. And despite my apartment looking a little untidier with her every visit, I'm entirely unfazed. Why would the disorder bother me when my other half is standing right in the middle of it, looking at me like I gave her the entire world?

Laying on my stomach as well, I lean on a forearm and throw my free arm around her lower back.

"Are you trying to distract me from my studies, professor?" she leads, nose in her book.

"I need to talk to you about something."

Maddie's deadlines are insane. Being abroad isn't helping, but at my serious tone, Maddie closes her book and eyes me warily. "Shoot."

"Santos will be at the conference tomorrow."

As most of my research was conducted whilst at Brownlow, Professor Santos the lead professor, it's only natural she would want to see its completion. To attend a conference where I share the discoveries I've made. Like all good things, there's kudos by association.

"Yeah, I presumed she would be."

Unsure how to phrase it, I say, "She thinks I'm to blame for your unsuccessful application."

Maddie absorbs my statement, her eyes conveying a sense of relief and anticipation. *Finally, we get to it.* Deflecting her concerns about this, hiding this from her *has* been cowardly, but only because I deeply regret my actions and have done from the get go.

"Would she be right?"

Steeling myself, I admit, "Yes."

Her face crumples. Her pain is like a sword to the gut. "How?"

There's no need to explain that Santos wanted her. Santos would've made that very clear in ensuing conversations, because, while Maddie might have denied reaching out to Brownlow to see why they rejected her, that's not the woman I know. What I don't know is if Santos threw me under the bus and named me as the person who sent the incorrect email—which I could lie about, saying there was a miscommunication—or whether Santos just referred to a mistake.

Needing a clean slate with Maddie, I state, "I sent the rejection email."

"Kit, no. Why?"

"Because I didn't want you to study at Brownlow."

She shifts away, sitting up. I mirror her actions. "*Why?*"

Although we've talked around the differences between our families recently, ones I've dismissed, reassuring Maddie as often as I can about the irrelevance of it all, her doubts and worries never go away. So I give her the worst possible answer I can, knowing there will be unforeseen consequences.

"You were a Devereaux."

It wasn't because she saw me leaving the ladies' restroom. It wasn't because I saw her in the bar, wanting to make a move on her before realizing she was my student. It went far deeper than that.

She sneers, getting to her feet. Then she grabs a pillow and hugs it to her lingerie-clad body. "I knew it."

Sucking in a lungful of air, I get everything off my chest. "I planned on telling you the night I was arrested. I was going to lay it all out there: the family heirloom; the convoluted family tree; the handed-down tale about a fated love. And there are many reasons I could give to excuse my behavior. To try and paint this as a positive thing, but fundamentally, in that moment, I rejected you. The only explanation I have is that it felt right, and out of my control at the same time. Like I had no choice. And it's because you were meant to come to Jacquard, to find me and for me to find you."

A pillow side-swipes my head before falling to the carpet. It wasn't meant to hurt, just knock some sense into me. To vent her frustration.

"You ruined my dreams! Upended all my plans! You put me in Harrison's path again, one I was desperate to avoid. Do you know how much I've struggled being around him again?! And I didn't even want to come to Jacquard!"

Still on the bed, I scoot closer to where she stands and wrap my arms tightly around her waist so that she can't escape. "I messed up Maddie, and I'm sorry. I regret it all, and even though I don't know how to make this better, I've been trying to make it up to you ever since."

"Make it up to me? That's debatable," she dismisses. "I recall you being up in my ass all the time with your non-stop questions and plucked from thin air essays and your interrogations. I mean, you even asked me to do the interview for the chair of the department!"

A lot of those questions were for class and necessary but I don't bite. Her unreasonableness is understandable. "You enjoyed our talks too. We were fighting our attraction, Maddie, learning about each other as we did."

"Yeah? What did you learn about me?"

"That you have the courage and resilience of a small army; you exist beyond normal boundaries, out-living everyone else like some kind of time-traveler; your vitality is awe-inspiring, your well of energy limitless; and loving you has been the greatest privilege of my life."

Maddie swallows, toying with a corner of the duvet she's grabbed to replace her lost pillow. The bubble of tension between us deflates a little, long seconds passing. Waiting for a response, for any kind of facial expression that will clue me in on her thoughts is like waiting for the guillotine to drop.

"Maddie," I murmur, my heart splintering. "Say something."

Seconds tick by, Maddie's face closed off, her tone sad. "You forgot about me."

The air is choked from my lungs. "W-what?"

"You forgot about me. There I was, unraveling a mystery, searching for you, and you just eviscerated my path to you like it was nothing. You forgot about me."

"Hang on a minute. You didn't know that when you applied to Brownlow. That only became apparent when you came to Jacquard, precipitated with us meeting in person. You've explained that everything became clear since August, when our paths crossed. Your thesis changed too," I point out, unable to miss how prescient her intentions have turned out. "You married another man, Maddie. I think you forgot about *me*."

Despite how right I am, she brushes me off. "Minor details."

"The devil is in the detail, Maddie, and you've made it very clear I'm a thorough, pedantic asshole. With all my heart I wish I can remember what *you* do, but I'm at a disadvantage there."

I'm reminded there's ten years between us when a glimmer of childish petulance streaks across her face before it dissipates. Maddie's maturity was one of the reasons I could picture us together. So I tell her, "I made two mistakes. You know what they are now. Rest assured, I will protect you until my dying breath, I will always put you first because when I look into your eyes, I see forever."

Her face is a mask of serenity, but I know I'm getting through when she says, "Stop saying such nice things. You're making it a habit."

Not sure what to do, I wait, barely breathing.

"I have two choices here," she whispers. "Rail at you for being the *biggest* jerk and get upset, or laugh at how your plan backfired. You tried to get rid of me, to destroy my ambitions, but all it did was bring me straight to you."

"Exactly," I say. "The universe had a plan for us."

"But you didn't know that," she pushes.

Sliding off the bed and sinking to my knees, I look up at her mesmerising features. "I fell in love with you. You had me on my *knees*. I've never felt what we've got here, Maddie. You hold my heart in your hands and you're everything I've ever wanted." Fingers glide through my shower-wet hair as she looks down at me. "Loving you is in my DNA." And it's reciprocated in hers. There's no way we can't overcome this.

Almost reverently, she says, "You've always looked so handsome kneeling for me."

The constant references to her past life shouldn't surprise me anymore, yet they still catch me. I'll never tire of hearing them.

The night she told me about knowing me *before*, when we stood in my bedroom, the landscape painting of Sherbrooke capturing all of my focus, I told her then and there that I would fight for her.

I repeat my words from that night. "I'm sorry if I ever made you think I wouldn't put you first. I'll fight for you, Maddie. With you, for you, against you if needs be. I'll make this work."

"You'd better."

Still on my knees, I accept Maddie's benevolent touch, her face soft, her eyes tender. "I adore you, Maddie. I love you so much. I've come alive since meeting you."

"I love you, too. And it's only because I believe your apology, that you mean so much to me, in this life and in all others, that I can forgive you."

Fractures in my heart reknit. "You can?" I press a long kiss to her heart, her skin soft and warm. When I look up, gleaming eyes drink me in. Gently, her fingers explore my brow or toy with my hair. All the while I press kisses into her body, my palms taking liberties, testing the boundaries and skimming over her ass.

"What are you up to?"

Her eyes are a total come-on and it has blood heading directly south.

"We need to make up properly."

A change in her breathing is all the approval I need. Grabbing the elastic of her panties, I pull them down, Maddie instinctively lifting each leg as I rip them free of her feet and toss them aside. Then I pick her up and throw her back onto the bed, her body bouncing on the mattress.

A yelp sounds.

"You accused me of being up in your ass."

"So?"

"And you mentioned something about reaming. Or was it railing? The only railing that's going to happen tonight involves me and this ass that I'm—apparently—all up in."

"Kit!" she admonishes on a laugh.

Joining her on the bed, I sweep her books to the floor.

"I need those! I need to study!"

I flip her onto her stomach. "Now I know you said I was forgiven, but I'd like you to take my apology fuck as it's intended," I say, unsnapping the clasp of her bra. "Or you can take it as punishment for *not* taking it as an apology. Your choice."

"Have you been reading *Psychopathy For Dummies* again? I'm not sure I wanna."

The rebuff has me smirking as she playfully glowers at me over her shoulder. Calling her bluff isn't in my interests, so I don't offer her an out. And as for the psycho back talk, it only makes me determined to live up to her expectations.

Tossing her bra aside I remind her, "You told Yves you like a psycho."

"Five percent. This is more like *ninety*," she insists as I grab her ankles and yank her closer.

"I need the reassurance, Maddie. Besides, you're going to love my brand of psycho. This is my mistake and I'm going to make it up to you. Now, ass up, beautiful."

Grabbing her hips, I lift her up so she's on her knees, her body angled down towards the bed. Her face rests against the mattress, her arms spread in front of her head to act as a counter point. Wet hair has been gathered into a messy bun; I'll keep it like that for now.

Rubbing my hands over her spread ass, I trail a finger from her wet slit to her asshole, rimming it. Maddie's gasp of surprise makes my blood gallop. I've not fucked her here yet but I plan on it.

Roughly, I ask,"Here?"

"Is it a condition of making up?"

Concerned by her question, I pause. Treating Maddie respectfully and equally in this relationship is a doctrine I live by. Do I push that when we're alone in my office from time to time? Sure, but only because we love it. But Tait didn't give her a choice. She was unable to say no to that fucker. So I say, "Of course not. If you'd rather cuddle it out, let's do that."

"We can do that after," she offers quietly. "I want you, and you can have me however you want."

Those final words, spoken with such commanding clarity has my body powering up like it did right before the Ordo Victor, ready to unleash. To defend the lady at all costs, to risk my life for her. "Careful," I warn. "Give me carte blanche and I'll lose restraint."

Her feminine scent hits me as I pepper kisses across her cheeks, dragging my tongue over the silken skin of her peachy ass. My cock is rock hard, throbbing with an urgency I only feel for her, my clever student, my one and only. And the sweep of her back, the helpless way she's positioned right here for the taking as my fingers drag through her pussy, is a visual I'm enjoying far too much.

"Kit, please," she begs. "Hurry."

Hearing that soft, husky whisper has my heart beating in victory. So, taking some pity on her, I scooch down and eat her out. Christ, I've never had her this wet. I gather some of her cream on my fingers, slicking them all the way to the third knuckle. Still eating pussy, I carefully slide a finger inside her ass.

"Oh God," she moans, rocking into my face.

"You like that, beauté?"

"Yes."

"You want to stop to study?"

An agonized, whimpered, "No. Soooo worth the late submission penalty."

Laughter rumbles from me as I lap at her slit, my tongue sliding deep in her pussy which wrings a moan of pleasure from her. Wriggling and writhing as I work her ass, I hold her down at the waist with a free arm. Her whispered *More* has me sliding two fingers inside as the tip of my tongue circles her swollen clit. Hands scrambling for purchase, Maddie pants into the sheets. My face is covered in her silk but all I want is more of her drugging scent and addictive flavor. Greedy, I pump my fingers inside her, licking and sucking every inch of her I can get to until she comes on my face with a series of soft cries that have my blood igniting.

Lining up my cock, I grit, "Taking your professor's cock gives you an extra day."

Her pussy is tight and hot from her release, my dick responding to the lush feel of her body around mine. Having her in this position means I can drive deep, drilling every hole I plan on having.

"Only a day?" She peers at me. "Not much of an apology."

Picking up the pace, the percussive slap as the back of her thighs meet mine is in tandem to Maddie's rising cries and sobs of pleasure.

"Oh God," she moans.

Hands on her hips, I hold her still and steady as I rail her sweet center. Now isn't the time for gentle or slow. Reaffirming our relationship turns my thrusts urgent, unleashing everything I have on this woman. When she's on the cusp of erupting, I smooth my hands down her bowed back, my cock enjoying every flutter and quiver as Maddie's orgasm builds and crests before sweeping her away on a tide of release.

As she sucks in lungfuls of air, I slide out of her pussy and press in further back.

"Taking your professors's cock *here*, gets you two days grace," I murmur, teasing and feathering my cock inside her tight channel.

There's a noise I can't translate. Then: "You feel so thick."

Squeezing past her ring of muscle, I keep pressing forward until I'm in an inch, then another. Carefully, I push until I'm fully seated, heat enveloping me.

"Good girl," I murmur before rotating my hips. Maddie releases a panicked sound so I reach forward and undo the clasp around her hair, letting it tumble loose. Grabbing a handful of chestnut silk, I pull her towards me, her peaked breasts coming into view.

"You get me so fucking hard. It makes me want to do filthy things to your body."

"Fucking my ass dirty enough for you?"

"Always got an answer." I bite her earlobe and she yelps. "I think about you sucking my dick, taking it wherever and whenever I want all day long. I fantasize about bending you over my desk, your knee propped on the surface to open you up nice and wide as I pin you down and show you what a first class education looks like. You are a *major* distraction in class, Maddie."

Using whatever leverage and tension the position of our bodies allows, I fuck her beautiful body, alternating between long, deep, slow thrusts and quick, shallow pumps. Consumed by her meadow-scent and raw passion, my vision goes black as I lose myself to baser, depraved instincts.

"I'm gonna work you so fucking hard."

Her breathing sounds frantic as I clutch her waist with one hand and pinch a nipple—hard—with the other, pawing at her delicious curves before I jam clean fingers in her sopping pussy and work her into a frenzy.

I'm everywhere. There's not a part of her toned body I've not had this afternoon as my lips and teeth maul her neck, as I take her tight ass and finger her pussy. All the while her songs of pleasure crescendo, letting me know she's close.

"Good girl, just a little longer," I encourage, holding off my release until hers comes.

"It's too much," she breathes.

I strum her clit with my thumb, her wetness coating my hand. "Like that," I encourage as she rides my hand, as our bodies move together in perfect rhythm.

Her core contracts, Maddie detonating like a small bomb underneath me. Around me. Convulsing, she exhales my name over and over as I ignite in her blast radius, our joining too much. The sight of her cataclysmic undoing on the end of my cock, too much. Sinking as deep as I can, I unload with a savage growl, long streams of hot cum filing her up and making a fucking mess of her.

"You make me so damn proud and happy," I pant. "You know that, right?"

Sucking in lungfuls of air, her face soft from coming, she sags. Holding her up with a hand wrapped loosely around her throat, I kiss the life from her, delving my tongue into her incredible mouth until her back bows from the force of my lust. Rocking into her ass until the last jerks of my cock subside, our kiss finally mellows, turning sweeter.

Lips red and swollen, Maddie pulls away and strokes my brow as we catch our breath. "Who said chivalry was dead?"

Her quip has me smiling like the devil. "You did good." I press a kiss to her temple. "Your man is meant to hold you down, not back."

She laughs hard at that.

"Let me run a bath. I promise to be tender now."

WHEN THE BATH is half full and the air is warm and steamy, we climb into the hot water. Maddie lies on top of me, her back to my chest, the tips of her breasts poking above the water line. Arms banded across her stomach, I hook my feet around her ankles and keep her under the warm water as much as possible.

Despite making up, there's still lots to discuss, so I'm unsurprised when Maddie asks, "If we don't find what we're looking for, is that going to change how you feel about me?"

The question makes me angry, but it's directed at myself, not Maddie. "I hoped I had erased any doubts about you and me."

Angling her head so that she's facing me a little more, she explains, "The history between our families is never going to go away, and if we can't locate this chest of yours, does that mean that you'll struggle being with me?"

I cup her face, the sound of water dripping from my hands mingling with my words. "No. I don't care about what happened between our families. I only care about now. About us. Please stop doubting."

"But it implies not good things. More betrayals, heartbreak. If you have the key to this chest, it must be yours."

"It might be yours," I object. "Whatever it is, we're the change, okay? We set the direction of this path from here on out."

Wary eyes regard me. "Okay," she agrees softly. "I just worry about what's around the corner. Stuff we can't predict or see."

"Like what?"

Her lips part but she hesitates. "More duels. More death."

"That's not going to happen," I convince her. "I'd rather lose that chest than ever lose you. We get to have this. I'm not risking you."

Slowly, Maddie turns so that she's lying on top of me, leaning her head on my shoulder as water sloshes around us. Taking hold of her left hand, I toy with her ring finger. Her questions trouble me, so I say without any sense of irony, "Besides, when we're married, whatever is in that chest will be both of ours."

Unsure how my declaration will be received—Maddie's experience and view of marriage may inadvertently sabotage a future proposal—I'm happily surprised when Maddie lifts her head and gifts a smile to rival all the smiles that have come before.

"That is one way around the problem," she answers, her eyes turning round with shock when she sees how serious I am.

I've completely thrown her.

"You did tell me to do better next time," she reminds me, trying to act cool. I don't need to point out that the *doing better* bit was not for financial gain, but to tie her life to a more deserving man. "And as I'm a penniless student, maybe it'll be me in the money when this chest turns up."

"Maybe," I agree, her eyes bright with mirth. "But whether it turns up or not, it's not going to change us."

She kisses me softly on the mouth. "I'm sorry," she murmurs. "For what my family did to yours."

"Not your fault."

"Still doesn't feel good."

I know a way to make her feel good but I keep that to myself. "It's wasted energy. Let's focus on our meeting with Sophie next week."

Sophie Bouchard, the woman in charge of Club VX, its members and activities, has agreed to meet with me. When she asked what it was about, I gave her a name: Madrigal Devereaux. Her response was *I see.* That was it. Holding back a million questions, I let the moment expand. If Sophie was confused about the topic she would've asked for further details. Encouraged by her non reply, we confirmed a day and time.

"She knows something. She has to."

"Let's hope so," I agree.

If Sophie doesn't, then the quest we've been on has all been for nothing.

29

MADDIE

I Miss You - Adele

Dawn breaks at my window, the sky a washed out pink. On mornings like these it's hard to understand why I began to dislike dawn. I thought it was due to a quiet dread of practice, forced to face Harrison and my confused feelings for him. But the reality is more profound, a hangover of my life as Iseult.

Every morning I leave Tristan and return to my chamber is an ever-present suffering. But knowing he's to wed is a horror that lives inside me, eating away at my soul.

Months have passed. My Lord Marc sent Tristan and a cabal of knights away for five months to fight in a battle I didn't think he'd return from, purely because he desires more land and seeks a title of count or duke.

When Tristan returned, scarred and weary, defeated in ways war and killing and death claim men, our joyful reunion was tainted.

Marc decreed the victorious Tristan would marry Gisèle DuPont.

At seventeen, she's older than me by two summers when I first met Tristan, but her family are of good standing for the highly-esteemed knight. Of what I can tell, she will make him a good wife with youth and health on her side. And it's obvious she finds him pleasing to look at.

As much as it hurts, it's only fair for him to have someone to be his. To love freely, with time, if not now.

And I'm pregnant. With Tristan gone, my life as Lady Devereaux had to continue as expected. The child was Marc's, the heir I had to conceive for the security of my marriage and kingdom. A child conceived while Tristan was absent from court, a child to keep him safe. The healer tells me I'm shy of three moons; an announcement to court has been made, and while many rejoice at the news, childbirth fills me with fear. My husband spends his nights with mistresses now I carry his potential heir.

Tonight there is a feast to celebrate Tristan's successful campaign, and that of his betrothal. Finding time to speak alone is nigh on impossible, but finally, thanks to the hard work of Lady Floquet, we steal a few moments alone.

The sorrow I felt at our enforced separation is replaced with nerves and happiness at our reunion. Our lives have digressed. Standing before him pregnant with a child that is not his, distresses me greatly.

"Are you well?" he asks, referencing the growing babe.

I nod, drinking in the sight of him, finally close enough to touch his body, to breathe in that forge and forest scent of him. But tiredness and slaughter are inked into his skin, leaving me pained.

"I missed you."

"I missed you."

Hurried touches are shared, his eyes soft and longing, but I can see the toll of his duty.

The key he gave me hangs low, between my breasts, hidden behind layers of fabric in this chill December air.

I picture the metal seal box that our keys unlock, both required to turn simultaneously to unlock the contents. The lord's seal box holds matrices, secure and safe, authenticating all his documents. But Tristan's, ours, holds treasured things. Our *treasured things.*

Soft kisses wake me from my dream-state, slow, explorative hands chasing away my dream and bringing me to consciousness.

"Tristan," I breathe, opening my eyes to find Kit's concerned face inches from mine.

"I'm here. You okay?"

"There are two keys," I relay. The hopeful look in his eyes has me sitting up, eager to share everything I remember. "Matching keys for a metal seal box."

A frown. "Keys to keep the seals safe."

"There's another key to find," I murmur, crestfallen.

"We already have it, remember?" He quirks his brows. "We made a copy. We can make another. More."

Relief is swift. "God, I love living in such a high tech world sometimes."

Kit smiles ruefully. "Right?"

Tugging me into his body, he holds me tight as we think and recap. Considering recent events, I picture the key inside the key, this soul of the heart. Oxford drew a blank, but we have a lead at the club. And while our time in England had highs and lows with respect to our quest, I remind myself that we're both here, together, and that we will solve this. We have to.

Kit's lecture on his research was extremely well received. As discussed, Professor Santos was present, eager to speak with him.

We'd already met at this stage, introduced by Kit who was owning the situation like he had nothing apologize for.

"I have to know," Santos addressed Kit. "Did you misunderstand my preferences for the program?"

"No," he clarified. "But your note said *I hope you agree*." A carefree shrug. "I didn't. Maddie applied to Brownlow because of me. I wanted her, and she needed to join me at Jacquard."

Our eyes locked, his expression conveying deeper meaning than the face value of his words. And just like that, despite Stephanie Santos' displeasure at the opening she gave him, the problem had been dealt with.

Kit makes coffee and breakfast while I shower and dress, my mind turning over. Returning from London two nights ago, I've only spent one of them in my dorm. Thanksgiving is around the corner, snow covers the streets, and I have four essays to hand in, two of which have an extended deadline thanks to my professor's benevolence and my tender ass. But importantly, we've secured a meeting with Sophie Bouchard.

Instead of our 8:30AM meeting in Kit's office, we battle rush-hour traffic and drive to the club, parking on the street. With the keys deep inside a jacket pocket, and our hands entwined in solidarity, we wait for Sophie in the formidable marble foyer.

She arrives with her usual panache, a burgundy pant suit complimenting her striking, red hair.

"Professor Chevalier. Mademoiselle Devereaux—how lovely to see you again."

Hiding our relationship seemed unnecessary. Kit nominated me, our connection through Jacquard easily identified. She knows he won me in the *conroi.*

Greetings over, we follow Sophie to her office where she directs us to her large, antique desk. The rearing stallion shield representing the society and the ornamental broad swords hanging from her walls instil me with confidence. We're on the right path, we have to be.

"Can I offer you a drink?"

We decline, eager for answers instead.

Siting opposite us, she asks, "How may I help?"

From his pocket, Kit pulls out the smaller key, the one hidden inside the larger, heavier key and places it on the desk. "Do you know what this key unlocks?"

Sophie's face is composed. "What is this key?"

"Let's not play games, Miss Bouchard. We know this key has a twin and that, together, they unlock a seal box, one repurposed into a personal treasure chest. We know it's linked to the société d'honneur." He runs a finger along the shaft, pointing to the words etched into the gold.

"Honneur aulx dignes," I interject. "Those words are the founding ethos of this society and I believe you can help us understand what this opens."

Sophie hasn't touched the key, but she eyes it with barely concealed incredulity.

"You were expecting to see a larger key," I surmise.

Dragging her eyes from said key, she looks between us, her lips curling ever so slightly. When she appears to ignore our questions, reaching for her desk phone and pressing a button, Kit and I exchange confused glances.

"Please bring our guests to my office," Sophie informs someone on the other end of the line before replacing the receiver.

"Who's joining us?" Kit demands.

"There are answers," Sophie informs us, getting to her feet, "but it's best that you hear them directly from someone other than me."

Nervous tremors skitter through me, my pulse fast. Twisting in his chair, Kit follows Sophie's every step. Reassured that he knows how to swing those swords stuck to the wall, Kit's dangerous expression makes me concerned for what will be required of him today.

"Kit," I whisper.

He reaches for my hand just as I reach for his. "It's okay. No one's going to hurt you."

"What about you?" I hiss back as the door behind us opens.

With disbelief, I turn to see Sophie greeting my mother. Instantly, I'm on my feet. "Mom?" Dad follows at her heels, his expression open and friendly. "Dad? What's going on?" I'm too stunned to move closer, to greet them with hugs and kisses.

"We'll explain." Dad says, nodding at Kit and resting a hand on my shoulder.

"Sit, please," Sophie beseeches, positioning two more chairs at her desk.

In shock, we all take our seats, my eyes flitting between Kit and my parents. "What's going on?"

Dad clears his throat. "It's time to give you your inheritance, Maddie."

Misunderstanding why he's bringing this up now, it all makes sense when he produces a key from his pocket. A twin, golden key to the one Kit holds.

"This is my inheritance?"

"Amongst other things."

"Like a chest?" I prod with no small amount of venom in my voice as I take the key from my father. I can't believe they hid this from me.

I catch an embarrassed nod, but the duplicate key in my hand draws my focus. Instead of a chevalier on the shank, there are wavy lines to represent water. And there are musical notes—minims, quavers, and crochets.

"Why didn't you say anything when we met to talk about this weeks ago?" Kit asks, his voice deathly calm. God, I wish I had his steely composure.

"They were not permitted to," Sophie answers.

All eyes swivel to the club's manager, now seated in her office chair, regarding the four of us with supreme confidence.

"You may remember, Miss Devereaux, that you enquired as

to who funded Club VX. Your ancestors founded this club. They have funded it ever since, ensuring the continued participation of the Chevaliers in competing here. Because it is only here, that we can guarantee that the Devereaux and Chevalier descendants might meet."

Then that means . . .

I turn, looking directly at my parents. "You nominated me." Proudly, my mother nods. "Before or after Kit?"

"Before."

Kit frowns, his words soft and just for me. "I thought your involvement was quick, but I put that down to your enthusiasm, the dates being in our favor, and Sophie's efficiency."

"Thank you," Sophie smiles. "But I had a head start. We hoped that seeing Maddie as an option would encourage you to participate, but thankfully, fate directed you to nominate her anyway."

And if he hadn't, I suspect he would've ended up in the *détachement,* his chances of becoming victor in the *conroi* bringing us together on the dais.

But Sophie's reference to fate has me sending her a questioning look. I've not shared my dream-memories with my parents, this knowledge that I've lived another life. When I spoke to them the day after Kit's short incarceration, I only referred to the connection between our families. That I was made aware of my professor being of the Chevalier line in the family tree, a copy of which existed in his family. Naturally, I had to mention the key too—we needed to see what it might unlock. My parents quickly deduced that we were involved, but now I know they were expecting it. Hoping for it.

Studying the gold key, I take stock of everything that's happened. Kit felt compelled to reject me, a decision that felt out of his hands. Perrie told me my father convinced her to apply here, no doubt hoping I would too.

"Was Kit's predecessor ill or did he get pushed out?"

"Poor health persuaded him to leave earlier than intended," Dad says unapologetically. "And I want to stress that you, Kit, are the perfect candidate, regardless of the need for you both to meet."

"Just how much involvement do you have with hiring and firing people here?"

"Only on this occasion."

"You lured me here by offering Josh Cusack a job," Kit guesses, shaking his head.

"Also a fine professor for the role," Dad stresses. "This is no trivial matter and although I'm sure you feel deceived, the pieces on this board have been in play for *centuries*—for both families. None of us got a choice."

The statement rings in my head. After acknowledging it, I press on. "Is this why your marriage was difficult?" I ask as kindly as I can, aware of the toll on their relationship. Today, although anxious, they both seem happy. Is this secret why Mom disliked Harrison so much? He was a distraction, and recently Dad suggested Harrison wasn't for me, no longer abiding by the no interference rules.

"It caused tension," Mom says. "Hiding this from you hurt us. Waiting for things to take their natural course was a constant worry. We were told to trust the process. No interfering. This had to come from you, a Devereaux girl finding honor in a Chevalier boy. Finding him worthy of her love."

"Why?"

"It was vowed. A promise. In 900 years we have never got this far," Sophie informs us. "Never a love that burns as bright and swift as yours."

Kit's palm, pressed against mine, tightens.

"What is your involvement in this, Sophie?" He's dispensed

with titles and games, seeking the root of this mystery. This sounds *orchestrated.*

Sophie looks to me. "Can you guess? Do you see me in your memories?"

I study her face, picking apart all the characteristics but unable to place her. The only option I can think of is my friend, Lady Béatrice Floquet. I tell everyone as much and am rewarded with a broad smile from Sophie, my parents passing ecstatic glances.

Sophie takes a notable breath. Full of pride, she reveals, "The honor society acts as custodian of the box and its contents. Its founders became aware of a vow, a promise between two people whose love went beyond earthly boundaries. Béatrice Floquet and Guy Vaudeville, of whom I am a descendant, secured your precious items until you were reunited again."

"I know the name Vaudeville," Kit interrupts.

Gathering us in her gaze, Sophie continues. "Your squire, Guy Vaudeville, who married Lady Floquet, sacrificing her position as a lady at court in order to safeguard your legacy." Her eyes fall to the keys resting on the desk. "A legacy built not only on what lies within the box, but on honor, duty, devotion and service."

Sophie stands and moves to the bookcases behind her. Gripping a cabinet door, she pulls it open to reveal a hidden door. Inputting a number into an electronic, green-lit key pad, beeps sound with each key press. The door unlocks with a click, Sophie pulling it open as dim lights flicker on inside the small room.

"Bring your keys."

Keys in hand, we round the desk and follow Sophie inside the three metre square, temperature controlled space. Sophie approaches a plinth, on which is a museum-grade display case. Inside is a metal seal box with rusted iron reinforcements along its edges and around its circumference. Shoe box sized, two keyholes are visible at the front locks.

It's hard to breathe. To take this all in. Will this change everything? Silently, I look at Kit.

Noticing the direction of my thoughts, Kit smooths a hand across my shoulders. "We've got this. There's no future for me without you in it. No existence worth living if you're not by my side."

"I love you."

Bending, he kisses me softly on the mouth. "I love you, too."

Behind me, Mom and Dad hold hands, happiness shining brightly in their eyes. My attention turns to Sophie who's been watching our heartfelt moment, pride on her face. Carefully, wearing curator's gloves, she removes the seal box from the cabinet and moves it to a nearby desk.

My nerves feel shot, my breath thin. No dreams have prepared me for what comes next.

Seconds pass as we survey the age-worn box.

"This has been in the club's possession since our founding. As preservation techniques advanced, we have done all we can to ensure the integrity of your inheritance, Miss Devereaux."

"*My* inheritance? I thought this was Kit's?"

"This chest and all its contents became yours. It was your family that secured it, with help from my ancestor."

"But they were *Tristan's* at one time. They still *are* Tristan's," I argue.

"Tristan was killed. On his death, they became yours alone."

"What does it matter? They would've gone to his family. He was married. He had a son, Williem."

"I am unwilling to debate this further. Now, it's time for you to swap keys."

Kit demands, "Why?"

Sophie regards Kit with steely eyes. "Because for almost a

millennium, the Devereaux family have safeguarded Tristan Chevalier's key, and the Chevalier family have kept and passed on Iseult Devereaux's key. The time to return them to their rightful owners has arrived."

Blankly, I look between Kit and Sophie unable to understand. Running the pad of my thumb over the musical notes and rippling water, I begin to understand. These attributes were engraved for Tristan, a reminder of me, our love, and where we'd meet. Because it makes sense that Kit's key denoting a knight with a personal message about honor would be a special keepsake for me.

Simultaneously, Kit and I pass over our respective keys; this is the first time Kit holds mine. As I lay it on his open palm he sucks in a sharp breath, his eyelids fluttering, his body shaking as if under attack.

"It means, chevalier," Sophie murmurs. "It's time for you to remember."

30

KIT

The Power of Love - Frankie Goes to Hollywood

The wretched man spins in a bloody arc from the heft of my sword, collapsing to the ground with a death cry as blood pumps from his thigh and gurgles from his mouth. Stepping over his fallen body I impale his thin chest with the end of Righteous.

Around me, four men lie dead at my hand. Their drab clothes and lack of armor denote them as thieves, opportunists. Wiping the blade clean on their dirty clothes, I sheathe Righteous and survey the two ladies who would've met a grisly end at the hands of these abominable men.

Dressed in attire fitting noble houses, they regard me with gratitude.

Chain mail tinkling, I sink to a knee. "Sir Tristan, at your service."

The younger lady who I know to be Iseult Auclair

approaches on swift feet, her voice flowing through me like cool water. "Thank you, good knight. We are in your debt."

When I glance up, she's rising out of a curtsey, her gaze inquisitive.

I cannot admit that our paths crossed twelve days ago. That I followed her, and that every day since I have waited and watched, tracking her as she roamed the woods and hills on horseback with her companion. It was dangerous for them to do so without armed men; it was my duty to protect them. To protect my Lord Devereaux's lands from sinister forces and all who dwell within them. Secret enquiries at court tell me her father is close to Lord Marc. She is Lord Auclair's only daughter, beloved and beautiful, a free spirit that he often chastizes her for.

He intends to being her to court soon, to be wed. An alliance to further her father's position, and to strengthen my lord's circle.

"Thanks be to God," her companion, Béatrice Floquet murmurs, smiling tentatively at me.

Standing, I nod to Mistress Floquet and turn to her high-born companion. She's beautiful. A necessary distance from previous days prevented me from the blood-warming sight. Of no more than fifteen, Iseult Auclair has long golden brown hair cascading down her back, torn from its neat coiffure as she fought off the attackers. Curious eyes drink me in, a jeweled, bloodied dagger held loosely in her hand. Her companion is older by a few years, thin of face, and brown of hair. Their fingers are interlocked.

"Are you hurt? May I escort you back to your lands?"

"We would be very grateful," Iseult replies. She's shaking, the fabric of her dress rustling.

I offer them water from my skein. Iseult accepts, sipping, as her eyes drink in my appearance. "Are you harmed?" she enquires.

Blood is splattered across my chest and face. "By the grace of God, no, Mistress Auclair."

Two horses, scattered by the sound of the attack graze nearby. I clean my face with a cloth as I walk to the mares. Gathering up the reins, I help the women mount.

"Sir Tristan," Iseult offers, her expression earnest. "Your name precedes you."

She speaks truth; I have made a name for myself, not only as a trusted sword for Lord Marc, but as a champion in tourneys. "Yes, mistress."

"If I see you I will cheer for you."

The words are confirmation of her imminent arrival at court and I accept the kindness she has bestowed me.

Slowly, we trek back, my ears greedy for Iseult's words and harmonious voice. We speak of many topics, her mind curious of people at court and the politics of our lands, despite cautionary words from her friend for her brazenness.

Iseult shrugs indifferently, a brow lifting in defiance. I understand then what sin is. At how God tempts man to leave the path of righteousness and to succumb to quiet seduction.

In the days that follow her safe return, I write to Iseult. My squire, Guy Vaudeville acts as courier. Often, I write no more than some lines of poetry, of religious texts that strike me as worthy, to aspire to. Sometimes, my words are complimentary to her fair looks and good graces. I vow to be a good servant to God, defending His name and her honor.

For three weeks, Guy delivers my messages, letting her know if I am indisposed. It is forbidden to meet alone, but with Guy keeping watch, she steals from her fortified manor and finds me in a pre-arranged corner of my estate, her companion ever-present. Here, where we are safe, Iseult avidly reads my letters, gifting me with tokens of her affections, including her knife.

She is all I think about.

It is on a fine late spring day when I first kiss her, a chaste kiss that burns through me nonetheless and smolders in my veins for the next seven days while I remain absent from her. On the eighth day we have barely escaped to our favorite spot before we fall to the grass, our kiss longer and heavier. Soft hands touch and caress my scarred skin, undaunted by the death of men these scars speak to. She's a purgatory I cannot escape. And even though it will damn us both, I do not stop her shy advances and whispered pleas. I make love to her sweetly, gently, pressing in beyond her barrier and making her mine for all eternity. She cries out my name to God and I feel torn in two, torn apart by my duty and heart.

By the laws of the land we are man and wife. Béatrice is witness but we can never document it thus.

For the next ten days we read Latin passages and psalms as if to cleanse our souls, to redeem ourselves in God's eyes. A rival to the skylark, her song enchants me. Endless stolen hours are spent together, quietly fearing discovery. Often we wish our lives were other; Iseult is destined for a marriage of politics not love.

"Love between a man and a woman is as good as any duty we owe to God," Iseult whispers to me as we lie semi-clothed by the brook. Today, she took my rigid flesh in her mouth, sucking until I spilled on her persistent tongue. Afterwards, I kissed the soft pink flesh between her legs and worked my cock inside her heat. I have lived in Heaven since our first meeting, but it is our lazy afternoons by the brook where my heart dwells. "He cannot forsake two souls who love as strongly as we."

Her father would never allow her to marry a knight—he has greater aspirations. And my marriage to Iseult is not advantageous to Marc—he would never agree. Besides, fever takes grip of Marc's pregnant wife. For a time, he has greater need of me, and to find balance between my selfish actions and my duty to God, I excel in all the tasks he asks of me. But I cannot compromise on Iseult. I never will. God would not join our souls together if He had other plans for us.

Before long Iseult is welcomed at court; her arrival causes waves amongst the lords and ladies as they strategize and plot who Lord Auclair will give her to. Until then, I must hide my interest, flattery and words of praise directed at married ladies of the court. Such actions pain me; my eyes only seek Iseult.

At the tourney to celebrate the birth of Marc's daughter, Iseult finds me in the stables through her usual stealthy ways. I'm preparing my stallion, Virtue, for the arduous tasks of the tournament ahead, his armor bright and freshly hammered.

"With you, my love is not pretend," I vow.

"I know," she agrees, fixing a ribbon of cream lace to the round end of my lance and wishing me good fortune. "What we have is real."

Attuned to her voice, I hear the tremor of worry for my well-being. It fills my heart with resolve. With care. I cannot disappoint or hurt her.

Knowing she watches me, that all eyes are upon me as I charge towards my opponent fills me with purpose. Shields shatter, knights are knocked from horses as I progress through the tournament.

In the end, I am champion, still.

Later, I am fêted at the feast. With the help of Béatrice, aware of how to move unseen and unheard through the castle halls, Iseult finds me and gifts me with a gold ring. It is a token of her faithfulness.

It will be treasured, kept with all the other declarations of our love.

Summer peaks and fades. Marc's wife is dead from the fever that never left, as is his infant. For a time, court grieves. To cheer my spirits, Iseult gifts me a small portraiture. Béatrice is a remarkable artiste and copies Iseult's striking visage with a deft hand. I ask her if she would paint me, as a token to my sweet Iseult. Four days later she presents it to me, the likeness strong thanks to her remarkable memory and keen eye. We lock the new painting with its twin in the chest, the two keys dangling from our necks.

We refer to it as a love chest. It has two keys to symbolize our two hearts. Two hearts in one body. As a love token, I carry her key and she carries mine, both engraved with meaningful symbols.

War is a constant threat. Other lords vie for land and position, causing unrest. "If anything happens to me," I tell Iseult, Mistress Floquet's presence meaning she is included in my order. "I will find you again. This chest, these keys, are testament to our bond. If it survives, so too, does our love."

"Don't trouble me with such images."

"Am I not to be troubled by Marc's interest in you, Iseult? He wants you. Your father encourages it."

Iseult looks stricken. Recently, she had her first bleed. She is a woman now, considered of marrying age. "I cannot deter him from this path—my father is ambitious."

My duty to God, to Lord Marc wars with my love for her. At times I struggle to understand how love between a man and a woman can be wrong. She was not meant for me but she is already mine. Our love is fierce and true and I cannot forsake her.

As the last light of the short summer day descends beyond the hills, I kneel before my love and present Iseult with a ring, one of many I have gifted her now. The gold is engraved with, *I desire to serve.*

The ring signifies our marriage contract. As I kneel before her with the vow I should not make but make all the same, she places a hand on the crown of my head, a gentle gesture binding us. After sliding the ring on her finger, I enter her hallowed warmth, my body, my heart wrapped around hers. Iseult's whispers and cries of love as she finds her pleasure is where my soul lives.

Basking in our passion, I trace her pale brown brows, her beguiling golden eyes, her rose-pink lips. Dappled sunlight filters between the leaf-laden branches of the trees above. The brook tinkles in the background. Pain in my stomach has me sliding a hand over where it burns with a breathless ferocity. Blood seeps between my fingers. My vision wavers and blurs.

Around me, the deathly cries of battle sound. Beyond the castle walls, horses shriek. Armor clangs and swords clash, the roars of dying men shake me to the core. Around me lie slain men, cut down by my sword as they came to steal Iseult and kill her son. Blood trickles between the flagstones, running in the grooves.

Iseult's knees give out, pleading to God as she slumps over me, tears falling like waterfalls. She shouldn't be here; it's too dangerous. Married to Marc, she was my wife first, unknown by any but two. Now she is his.

Wailing, Béatrice drops to my other side. She has been a most faithful friend and companion to Iseult and myself. I pray that she be rewarded by God for her steadfastness.

Cloth from their dresses is pressed to my stomach but I bleed and bleed, faint and heavy-bodied. I think of my son; two years is no age to lose your father. I think of Gisèle who I will leave a widow. But my eyes find Iseult as I reach for her with shaking hands. I have failed her. My honor is broken, my promises too.

Vehemently, she shakes her head. I must've spoken the words aloud but I cannot feel my body.

"We didn't have long enough," I tell her.

"As God as my witness I will follow you, Tristan."

Angrily, I mumble a *no,* shaking my head.

The blade of Righteous lifts in her hand, angled to her body.

Béatrice's voice is a shrill command. "My lady, no!"

Tears splash my face, my vision darkening.

"I cannot live in a world without you."

"You must," I grit. "Think of your son. Love is stronger than death. And you are strong, Iseult."

Injured, Guy Vaudeville staggers towards me, stepping over those I felled by my sword. Falling against a wall, Béatrice crawls towards him, helping him as best she can.

"Guy," she croaks fearfully.

"They're dead. You killed the last, sir. The castle is secure."

At least I have protected her. I always vowed it so until my dying breath.

"Please God," Iseult sobs, "do not take them. Do not take Tristan from me. If you do, then rip my soul from my body and bury it with his! I am not Marc's. *I am Tristan's!*"

My vow by the brook returns to me like a clarion call. We are bound together like time eternal. This life was too short but this love will endure.

"The Lord Jesus died for us that we might be re-born. I will find you, Iseult. I will live again. This life is preparation for the next. The new. For a life where we are free to love with our *whole soul.*"

"Where we do not need to hide."

"Never again," I vow.

"I have loved you since I first saw you."

I know this. I felt it in her touch and saw it on her face. "And I you. You are the soul of my heart."

I can barely hear her broken words before she furiously kisses my face, my mouth. Pressing her lips against mine for long seconds, I feel breathless.

I am dying.

It's hard to speak. To see. I press the key from my neck into my love's palm. "On my honor we will . . . be reunited. And I will serve you . . . better than I have in this life, Iseult. I . . . will be worthy."

Throwing herself onto my chest, her voice breaks as my lungs rattle. "I will love you until I am dust."

"And we will have again." My body is weightless. My eyes sightless. With my last breath I whisper, "I will f-find you."

SHUDDERING, it feels like a spirit has passed through my body. What do they say? *Someone walked over my grave*. Eyelids fluttering as I process, as I recall and *remember*, I become aware of four people around me. Sophie, Pippa and John watch with rapt, tense expressions. Tears line Maddie's cheeks, her eyes blinking furiously. Has she remembered more? Has she seen what I have?

"Kit?"

The haunting, soft, familiar voice is almost my undoing. But the sight of her, of my Iseult standing in front of me, breathing and beautiful and so heartbreakingly alive, sends me to my knees in catastrophic relief. Tears flow as my arms wrap around her thighs like steel bands. My cheek presses against her abdomen, every part of me aware of how her chest heaves with ragged breaths, of her beating heart and rapid pulse.

"Oh my God. You're here. You're real. You're alive."

Gentle fingers stroke my scalp and run through my hair. And naturally, the answer is simple for Maddie. After all, she's lived this for months. "I'm here." Softly, with a smile in her voice, she adds, "You found me."

. . .

It might only be ten o'clock in the morning, but Sophie orders a bottle of champagne from the club's bar. We knock it back as I recount the most pertinent memories to Maddie's parents, leaving out some of the more private details.

Sophie Bouchard's family tree goes back as far as mine, all the way to Lady Floquet. It's preserved—alongside a patchwork diary—inside the vault, more evidence of our connected lives. Of the enormous quest Lady Floquet's family have courageously weathered.

"Béatrice was a devoted friend."

Iseult—Maddie—nods, smiling at Sophie and enveloping her in a long, heartfelt hug. Then she walks to her parents and does the same. "I like to think we were soul sisters. I was an only child, even then. So was Béatrice."

It's hard to comprehend all that's been preserved and passed on. The descendants of the Vaudeville's have acted with remarkable generosity and devotion. Selling the chest and its contents would be easy. Forgetting to share this knowledge and fate to descendants all too simple. Their dedication to the cause is beyond exemplary.

Already, I know the chest's contents and they will be the find of a thousand years. The items and texts will be debated for decades and researched to death. It will change and divide opinion. It is an outstanding find, depicting a love story that transcends time. I tell the others as much, all of us awed and grateful and so bewildered it will take time to sink in.

Pippa and John must feel this hardest—unable to rely on memories, they have to go by the word of Sophie Bouchard, the diaries of the Floquet/Vaudeville line, and whoever she inherited this monumental task from.

At length, Sophie explains the role of the society. Hundreds of years ago it was only known to a small number of people who made records of our descendants, hoping paths would cross and souls would reunite. Béatrice was what we would call a hopeless romantic. She had watched Tristan and Iseult fall in love, evidently heartbroken when Tristan died.

I get the impression she was a little in love with him.

A year after Tristan's death, Iseult died in childbirth. Her daughter survived, but according to Sophie, Iseult had given up on life.

With swords and armor surrounding us, I share a seat with Maddie as history unfolds around us, our hands and fingers laced together.

"Béatrice was certain you would find each other again. It became a passion project, so to speak. She had her own family —with Guy—and ensured their children and grandchildren and all that followed tracked your lines until you met again."

"Ideas like that would have had her burned at the stake or sent to an asylum," Maddie notes.

Sophie nods. "It was kept close to their chests. Until roughly two hundred and fifty years ago, when my ancestor, Henri Vaudeville, took the chest from Oxford when he moved to Canada."

"We thought we hit a dead end in Oxford," Maddie shares.

"Vaudeville knowledge was pooled with Devereaux finances —after some convincing to the validity of Henri's claims," Sophie adds wryly. "But he was very persuasive, and thankfully," Sophie looks to Maddie's father, "John's ancestors were convinced. Alongside the family trees that were painstakingly recorded, the chest's contents were unequivocal in their origins."

"I can't believe you kept this from me," Maddie presses her parents.

"It had to be authentic."

Maddie argues carefully, "Did it though? Why not just share

all of this with us?" She sweeps a hand towards the chest, still unopened on the desk. "Maybe love would've blossomed from seeing the letters and gifts."

"Non," Sophie barks. "Lady Floquet's instructions were very clear. Reunited souls. Souls of the heart only. Tell me you were not drawn to the essence of Club VX. That a knight did not appeal to you more than any other fantasy. That French medieval literature was not a calling for you. That you did not feel a pull when you first met your professor, in the bar or in college."

Maddie's eyebrow is arched. "Were you spying on me? On us?"

Sophie's mouth purses. "The authenticity of the chest's contents will be incomprehensible to many. They are beyond treasure. They are of insurmountable value financially, intellectually, and historically. Do not underestimate the lengths the société d'honneur has gone to to protect your inheritance and to see your death-vows realized. It was my ancestor's greatest wish to see this to fruition and that honor was restored."

I want to ask about the family feud but it really would be petty and ungrateful and sour the mood. And part of me wonders does it even matter? Can I forget what happened when I've been reunited with my first and only love? My blood flows through me like a golden river. The air in my lungs tastes silver bright. Facts and statements and words are my currency and I find myself unsure how to deal with the paranormal or the Godly. Was this God? Have I been rewarded by Him in this life?

Positives aside, it hurts like a motherfucker knowing that it was me that broke Maddie's heart. An echo of that pain carried into this life, her sights set on the wrong man. Harrison might've been a wretched fuck, but it was my death that had her crawling this earth, seeking the other half of her heart.

"We are very grateful for your tireless work, Sophie. Truly. But what now?"

Smiles of agreement from my future in-laws. Or are they my in-laws already? I can't decide.

"Now," Sophie says getting to her feet and raising her flute, "now you open the chest."

31

MADDIE

Sweetest Devotion - Adele

Six years later

Beyond the verdant hills the sun sets, painting us in warm orange and crimson. Under cover of maples, ash trees, and lindens, the branches thick with birds and the air filled with insects, Kit and I absorb the view that featured so strongly in our memories.

"It was here that I declared you my sworn love, in this life and in all others."

I trace Kit's brows and cheekbones, running my fingers across ten day stubble—my favorite. "I know."

At the beginning, Kit said it felt like every day was a dual life. He was teacher and warrior, researcher and writer, but he protected and loved and honored too, flitting between lives.

The one constant in this crazy alternative world he inhabits is me, a replica of Iseult at his side while he learnt of his life as Tristan, a life of déjà vu and knowledge beyond our realm. We recalled conversations, relived memories. Some afternoons we lay by this brook and fucked like it was still forbidden and time was running out.

Bit by slow bit those memories of *before*, faded, leaving us to live only in the now.

I am his wife. Again. For always. Mother to three adorable children. First came the twins, Béatrice and Sophie. Guy came fourteen months later. Somehow, amongst the marriage and pregnancies, and not least the madness that followed the chest's existence, I completed my doctorate, my academic ambitions realized.

Life is too short. Grabbing happiness with both hands and hanging on for the ride, wherever it takes us, is our motto.

The contents of the chest created a frenzy of academic, media, and international interest. So far we have managed to conceal the hows and the whys, merely stating that it was left to Kit by the family of Henri Vaudeville. The family tree was proof enough of his ancestry, and with Henri's will stating it had to go to a descendant of Sir Tristan Chevalier, it was Sophie's choice to make.

Keeping it was inconceivable, the contents priceless. Our love story belongs to everyone, but it came at a steep, personal price. Museums and collectors and nations all wanted a piece, but they were outbid by the Devereaux Foundation. In some respects, it's only fair; these heirlooms belong to us, and this way we get to keep them, even if they are preserved in perpetuity in museums around the world.

Aside from brooches, necklaces, and precious stones, there were seven rings inside, all of them inscribed with words of favor, love, or service. Some were set with jewels but nothing like today's glittering sizes or clarity. But it's the love notes, texts, and poems that thrill us most; they're extraordinary, a gift beyond measure, an insight into a knight's agonizing dilemma and the difficult choices he faced. At what we risked, together. But the icing on the cake is the complete manuscript of an unknown epic romance, gifted to Tristan by Iseult.

With Béatrice and Guy's diary—sheets of barely legible parchment added to over centuries—acting as authentication of the contents, the origin stories, and the sentiment behind them, our items have been heralded as the find of the millennium. It's all thanks to my good friend and to Kit's squire that any of this exists.

We trek back to the stables on our favorite horses, the path through the woods lined with motion detector lights to guide our way. Unfamiliar with horse riding, it's taken me some time to find confidence. Kit incentivizes me by wearing the black jodhpurs he looks too good in, and depending on the time of year, sits atop his black stallion sans shirt.

Still, it's not often we get moments like this to ourselves. But with Kit's sister and her young family staying, Hélène offered to take control.

The stablehands greet us when we dismount and, after saying goodnight, we head into the house.

Sherbrooke, with its two hundred and four acres of rolling pastures, woodland, and hills, was a wedding gift from my parents. Thanks to the accounts of Sophie's family, I learnt that this land belonged to the Chevalier's at one time before it was gambled away. An altercation ensued, a great-great grandparent giving the Chevalier ancestor a chance to win it back. It didn't end well, a mess of pride and hurt feelings and affairs shrouding everyone's good senses. A duel was called. A death followed. Ashamed at believing the tales of endless feuds, Kit feels Sophie was kind in her explanation.

And it's perhaps why he didn't push for Erica to be pursued

by the law, ensuring the police stopped at fining her for false reporting. It was an act of generosity I came to accept in the end, though I struggled with it.

As for Harrison, our paths rarely cross. When they do, we're civil, but I have no interest in his life anymore. He's my past, Kit is my future. My forever.

Two years ago we built a huge stone and log house near the ruins of the original cottage. The proportions are insane, with tons of glazing, balconies, and modern architecture making it more than enough for our large family. Gramps lives in an annex, his old house knocked down and a new stable big enough for fifteen horses built in its place. With funding from the Devereaux Foundation, and with proceeds from the sale of our chest, we have more money than we could ever need to keep the riding school a viable business.

Ecstatic doesn't begin to describe Hélène's emotions when she's here, working with vulnerable children. Seeing her fulfilling her dream, her mom's, makes Kit happy. Also recently married, we find Hélène and her husband, Ryan, in the kitchen, somehow managing to wrangle five children under six to the dinner table.

We didn't know how long it would take to have the family we envisioned. Would I take after Mom and have my own struggles? And waiting until I finished my doctorate seemed nonsensical with Kit so keen to wife me up and put a baby in me.

Gramps is stirring a pot on the stove while Ryan and my sister-in-law sort the children into age-appropriate seats, the noise and mayhem a stark contrast to our peaceful horse ride.

"This place is a zoo," Gramps remarks, offering me a taste of the spoon.

"You don't get to grumble, Gramps," Kit jumps in. "You wanted great-grand kids, remember?"

He winks at me. "So I did. If only I could remember their names," he jokes.

"There's nothing wrong with your memory," I tell him because it's true, though I do allow that Bea and Sophie might be tricky for others to tell apart—they're identical. But he's like those old golden retrievers who find a new lease of life when young pups arrive. Seeing his great-grandchildren arrive, having everything squared away for Kit and Hélène gives him peace and renewed purpose. Watching them grow up happy is all he wants.

After sorting food and drinks, we join everyone at the table. The double height kitchen, the last of the sun coming in through the floor to ceiling windows, is my favorite room in the house.

"Thanks guys for taking point," Kit says. "It was good to get out."

"Yeah? Bruno and Sabrina behave themselves?" Hélène asks while popping a cherry tomato in her mouth.

The horses are named after singer/songwriters. I'm not entirely sure why other than Hélène and I cooked up the idea at her bachelorette party. All are impeccably behaved, selected for their calm characters and pedigree.

"Good as gold," Kit answers.

The grown-ups barely get a chance to talk as we cajole our children to eat, to eat *nicely*, and to not drop food on the floor. It's all a lost cause. As Ryan passes round beers for courage and fortitude, we're all quite pleased when it's bath time.

"Can we swim in the pool?" Sophie asks, her blonde ringlets framing her angelic face.

"Tomorrow you can. When Josh and Perrie are here."

My children love our friends, referring to them as Uncle Josh and Aunty Perrie. To squeals of happiness at the idea of visitors,

Kit rounds up as many children as he can and hauls them upstairs, heading for the bathroom. Béatrice clings to his back, Guy is tucked under an arm, Sophie the other. Ryan scoops up his two boys and takes them to the guest quarters.

It's an hour before they're in bed. Stories are a big part of our routine and it's unsurprising that knights and dragons are a big hit for the four-year-old twins. Still two, Guy's tastes are a little less sophisticated.

Once they're snuggled down, Kit and I walk wearily to our bedroom and collapse on the bed. Save for the distant lights of the stables, it's pitch black beyond the balcony doors.

"I feel that I didn't give Mrs P enough credit for looking after Cody. My body *aches.*"

Mrs Pantazis remains Kit's steadfast PA and has been a wonderful friend over the years. Cody loves visiting and meeting the horses, though Elvis is his go-to.

"She didn't have three beautiful kids to look after," Kit points out. "Or the million other things you do." He turns his head to find me looking at him. "I can run you a bath," he offers. "Or," he suggests, rolling on top of me and wedging his hard cock against my pussy, "I can kiss the aches better."

A mischievous smile blooms. "I am a little saddle-sore."

Kit's low laughter warms my heart. "Little liar, but as I've said before, I will accept all and any excuse."

I dissolve into laughter as he ravishes my neck and face and lips, my body slowly melting as the kisses turn heavier, a moan of want purring from my throat.

"It still bothers me," he begins, tonguing my neck as his fingers strum my nipple. "That I couldn't save you from Mark, before or now."

I rock into his body, undulating underneath him with growing persistence. "You did, Kit. I'd already met and married him when you got the first job offer—nothing was going to change that. But the second time," I whisper, gripping his ass and moving him harder against me, "you were there, protecting me. Directing me towards you, lesson by lesson."

His lips are tender and drugging, but suddenly he pulls back, grabs my waistband and yanks off my leggings. My panties follow, then he's tugging my ass to the edge of the mattress. Dropping to the floor, he places my feet on his shoulders and *feasts*. Clutching his head between my hands, I direct him how I need him, tortured *yeses* falling from my lips. Rocking against his devious mouth, he works his tongue inside me, soothing my aches until I implode underneath him.

Meeting Kit when I was teenager was an impossibility. Considering my family's knowledge of the task, they never sought him out, never engineered our paths to cross. Until later. Considering my age, it would've been weird, not that it stopped me from seeking a relationship with an older man at the time. I pursued him because I thought he was Kit, an echo of my grand love driving me forwards.

"There had to be three of us, circling each other. It was a mirror-life."

Standing, Kit pulls his cock from out of his sweats and guides himself home. "But with a better ending. What did I do to deserve you?"

"You loved me," I answer on a moan as Kit fully seats himself. "You stole my heart."

The thieves would've taken my virtue along with my valuables. But he was watching, protecting, stealing me for himself. Those behaviors ran in parallel where Harrison and I were concerned, though this time I wasn't stolen, just reclaimed.

The minutes dissolve as we chase release. When we fall, when the high dissipates and we've recovered our breath, we don't get to lounge or linger in the afterglow. We just hop in the shower and get ready for our guests.

Josh and Perrie are driving up tonight. Josh is still at Jacquard and has been in love with Perrie ever since she gave him hell for not knowing any female soccer players. Perrie tells me she fell for Josh after Kit's prison break, the common ground of Kit and I their favorite talking point.

A little while later, as Gramps retires for the evening and Kit opens some champagne, Perrie and Josh pull up.

Seeing Perrie again brings a wide smile to my face; I've missed her. Having them stay the weekend is going to be such fun. We'll swim and sunbathe and go horse riding, drink and eat and catch up like the old days. That they'll happily include my sister-in-law and Ryan into our double celebrations means a lot to both of us.

"Happy anniversary!" Perrie shouts as she walks through the door. "Here's to five years married!"

I pass her a glass of bubbles, giving her a hug before greeting Josh who's finished bro-hugging Kit.

"I can't believe it either! Time flies, *Dr* Secker."

A quick grin. "Sure does, *Dr Chevalier*. Three kids to grow, birth, and nurture, a doctorate to finish, a new home, a business venture with your new family," Perrie says, throwing her arms around Hélène and Ryan as we enter the living room, "I feel under accomplished."

"Nonsense," I say, knowing how much effort the last years have taken.

"Honey, do you have our presents for the happy couple?"

Carrying a large, heavy gift bag in his hand, Josh passes it to Perrie.

"Okay," she says, putting down her glass and bringing something out of the bag. "So, to remind everyone, five years is wood."

Josh snickers and I think I know what's going through his mind.

"This was Josh's pick. As you know, I have superior taste, but I was overruled." She winks at me. "It was too fun an opportunity to pass up."

With a very satisfied grin, Perrie hands me a rectangular package. It looks like it could house a slim, tall vase or a flask. Tearing off the paper to reveal the plain box, I pick open the tabs at the top and peek inside.

"Dear Lord," I whisper, fighting a laugh. Perrie is cracking up, so I pull out the wooden cock, one that's at least ten inches long and far broader than a cucumber. I hold it aloft for all to see.

Josh grins. Kit chuckles. They both speak at once.

"—We went larger. Didn't want to embarrass you."

"—Way too small. You should've asked for a picture as a buyer's guide."

"Where am I supposed to put this?" I say to Perrie and regret it immediately.

"Up your ass?" she suggests to hoots of laughter. "It has a base in case you want to display it, or use it."

"I meant, how am I going to hide this from the kids!" Heat rushes to my cheeks and I throw the gift to the couch as if that can save me.

Despite laughing, Hélène slowly steps away from where I threw the offending item. "I don't want to know."

Josh's laugh is deep and sonorous. "Let's move on to our second gift which is equally practical."

Kit scoffs. I shake my head in disbelief.

A bigger parcel is pulled out of the bag. Kit opens the package which turns out to be a beautifully crafted memory box. The colours are warm and beautiful, two woods dovetailed together, the veneer creating a soft sheen under the lights.

"It's rosewood. It's guaranteed to last at least fifty years in the ground, though stick it in a plastic bag and you'll double the life of it, maybe triple."

There are two gold keys for the lock, lovely, personal details etched into the lid and sides. There are waves, hearts, stars, and latin text that speak of enduring love.

"It's too good to bury," Kit says.

"I agree."

It'll be a keepsake box for sure, but one we don't have to hide. Unlike before, my wedding ring sits proudly on my finger. Although modern and set with diamonds, it has a familiar vow engraved on the band's inside: *I desire to serve.* It's only fitting for the man who is consistently *extra*, who gives me the fully loaded version of him at all times.

Hugging Perrie and Josh, I tell them, "Thank you. It's perfect and beautiful and we're so grateful."

"It's also big enough to hide your first present in, in case you were wondering," Josh imparts.

"Wasn't," Kit answers for me, "but thanks for the tip, man," he murmurs.

Perrie asks, "Where are the little cherubs?"

Our children are going to be ring bearers and flower girls for their wedding next year. "Asleep," I tell her, shoving the glass of champagne back in her hand. "I know we've already celebrated, but we should raise a glass to your happy union tonight too," I announce, Hélène and Ryan raising their glasses in toast.

Kit refills glasses, everyone taking a seat on the couches. Music plays in the background as the night draws on, laughter and chatter filling our home. The overloaded charcuterie boards with a range of meats, cheeses, and speciality breads are slowly consumed.

Life is good.

Several times, Kit and I lock eyes, conveying so many emotions. And when, eventually, we retire to bed, knowing the children will be up at 6AM if we're lucky, 5AM if we're not, Kit and I sit on the day bed on our balcony and inhale the mild night air. Stars and a crescent moon shine down on us as we examine our memory box.

"The cock is *not* going inside."

"Agreed. A copy of your bound thesis should—a different kind of manuscript but just as valuable as Iseult's. It was your doctorate that brought us together."

I nod. "I'm going to add the first essay I wrote for you. You had written: *A well-deserved A plus. An excellent use of comparative judgment, Madrigal.*" He was always so good to me, my champion in all things.

"Iseult's favor to Ronin also goes in," he suggests to my ready agreement. "Our wedding photos. Your picture as Iseult."

"You in your armor."

As unique wedding presents go, I hit the jackpot. The company I bought Iseult's dress from also made high quality, bespoke armor. Crafted from metal that's more charcoal than silver, the deep chest plate is light-weight and covered in designs straight from the medieval era. Pauldrons protect both shoulders, the material layered like armadillo scales. There are tassets for the thighs and bracers for the forearms. With his sword attached at the belt and a deep green jacket underneath that compliments his dark honey eyes, Kit gets devoured whenever he wears it.

A nod. "What else?"

"The detention slips you so eagerly gave me."

An amused chuckle. "Someone was *eagerly* bending over my desk if I recall. Besides, the girls were conceived on it."

"They were," I agree. "The print out of the text message you sent Gramps saying *she's the one*."

Kit smiles contentedly. "You were. You are. I knew it quickly."

Contemplating on our new love chest, Kit gathers up my

hand as we look up at the silver dots in the sky. Whether it was God who set us on our path, or the particles of stars which live on inside us, a gift from the crucible of the galaxy guiding us back together, I cannot say. I just know that the man I was meant to love for all eternity is at my side, that his strong heart beats anew, and that Iseult and Tristan can finally rest in peace.

We are home.

ACKNOWLEDGMENTS

Thank you for reading Lessons in Love!

If you liked it, please consider leaving a review on Amazon :)

Tales of courtly love and epic poems, of knights adhering to a chivalric code from medieval days have fascinated me. I studied medieval literature at college so it's no surprise I wanted to write a love story on this theme. And while this isn't meant to be a history or language lesson, you might be interested to know what else has inspired me.

East Anglia, in the east of England, is a treasure-trove. It is in this part of Great Britain where many Roman finds have been unearthed through metal detecting, alongside treasure from Viking and medieval eras.

Medieval jewelery, such as brooches, were used as tokens and given by champions to lovers; rings were engraved with French chivalric mottos such as "I desire to serve you" and "I wish to obey." Others were adorned with images of saints, or shaking hands - a symbol of faithfulness, which featured in my book.

England was once ruled by Dukes of Normandy, an area in northern France. As a result, Old French was the common language of the English courts for several hundred years, jewelery, and ultimately treasure from this period with French inscriptions.

The Spanish chivalric romance Maddie references **was** found in Norfolk, England.

The suitcase tale I heard on Radio 1. The segment about people trying to be helpful but making it ten times worse had me howling with laughter. Kit's intentions were definitely good, but I did embellish the story. Thanks to the caller!

And finally, the fact I really love, as confirmed by Professor Brian Cox and Professor Hannah Fry; our origins are entwined with the stars. Atoms in our bodies were 'forged in the hearts of dying stars' and spread across the universe through cosmic events, such as a supernova.

It is only fitting that Kit and Maddie would reunite with this otherworldly force driving them together.

Finally, thanks to all the book bloggers, reviewers and readers out there and for your support for Kit and Maddie's story. And to Scott Gaunt for my fab cover and supporting artwork.

ABOUT THE AUTHOR

This is Penny Asher-Darke's third book, but she has written several contemporary romances as Autumn Miller.

Please get in touch; she would love to hear from you on Facebook, Instagram and email: pennyasherdarke@gmail.com. You'll also find her on Bookbub, Goodreads and TikTok too.

Printed in Great Britain
by Amazon

61783144R00238